SECRETS

OF

THE

MAGDALENE

SCROLLS

Life is a Journey of Discovery,

Enjoy!

Bettye Johnson

To Be Published Soon

A Christmas Awakening

The Secret Behind the Door

Coming in 2006

The Legacy of the Magdalene Scrolls
Sequel to
Secrets of the Magdalene Scrolls

SECRETS

OF

THE

MAGDALENE

SCROLLS

The Forbidden Truth of the Life and Times of Mary
Magdalene

Bettye Johnson

Published by
Living Free Press
P.O. Box 97
Rainier, WA 98576

Revised Second Edition
ISBN 978-0-9650454-1-4
June 2005

Words to *Gift From Me*© by permission from Bill Dallavo

http://www.magdalenescrolls.com

Dedication

For Seekers of Truth
For Seekers of Knowledge
And to those who have said,
"I believe in you"

I also dedicate this to
Mary Magdalene
and what she represents.

"I felt I had been given a chance to be of service to the world.
Here at last was a woman writing a truth that the world has a
right and a need to know."
- Sebastian – *Secrets of the Magdalene Scrolls*

CONTENTS

INTRODUCTION

For a number of years I have had a deep interest in Mary Magdalene and have wondered why so little is known about her. There is a blank spot in history surrounding the period Jesus and Mary Magdalene lived. I have read scores of books and searched the Internet to glean an understanding of why this exists. What I have discovered is that the only documentation of their time comes from scrolls and materials written at least fifty years after the events. I have concluded their message was threatening because it would bring down the old religions and upset the politics of the world during that period. The same attitude continues today.

I have also realized that while many writers may read the same material, each one's interpretation will be different. Therefore, it takes great effort to attempt to ferret out what happened during the time the events of the New Testament took place.

From my research it appears those who wrote about Jesus, a Christ, did not absorb his message. Some researchers claim Jesus was never crucified. Others claim he had more than one wife. Many are only concerned with disproving his miracles. I call these people "naysayers."

There is no one authority on the Ministries of Mary Magdalene or of Yeshua ben Joseph, also known as Jesus who became a Christ.

He gave his message with meanings within meanings. The mysteries are there for those who have an open mind and are seeking knowledge. It appears many have simply missed the point.

In asking myself why so much has been written concerning Jesus and Mary Magdalene, the answer came that the gaps in historical documents keep their time a mystery. People love mysteries and hope that by examining the clues left, they can arrive at the solution. However, the biggest clue may have been missed. The teachings of Jesus in the New Testament are ancient teachings that he came to reiterate. Perhaps the answer to the mystery is to seek our own interpretations instead of adopting someone else's.

The following is my perception of the legacy Mary Magdalene left for us. From my research, any documents from her time would have been written in Greek. *Secrets of the Magdalene Scrolls* is written as fiction, however it contains an important clue for those who love the mystery and have an open mind.

Bettye Johnson
March 2004

INTRODUCTION TO THE SECOND EDITION

*Whoever undertakes to set himself up as a judge of Truth and
Knowledge is shipwrecked by the laughter of the gods.*
- Albert Einstein

I have gained many great insights since the first edition of
this my first novel was written in 2003 with re-writing and
publishing in December 2004. This second revised edition is a
polishing of the first. The revisions made do not take away from
but actually enhance the story.

I pay homage to Dan Brown for setting the world on fire
with his novel, *The Da Vinci Code.* I was two-thirds of the way
through writing the *Secrets of the Magdalene Scrolls* when I first
heard of Dan Brown and his book. I chose not to read his work
until after I had completed my manuscript. When I did, I was
delighted with the information he gave.

Truth cannot continue to be suppressed. There are too
many knowledgeable people who hunger for it. To suppress it any
longer would be like trying to get the chicken back into the egg.

Historical records are sketchy. The great library located in
Alexandria, Egypt was destroyed and also the Temple of Serapis[1]
later was destroyed, Rome was destroyed by the Visigoths.
Additionally the Celts handed down their history in unrecorded
stories.

The Bible has undergone many changes and
translations since Constantine convened the Council of Nicea
to create it in 325 A.D. Today it can be used as a roadmap,
however the road taken is up to the interpreter. I have learned
that anyone can prove his or her point of view by using some
part of the Bible.

After King James commissioned theologians to
translate the Bible into English so the common people could
read it, he gave it to Sir Francis Bacon for editing. It is said

---

[1] When Julius Caesar set the harbor on fire and destroyed the Great Library
of Alexandria, there was a branch of the Library in the Temple of
Serapis. In 391 A.D., Emperor Theodosius of Rome ordered it burned in
order to stamp out paganism so Christianity could be promoted.

Bacon encoded the King James version with secrets of the sacred mysteries.[2] The sacred mysteries had to be hidden and passed down in code so that the mystery teachings of the ages would not be destroyed by ignorance or by the Church. Therefore the mystery teachings were "for those who have the eyes to see and the ears to hear."[3] Francis Bacon is also deemed to be William Shakespeare,[4] although there are some who would dispute this.

It is alleged that the Vatican has old and ancient documents in its archives. The validity of even these is suspect because of the Church's history of suppressing the role of women. It stands to reason that many of these documents would not give credence to the true contribution to life made by any woman.

Thus, there are virtually no public records from the time of The Magdalene and Jesus, except what was created at the Council of Nicea.

There is a huge gap between the time of Mary Magdalene and Jesus and the known records of the Merovingian lineage, which many claim descends from them. The first mentioned king of the Merovingians is Clovis I who lived from 481-511 A.D. The lineage of the queens for the most part has been omitted from their records. It makes me wonder where the wombs came from to create their kings.

Today's science of genes and DNA has discovered that to trace our lineage, it is important to use the mitochondrial DNA,[5] hence it stands to reason that the bloodline comes through the maternal.[6] With this knowledge, it becomes obvious how important it was historically to marry daughters to kings, to princes and to royalty. Perhaps our ancestors knew

---

[2] Psalm 46. Bacon allegedly encoded that chapter with the knowledge that he was actually William Shakespeare.

[3] Bible, Matthew 13:13-17, John 12:40, Mark 8:17,18, Luke 7:10

[4] Manly P. Hall, *The Secret Teachings of All Ages: An Encyclopedic Outline of Masonic, Hermetic, Qabbalistic and Rosicrucian Symbological Philosophy*

[5] Mitochondria is the power source of body cells and contains its own DNA. By tracing the mitochondrial DNA, which individuals can only inherit from their mothers, genetic links can for the most part be determined.

[6] Olson, Steve. *Mapping Human History: Genes, Race, and Our Common Origins.*

something about genetics that is just coming to light again today.

When one understands genealogy from the DNA perspective, one realizes that any of us could be of the bloodline stemming from The Magdalene and Jesus. I have found this a worthwhile contemplation.

All women carry the mitochondrial DNA and the shame of His-story is that Her-story has been suppressed or omitted.

So what is the truth? I have written my interpretation of Mary Magdalene based on my research; and whether you agree or disagree with it, it is your perception. Women need a hero and my intent in writing this work as fiction, although basing it on research is to give to women and to men a much-needed heroine.

Bettye Johnson
May 2005

PROLOGUE

Repeatedly Jill and I have been asked to tell the story of our discovery of the scrolls written by Mary Magdalene. After much contemplation regarding our part in bringing the scrolls to public awareness, we made a decision to write our story. My name is Ellen Montgomery and my co-writer is Jill Ashland. There will be chapters where I tell the story and others where Jill narrates the tale. I will begin.

It was early April when we arrived in northern Spain and joined a group of hikers in Santiago de Compostela in Galacia. We had read much about the Walk of the Pilgrims from Compostela, which many followed into France, and we wanted to do it. Knowing the hike through the Pyrenees would be a challenge, we prepared for all kinds of weather and temperatures. There could be snow, rain or sunshine.

Ten of us were in the hiking group led by a Frenchman named Henri. The only Americans were Jill, myself and a man named Peter Douglass. The rest of the party was British, German and Dutch, and the group was made up of four women and six men.

Two months later we descended on the hiking trail through Andorra to Mirepoix, France, where Jill and I separated from the group, going our own way.

And that was how it all began.

Chapter 1

THE DISCOVERY

Somewhere, something incredible is waiting to be known.
- Carl Sagan

It was now early June, with the day already warm as Jill and I hiked our way out of Mirepoix in the foothills of the French Pyrenees. We began early in the morning because we had been told that in the afternoon there was always a chance of thunderstorms.

While resting for a couple of weeks in Mirepoix, we had learned of the transhumance. Jill and I chose to have that experience while Peter and the others opted to go in other directions.

We were following the transhumance, a tradition where the farmers take their cows, horses and sheep up to the high pastures for the summer months.

There were other hikers on the trail, and the previous evening we had become acquainted with them at one of the refuges where we had spent the night. We were an interesting mix of different nationalities. In the morning each group wended its way up at its own pace.

Because we started early, Jill and I decided to eat breakfast along the trail. We had taken cheese, bread, water and wine, plus olive oil, recommended by other hikers to replenish the body's moisture loss from sweating.

It was an awesome sight to see the herders maneuvering their livestock and we could hear their laughter and singing. The wildflowers were in bloom; and set against the blue sky with the rocks and crags of the mountains, the area was more beautiful than any painting I had ever seen.

Having hiked the Pyrenees mountain trails and entering France by way of the tiny country of Andorra, we were now contemplating hiking to western France on the GR10[1] trail, also known as the Chemin de Grande Randonnée. The hike we were on was a prelude to our decision. We had heard the GR10 was a demanding route with difficult terrain. Our other contemplated option was to explore further the many caves in the area of Mirepoix.

The position of the sun indicated it was close to noon, and hunger pains were beginning to gnaw at me. We walked off the trail to rest and eat, and in the distance we could hear the cowbells as the herds made their way up the mountains to the summer pastures.

I had read there were griffin vultures and chamois in the Pyrenees and had been thrilled to see a chamois, a small goatlike antelope. Now I wanted to see a vulture. I took my binoculars out of my backpack and began scanning the sky and the surrounding mountains, while Jill was busy taking photos of the panorama and the flora and fauna. She had read there were orchids growing in the Pyrenees, and she wanted to find some.

Stepping up on a rock, I trained my binoculars on a moving black dot in the sky hoping it was a griffin vulture. Then I did what I would normally have thought was a foolish thing. I lost my balance and fell into some brush. The brush gave way and I found myself falling down into a hole.

Jill had turned just in time to see me disappear and came running.

"Ellen! Ellen! Are you all right?"

Although stunned I managed to grunt an answer. "I think I'm in one piece. It doesn't feel like I have broken anything." Groaning, I managed to say, "I'm getting the flashlight out of my pocket to see what kind of place I'm in."

I scanned the hole and was stunned. "Oh my gawd! Jill! Jill! You have to see this! It's a cave!"

Jill was peering down into the hole and could see the light coming from my flashlight. "Can you stand up? How big

---

[1] Long national paths called *Sentiers de Grande Randonnée* are numbered and shortened to GR. The French trail system is 180,000 kilometers long.

is it? Is there room for us both down there? If I come down will we both be able to get back up?"

"Yes, I can stand up and it looks like a chamber of some kind with an opening leading away from it. I want to explore."

"Wait for me. I'm going to tie my rope on to something so I can come down."

Within minutes Jill had joined me. "Are you okay? You look like hell," she said as she shined her flashlight over me.

"Thanks. I feel like I've been hit by a truck, and my hand is bleeding. Will you help me wrap it up with this?" I took a kerchief off my hair and handed it to her.

After my hand was bandaged, we crawled through the opening and found another chamber larger than the first.

"I'd read the Pyrenees are riddled with caves, but I never thought I would fall into one," I muttered. "I also heard somewhere that the Pyrenees were the home of Mordor in Tolkien's *Lord of the Rings*."

Shining our lights around, we spotted three pottery jars against one wall. Each jar was about three feet tall. Jill walked closer and without touching any noted that it was very odd there were only these three jars and nothing else that we could see.

"I wonder if anything's inside?" she murmured. For some reason we were both loathe to touch them with our bare hands. She thumped the side of one. It didn't sound as though it were full.

When we weren't wearing our mountain gloves, we always attached them to our belts. Jill put hers on and began twisting the stopper on one of the jars.

"Do you think you're going to get bitten by a snake or something?" I joked.

"No, but there is no telling what's in these. Do you want to put your bare hand in and find out?"

"I get your point." Putting a glove on my unhurt hand, I joked, "I'll take the plunge."

Aiming my flashlight into the jar, I saw what looked like rolled up cloths. Gingerly I drew one out. There was something wrapped inside the linen. With Jill holding the light, I carefully unwrapped it and found a scroll of some kind.

"Gawd, it looks old," Jill whispered. With shaking hands, I continued pulling out linen-wrapped scrolls. When the first jar was empty, we began on the second and then the third. They both contained additional scrolls.

"Ellen, do you think this is a hoax or something old and real?"

"I don't know, but I want to find out and I don't want to leave them here."

"Shouldn't we leave them and notify the authorities?"

"Oh Jill, reason it," I said. "If we leave them here and call in the authorities, these will get lost in the files of bureaucracy, or some archaeologist will come and take all the credit. No, I want to know what these are before I turn them over."

"But, isn't that illegal? After all we are in a foreign country."

"Jill, I have no intention of stealing them. I only want to delay turning them over until I know what they are. Did you bring your camera down with you?"

"No, I'll climb out and get it. Good idea to take pictures of the cave as we found it."

As Jill was going after the camera, I told her to bring back the large plastic bags we carried for our trash. Now they had another use. While she was gone, I scanned the chamber again, that time noting a few drawings in one area. They were similar to ones we had seen in other caves recently.

After what seemed like an eternity, Jill returned and told me she had placed our backpacks under a ledge because a sudden shower had come up. With me shining the light on the three jars Jill took flash photos. I also directed her to the wall with the drawings. She first photographed the ceiling, in case our light had missed anything, and then the rest of the chamber. I noticed one of the drawings looked like a ram's head.

I held the light and Jill carefully placed the scrolls in two plastic bags. With her carrying one bag and me the other, we managed to get through the hole and back into the outer chamber.

Climbing up and out I realized my body ached like a steamroller had run over me. My wrapped hand screamed with pain, and it was all I could do to stifle the agony as I hauled my body up the rope. When we emerged, the rain had passed over and the sun was shining again.

Retrieving our backpacks, Jill lashed a plastic bag to each one while I covered the hole with brush. When I finished, it was hard to tell it had been uncovered. Jill took photos of the brush-covered area.

"Ellen, you look awful. Do you want to stay here awhile or start walking? It doesn't make sense to continue going up the trail."

"You're right. Since I don't have any broken bones, let's head back to Mirepoix. We can't make it all the way back there today so let's try for a place where we can set up our tents."

The return trip was agony for me. When we stopped for the night, Jill put up our small bivouac tents in a sheltered area. Taking out a bottle of wine, we drank to our treasure find.

"Ellen, let me look at your hand. You also have a nasty bruise and scrape on your left cheek." Pulling the kerchief off, I winced.

"Hmmm, looks like a small cut and bruises. Hold still while I pour some wine on it. It's a good thing it's your left hand."

"Holy shit! That burns!"

"It's supposed to. It disinfects. Here, have another drink," she said pouring some wine in my plastic glass. Taking her first aid kit out, Jill put some antibiotic ointment and a bandage on my cut. Then she asked, "Do you want to look at one of the scrolls and see what's on it?"

With curiosity, I unwrapped a scroll. It was covered with writing. "It looks as though it could be Greek."

"Are you serious? Or do you mean it could be all Greek to you?"

Laughing, I said, "No, silly. I think it's Greek writing."

"How do you know?"

"I once had a boyfriend who was of Greek descent. He took pride in being able to speak and write his native language."

"Oh. Well. Where are we going to find someone to translate these for us?"

Sighing, I said, "I need to sleep. When I wake up maybe the answer will come to me. In the meantime, I think I'll have some more wine."

Wrapped in my sleeping bag, I was soon out like a light. It was a dreamless sleep. As the night began to fade into morning I woke up stiff and sore. Jill was awake a few minutes after me.

Crawling out of our tents, we used some of our precious water to wash our faces. Jill brought out our cheese, bread and olive oil. While eating we silently watched the sun come up. Sunrise has always been a special moment for me. I feel it is one of the holiest moments there is.

After breaking camp, we looked around to make sure we had left no trash. Slowly we made our way down the trail, waving to those who were making their way up as the transhumance continued.

During one resting stop, Jill asked what I had in mind once we reached Mirepoix. Pausing for a moment, I replied, "I've thought about this, and the only viable solution I can think of is to see if we can find Peter."

During our walk from Santiago de Compostela the three of us had become good friends as well as compatible hiking companions. Peter and I seemed to gravitate to one another. In fact, I was more than attracted to him. But the relationship had not developed beyond friendship. We also shared common interests in the history of the Knights Templar and both liked to research history. We had all read the book *Holy Blood, Holy Grail* and it had inspired us individually to make the trip.

Peter was at least 6' 4" tall with a shock of long brown wavy hair he wore in a ponytail. His frame was what one would call lanky. He had sold his thriving business in Massachusetts after his pregnant wife was killed in a single car accident several years before. They had no children. As a result of all this, he had made a decision to find out what life was all about and had developed an interest in the Knights Templar as well as the Cathars. Having read many books similar to *Holy Blood, Holy Grail*, I was also interested in learning more of the Templars and the Cathars.

Jill and I had been roommates at Stanford University in California and we had continued our friendship throughout my disastrous marriage to Walter Montgomery, which had ended the year before. I was divorced and I was a disenchanted research lawyer.

Jill had never married and was a schoolteacher, or I should say had been a schoolteacher. Her mother had passed away the previous year and left Jill enough money so that she felt she could take a year's sabbatical. She also received funds from a trust her deceased father had set up for her.

Jill thought a moment then said, "Do you really think it would be wise to tell Peter about the scrolls?"

"Do you have a better idea?"

"No. Oh, why not. After all I noticed you and Peter have an eye for each other. Nothing ventured, nothing gained. All he can do is say no and turn us in to the authorities."

"Oh, you and your authority kick, Jill. The authorities will get these scrolls after we know what they contain. A few weeks won't make that much difference. And yes, I do like Peter."

Arriving in Mirepoix, we found a telephone and called the Maison de Larche where Peter had been staying. We were hoping our luck would hold and he would not have departed for Foix as he had planned.

Fortunately Jill and I spoke enough French to make ourselves understood. We learned he had not checked out and breathed a sigh of relief. So we left a message saying we were on our way to see him and set out on foot.

The Maison was only several kilometers from Mirepoix and when we arrived, we found Peter waiting in the garden where there was a magnificent view of the mountains.

Unfolding his lanky frame from a bench, he put his pipe away and gave us each a hug. "Why the change of plans?" he asked. "If you had come tomorrow, I would have been gone."

Jill looked at me, and even though I had rehearsed my speech, I felt tongue-tied.

Peter eyed us quizzically and said, "Oh, come on. You two look as though you have been caught with your hand in a cookie jar. And by the way Ellen, you look like you've been mauled by a bear or something."

"Ummm, I feel like it, but it was nothing alive," and then I began. "What if I told you Jill and I had stumbled into a cave and discovered something that had been hidden for many years?"

"This sounds mysterious. Why not begin at the beginning."

Taking a deep breath, I related the entire story with Jill interjecting her part. The whole time, Peter's face was expressionless. He would puff on his pipe and then relight it.

When the story was finished, we sat there for a few moments until Peter broke the silence, "And what do you want me to do? Have you gone over the repercussions of hanging onto the scrolls?"

I replied we had. "What we want to know is if you have any idea how we can get some of these scrolls translated? We want to know what they are."

"Hmmm. I see." Peter puffed away for what seemed an eternity. "Tell me. What is the honest reason you don't want to go to the authorities now?"

Jill spoke up. "Since it is really Ellen's discovery, I think it best to let her voice her reasons."

"Okay, you two," I said. "I thought of this all the time Jill and I were hiking back to Mirepoix. I remember what happened to the documents found at Nag Hammadi as well as the Dead Sea Scrolls. Selfish interests kept them from the public for years. If these scrolls are indeed written in Greek and are not a hoax, then the find could be as important as Nag Hammadi and the others. There is something within me telling me it is important to get them translated as soon as possible."

Peter grinned. "Well put Ellen, and you have a valid point. I like your reasoning also. There is perhaps someone who might be able to do this. Now, hold on. I said might. He happens to be a French priest I met last year in Paris at the Louvre. We struck up a conversation in front of the portrait of the Mona Lisa and ended up having dinner together. As I recall, his specialty is ancient Greek, and he told me he had translated many documents for the Vatican."

"A priest? You must be joking!" I exploded.

Jill was surprised, and I was shocked. A priest was the last person I would have thought Peter would recommend.

Peter shrugged his shoulders. "Somehow I don't think the Father is like your stereotype priest. I can't guarantee how he will respond, but I have a strong sense he is honest. Do you have a better idea?"

24

"I don't know, Peter. I want to think about this; don't you too, Jill?"

"I agree with Ellen, unless you can give us more information, Peter."

"Well, when I met him Father Sebastian was on medical retirement for an illness, and I don't even know his state of health now. I think I have his address and phone number in my wallet. All I can do is call him. Perhaps we can meet and feel him out."

Putting his pipe down, Peter reached into his back pocket and brought out a black wallet. While Jill and I sat back in silence, he rummaged through many cards, at last pulling one out. "Yep, here it is. Father Sebastian Gontard with his home address and phone number. Will you agree to meet him if I don't mention the scrolls?"

Jill and I said yes, so the three of us made our way into the Maison where Peter asked to use the phone. He placed the call using his phone card. Father Sebastian's housekeeper answered and told Peter the Father was in Lourdes taking the cure. If it was important, she said Peter could reach him there and she gave him an address.

Turning from the phone, Peter smiled, "I guess it's off to Lourdes tomorrow if you two want to go. I'll ask if there is a room for you here and then we can walk into the village for dinner. That is, if you're up to it." We were.

There was one room available with a standard double bed, but at that point Jill and I didn't care. We would have taken anything. After freshening up, we hiked back into Mirepoix.

Since Peter had been there awhile, he already was familiar with the cuisine and had said it was quite good. We settled for a small restaurant and chose the region's specialty, foie gras, followed by a robust savory dish of mounjetado. We shared a lovely regional wine, Minervois. After the entrée, we had a green salad followed by an Ariege cheese course and for dessert, a fruit-filled croustade.

Later Jill told me that it was obvious something was developing between Peter and me because at dinner we only had eyes for each other.

After stuffing ourselves, we walked back to the Maison. Saying goodnight to Peter, we went to our room. I knew I had

25

to have a bath so I gathered up my towel and soap and padded down the hall to the bathroom. The hot water was heavenly. Afraid I would use it all up; I reluctantly got out of the tub. Jill was ready to take her bath, and before she returned, I was fast asleep.

It seemed as though I had just put my head to the pillow when there was a tap on the door. Sleepily I answered, "Yesss."

"Get up you sleepyheads. It's morning. And we can catch a ride to Foix in thirty minutes. The owner of la Maison is driving in for supplies and has offered to give us a lift."

Jill and I quickly got up, and we were dressed, packed and outside ready to depart in less than thirty minutes.

"Hey, that was quick," Peter said. He picked up our backpacks and gear and put them in the trunk. I noticed he took great care with the plastic bags. We had paid our tab the night before, so there was nothing to keep us.

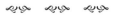

FATHER SEBASTIAN

Knowledge comes, but wisdom lingers.
- Alfred Lord Tennyson

During the ride to Foix there was very little talking among the three of us because the owner of la Maison spent the trip extolling the virtues of the region. He was very proud of his area and pointed out places he thought would be of interest to us. I surmised he did this in order to entice us back for another visit.

The winding road allowed us to have magnificent views of the mountains, gorges with small waterfalls, small rivers and the quaint villages that we passed through.

Arriving in Foix, our host and driver drove us to the bus stop where we would be able to catch a bus. It was near the center of the small city that I estimated to have a population of around 6,000. However, Peter and Jill thought it could be closer to 8,000.

Close by the bus stop we were fortunate to find a small café serving croissants and coffee. Once we were replenished, we made our way back to the stop. It wasn't long before the bus came.

Again we were rewarded with panoramic vistas of the mountains, forests, villages and farms on the trip to Lourdes. It was rather wild country. To the south was Andorra, which we had recently passed through. We saw deserted villages and half-deserted villages, and as I looked toward Andorra, I was amazed we had hiked through those mountains. All of it had once been part of the Cathar country, and I could imagine the possibility of Mary Magdalene having once traipsed the same mountains.

Coming into Lourdes we were greeted with a spectacular view of a castle sitting atop its rocky perch. To the west was the valley of the Gave de River Pau and to the east, the sanctuaries. Jill had her guidebook out and read to us that in 1844 a marble head had been discovered in the castle and it seemed a Phrygian[1] cap was perched on it. Phrygian caps are associated with the god Mithra.

As we entered the town of Lourdes, we could see the great Basilica that was built over the grotto where Bernadette supposedly had her visions. We learned the grotto is called Massabielle. The town was teeming with pilgrims, their families and tourists.

We selected an outdoor café where we could wait while Peter went to see the priest. It had been agreed that he would approach Father Sebastian alone. Sipping our café au lait, Jill and I welcomed the opportunity to people-watch and relax. However we didn't do much relaxing. We were too nervous about meeting Father Sebastian.

It wasn't until much later that Jill and I learned what had transpired when Peter and the priest met. Perhaps it was just as well. We were skeptical of anything good coming from a priest regarding the scrolls.

---

[1] Phrygian cap: A symbol originating from the Romans. A red cap with a tapering end was placed on a pike to denote a freed slave. During the French Revolution it became a symbol of republican liberty and is usually made of red wool.

When Peter arrived at the Basilica, he asked directions for finding Father Sebastian. At the information desk, he was told the Father would soon be returning from the grotto where he had been partaking of the healing waters.

Before long Peter saw Father Sebastian approaching. As the priest came nearer, Peter noticed a grayish pallor to his skin. He was rather nondescript, about 5' 7" tall with graying brown hair and rimless glasses that sat on a rather aquiline nose. Greeting each other with a hug, the Father kissed Peter on each side of his face, and then asked what had brought his friend to see him.

Peter suggested they find a place where they could talk privately. The Father led him to a garden where they would not be disturbed.

"Now my friend, tell me why you have sought me out. I think it could be more than you only wanted to see me," the priest said with a twinkle in his eyes.

Peter related to me later that he had a strong compulsion to tell the priest the truth.

"You're right Father. I must request that you keep in confidence what I am about to tell you."

"Ah, like a confession?"

"Yes, Father."

"Very well, Peter. I will keep it sacred, like a confession."

Peter told Father Sebastian that Jill and I had come to be in possession of the scrolls and had sought out Peter in our desire to have them translated. He told him the three of us were reluctant to turn them over to the authorities before we knew what they contained. When Peter finished, Father Sebastian stroked his chin. Peter noticed there was a great sadness in his countenance.

"I am about to tell you something that I have told no one.

"As a young man, I had no means to go to a université to study languages, which were my passion. I sought out the parish priest and he advised me to become a priest and ask to be sent to a université where I could pursue my passion."

Pausing a moment, the Father continued.

"With a word placed in higher places, it was agreed I would be sent to a université once I had taken my vows. With

28

trepidation, I accepted. I fell in love with the Greek language and specialized in ancient Greek. Ah, the Church was well pleased to have me. I could translate old documents that for years had lain in the bowels of the Vatican.

"For a period of time I was happy with my work. I lived at the Vatican and worked in the archives. However, what I saw occurring inside the Vatican was not in keeping with what I had been taught that the Church represented. Oui, I became disillusioned."

Peter interrupted, "Father, why didn't you quit?"

"Ah, that is the stain upon my soul. I did not have the courage to reveal what I had learned about the deceptions of the Church.

"Are you aware the Inquisition is still going on, under the guise of another name? It has a very long reach." Peter shook his head no.

"I did not have the courage to be named a heretic. So, I continued my work until I became ill and was placed on medical retirement. An opportunity to become a université professor in France arose so I returned to my country of birth.

"To bring up another matter, are you aware there is an arm of the Church called the Opus Dei?"

Shaking his head no again, Peter allowed the Father to continue.

"So what does all this have to do with the scrolls you and your friends have acquired? Not only did I teach Greek, together with ancient Greek, but also I became enthralled with computers. I learned all I could about them from my friend, Paul Leseur. With him I developed a computer program that could translate ancient Greek into French." The Father became quiet, allowing this to sink in to Peter's awareness.

"My god!" Peter whispered. "This means you can translate these scrolls yourself!"

"Ah oui, and as I have shared my story with you, I think you can understand why I am agreeing to assist you. Call it redemption, if you like. I have had this sin eating away at my soul, and I know that is why I am ill. Even the waters of the sacred Lourdes cannot heal me. Before I die, I want to do something that is of service to mankind. Oui, I will agree to translating these documents, but only if we give the translations to the world at the same time we hand them over to the French authorities."

"I think Ellen and Jill will agree with that idea. I know I do. I can't tell you how relieved I am especially since you have given me your sacred word that you will not divulge our conversation to anyone."

"Peter, I mentioned the Opus Dei and the Inquisition, now known as the CDF.[2] The Vatican controls them both, and they are extremely powerful. They will use any means to get what they want. If word gets out before the scrolls are translated, all could be lost."

"Surely, Father, you jest."

"Non, Peter. I cannot undertake this unless you and your friends fully understand the potentials for danger that exist. Are you still willing to proceed?"

"I can't speak for Ellen or Jill, Father. But will you come with me, meet them and tell them what you think necessary?"

"Oui. I had already decided to leave here and return home. Since my computer with the Greek program is at my home in Toulouse, I suggest you three travel there with me, if that is agreeable with the ladies. Do you have a car here? Non? Très bien. We will travel in mine."

Waiting for Father Sebastian to check out of his accommodations and gather his belongings, Peter thought about his own motives and came to the conclusion he could not let fear be his deciding factor. No, he wanted to proceed with the translations. He had a sense it was the right thing to do. However he also realized that being with Ellen was a major factor in that decision.

Returning shortly Father Sebastian suggested that Peter go and wait with Jill and me while he brought his car to the café, which he knew well.

Peter found us relaxed and having a splendid time watching the people passing by.

"Peter! Tell us. What came of your meeting with Father Sebastian?" I asked.

---

[2] CDF: Catholic organization, Congregation for the Doctrine of the Faith

He sat down in one of the chairs and looked at each of us. Taking a deep breath, he said, "I met with Father Sebastian, and it seems I was just in time. He was about to check out and leave. We had a deep sharing, which I won't go into now. However, without intending to, I felt compelled to tell him about the scrolls. I know I had said I wouldn't, and all I can say is that it felt right."

There must have been sparks blazing from my eyes. I was speechless. "Peter! You gave your word! How could you?"

Jill was as angry as I was. It was easy to see Peter was having second thoughts.

"Yes, I said if you agreed to my meeting with him and setting up a meeting between you two and him that I wouldn't mention the scrolls. I apologize. All I can do is reiterate that when he and I began talking I felt an overwhelming compulsion to tell him about them. I urge you to meet him and hear from him why he wants to help. He has accepted what I told him as a confessional, and he gave me his sacred word the information I gave him would not be revealed to anyone."

Jill snickered. "Yeah, his sacred vow. Do you realize how many priests have broken their sacred vows?"

"Before he makes his final decision to look at the scrolls, he wants to speak with each of you. It seems there is a lot at stake."

"What does that mean, a lot at stake?" I asked.

We were almost whispering so we wouldn't be overheard.

"He talked about the Inquisition, the Opus Dei and other organizations."

"Well!" I whispered, "He can't be all that bad if he knows about them and how dangerous they are."

Jill interjected, "Who was it that said, a faint heart never won a battle?" This brought a chuckle from Peter, but I was still dealing with my anger.

"I don't think that's the exact wording, but it's the same message," he said. "The Father is on his way here, and if it is agreeable with you, we will ride with him to Toulouse. He has a program on his computer at his home there that can translate ancient Greek into French."

Before we could react to that bit of information, Father Sebastian drove up in his black Peugeot, motioned for us to get

31

in and Peter made brief introductions. Peter stowed our packs in the trunk and got in the front seat with the Father.

I felt a sense of relief. We were beginning to do something. At the same time, I felt a residual anger even though I had reversed my earlier decision about not telling Father Sebastian about the scrolls, and I was also experiencing an inner excitement along with trepidation. Later Jill told me she was feeling the same way.

"Tell me ladies, how did you make your discovery? And why are you hesitant to turn these scrolls over to the authorities? Peter has told me some, however I want to know the story from you."

What the hell, I thought. *All that can happen is for the authorities to get the scrolls before we know what they say.*

Since I had fallen into the cave, I began telling the story; and then Jill told hers.

By the time we were done, we were well past Tarbes and on the priority road to Toulouse. Father Sebastian had made no comment.

There were many trucks on the road, and he negotiated the traffic quite well. The rest of our conversations were light and sparse. We were all into our own thoughts.

Approaching Toulouse I could see why it is known as the "ville rose." It's because of the pink-brick buildings. Father Sebastian roused from his reverie and told us it was the home of an 800-year old université as well as France's aeronautics industry.

His home was near the université and soon we were driving down long narrow streets, which at times seemed too narrow even for one car. Turning into what looked like a small alley, the Father drove to the back of it and while making a turn touched his garage door opener.

After the car was parked, we followed Father Sebastian, through the one-car garage into a small well-tended garden. Smiling, he looked at us and said, "This is my place of contemplation. You like?"

We all nodded. There was a small fountain gurgling as water poured over rocks into a small pool.

He lived in a small two-story house. We trailed him in through the kitchen and on into what Americans would call a living room. Off to one side was a desk with a computer and shelves with books and stacks of papers. It was definitely a masculine room.

Pointing to a small hallway, the Father told us where the lavabo was and I remembered that in France it was the name for a bathroom with only a toilet. It was more like a closet with room for one person. There was only the toilet with the tank up near the ceiling, and it was flushed by pulling a chain.

Once we had all relieved ourselves, he asked Jill and me to sit on the sofa and motioned Peter to the one chair. Pulling up his swivel chair from his desk, Father Sebastian looked at each of us. I was the first to speak.

"Father, I want to be open and honest. I had reservations about Peter contacting you. I have a low opinion of the Catholic Church and priests."

Responding the priest said, "I understand. Since I know nothing of your background or your reasons for distrust, I do think what you told me about the scrolls to be true. For me to translate for you, there is something you should know.

"Perhaps Peter told you of my work at the Vatican. While there I learned many things, and by revealing them to the three of you, I could be signing my death warrant. This is ironic, since my doctors have already given me a death warrant. This is why I was at Lourdes.

"All of you must understand there could be danger and consequences, and I have already told Peter some of them."

He launched into telling us about the power of the Church and the Opus Dei, an arm of the Church.

"If word leaks out before the translations are done and the documents are turned over to the Bibliothèque nationale, these church organizations will stop at nothing to get them. Also, there are other organizations that could have an interest in the scrolls. There are rumors of people dying for less than this."

Jill later said she was wondering about paranoia. Speaking up she asked, "But Father, why would they do that?"

"Power. Power can be very dangerous if one pursues it only for power. It can become as addictive as taking a narcotic. There are others, such as very wealthy men, who seek to hoard antiquities that should be shared with the world. In addition, there are those in the archaeological world who would have an interest in getting the scrolls. There are many vipers of power.

"Do I make myself clear as to the possibilities of danger? And if I have, are you willing to proceed?"

I took a deep breath. "Before I answer that Father, I want to say that for years I have been interested in the Black Madonna. Do you have any interest in her?"

"I am familiar with the Black Madonna in the sense there are many churches in France and in Spain that have statues of a Black Madonna with a child. For the most part these are displayed unobtrusively. There are Black Madonnas in other parts of Europe, also, including a famous one in Czestochowa in Poland. It is a known fact the current Pope has a painting of this Madonna in his private chapel in the Vatican."

Looking at the priest, I began laughing.

"You can't be serious, Father. Why would the Pope have a Black Madonna?"

"Ah, he is from Poland. Many miracles of healing have been attributed to this ancient painting. Supposedly St. Luke himself painted this portrait on wood."

Jill was almost sputtering. "But Father, if one studies the beginnings of the Christian religion, there is no validation of a Luke."

"It is true. A chance remark can become a belief. It isn't that I haven't taken an interest; it is I have been occupied with other things, such as developing the translation program for the computer."

Jill asked if he could tell us anything of why he had became disillusioned with the Church.

"Oui. You have a right to know.

"In my research, I observed and learned the hierarchy of the Church has many faces of lies and deceit. What the people are told to do is not what the hierarchy does. I have studied the works and the words of Jesus. What I read as being attributed to him is not practiced."

The priest was beginning to get agitated. "Forgive me. I am filled with remorse and anger. If you will trust me, I will do the translation for you; that is, if after I view the first document I deem it to be reliable. Do you want me to proceed?"

"Before I agree, are you aware one of the early Church fathers was a transvestite?" Jill asked. I sensed she was testing him as I had when I asked about the Black Madonna.

"I am not sure of the word transvestite," he replied.

"As I understand, it is a person who gets sexual pleasure from dressing as one of the opposite sex," replied Jill.

Smiling, the Father said, "Oui. I cannot recall his name at this moment; however the information I came across was of an early Church leader who retired to bed one night. A fire broke out in his residence. Groping in the dark for his clothes, he donned a woman's dress, which was bright red. So the story goes that henceforth that is why Cardinals wear red and also long skirts and cassocks."

Peter sputtered, "Now, you're pulling my leg."

"What do you mean, pulling your leg?"

"Forgive me Father. It means joking."

"Non Peter. I do not jest. There are many other records such as this. I have not exaggerated. The early popes married and had children. They also had illicit relations and had children from those encounters."

Until then Peter had been quiet. He knew the decision had to be Jill's and mine, and I appreciated him for not interfering.

Making up my mind I said, "I cannot speak for Jill, however what you have told us only reinforces my gut feeling that these scrolls must be translated before being released to the authorities. I am willing for you to see one of them."

Jill agreed. "I have also wondered about the Church and its hypocrisy. With the latest revelations of priests sexually molesting young boys and even young girls, I'm beginning to think I would not be shocked anymore at anything regarding the Church."

"Jill, not only am I scholar, I am also a priest. Do you think you can trust me?"

"Yes, Father, I do," she answered.

"And you Peter, are you willing to trust me and to go along with this?"

"Yes, Father. And I will do whatever I can to assist you."

"Good. We are all agreed. Now, we need to move to a location more secure than my home, and I have just the ideal place. My friend Paul Leseur is in South Africa for six months. He teaches computer science at the université and has entrusted me with finding someone to live in his house while he is gone. The couple that had agreed to rent it has now backed out due to a death in their family. So, we have a place to work from. Fortunately for us, I had Paul's housekeeper stock the kitchen with food before she left for her vacation. Providence is with us and I have the key."

"Father, where is this home?" I asked.

"It is outside of Toulouse in the country. My housekeeper is also going to take a vacation, however we would be more visible here. Therefore I prefer to go to Paul's, as it is more secluded. We will be hidden away from prying eyes. I am not much of a cook, but we will manage. Now, I will gather a few things.

"Forgive me if I appear to be overzealous, but I must request you leave nothing here and wipe your prints where you think you have touched."

Jill gave Peter and me a wondering look. "He really means business. I'm willing to see this through." Turning to Father Sebastian she asked, "But how do you know to be so careful?"

"Ah, when I lived and worked at the Vatican, like I said, I saw and heard many things which I cannot discuss, including the possibility that even a pope was murdered."

Having read much regarding the Church and its repression of historical information, I had an inkling to whom he was referring. There have been books written alluding to the murder of the pope before John Paul II, the present pope.

By now it was evening and the sky was overcast, promising perhaps a shower or two.

Driving through Toulouse, it was difficult to see much of what the city looked like. Once we were out of the city, we had gone only a short distance when the Father turned off onto a small dirt road. He drove through woods and came to a clearing where the house stood. It appeared to be a typical French farmhouse with a circular driveway in front. The Father drove around to the rear of the house where we saw a large barn.

Quickly he got out while pulling a key ring from his pocket. Selecting a key using the light from the car's headlights, he opened the barn door. On the right side was Paul Leseur's car. Pulling in on the left, the Father stopped the engine and told us bring our packs and the scrolls and to follow him.

Using the flashlight from his car, he led the way to the house, making sure he did not trip the burglar alarm. The Father paused and told us that he had shown the house to prospective renters a number of times, which was why he knew about the burglar alarm.

The second key on the ring fit the back door. After the lights were turned on I saw that the door opened into a large kitchen. In addition to the stove, counters and cupboards, a round table with four chairs stood in the center. It was most inviting. What seemed out of place was a small television set on the counter.

Going through the kitchen, we followed the Father into the heart of the house. The living room had a massive fireplace flanked on either side by chintz-covered couches and two matching chairs. The room gave off an ambiance of comfort and serenity. At the opposite end was a large dining table near French doors, which Father Sebastian said opened to the garden outside. The room was inviting and reflected the love and care that had been given it.

Switching on other lights, the Father continued our tour down a hallway where there were three bedrooms. He indicated Jill and I would share the one with the twin beds while he and Peter would each have their own.

There was one massive bathroom, with a Jacuzzi tub of all things. Smiling, the Father told us Paul enjoyed his comforts and had upgraded the house from its original structure. He told us there was also a lavabo just off the kitchen.

We returned to the living room and Father Sebastian asked us to remove the scrolls from the plastic bags. I could tell that he was horrified with the bags, however they were all we had at the time. At least we'd had the good sense to wrap the scrolls in the towels we carried in our backpacks.

Clicking his tongue in a tsk, tsk sound he muttered, "We must secure decent tubes for these."

We put the scrolls on the dining table, and the Father could see all were wrapped in linen. He commented the linen coverings appeared to be treated with something similar to what ancient Egyptians used to preserve cloth. One was much smaller than the others, and with trembling hands, he picked it up and began unwrapping it. With a perplexed look, he noted that it was something like old linen with what appeared to be a rust-colored stain on it. There was nothing inside.

"Mon dieu? What is this? This is not papyrus, but it seems to be ancient linen. There must be an explanation in one of the other scrolls. This one is only cloth. There is nothing inside. There is no writing."

We were all puzzled and agreed to set it aside until we saw what the rest of the wrapped scrolls contained.

With our permission, he continued to unwrap each one. His hands were shaking, revealing his excitement. "Hmmm. They *are* written in ancient Greek. There appears to be a sequence." Looking at each scroll, he arranged them on the table. "Ah, oui," he said as he began to scan some of the scrolls. "They seem to be numbered, and ah, oui. This one must be the first."

The rest of us refrained from talking. The moment was intense. I noticed I was holding my breath. Slowly I let it out. Looking up at us with tears in his eyes, he began speaking in French, then caught himself and switched to English.

"Mes amies, I think we have the Holy Grail here. If these scrolls are authentic, these words were written by Mary Magdalene." The air was pregnant with the import of his statement.

"Oh god! Can it really be?" asked Jill.

"Oui, Jill. This has the feel of old papyrus, and there is some damage from age here. We must be extremely careful of how we handle these."

With tears streaming down his face, the Father shakily told us he had asked for a sign of redemption when he was at Lourdes. "This must be the miracle I asked for."

Peter got up, opened the French doors and went outside. I was too stunned to move. Through the doors I could see him lighting his pipe. Jill and I sat, allowing this information to seep into our consciousnesses. I was in awe of our find. In the past year I had begun questioning what Mary Magdalene was about and who she really was. Before coming to Europe, I had read Laurence Gardner's book *Bloodline of the Holy Grail* and it had intensified my interest.

After visiting many churches and cathedrals in France, especially in the French Pyrenees area, I had become entranced with the Black Madonna. Within me I knew she was not Mary, the mother of Jesus. As a feeling of exhilaration swept through me, I found myself praying, *Oh god, let these be authentic.*

The Father arose, going to one of the two computers in the alcove off to the side of the large room. Turning it on, he typed in a password. I asked how he knew it, and he replied he and Paul had exchanged passwords in case a need ever arose. Taking a disk from his briefcase, he inserted it in the CD drive. Turning to us he said he was installing the program that translated ancient Greek into French and that it would take some time.

Sitting there, I was tingling with excitement and knew I had to get up and do something while the installation was progressing. Realizing I was hungry, I spoke quietly to Jill and suggested we go and check the kitchen out. Apparently Peter had the same idea because he was coming into the kitchen through the door leading from outside. We laughed at our timing.

Not saying anything about the scrolls, we began exploring what the kitchen had to offer. In the refrigerator there were eggs and various kinds of cheese, so we settled on an omelet. Jill loves to cook and volunteered to be the chef. I set the table, and Peter said he would find some wine and help in the clean up.

I went into the living room and told the Father that we were preparing dinner. He smiled and responded with a "Merci."

When Jill announced dinner was ready, he came into the kitchen still beaming, and his eyes danced with joy. It made him look years younger. I learned later he was only fifty-four.

Pouring the wine with a flourish, Peter suggested we toast to the success of the translations and satisfaction for all. Clinking glasses, we honored the unfoldment of great knowledge and a completion of the translations.

Jill had outdone herself on the omelet using various cheeses to which she had added a small tin of mushrooms and some spices. Her ingenuity also included hot flour tortillas that she made from scratch. The priest was impressed. It was his first time to eat the delicious flat breads.

While we were eating dinner, I asked Father Sebastian where he had acquired his excellent command of the English language. With a big smile he replied, "When I was studying Greek at the université, an American priest was teaching an English class there, and I studied with him. However when I speak English I find myself lapsing back into French from time to time. I hope you will excuse me when I do."

"Of course we do," I replied. "Do you speak other languages?"

"Oh, oui," he answered with a smile. "I have some command of Latin, Italian, Spanish and German."

I thanked him and we changed the subject, discussing the potentials of what could happen if we had the scrolls translated before releasing them to the authorities. I can sum it up by saying we were willing to take the risks. The Father said he would like to begin translating then, so we told him to go ahead.

The computer program had finished installing. Picking up what he had said was the first papyrus, the Father gently opened it. After stabilizing the scroll, he began typing the ancient Greek text of Mary Magdalene into the computer.

I found myself again holding my breath. There was an excitement in his demeanor, and none of us dared to talk or interrupt him. The air was electrified. Later the three of us agreed we had sensed a divine presence in the room.

Peter got up. It was obvious he was restless. Walking through the kitchen to the garden, he returned shortly saying a spattering of raindrops was falling. I had intended to follow him and just as I was entering the kitchen, he was returning.

When he said it was raining, I responded, "Oh, it is?"

Suddenly I felt self-conscious. "Peter, why are you helping us?"

Drawing on his unlit pipe, he sighed. "I've asked myself that question. Perhaps it's because I'm interested in you."

"What do you mean by interested?

"Hell, Ellen. I'm feeling something about you that I don't have words for. There! I've said it."

Within me I felt a tingling of electricity. All I could say was, "Oh."

"And what do you mean by oh?"

"I suppose I'm interested in you also. Uh, Peter, if our friendship is going to develop into something closer, I ask that we just let it flow."

With a grin on his face, Peter let out a sigh. "I accept."

At that moment Jill came into the kitchen and looked at us. "Am I interrupting?"

Peter was the first to answer. "Not at all Jill. We were talking about going with the flow."

"Good idea. Father Sebastian is totally immersed in his translation, so I came in to make coffee. It could be awhile."

We chatted while the coffee brewed, and each of us agreed we were too wired to think of going to bed.

Returning to the living room, Jill told the priest she was making coffee and asked if he would like some. "Ummm, I'm almost finished with a portion of this, so your timing is très bon."

About the time the coffee was ready, the Father came into the kitchen with a sheaf of papers saying he wanted to read us the translation of the first papyrus. Knowing we would not understand the French, he translated into English as he read.

Haltingly he began, and this is what he read.

∽ ∽ ∽

MARY MAGDALENE'S CHARGE
Scroll 1

Hail unto you who uncover these writings. I have placed my story in these containers for you to find. I have written in the language of Greek, as it is the language I have foreseen lasting.

These words I write are for those who have the eyes to see and the ears to hear. Who am I? I have been called many names, the last being The Magdalene. This is my record. I have written it in pieces over the years. Now is the time to share it with the world.

You may well ask why I have hidden my story in this way. I have foreseen the suppression of the knowledge of me and my teachings, by men who have a great fear of what I taught, of my womanhood, of what I represented and of the Mother Goddess.

For you who have found my legacy, I charge you with this responsibility. Let no man or group of men hide me away again. It is destiny for my writings to be revealed to the world.

Hail women! Hail men! I salute you. My blessings will be with you.

Chapter 2

DECISIONS

*One's mind has a way of making itself up in the background,
and it suddenly becomes clear what one means to do.*
- A.C. Benson

When Father Sebastian had completed his translation of the first scroll, we sat a few moments in silence.

"Oh god!" Jill muttered. "Do you realize the implications?"

The Father thoughtfully and slowly nodded yes. "It appears you two women were led there by Divine Providence so you could discover these scrolls. I am honored you were then led to me, and that I have this privilege."

Tears trickled down my face. I was choked with emotion. Peter reached into his pocket, brought out his kerchief and began dabbing my eyes. "Well, Ellen, it would seem that some guiding angel directed you to that cave."

In the midst of my tears I began blubbering, "I know. I know. Perhaps it was her, The Magdalene. I know I felt a presence in the cave."

Peter broke the moment by getting up and getting a bottle of wine and glasses. After pouring a glass for each of us, he held his glass up to give a toast. The ruby red wine reminded me of the communions I had partaken of as a small child. Laughing, I stood up with Peter and said, "When I was little, I took part in communion where we drank grape juice as the blood of Christ. Now, I say we toast to Mary Magdalene. May this wine represent her blood and her legacy." Little did I know the full import of my words.

The Father and Jill had also risen. We all touched glasses saying, "so be it" or "amen." Although we each were rather subdued, there was exhilaration in the air with what she had charged the finders of her scrolls. Father Sebastian was eager to return to his translating and went back to the computer. Peter and I told Jill we would take care of the clean up in the kitchen.

While I was washing the dishes and Peter was drying, I asked him what he thought the repercussions of our find would be.

Leaning against the counter, he folded his arms and looked at me. "If these scrolls are not a hoax, and I think they are the real thing, I would say this will create a major storm in the world of Christian religion. It is a travesty that Mary Magdalene has never had her own voice or recognition before. There may be some penalty for not reporting the find to the authorities, however we can use her opening statement that she wrote these scrolls to be revealed to the world. If we can keep the lid on this find until they are all translated, it will be to the benefit of the entire world."

"I agree with that, Peter. I wonder how long it will take Father Sebastian to translate the Greek into French? I also want them translated into English."

"Good suggestion. How adept are you and Jill with computers?"

"I would say Jill has more expertise than me. Of the two of us, she is the most capable. Are you suggesting she and I translate the scrolls from French to English?"

"Yep. That is if the two of you are willing. Let's see what The Father has to say about this." Quickly Peter and I finished our kitchen duties and went into the living room to speak with the others.

Jill was thumbing through a magazine while Father Sebastian was working diligently at the computer. Looking up at us she could see we had something on our minds.

Peter spoke first. "Father, could we interrupt you for a few moments?"

Turning, he said, "Oui." Peter asked how viable it would be to set up the other computer with a French to English translation program, saying that I also wanted the scrolls translated into English. A big smile broke out on the Father's face. "But of course. Using two computers would help immensely. It is my understanding Paul already has a French to English program installed on the other computer. Which of you is willing to take on the job?"

All three of us held up our hands. I looked at Peter. "I didn't realize you had computer skills."

"Ha! There are a lot of untapped resources in me. I may not be fast, but I can be accurate." Jill spoke up saying she would like to go first, and since I didn't consider myself too speedy, I agreed. Peter told her, "Go for it."

"Before we continue further, there is something I want to know from you Father."

"What is that, Ellen?"

"Are you aware of and is the Church aware of the contention that Jesus and Mary Magdalene were married and had two children?"

Looking me in the eye, the Father answered, "Oui. It is known and was also known throughout Europe until two hundred years ago." I was taken aback because he had answered so matter-of-factly. His credibility went up a notch for me.

He turned on the second computer and was opening the program when he stopped and turned around to look at us.

"Mes amies, I want to make a request. No more calling me Father. I now renounce the title and request you call me Sebastian. Bien?"

We agreed and it seemed to me the energy between us all lightened up. Jill took the printouts of the French version of the first Magdalene scroll and began typing. Peter and I wandered outside since there was nothing for us to do indoors.

The evening was warm, and we could see the scudding clouds against the darkening sky, giving a strong indication of more rain to come. A glider swing beckoned us, but before we sat down we wiped off the water from the previous shower. Peter pushed us to and fro with his long legs. It felt like we had known each other for a long time, and the silence between us was comfortable.

At times I can be very practical. "Peter, tomorrow we must devise a way to get more food supplies in. This could be a long haul." We discussed how to do this while not calling attention to ourselves and decided to ask Sebastian for his advice.

Returning to the house, we found Sebastian and Jill concentrating on the translations. When I said I was going to turn in, neither of them looked up. Saying goodnight to Peter, I retired to the bedroom Jill and I would share.

During the night I awoke to hear rain on the roof, a sound I've always enjoyed. I snuggled back to my sleep. When I awakened in the morning the sun was shining brightly. I did my stretches in bed, looking over to see Jill still snoring away. Apparently she had worked late into the night.

Heading to the bathroom for a shower, I could hear no sounds in the house. As the warm water pelted my skin, I pondered what the next translation would bring.

After dressing for the day, I went into the kitchen where I smelled coffee. Peter was there. He looked down on me with a smile and handed me a cup. "Good morning, you're just in time for a fresh pot." Gratefully I thanked him. Coffee was the one thing I had missed on the trails.

Just as I was taking my first sip, in walked Sebastian all full of smiles. I thought *Gawd, he looks like a new person, like someone with a purpose to live.* Saying good morning, he poured himself a cup.

"Okay Sebastian, what is the beaming all about?" I asked.

"Ah, Ellen, the translation is going magnificently. Wait one moment. I will get what Jill did last night. I give you the privilege to read it aloud."

In a moment he returned with several sheets of paper and placed them in my hands. Shakily, I began to read.

MARY MAGDALENE - MY BEGINNINGS
Scroll 2

I always had memory of my birth. Does that sound strange? As I came out of my mother's womb, two women held my mother as she, in a squatting position on two birthing bricks, began pushing down. The midwife coaxed my head and body through the channel. I came out with my eyes open because I wanted to see everything. My first eye contact was with the Priestess standing behind my mother with her hands resting on my mother's shoulders.

As our eyes met, there was a momentary shock of recognition between us. I remember hearing her say, "Here is another Sophia." The midwife, handing me to another woman, gasped as she saw my eyes. It is very rare for a newborn babe to have its eyes open at birth. Before relinquishing me, she exclaimed that my eyes were of two colors. One eye was green and the other, blue.

The Priestess smiled and said, "Yes, she is a Sophia coming back to teach us. She has the mark of a Sophia."

"Ah, Sophia," the other women murmured in a voice of awe. Another woman appeared closer to me and I would later realize she was my grandmother. "Are you sure?" she asked with the Priestess replying, "Kandake, I am sure."

Quickly the umbilical cord was severed and the afterbirth taken. My mother was assisted to the cot prepared expressly for the cleansing of her. I was wrapped in a clean soft cloth and placed on her belly. One of the assisting women handed the Priestess an alabaster jar of oil for my anointing. The aromatic oil of spikenard was gently rubbed over my body until I was clean. As the Priestess performed this act of anointing and blessing, she sang this song:

> *Praise be to the Creator of All.*
> *Praise be unto this Life*
> *For she is the one foretold*
> *To be the Messenger of Hope.*
> *She is the Anointed One*
> *To bring the Message of the Remembrance*
> *Of who we are.*
> *Rejoice, rejoice, rejoice!*

Thus began my life in this incarnation. The name given to me was Makeda. I am also called Magda as well as Mariam. Perhaps I should give an accounting of my lineage to explain these names.

Chapter 3

A SHOCKING REVELATION

Feel the fear and do it anyway.
- Anon.

When I finished reading the translation aloud, the tears came. Jill had walked into the kitchen just as I read the last words. With his arms folded Peter stood as if stunned.

Jill spoke up, "Pretty awesome, huh?"

"Awesome doesn't describe it. Oh my gawd, she was declared a Sophia. Now what does that mean?"

Sebastian answered, "Sophia is another name for Wisdom with a capital W. Some say she was a goddess and others say she represents the feminine principle. I personally tend to go with the feminine principle theory. It is difficult for me to accept the goddess theory at this time."

Peter shook his head yes. "From my reading, the creator is both the male and the female. The feminine has been represented by the Greek name Sophia. The male has been represented by the Sun, also called Ra."

"Yes," Jill interrupted. "From my understanding the Catholics believe Sophia is another word for the Holy Spirit."

I had to laugh. "Father, Son and Sophia. Well, I guess they must give some importance to the feminine, but look at the symbology. The sun represents power, the giving of life."

"Non," Sebastian said. "Not the giving of life. Look at nature. Mother Gaia gives forth life while the sun nourishes its growth."

"I wonder what The Magdalene meant when she said she had the mark of a Sophia? Perhaps her one blue eye and one green eye meant duality, and she was here to show it could be overcome?" Jill offered.

"Oui, oui," Sebastian replied. "That is possible. I go for that interpretation." The rest of us agreed.

Peter said he would take over for Jill while Sebastian returned to his translating.

Jill and I talked about the need to go into Toulouse and purchase supplies. However, after taking inventory of what we had on hand, we found we could delay the trip for awhile.

We all slipped into daily routines and the days passed quickly. I was rather at loose ends as Jill and Peter alternated on the computer. Jill finally gave up her need to cook so I took over and Peter helped. We could see Jill was becoming as passionate about translating as Sebastian.

One morning after breakfast Jill announced the day for shopping had arrived. Sebastian gave us the keys to his car and suggested we not purchase a large amount at any one place since that was not the French way of shopping. He gave us directions to the various supermarchés, also called hypermarchés, which by American standards were sparse in some locales. With me driving, Jill and I set out for the day.

It was pleasant and warm as we drove into Toulouse following Sebastian's directions. Jill and I needed to find an American Express or a bank where we could exchange traveler's checks for euros.

"Wouldn't you think it might be best to go to the université area to locate one?" she asked.

"No. What if Sebastian's car is recognized? Perhaps it would be better to go near the aeronautics industrial area first."

"Good idea." Soon Jill pointed out a bank as we neared the industrial area. Parking the car in front, we walked in and the exchanged our traveler's checks. The rate wasn't too bad, and our transactions were done easily. With euros in our pockets we followed Sebastian's directions and headed out for one of the hypermarchés. We laughed at our attempt to follow directions but managed to arrive at the one we were drawn to.

We knew that in many locales, the French still clung to their local specialty shops and open markets. However Toulouse boasted six or seven hypermarchés. We chose to go to the Carrefour at Portel-sur-Garonne, since it was purported to be the largest in France.

It was a regular shopping mall, and we knew from experience that we needed a 50-cent euro coin to get a shopping cart. The French were smart to lock up their carts. In many U.S. cities they are stolen or never find their way back to the store. To get one, a 50-cent euro coin was inserted into a coin box slot; to get the 50-cent euro coin back, the cart had to be returned and secured into the cart stand.

We also knew that French stores were usually closed from twelve to two in the afternoon, so we wanted to make the most of the morning. A clothing store caught my eye and Jill agreed to some additional shopping. We each purchased several skirts with tops to match and underwear.

We were pleasantly surprised by the selections at the hypermarché as we made our way through the aisles choosing items we thought would be suitable for future meals.

The produce was excellent. And we purchased a variety of cheeses along with spices to replenish what Paul had left. Fortunately Paul had a freezer so we stocked up on meat and chicken.

Jill reminded me we had to have coffee, sugar and flour, and I added that we mustn't forget some chocolate and wine.

While waiting in line to check out, we were contemplating taking the subway down to the city center. Just as we reached the check out, I noticed a rack of newspapers and paused to see if I could read the headlines.

When I saw a photo of the hole I had fallen into, a shockwave went through me. The photo showed a young grinning boy standing beside it. Quickly I added the paper to our purchases.

Oh gawd, I thought to myself. I didn't want to say anything to Jill until we were out of the parking lot. Once we had our purchases stowed in the car's trunk, I asked Jill if she would drive. I said I didn't think we should leave perishables in the trunk and attempt going to the city center on the subway.

Taking the keys, Jill slid into the driver's seat and we started out. "Okay Ellen, what's really going on? You look like you've seen a ghost."

"I have." I pulled the newspaper out and showed her the news photo.

"Oh jesus christ!" she moaned. Fortunately she didn't run off the road. I began translating the best I could while she drove us back to Paul's place.

According to what the article said, a young boy was helping his family move cows to the higher pastures near Mirepoix when he missed a young calf. He began tracing back the way they had come. He had stopped to look for the calf when he saw two people emerge from a hole in the ground. He said they were carrying bags of some kind. The boy, Etienne Ducat, continued to look for the missing calf. When he found it, he returned to his family who was moving up the trail with the herd. He told his father what he had seen.

Knowing this was most unusual, his father sent Etienne and his brother Jean back to Mirepoix to report it to the police. In making an investigation, the police found an unknown cave and inside three large ceramic urns. On the floor of the cave were two parchment scrolls wrapped in linen cloth. The Bibliothèque nationale de France has been notified and was now also investigating.

The article didn't mention that the two seen emerging from the cave were women. We both breathed a sigh of relief. So far we had not been identified, however we were aghast that we had dropped two scrolls.

On the way back to Peter and Sebastian we discussed what this could mean for us. Jill almost overshot the driveway into Paul's property. When we got to the garage, she tooted the horn and out came Peter with Sebastian following on his heels.

"Hey, we weren't expecting you back until evening." Jill opened the trunk and Peter began unloading the packages. Sebastian joined in and soon the car was in the barn. Jill and I went into the kitchen where Peter and Sebastian were, having brought in the final load.

"You two look as though you have had a shock. What gives?" Peter asked as he moved towards his favorite spot by the sink. Folding his arms he looked at each of us. Sebastian was also staring at us.

I brought out the newspaper and handed it to Peter. He gave a low whistle and passed it to Sebastian who read the article. With a sound that almost sounded like "aha," he commented the story was dated that day, yet Jill and I had made the discovery some weeks ago. He said perhaps we should sit around the table to discuss this. Peter pulled a chair out with one of his feet and sat down.

After telling the story of how I discovered the article on a newsstand by the check out at the market, we began discussing what this could portend for us. Sebastian picked up the paper again saying, "I went through the scrolls carefully today and I found two were missing. The Magdalene was clever. She numbered them."

"What can this mean for us?" I asked.

"I don't think there is any immediate danger since all that has been reported is only what's in this story. Let's continue on with our translations. Bien?"

Peter picked up the newspaper. "There is something wrong with this. The article indicates the discovery was within the past few days. I want to know what has happened in the interim."

"Pardon. What is interim?"

Peter chuckled. "Interim means the time between the discovery of the scrolls and when the article was printed."

"Oui. I understand now. There are perhaps reasons such as the Bibliothèque is waiting to examine and authenticate the jars and the scrolls. There will probably be politics involved."

"Or," Jill put in, "It could also mean it is a maneuver to get us to reveal ourselves."

"Très bien, you think well Jill. Yet, I still think there is no immediate danger, and I desire to continue with the translations."

With a sigh of relief we all agreed we should continue our work on the scrolls. We talked of our shopping trip. Then I got up to put the kitchen items away, and Peter said he would help while Jill was going to follow Sebastian into the alcove off the living room to see what had been accomplished while we were gone.

Before leaving the kitchen, Sebastian asked if we wanted to hear what had been translated. Of course, we said yes and that postponed our kitchen duty.

MARY MAGDALENE – MY HERITAGE
Scroll 3

My mother, Princess Amanitore was the daughter of the reigning Kandake[1] Amanishakheto of Ethiopia. My father was Prince Natakami. Our lineage were people quite tall with beautiful shades of dark skin. The shade of my skin grew to be a beautiful dark cinnamon color. The Greeks gave us the name Ethiopians meaning the "burnt skins." Some of us had hair the color of burnt copper. I inherited the copper hair. Our beautiful hair could be tight with curls or straight, but mine was somewhere in between.

Through my grandmother Kandake Amanishakheto, I was descended from a great Queen for whom I was named. She was the great Queen Makeda also known as Magda of Sheba. In learning of my great heritage, I was told the Queen Makeda had traveled to the land of a great king named Solomon. While there, this great Queen became pregnant, and she gave birth to a son named Menelik and it is through him that my Grandmother, Mother and I descended. I have a great lineage.

I am of the House of Solomon by way of my ancestor Menelik the son of Solomon and Queen Makeda, the Queen of Sheba. Ethiopia and Egypt were called Sheba or Saba during her reign. I have chosen well my lineage, the choice being made when I was living on the plane of contemplation before I was born into this lifetime.

---

[1] Kandake, an ancient Ethiopian word for queen

Chapter 4

INTENSIFIED ATTRACTION

*Love is a perky elf dancing a merry little jig and then
suddenly he turns on you with a miniature machine gun.*
- Matt Groening

It was difficult not to be emotional over these revelations. I noticed the others were feeling what I felt. From scrolls written over 2000 years ago, we were at last learning about Mary Magdalene.

Peter was the first to speak. "She's a descendent of the Queen of Sheba? That goes back a long way. Sebastian, do you know anything about the Queen of Sheba?"

Clearing his throat, Sebastian replied, "If my memory serves me correct, there is an Ethiopian bible named the *Kebra Negast*. It along with the Old Testament tells the story of the Queen of Sheba and Solomon. The issue of their union was a son named Menelik. Supposedly it is regarded as the ultimate authority on the history of the conversion of the Ethiopians to the God of the Jews. Before this conversion, it is said they worshiped the sun, the moon and the stars. As a side note, the *Kebra Negast* is the bible of the Rastafarian religion in Jamaica and also in the West Indies."

"Okay," I said. "So, it is pretty well established there was a Queen of Sheba, but has anyone heard of those queens of Ethiopia? She writes saying they were her grandmother and mother."

"The Internet has all sorts of information. I think we can probably find out something if we do a little research," Jill offered.

"Holy moley!" Peter exclaimed. "This would mean she was black skinned! It also explains the many Black Madonnas in France, Spain and parts of Europe."

"Perhaps you are right. Perhaps this is one reason the Church wanted to destroy her greatness by making her into a white prostitute and a whore," said Sebastian. "There is no mention of her being a prostitute or whore in the New Testament in the Bible, because this is a myth created by Pope Gregory I and perpetuated by the Church."

"Do you realize the repercussions this will cause when the age of these papyri are established?" I asked.

Jill spoke in a contemplative voice. "It's beginning to sound as though she wrote these as a diary, and she really wanted the world to know about her."

"You're right," I said. "I wonder if these scrolls were written at various stages of her life? Perhaps you are correct."

Jill was eager to continue with the French to English translations while Sebastian worked on the Greek to French ones.

He commented he was happy The Magdalene's papyri were not as long as some ancient Egyptian ones. When asked what he meant, he said that some of the ancient papyri scrolls were 35 feet long. These were much shorter.

Peter and I volunteered to take care of the meals and clean up, and we agreed that in the evening we would work out a schedule of what we could do to facilitate household maintenance and cooking. Sebastian suggested we turn on the early morning news each day to see if there were any new developments, and of course, we all thought that was a good idea.

The following morning after breakfast Peter and I planned the evening meal then set out for a walk through the woods. Splotches of sun were peeking through the branches of the trees. The forest appeared magical as the sunlight hit the residue of rain on the leaves of the lower branches, making sparkles that gave off minuscule rainbows. With the aroma wafting up from the soil along with the smell of wild strawberries and violets, I felt at times like we were in a different world.

Soon we heard the gurgling of running water as we reached a Y in the path. I noticed a marker attached to a tree. It was painted with a yellow stripe on top and a red stripe on the bottom. It wasn't very large, but big enough to be spotted. I stopped, commenting that here was one of the officially marked trails.

"Yes. This is apparently a regional marker. Did you know there are close to 180,000 kilometers of walking trails throughout France?"

"That's a long hike!" I exclaimed. I had read something about the marked trails before coming to Europe. "What else do you know about them?"

Peter said there were four types of walking trails maintained throughout France. There were the national trails whose markers were white on top and red on the bottom. The regional trails' markers were signs like the one we were looking at with yellow and red stripes. The third were the local trails, which had single yellow stripes. And the fourth were international trails that overlay or use the French trails.

We chose to take the trail to the right and within a short distance came to a small footbridge across a running stream. It was the source of the gurgling water we had heard. Walking onto the bridge, we looked down into the clear water and watched various fish swimming about. Since I don't fish, I couldn't make out the species, except I knew they weren't goldfish.

I told Peter that and he laughed. As I turned to walk on, he caught me by the elbow turning me around. I looked up into his eyes, and I swear my heart began to pound. Cupping my chin in his hands he asked, "Do you know when I first fell in love with you?"

"No. Tell me."

"Remember during our trek from the Spanish side of the Pyrenees when Nancy fell and broke her leg?" I nodded. "When I saw you take charge telling us to make splints until we could get the medics in, I knew I loved you. You are one helluva woman. When you sought me out at Mirepoix after your discovery, I knew I had to follow you no matter what."

"Oh Peter! I can't remember when I first knew I loved you. It's as though I've loved you from the first moment we met."

Still holding my face in his hands, Peter bent down, gently kissing me. Time stood still. The kiss became a long passionate one.

Suddenly we heard an "Ahem." Jumping apart, we saw two walkers standing at the entrance to the footbridge. The man and woman were beaming, and I felt a flush of scarlet rise up in my face. Peter held my hand tightly as we stood aside allowing them to pass.

After they had gone on their way, we began laughing uproariously and while holding hands, we returned the way we had come. We were like two giggling school children and stopped to kiss, again and again. Eventually we made it back to the house. But before we went in, Peter took me in his arms, passionately kissing me again.

"Hey, guy, this is pretty heady," I whispered.

Reluctantly, we pulled apart and went inside. Holding hands we walked into the living room. Jill was the first to look around.

"Back so soon?"

Soon? I thought we had been gone hours.

Jill looked at us again. "Looks like Cupid's dart has found its mark at last."

Sebastian swiveled around, and I assume it was apparent Peter and I were in love. Getting up, he embraced us while congratulating us.

"Is it that evident?" I asked.

Jill laughed. "Oh my dears, I've been watching this happen ever since we met Peter on the GR trail. I was waiting for the realization to hit you two."

Sebastian told us it was a time to celebrate. Going to the kitchen he returned with four goblets and a bottle of champagne. In answer to our quizzical expressions he said, "One must always keep a chilled bottle of champagne for celebrations, especially for those of professed love."

Clinking our goblets, Peter spoke first. "I accept your blessings and I am blessed. I have exposed for all the world to see that which I have thought I had kept hidden for these weeks."

Feeling like a star struck kid, I was overwhelmed. Seemingly, it had happened so fast for me, although for Peter it was a natural evolution from the moment he laid eyes on me at the beginning of our hiking trip. Or so he said.

Stooping down, Peter kissed me, and then we were all talking at once until Jill got up and put together a plate of cheeses, cold cuts and bread. Once we had finished the champagne, Jill suggested she begin preparations for our dinner, with Sebastian volunteering to help her.

Peter and I wandered out into the garden. To me, it looked so different. I realize now that I could have been in an altered state of consciousness. We didn't say much because walking hand in hand was enough. It was the moment to experience the magic of our revelation of love.

Before dinner I went into my bedroom, changing to a skirt and knit top. Jill came in and hugged me. She also changed. When we emerged, both men clapped, telling us how beautiful we were.

The meal was a gala affair. They brought us up to date on what had been translated thus far. Jill went and got the printout, and while we sat drinking our coffee and cognac, she read.

৵৶৹ ৵৶৹ ৵৶৹

MARY MAGDALENE - MY FIRST SIX YEARS
Scroll 4

At the time of my birth it was the custom for the mother and child to remain secluded in a section of rooms for six weeks or until the mother's menses ceased. It was a period of rest for both mother and child and a period of purification for the mother as the menses were regarded as residue of the birth matter, and it was necessary that her body rest and become renewed.

Two weeks before we were to leave this bower,[1] my mother, having suckled me, gave me over to a wet nurse. Her name was Hadja, and she became my nurse. Hadja was tall with skin of ebony. Her white teeth gleamed when she smiled. She smiled often unless I did something she thought was unworthy of my royal status.

There was an abundance of attention given to me by my grandmother as well as my parents and my two older brothers. With all the attention, I knew I was loved.

---

[1] Bower: meaning, a retreat

Those first six years of my life were years of joy and happiness. My Father took a delight in my growth and antics, and called me Re-Re saying I was indeed a sun in his life. Mother and Grandmother Kandake also delighted in my growth, and they were quick to recognize the potentials in me. It was discussed and a decision made that I was to attend the Temple of the Lion upon attaining age six. However, until that time I was allowed the freedom to explore to a certain extent.

Accompanied by Hadja, I had the opportunity to explore the grounds of the Palace and my happiness was truly in Nature. The gardeners delighted in my coming, as I was inquisitive, asking many questions. I could have spent hours observing a caterpillar eating leaves before weaving its cocoon. As patient as Hadja was, there would be a moment when she felt I had observed long enough, and I would be pulled away to a meal or something else.

The keepers of the royal animal compound were also happy in my coming. One particular day when I was age four, Hadja took me to the compound, and while there, one of the massive lions was roaring with agony. Hadja attempted to restrain me from getting close to the enclosure where the lion was held. Nimuji, the chief of the animal enclosures was beside himself as to what to do.

Silently communing with the great male lion, I learned he had been given poisoned meat by one of the animal keepers. Upon relaying this to Nimuji, he hissed with great anger, that someone would poison one of the Prince's favorite lions!

Quickly the lion was given a substance to induce vomiting of the vile poison from his system. Hadja attempted to pull me away, but I would not go. This was far more interesting than anything else there was to do or see. Nimuji called all his animal keepers together, and he set about interrogating each of them. Scanning the light fields of energy surrounding their bodies, I knew which was the guilty culprit. Tugging at Nimuji's clothing to get his attention, I whispered which one had done the deed.

Being a wise man, he dismissed all the keepers except for the guilty one. Nimuji asked Hadja to take me away and I went willingly since I knew the lion would live. Later I learned the man had confessed he was jealous of Nimuji's position, and he wanted it himself. He thought if one of Father's lions died,

Nimuji would be dismissed and he would get the position. Without being told, I knew the guilty man had been taken out into the jungle and staked as a lure for lions. The next time I saw Nimuji he smiled, telling me I was gifted with the sacred sight. Naturally my father had been told what happened. He smiled saying to me, "Truly Re-Re, you have the gift of the gods."

Later my Mother and Father discussed the gifts I had. Each expressed their concern others would misuse my gifts, and both agreed to observe and take no action until necessary.

From the lion episode, the word spread rapidly throughout the Palace and the surrounding territory. It wasn't long before everyone I came in contact with, except the servants who had been given explicit orders, wanted me to foresee the future for them.

My parents were wise in turning down all requests, and at last the callers and requests ceased. I was content to explore the gardens where I talked to each plant and the plants responded. The gardens were said to be the most abundant and the most beautiful in the memories of everyone.

For the most part, my playmates were those in the unseen. Hadja thought I was pretending when I carried on lively conversations with them. She seemed always to be scolding me, as I would wander off to a new interest – a new exploration. Life was a marvel to me and I wanted to savor each moment. It was as if I had returned to greet old friends. What I was feeling could not be explained to my family or to Hadja.

Father would sit listening to my stories that seemed outlandish to him. Laughing, he would tousle my copper hair. Father was kind and I knew he was humoring me, however I didn't cease. In my mind I knew what I had seen, and I knew what had transpired was real.

These brief six years gave me the opportunity to be a child without a care and I was able to connect with Nature. Yes, I did have abilities to foresee the future some of the time. I also read the lights around people when I wanted to. For the most part it was a time of learning. I wanted to know what Grandmother did. There were times I would sit in on her arbitrations with the people she ruled. The decisions she made were based upon the seriousness of the issue at hand. My

Mother and Father also sat in on these sessions. The times Grandmother was away inspecting her kingdom, they would take over, and there always seemed to be unrest with the Roman occupation in the north and it disturbed them. Grandmother was a great warrior, passing this trait to my Mother, and in one respect to me.

Other times I could be found in the great kitchen learning to bake and know the spices to use in different foods. My mother saw to it I was taught the art of sewing and the ways of women. Or I should say she attempted to have me taught because my mind was elsewhere. However, Mother would sometimes gently and not so gently pull me back to the present when my instructors came to her complaining of my truancy.

Our primary palace residence was located in the capitol named Meroe, near the sixth cataract of the Great Nile River. The palace grounds were on a large island in the Nile River where I spent hours at the river's edge watching the birds as well as the various fish in the water. I loved watching the numerous barges carrying trade goods moving up and down the Nile. At times I could smell the frankincense and myrrh as well as other delicious smelling spices. There were also barges carrying gold, amber, copper, ebony and the spices from the East.

Hadja attempted to keep me near her because she had a great fear of the crocodiles that came to our waters from time to time. She would roll her beautiful eyes when I told her I spoke with them, and they assured me no harm would come from them.

The trips to the great Temple were always looked forward to with great anticipation. I loved going through the Avenue of the Rams that my parents had duplicated from the Avenue at Karnak. Always when I gazed upon the sphinxes with the ram's head, a memory would tug at me of some forgotten time and a teacher.

Grandmother was primarily occupied with the growing threat of the Romans encroaching into her territory. Therefore, Mother and Father made many trips to inspect the territories claimed by Grandmother, Mother and Father. However, there was one memorable trip to Lake Tana in the highlands and our palace at Magdala.

We departed at the beginning of shemu, the harvest season when the rivers would not be flooding. It was also a time of celebration. We began by traveling north on the royal barge with a retinue of many servants requiring many additional barges. We were also taking with us goods to trade, as Magdala was a great trading center.

We sailed north until the great River met the Atbara River, which would take us into the highlands. It was not wise to travel south as the second Nile, or the Blue Nile, was impassable for our barges. I was told there was a great waterfall preventing the way.

We were several days away from Meroe when we passed a splendid barge on its way north. We passed so close I could almost reach out my arms and touch another on the passing barge. As I was contemplating this, my attention was drawn to a young boy about the age of 12. He was looking at me, and our eyes locked for what seemed an endless time. I knew I knew him, however I knew not whence. His hair was to his shoulders and a beautiful shade of copper. His blue eyes were set against skin that was of a lighter shade than mine. I thought of it as a shade of bronze, and I thought him most beautiful.

Finally my gaze shifted, and he laughed a wonderful laugh. Smiling in return, I felt a great joy welling up inside of my chest because I knew we would meet again. It was my destiny.

Calling to Hadja, I asked her where the barge was going. She replied, "To the Temple of Isis, my Princess."

"Do you know who that young boy at the rail is?" I asked.

With a mischievous look in her eyes, she asked, "Do you mean the one with the red hair and blue eyes?" She knew he was the one as there was no other boy on the deck.

"Yes," I replied. "Find out his name." With a slight bow, Hadja left to do my bidding.

It wasn't too long before she returned and with a slight smile told me, "His name is Yeshua ben Joseph of the land of Judea."

I instantly replied "Not Judea. The correct name is Canaan."

Hadja's eyes grew wide, and she asked, "How do you know my Princess?"

I thought a moment. "I do not know how I know it, but I know it is true."

As if anticipating my next question, she continued, "It is said he is on his way to the Temple of Isis for further schooling in the school of mysteries."

I thanked her. Seemingly it appeared I dismissed the information as if it were of no importance. However, I felt a great excitement because I knew I also would be attending the same school.

The days passed with a splendor of sights. The vegetation was lush and thick. The air was humid although I knew we were climbing towards the mountains. I marveled at the birds, and among them were the great blue herons and the smaller sunbirds, rosy finches. The myriad of colors were dazzling; intertwined with a cacophony of sounds, the odors emitted by the flowers were heady and sweet. I felt it was another world.

All too soon we arrived at a high plateau amidst towering mountains. The river had dwindled, making it necessary for the barges to be left behind. We were carried by litter while donkeys and camels brought our supplies. It was an exciting time for me. Sometimes I chafed at being confined because I loved the freedom of exploring.

At last the city of Magdala appeared on the horizon. Tingling with anticipation I could hardly contain myself. The sights and smells were scented with spices and camel dung along with the sweet smell of frangipani. I marveled at the tilled grapevines, the olive trees and the fig trees. At my small age it was a paradise.

The Palace was smaller than the one at Meroe, however it was comfortable. My rooms opened toward the majestic snowcapped mountains. Every part of me moved with excitement and I wanted to go and explore these new surroundings. Hadja scolded me, telling me I had to wait until she was sure our garments and belongings were put away properly.

Every day was a new experience, with my father often taking me into the market place where I viewed the comings and goings of the traders from the deserts and the east. There were many different languages spoken and I found I could follow most of them. I was blessed with having an ear for languages, thinking it natural and everyone should be able to understand them too.

One day I asked my mother why Magdala was so different. She was taking her rest period and looked at me with her eyes full of love. I could tell she was making a decision. Mother took me by the hand leading me to a garden seat, telling me she would tell me as it had been told to her.

"Magdala was named for our great ancestress, the Queen of Sheba a country also known as Ethiopia. This area was unique as it was the birthplace of humanity. The gods, having come from a far away other place, settled here. It was virtually a fertile paradise. There were many treasures here, which they mined, taking them away in their great air ships. Sometimes if we look up into the sky at night, we can see these air ships mingled among the stars.

"This all began many thousands of years ago, and these gods were called the Annunaki. It has been said that after thousands of years they began to grumble because they were tired of mining gold and other treasures. A great call went out to one of their great goddesses named Ninhursag, and she was well trained and knowledgeable in creating new species.

"On this land were beings that walked upright, however their intelligence had not developed. In her place of work, Ninhursag mated a seed from one of the female beings with the seed of one of the Annunaki. Ninhursag planted this seed in the womb of one of the female Annunaki, who birthed a new being in nine months. There was great excitement. And with the first success, she created more. However, these new species were not what she really wanted, and it took many attempts to bring forth a being that could be trained to be a worker for the Annunaki.

"There was one thing wrong. These beings could not mate, so Ninhursag went back to her work place and taking a bit from one of the species, she created an evolution of these beings, which became the female. Now the two could mate and bring forth new beings. These were named the humans or the male and the female. Thus began our race of people."

"But Mother, how did we get to be so intelligent?" I asked.

"The story told is that Ninhursag could not bear to kill off her creations who did not measure up to what was wanted in the worker human. She turned them out of the place of creation, and they were sent off to fend for themselves. And through many experiences and learning became intelligent."

"But Mother, who occupied those humans? I mean, did they have a soul?"

"Ah," she replied. "Yes, the gods had new bodies to explore and be born into. As some of the new humans quickly learned, they had a part of the gods in them. Now, my beloved Mariam, it is the hour when I must attend to my duties."

Left alone, I pondered this. I was in awe that here in this area were the beginnings of our people. I longed to know more. The opportunity did not arise for me to ask Mother for more of this story. With the business of my Mother and Father completed, we began our return trip home.

Chapter 5

DOWN THE RABBIT HOLE

*The rabbit-hole went straight on like a tunnel for some way,
and then dipped suddenly down.*
- Alice in Wonderland, Lewis Carroll

When Sebastian ended his reading, we sat for a few moments mentally digesting what he had translated. I was the first to break the silence.

"Well, she was truly of royalty, and this would explain in part why the Knights Templar purportedly revered her. Information alluding to what The Magdalene had written must have been placed in the supposed Temple of Solomon where they found it."

Sebastian agreed. "I think you are correct Ellen. There are many documents in the archives of the Vatican that I was not privy to. It is possible all this was known until the Emperor Constantine called the Council of Nicea."

"Wasn't that in 325 A.D.?" Jill asked.

"Oui," Sebastian answered and continued, "Constantine created the Byzantine Empire, and he needed something to empower his position. His assistant, Magyaris, suggested he consult the prophecies of an oracle[1] of Delphi. As the story goes, he consulted the writings of the prophecies, and these writings were said to have been given 500 years prior. According to this particular Oracle, she foretold that the emperor who was head of the Roman Empire 500 years in the future would need to form a new religion."

Mesmerized, we urged Sebastian to continue. "Constantine was not a Christian. In fact, the people who believed in the teachings of Jesus were not called Christians until after the Council. They were known to have gnosis, which means 'to know.' In other words, they were gnostics.

---

[1] Refers to *The Sibylline Books*

Constantine claimed he had a vision of Christ on the cross, however it was more after the fact when he formed the Council to create a new religion. Of course it was done as self-serving, to enhance his power and position.

"As it is known in some circles, there were men traveling all over telling stories of various religions such as those of India, Egypt and the Jews. These storytellers were called presbytères.[2] These presbytères were called to the Council by Constantine and were told to bring any old manuscripts they had. Of course after the Council met, the meaning of presbyter changed, and it evolved into what is known today as bishop and priest.

"From these manuscripts, which contained stories from all religions, a new religion was created. There was great conflict among them as to who would be declared a god, and Jesus narrowly won out. There were other Christs known at that time. From my reading, a myth of Jesus being the only Son of God was created at this Council. Thus was born Christianity."

"So," I said, "history became a distortion due to the power and control it could bring."

"Ah oui, you are correct, Ellen," Sebastian replied.

Jill asked, "Who were the other Christs?"

"Ah, Apollonius of Tyiana. It is also written he was a Nazorean,[3] and another was Buddha. It is documented Apollonius was in chains before a Roman Tribune when he disappeared into the air, leaving his chains on the floor."

We paused for a few moments to think of what Sebastian had told us. I knew some of it, but not all.

Jill told us that she had read Zechariah Sitchen's books, *The Earth Chronicles*, and that he wrote about the Annunaki as well as Ninhursag.

Peter spoke up. "What do you think of her mother mentioning air ships? From The Magdalene's writing, it would seem it was a common occurrence."

Sebastian almost exploded. "Non! C'est impossible! Air ships two thousand years ago? Non, c'est impossible."

---

[2] Presbyters, wandering public orators
[3] Nasorean, Nazorean are variations for Nazarene

Smiling at him, Jill asked if he had heard of UFO's. He looked perplexed. "UFO's? What are those? Ah oui, now I understand. The French word is ovni. But do continue."

Peter and I asked Jill to go on since she had read the books.

"Sebastian, these UFO's or ovni's were the space ships of beings visiting this Earth from other planets, universes and galaxies. Sitchin translated the information from Sumerian tablets that archeologists found."

He shook his head in disbelief. "Perhaps what you say is true. I must think on this information, but now, I will return to my computer work." Jill excused herself and said she was going back to work also.

After completing our chores, Peter and I went out into the garden. The night air was warm and there was a slight breeze. We sat in the glider swing with neither of us saying much until I spoke up. I said I didn't want there to be any hidden past between us. Peter agreed and began telling me about his life.

He had known after the first year of his marriage to Shelia that it was a mistake, but he was too proud to admit it and thought he could make it work. His wife didn't want children, preferring to pursue her career as a psychologist. Peter began his business and threw himself into it. As he related this to me, he said it was an empty relationship with many quarrels. They had talked of divorcing, however by then she enjoyed being the wife of a very successful businessman. Peter had developed a new software chip. And when his business hit NASDAQ, his fortune soared.

Coming home late one night, he found Shelia sitting in the darkened living room. She began laughing, telling him she was pregnant.

"I didn't know whether to laugh or cry," he said. "When I got over my shock, I told her how pleased I was. Her response was, 'Don't be; it isn't yours.'

"I was stunned and left the room. She left the house but I didn't know it. The next thing I knew, the doorbell was ringing, and I went down to answer it. A highway patrolman stood there and with a sinking feeling I knew something had happened. He told me there had been an accident and asked if he could come in. I nodded yes and stepped back from the door. He told me there had been a one-car accident, and Sheila had been killed instantly.

"After that, I began questioning my life and the purpose of it. A year later I sold the business, setting out to learn what life is supposed to be about."

I reached over and kissed him. "Thank you my darling."

Then I began my story. "Walter and I met while at Stanford. He was handsome and could be very charismatic. I knew he had slept with half of my sorority sisters but I didn't care. Walter and I graduated and married while we were in law school.

"My father was a prominent attorney and it was the prestige of marrying the daughter of Fred Lassiter that attracted Walter to me. I was a plum in his eyes, and it opened doors for him. It wasn't too long before he began drinking, and I realized I had married a man with few scruples. I was heartsick but too stubborn to walk away from it.

"When my father died, I was bereft. We had been very close. On his deathbed he urged me to leave Walter and never look back. After the funeral, I went home, packed the belongings I wanted and left. I don't think Walter even knew I was leaving; he was too drunk. Fortunately my Dad left me an inheritance that Walter couldn't touch and here I am."

Peter and I talked long into the night, and when we decided to turn in, it was agreed I would still sleep in the room with Jill. Somehow it didn't seem the right moment for us.

The following morning after we had cleaned up the breakfast dishes, Peter and I did the laundry for the four of us and dusted all the rooms. By lunchtime we were ready for a walk and left Jill and Sebastian deep in their translations.

Peter carried the picnic basket, which contained a bottle of wine, bread, cheese and fruit. We were walking in silence when he stopped, pulling me off onto a barely noticeable trail that led to a small clearing. "Now is the moment," he said, setting the basket down and reaching for me.

I nodded yes. We began kissing and then he stopped, reached into the basket, and pulled out a sheet. Grinning, he said, "I came prepared."

We spread the sheet on the ground and he began unfastening my shirt. I allowed him to undress me and then I began undressing him. Slowly we sank onto the sheet and our lovemaking became passionate and breathtaking. "I don't give a damn who sees us, I want you," he whispered.

How can I describe the ecstasy I felt? With his mouth on my nipples, and then kissing me all over, I felt a wave of electricity shoot through me. Finally Peter entered me, moving in and out not too fast as he was seeking my clitoris. I know I moaned in sublime ecstasy while he maintained his hardness as his penis stroked my clitoris. I cried, "Now!" and we climaxed at the same moment.

Never in my life had I experienced an orgasm such as that one. Walter was the only man I had had sex with and it was most unsatisfactory. With Walter it was "wham, bang, thank you ma'am." Spent, I lay in Peter's arms while he kissed my hair. I allowed tears of joy to flow down my face and he kissed them away. "Oh Peter, it was wonderful. I never dreamed it could be this magnificent."

"Sweetheart, my most precious one, I never thought it could be this wonderful either. It's only going to get better." Peter began stroking me and kissing me, and he entered me again and I was brought to a new height of orgasmic splendor. When at last we were filled, Peter pulled out another surprise – two cloths which he dampened from his water bottle.

"You knew we were going to do this!" I teased.

"Yep," he replied. "I plotted this last night after we went to our separate beds."

After cleaning each other, we dressed and realized we were both famished. It was time for the lunch we had brought. I was in a timeless, magical state of being. And for the next few days we maintained our picnic routine.

Jill and Sebastian were totally immersed in their translating and didn't seem to notice our absences. At times I felt a rush of guilt because they were doing all the work. When I aired my feelings to Jill she laughed, telling me she was thoroughly enjoying what she was doing.

THE TEMPLE OF THE LION
Scroll 5

It was all so strange, the first year. Suddenly I was thrown into a very different way of life because I was required to live at the Temple of the Lion, as this was the first level of preparation for greater learning.

At home in Meroe there had been Hadja to wait upon me, along with a host of other servants to do my bidding. I always had free time to explore Nature and the grounds of the Palace; but all of this changed.

After the departure of my parents, the Priestess explained to me it was a requirement to wear the robe of a novice, which was white. She gave me a verbal list of what my duties were to be. A gong would sound one-half hour before sunrise. This was the signal for all to rise to greet the day while paying homage to Ra. At the sound of the second gong we were to make our pallet, followed by making our morning ablutions.

The list seemed endless. Make my pallet? I had always had a maid to do this for me. I knew enough not to interrupt the Priestess as she presented a formidable countenance to me. After the seemingly endless list of do this and do nots, she clapped her hands twice, and immediately a young novice appeared. She was introduced as Meesha, and she would guide me through the procedures and responsibilities for novices.

From being a pampered darling princess of the household of Kandake Amanishakheto and Prince Natakami, I was thrust into an environment of self-responsibility. It soon became evident to the High Priestess and others that I was not one to conform to rules which I deemed to be stupid.

In the beginning I would run away to explore the gardens while my duty to help serve meals or to assist in the kitchens was forgotten. The Priestess Semare would soon find me, pulling my rebellious body to see the High Priestess Aseroth.

The High Priestess would explain sternly I was there to learn. One of the most important lessons was to master self-responsibility, and oh how I hated those words. I was given additional duties to perform, thereby missing out on the rest periods we were given.

Meesha would click her tongue, becoming exasperated with me until she lost her temper, telling me I was selfish and I was placing undue hardships on the others because they had to assume my responsibilities. Chagrined, I began changing my habits thus falling into the rote of compliance. Inside I felt like I was a bird striving to break out of my prison.

One morning Meesha and I were on our way to the kitchen garden supposedly to gather vegetables for the kitchen. I stopped, becoming entranced with a caterpillar. I became enthralled as I watched it slowly weaving its cocoon on a low branch of a mulberry tree. Meesha turned back. Grabbing me by the arm, she admonished me, "Mariam! Do you want to get us into trouble? Oh, don't look at me with those eyes!" I stuck out my tongue winking with my blue eye and again with my green eye. Meesha giggled, telling me I looked funny. Sighing, I resolved to pay more attention to my work assignments.

I progressed through the years. In addition to our duties, we were schooled in history of religion, mathematics, alchemy, astronomy, science, divine geometry, history, philosophy, languages, writing, the functions of the body, agriculture, art, music, dance and various other subjects. I was educated according to my progression, and I was introduced to breathing exercises, which continued each year.

We were also schooled and drilled on the value of what we thought; on the importance of being kind to one another; on not faultfinding and on being generous. We were taught that, to be godlike, one must be a giver as well as a discerner. For one who is wise in discerning knows when to give and when to withhold because the giving could be crippling to another.

During these years I returned to my family for short visits. During these times Mother, Father and Grandmother each took me aside and away from the others, to question me as to what I was learning. My Grandmother was a great warrior queen whom I admired greatly. She had no fear of leading her armies against the Romans, although there had not been a major battle yet. All too soon, I returned to the Temple.

Semare was assigned to me as my primary teacher for the first several years. When we were first introduced, she boldly looked me in the eye telling me, "At the Palace you may be Princess Mariam, and here, however, you are only one of the novices. Do not expect to be pampered." I wanted to retort but my knowing told me to keep my thoughts to myself. Yet I also knew she could read my thoughts. This was most unsettling. After our initial meeting, she gave me the most menial duties, speaking to me with a look of contempt. Of course I bridled at her treatment because it was as though there was nothing I could do to satisfy her.

Each morning we would gather in the main courtyard singing a Hymn to Ra.

Bright is the earth when thou riseth in the horizon.
When thou shinest as Aten by day
Thou drivest away the darkness.
When thou sendest forth thy rays
All lands are in daily festivity.
Awake and standing upon their feet
When thou has raised them up,
Their limbs bathed they take their clothing
Their arms uplifted in adoration to thy dawning
Then in all the world they do their work.[1]

In the evening we would gather and sing the following hymn to Maat.

O Re, Lord of Maat
Who lives by Maat
Who rejoices in Maat
Who is complete because of Maat?
Who persists because of Maat?
Who is praised by Maat
Who is powerful through Maat
Who rules through Maat
Who is crowned by Maat
Who ascends in Maat
Who descends in Maat
Who nourishes on Maat
Who is joined with Maat

---

[1] This could be a composite of the ancient Hymn to Aten and Psalm 104. It is purported in some circles that the Psalms were derived from ancient Egyptian texts.

O Ra eternal in deed, perfect in plans

*Righteous in heart, who establishes Maat
In everything which she creates.*[2]

In my second year I rebelled at singing these hymns. It seemed as though we were singing from habit instead of from our inner praise. I wanted to rise up, dance and sing my own song, but Semare did not take this too kindly. In addition to my lessons and duties, I was to spend one hour in the Room of Contemplation to contemplate the Goddess Maat.

Actually I was delighted because that gave me time to be alone. Of course I already knew Maat was the Goddess of Intelligence, Truth, Balance and Justice. At the end of the hour Semare questioned me as to what I had learned. I repeated what I thought was an appropriate answer. My answer did not please her and I was given another hour to contemplate.

For over a week none of my answers pleased Semare. Each day I would contemplate Maat. At my young age I wanted to be out in nature and to commune with my friends in the plant world.

With great resolve I began seriously to contemplate Maat, and I realized the word goddess did not mean a person. The word goddess indicated a principle of life. Maat was a principle of Intelligence, Truth, Balance and Justice. With this realization I became inwardly engrossed. I asked myself what Truth is. The answer came that Truth is the result of one's own experience. There is no one Truth. There are only individual truths.

At the end of this hour, I met with Semare and told her of my realization. Her eyes narrowed and she snapped that there was more and I had to return the following day for another hour.

The following day I again contemplated the principle of Maat. This time I concentrated on Intelligence. Intelligence was not the brain nor was it necessarily the mind. Perhaps

---

[2] Maat was the personification of the fundamental order of the universe, without which all of creation would perish.

intelligence was similar to a cup or a chalice. If we fill it halfway up with knowledge, we only have a small amount of intelligence. If we fill the cup up with a great amount of knowledge, we will have greater intelligence. Therefore, Intelligence is the knowledge we seek and attain along with its application.

Pleased with myself, I met with Semare, giving her my latest realization. She made a sound like a snort, and with her eyes narrowed, she told me to return the next day to contemplate the principle of Maat again. I had not finished, she informed me.

Inwardly sighing, as I dared not by this time do it out loud, I left. The following day I again returned to the Room of Contemplation, giving thought about Maat. The word coming to me was Balance. I already knew we live on the plane of opposites or duality. I thought of examples such as up and down, good and evil, dark and light. I asked myself, "How does one find the balance?"

My hour was up and again I met with Semare. Looking at me with scorn, she spoke, "Mariam, you may come from a great lineage, but it does not indicate your level of intelligence. Your blue eye and your green eye may indicate you are a Sophia, however you have done little to bring this forth. You will return tomorrow and if necessary, again and again until you know the answers."

Turning her back on me, she strode out of the room. I continued standing, as I was perplexed. I had almost forgotten my birth and the moment when I came from my Mother's womb. I again remembered Priestess Aseroth saying, "She is another Sophia." So, I thought, that was important enough for her to tell Semare. I knew Sophia represented Wisdom, but how did that apply to me? I decided I would contemplate this at another time.

Returning to the Room of Contemplation, I again sat and pondered the word Balance. It came to me that Balance must be the place where good and evil met, becoming the center. If one were to say one thing was evil it would throw off the balance. If one were to say one thing was good, that would also throw off the balance. Therefore, one must be the watcher while being aloof of good and evil. Ah, that must be Balance.

Balance must be detachment. Yes, that is it. Balance is detachment.

Again, the following day I was sent back to the Contemplation Room as Semare in a scathing tone of voice told me I had not contemplated enough on the meaning of Maat. The silence of the room lifted me. Ah yes, I had not contemplated the word Justice. Deeper I sank into the Void of Nothingness. Justice could mean punishment, however this did not seem correct for me. No, Justice was not punishment. I knew there had to be laws to prevent the people from becoming unruly and uncivil. Justice must be a form of mediation because I already knew that what was done to another will be returned to the perpetrator. On the human level, justice could mean fairness. There were times when a mediator was necessary to settle differences.

And yet, I knew this was not the deeper meaning. Ah, the meaning came to me! Justice meant the settlement of one's karmic debts written within the soul. Any uncompleted experiences in one lifetime would be scheduled for the next lifetime. Instantly I knew these incompletions were what kept us on the wheel of reincarnation. For one to bring Justice to the soul, there must be forgiveness, which dissolves karmic debts.

I also realized that in contemplating one word or one symbol there were outer layers. If one contemplated long enough, the deeper meaning would come. Now I was ready to face Semare. When I reported my findings, she had me go over the realizations I had about Truth, Intelligence, Balance and Justice. Semare looked at me for what seemed to be a long time and I gazed back into her eyes. I knew my realizations were the correct ones and I also knew she knew. At last she said, "You have realized correctly. You will report to me each day at the same time. Go now."

I was speechless. What had I done to deserve more of Semare! I had the impulse to stick my tongue out at her departing back. I dared not as I was sure she had eyes in the back of her head. I left fuming, almost bumping into Meesha. "Mariam let us go to the garden to see what we can find." Of course I was ready, as I wanted a change from my contemplations.

Laughing with arm in arm we walked to the great garden. By this hour the gardeners had completed their labor, and it seemed as though we had it all to ourselves. I felt I had been away from the garden and my friends, the nature spirits, too long. Meesha questioned me as to what I had been contemplating. Of course I shared with her my realizations. Sighing, Meesha said, "Oh you are so wise Mariam! I can understand why you are so special."

Me, special? I was shocked at her statement. I had never thought I was special. "Why do you think I am so special? Don't I do the same studies as you and don't I do my share of responsibilities?"

"Mariam, forgive me. I did not have the intent to imply you were not doing your share. And it certainly isn't that you are a Princess. No, I sense there is greatness to you beyond royalty. Besides, none of the others, and me included, has Semare as our private tutor."

Bursting into laughter, I could not contain myself. "Why are you laughing?" she asked.

"Oh Meesha! Semare tutoring me? No, I don't think so. For some reason she appears to be doing more spite than tutoring. She finds fault with everything I do. Even when I arrive at a great revelation, she only sniffs while looking at me through the slits of her eyes."

"Perhaps," Meesha answered. "However, I do not think her harshness has anything to do with a dislike for you. We have a few moments before the signal for our evening meal is called. Let us race to the pond and see who will get there first."

"Done!" I cried and we sped across the great garden to a pond filled with lilies and beautiful fish of gold. Later, I pondered my conversation with Meesha and yes, I knew I was different but I did not equate that with greatness.

During my studies I became adept at speaking five languages as well as writing each language. I was trained in the languages of Coptic, Latum, Greek, Aramaic as well as my own. I spent many hours in the Contemplation Room contemplating my limited thinking. It seemed as though Semare was harder on me than the other girls. In retrospect I can see she was pushing me toward my destiny.

I loved the sciences, devouring all knowledge given to me. I knew the meaning of "as above, so below." I learned the meanings of the natural laws of the universe, The Law of Rhythm, The Law of Opposites and The Law of Attraction.

By the end of my education at the Temple of the Lion I knew I had far more knowledge than when I first came. When I entered the Temple I felt unprepared and had not fully been told what to expect.

Chapter 6

CONTEMPLATION

If something is to give light,
it must first endure burning.
- Anonymous

The next morning I awakened early and lay in bed contemplating the change in my life. I realized I had never felt so alive. My life before stumbling into the cave and finding the scrolls seemed drab and uninteresting. *Perhaps I have been one of those people called the walking dead. Yes, I was dead to the wonders in life. Where have I been all those years? What have I accomplished?*

I turned towards the bed where Jill was sleeping. I felt so blessed to have her as a friend. She was truly the only friend I really ever had. The others were like ships passing in the night.

Knowing she had worked on the translations until late, I quietly got up, showered and dressed. Going into the kitchen, I found coffee already made. *Peter must be up.* Pouring myself a cup, I quietly went out the kitchen door into the garden and there he was.

Seeing me, he quickly got up from the glider and greeted me with a warm hug and a lingering kiss. "Hey," I said. "Careful of the coffee. I don't want to burn you."

Pulling apart, he took my cup and led me to the glider. After I was settled, he handed me my coffee. *Gawd, it tasted good.*

"Peter, you make the best coffee. What is your secret?" Chuckling, he told me his grandfather had taught him how to brew a good cup of coffee.

We were silent for a few moments. I was the first to speak and shared with him my morning contemplation.

Peter listened until I had finished, then he spoke up.

"My dear, what do you mean by the 'walking dead?' I'm not sure what it means, however I have heard the phrase."

I thought a moment before answering. "As I understand it, it means someone who remains in ignorance or is ignorant of greater knowledge and potentials. Am I making sense?"

"Yes. Now I understand. I seem to be more alive and awake since you sought me out in Mirepoix. I have even thought that The Magdalene might be working her magic on us. It really is difficult to remember what I was like before I began the trek through the Pyrenees."

"Is it her magic or is it that we are learning something that innately we have always known?" I asked.

Lighting his pipe, Peter took several puffs before replying. "Perhaps it is a little of both. Have you ever read the book *Flatland*?"

I shook my head, no. "What is a flatland?"

"Well, it is what one would call a classic fable. It's a story about a land called Flatland. To get a picture in your mind of it, imagine a flat sheet of paper with lines, triangles, squares, pentagons and other figures. Suddenly they become alive and are people. These people move around on this flat sheet of paper which is a two-dimensional world and that is all they know."

"It sounds mathematical to me." I interjected.

"It is, and what the fable is talking about is that we stay stuck in the limited dimension until a revelation comes along. In the fable, the person called Square gets such a revelation and realizes there is a third dimension. When he attempts to share this with the others they label him a heretic and shun him. Does that sound familiar?"

Chuckling I said, "I think you just described me before I had this encounter with The Magdalene's scrolls and you."

"Ah, my love, I think it describes us both. If we were to return to our old mode of life, don't you think we would be considered odd and shunned?"

"You're right Peter. I would think our old way of life would be boring. From what you've told me, our everyday reality has been challenged, and now I do have a broader perspective about life."

At that moment Jill came out and asked us if we were hungry yet. We were. Entering the kitchen we found Sebastian sipping on his coffee. Jill had set the table and laid out a continental breakfast.

While we ate Peter and I shared the discussion we had in the garden. Sebastian looked at us quizzically, "What is this flatland you're talking about?"

Since Peter had read the book, I let him answer. "*Flatland* is a short fable about limited concepts and thinking using mathematical terms to represent the people in a satire of their reality. An example is that Flatland is a two-dimensional world. One of the people named Square has a revelation that there could be another dimension, thereby making it a three-dimensional world. Anyone thinking differently from the usual two-dimensional concepts and beliefs is labeled a heretic."

"Ah, I think I am grasping what you are saying. If I am correct, this is what the Church has done to most human beliefs. N'est pas?"

I interjected, "This can also apply to many politicians and rulers. This limited view of reality has permeated most societies through religions."

Jill had been quiet until now and suggested we hear what the fifth scroll was about. We urged her to read it to us, and she went to get it. In the meantime I brewed a fresh pot of coffee.

We heard about The Magdalene's education in the Temple and sat still for a few moments digesting it all.

"Mon dieu!" Sebastian was the first to speak. "This woman was only a little girl and yet she was subjected to such an intense discipline!"

"Correct, however this little girl was destined to greatness and from my perspective, it was necessary for her to have a teacher such as Semare," Jill responded.

I spoke up, "Semare was a great teacher and I would venture to say she exhibited a tremendous love for her student."

"Yes," Peter said. "From my limited knowledge and observations, I would say that greatness probably has to be tested by fire."

"What is meant by fire?" asked Sebastian.

"Fire has as many faces as everyone has different experiences. However the bottom line is – fire is adversity and the rising above it. Think of all the great minds of history and I think you will find they all had to overcome adversities."

"Ummm," Sebastian paused for a moment. "Then what I hear you saying is that one must not shun adversity."

"Correct," answered Peter. "I think there are times when we run away from it thinking we will escape it. I know I have. Hmmm, in retrospect that's exactly what brought me here."

I asked, "Isn't it that adversity has within it the opportunity to gain wisdom? How else would we learn from our experiences?"

"Well stated," Peter answered.

Jill brought us back to the scroll. "The Magdalene's adversity was a stern teacher who recognized her potential and it was through contemplation that The Magdalene came to great realizations."

"Oui!" Sebastian said excitedly. "If she had not had to contemplate the meaning of Maat, she would not have realized the many layers of its meaning. So, each of us should be grateful for any adversity we have had in life. In other words, adversity is another word for change."

Chuckling, we all applauded Sebastian for his insight. Peter got up, poured us each another cup of coffee, and then sat down. "Wouldn't it be safe to say that the people living in a flatland want to avoid adversity and only end up with more of it?"

"Perhaps most of our cultures and societies are flatlands and the more change is resisted, the more adversity comes knocking at the door," I speculated.

"I think you're right," Jill said. "I would say that adversity can bring out greatness in us if we allow it to."

"Well, it certainly offers opportunities!" Peter laughed. "I am impressed with her realizations of the meaning of Maat. I had never thought of balance being the same as detachment, or as defined in quantum physics, the observer."

"You're right, Peter. I take it you have studied quantum physics?" Jill said.

"Ummm, yes I have studied quantum physics," he replied.

Later I understood that Peter was keeping a low profile. He really didn't want to go into his background in quantum physics or to discuss the business he had sold. He was on holiday.

Nodding her head, Jill went on to say, "I also had never thought of justice as dissolving karmic debt. It makes sense."

We all agreed it was a scroll to be gone over again and again.

Peter got up saying, "I think I'll go outside, contemplate and smoke my pipe."

Jill and Sebastian returned to translating while I tidied up the kitchen.

As we did almost every day, I turned on the news and breathed a sign of relief that there was still no further mention of the discovery the scrolls. I knew I was pushing the fear of being identified away from my conscious mind.

After I turned off the TV, I enjoyed the quiet moment to be by myself. And the thought came: *Few children of today could hold up to the discipline Mary Magdalene was subjected to.*

～∽ ～∽ ～∽

QUEEN MAKEDA
Scroll 6

The years sped by, and I am eleven. This will be my last year perhaps studying at the Temple of the Lion. There was a choice to be made. I could marry and bear children or I could pursue the studies of becoming a priestess and serving in a temple one day. Then too, I could assume the role of Princess in my Grandmother's court.

It was the time of my yearly visit to my parents and Grandmother whom I called Kandake. One day I was asked to come to her apartments as Kandake wanted to speak with me. I intuitively knew it was about my decision.

"Ah, Makeda, you have become a wondrous beauty. Tell me how it is at the Temple?" Kandake always called me Makeda and not Mariam like the rest of my family called me. I knew this was only a preliminary as to the true reason for my visit. I shared with her what I was learning, and she nodded from time to time to acknowledge what I was saying. We nibbled on sweetmeats and drank a bit of wine.

Kandake asked me if I knew that when I was born it had been noticed I had the mark of a Sophia. I replied I was aware. Kandake reminded me I was a direct descendant of the great Queen Makeda also known as the Queen of Sheba.

Kandake told me that for many hundreds of years only women could rule Ethiopia, and that had also been true in many other countries. She was concerned over the erosion of the positions and power of women that was occurring. In some countries they had been relegated to being no more than breeding objects.

She went on to say she wanted to share with me what had been handed down regarding the Queen Makeda when she was about to depart to the land of the great King Solomon. This is what I was told.

"Queen Makeda was addressing her people as to the purpose of her trip. And this is what has come down to us from old papyri. Perhaps one day I will show them to you," Kandake told me.

As for a kingdom, it cannot stand without wisdom, and riches cannot be preserved without wisdom, the foot cannot keep the place wherein it hath set itself without wisdom.

And without wisdom that which the tongue speaketh is not acceptable.

Wisdom is the best of all treasures.

He who heapeth up gold and silver doeth so to no profit without wisdom, but he who heapeth up wisdom — no man can filch it from his heart. That which fools heap, the wise consume.

And because of the wickedness of those who do evil, the righteous are praised; and because of the wicked sets of fools the wise are beloved.

Wisdom is an exalted thing and a rich thing.

I will love her like a mother, and she shall embrace me like her child.

I will follow the footprints of wisdom and she shall protect me forever.

I will seek after wisdom and she shall be with me forever.

I will follow her footprints and she shall not cast me away.

I will lean upon her, and she shall be unto me a wall of adamant.

I will seek asylum with her, and she shall be unto me power and strength.

I will rejoice in her, and she shall be unto me abundant grace. For it is right for us to follow the footprints of wisdom, and for the soles of our feet to stand upon the threshold of the gates of wisdom.

Let us seek her, and we shall find her.

Let us love her, and she will not withdraw herself from us.

Let us pursue her, and we shall overtake her.

Let us ask, and we shall receive.

And let us turn our hearts to her so that we may never forget her.

If we remember her, she will have us in remembrance.

And in connection with fools thou shalt not remember wisdom, for they do not hold her in honor, and she doth not love them.

The honoring of wisdom is the honoring of the wise.

Queen Makeda's nobles and her slaves, and her handmaidens and her counselors answered and said unto her.

O our Lady, as for wisdom, it is not lacking in thee, and it is because of thy wisdom that thou lovest wisdom. And as for us, if thou goest we will go with thee, and if thou sittest down we will sit down with thee. Our death shall be with thy death, and our life with thy life.[1]

When Kandake completed her story of Queen Makeda, we both sat in silence, and I was quite moved by this new knowledge. After a long pause, Kandake spoke. "Makeda, in my heart of hearts I know you are not destined to return to this court to take your rightful place. I know also you are not destined to become a priestess of the Temple nor is it at this time your destiny to marry early and bear children. No, there is a greater destiny. Where it will lead you, I do not know."

"Kandake, if those choices are not in keeping with my destiny, what other choice do I have?"

"I have spoken with Priestess Aseroth of the Temple of the Lion, and a decision has been made to send you for further training and knowledge to the Temple of Isis where you will dwell for a six-year period. It is my understanding it will not be easy, however it is a step towards your destiny."

The Temple of Isis! There was an air of mystery regarding the Temple of Isis. My heart quickened at the thought that I would receive further training. The mysterious mystery school! I had a sense of coming home.

---

[1] This has been handed down from ancient times and is now part of the Ethiopian Bible, *Kebra Nagast.*

Chapter 7

IN SEARCH OF WISDOM

The doors of wisdom are never shut.
- Benjamin Franklin 1706-1790

Peter and I had just returned from our daily walk in the woods when a sudden shower burst forth from the skies with the impactful force of nature. I'm sure Jill and Sebastian weren't fooled by our outings, but they were deep into their translations and did not ask questions, for which I was grateful. We found Jill in the kitchen whipping up a lovely dessert concoction that would turn out to be a chocolate lover's idea of decadence.

"Hi, you two," she greeted us. "Have a seat while I finish this up. I just finished translating scroll six."

"What is this one about?" I asked.

"Ah, wait until it gets read. I want your input," she replied.

Peter excused himself to go to the bathroom and I sat down for a brief chat. Our conversation covered mundane topics such as the need to shop for more food and the menu for dinner. Soon Peter returned with Sebastian right behind him.

We all opted for a glass of wine while Jill left to get the latest translation. Upon returning, she began to read to us and as she finished, Sebastian asked, "Do you think the Queen of Sheba's departure was to seek out Solomon for wisdom?"

"What are you getting at?" Peter asked.

"Ah, perhaps I should make myself clearer. As I was doing the Greek to French translation, I received a sense that there was more to this than what is given in this scroll."

"I think you are onto something," Jill said. "My research has shown that there is no historical evidence of Solomon or his great Temple. Scholars have said it is only in the Bible that Solomon is mentioned."

Sebastian replied that he had not personally come across any evidence of Solomon or his Temple, however he had heard there were documents other than the Bible that did refer to Solomon and his Temple, and yet, here was The Magdalene writing about it in the scrolls. We all agreed it was an intriguing mystery.

Peter asked if any of us had read *King Solomon's Mines* by H. Rider Haggard. Jill said she had.

He went on to say, "In the book the mines were located in mountains in Africa and held a great treasure. It says on the mountains where the mines were located there were two peaks, and they were called the Breasts of Sheba."

"Hmmm," I said, "Perhaps Solomon and his Temple were actually in Africa and not Israel as most of the historical scholars contend."

Smiling Peter said, "It is interesting how most Biblical scholars want to lump everything into Israel."

With a twinkle in his eyes, Sebastian asked, "Would that be what you call flatlander thinking?"

We all burst out laughing. I was laughing so hard that I thought I would wet my pants. Wiping tears from my eyes, I commended Sebastian for his levity and said I thought his statement was pretty close to the truth.

Once our laughter subsided, Jill told us that after she had finished that translation she had gone on the Internet and found that most of the search engines gave variations of the Biblical version of the mines. However, she found one site she thought most interesting. Someone, and don't ask me who because the name escapes me at the moment, had studied the Old Testament from a different perspective than most scholars who kept to the traditional interpretations, and from extensive research he had come to the conclusion that the descriptions in the Bible of Solomon's Temple meant that it was built in the shape of a man's body with each limb and part of the body being a part of the Temple. He claimed it was the composite of three biblical figures. However, Jill didn't remember who the figures represented.

Peter said that would be in keeping with the freemasons' construction of the gothic cathedrals in Europe as symbolizing man and woman's connection to God.

And Jill reminded us that Leonardo da Vinci had a famous drawing of a man with his arms outstretched, and that the symbol of a pentagram would fit perfectly over it.

We all agreed that much of ancient knowledge had been hidden away and perhaps it took great beings to be born and become golden threads of this knowledge in the hope that humankind would awaken to something greater within.

"What if," I interposed, "what if, the Queen of Sheba was saying farewell to her people because she was leaving to go to a Mystery School?"

"Well, now that's quite a hypothesis," said Jill. "I like it. And what if, Solomon's Temple was actually the Mystery School and located in Africa?"

Peter gave a whistle. "Some hypothesis! It makes more sense than the others. Of course, going to seek wisdom could be another way to say, going to a Mystery School."

"Pardon," Sebastian said, "but what of her son Menelik supposedly sired by Solomon?"

"Another what if," I said. "Perhaps she took part in the hieros gamos[1] fertility rite and that is how Menelik came to be?"

"C'est plausible," responded Sebastian. "Truly, I am in the midst of very wise people and I honor you."

"Sebastian, I urge you to include yourself as one of the very wise people. Speaking for myself I am honored to have you among us," said Peter.

Sebastian flushed when Peter uttered this. Jill and I agreed with Peter.

It was then I proposed a toast. "To each of us being a wise person and honoring the god within."

Jill murmured, "It is the obvious, unobvious that often contains the actual truth."

৵৩৵ ৵৩৵ ৵৩৵

---

[1] *Heiros gamos* was an ancient fertility rite celebrating the unification of the male and female as the acknowledgement that it takes both male and female to bring forth life. This rite was celebrated 2000 years ago and prior to the time of Mary Magdalene.

THE MYSTERY SCHOOL
Scroll 7

There is much I cannot divulge, as it would be unwise of me. There are too many who have not the capacity to accept or understand the great mysteries. But there is some information I can write about.

The first year was spent in learning the workings of the body, especially the head and how it all works together. The nous[2] is all important.

I can tell you we were schooled in the teachings of the god Thoth. If I had any thought of Semare being hard on me, I now realized how important her training had been. In retrospect she had been very easy on me.

The studies here included alchemy, astronomy, mathematics, science, wisdom, magic and other sacred topics with the emphasis on their application for personal experience. We learned the god Typhon represents the dragon of ignorance and also the perversions of mental, moral and the physical self. We were required to read the writings of Iamblichus and Manetho as well as study the works of the great scientist Democritus with his theory on what makes up the aether and the world of matter. We studied the great Persian scientists as well. What most would call magic, we learned was only the natural laws of the universe. These laws are available to those who seek to know, and it became second nature for us to know and understand the age-old saying "as within, so without" or "as above, so below."

We were schooled in advanced breathing exercises, whose purpose was to push energy up to the head. We were also taught a special method of breath, and it took many hours to perfect it. There is a path along the spine called the serpent energy. Actually there are two paths, which are connected once the energy reaches the head. Each path must go through seven doors in the body. And we used the intertwined serpents as our symbol because the serpent is very sacred. As always, it is said, there is a meaning within a meaning.

---

[2] Nous is an ancient Greek word for the intellect or mind.

I also was taught that the head, which contains the nous, has a grander purpose than most people deem it. The head contains avenues used to communicate with the Great One. There are many paths in the head to explore, and the more one has knowledge, the greater the communication. Our imagination, perceptions, and thoughts determine which path we will take. All of our thoughts create mind. As within, so without.

There were symbols we used for contemplation. One was the magical Eye of Isis or as some say, the Eye of Horus. There is a left eye and a right eye. Both represent an inner view of the head holding within it the nous.

My people of the lands of Egypt and Ethiopia had always known to study nature, and that the ways of animals would lead one to the Divine. They knew the lowly worm could be sliced in half and grow another body on each half. If the lowly worm had the knowledge to do this, why could not the human do this? I pondered this, realizing the knowledge had been suppressed when people began worshiping a god or gods outside of themselves. The human was projecting outwardly not inwardly where the Divine resides.

As I continued my disciplines and studies, I examined the thoughts and the emotions I held onto, knowing I could make choices. Those that no longer served me I would discard. Each of the seven doors in the body had to be mastered before one could leave this plane. All people with knowledge are able to ascend into the One. Every discipline had a purpose, and I advanced by learning to control my body. I learned to become invisible, and I was able to reappear wherever I chose. I did this by learning the secret of vibrations.

These years were spent in strict disciplines for initiations into the mysteries. There were different levels of initiation. There was an initiation to indicate the mastery of each discipline. I was initiated into the mysteries of becoming invisible; to see into the future; to be in two places at the same time; to know what others were thinking; to place my thoughts in another place and to see in my mind what was there. There were other disciplines I learned also.

There came for me, a great initiation in water. It was the initiation of death and rebirth. When the moment came for me to undergo this initiation, a few others and I were led into a

91

sphinx and through an opening into a secret chamber. We were led down winding steps much like a spiral, and soon I could hear the sound of rushing water.

Fear grasped me by the throat almost paralyzing me. I remembered I had gone through this initiation in a previous lifetime. I had died during that initiation because I had let go of my concentration. Now I had the opportunity to do it differently.

After what seemed to be an endless descent, we arrived at the bottom by the edge of the rushing water, and we were not told where it would lead us, only that when it was over we would know. We were told to disrobe and go into the water. It would be our concentration and our knowing that would take us through this labyrinth.

I knew I could not hold onto any hatreds, anger, judgments or emotions of the past. I could only be in the present. In the beginning I allowed the current to carry me, and I had a flash of insight that there was a waterfall ahead. Knowing I could not resist, I allowed myself to be carried over and down into this torrent of water. It felt like I was being catapulted down into the bowels of what I knew not.

My next sense was of being in a spiral of water. Immediately I was sucked under, and it felt like I was in a swirling powerful grip of something I had never experienced. Suddenly it ended and I was carried along and at unexpected moments I would come up into a pocket of air. I gulped greedily before being pushed along under the water.

Time ceased to be. I only knew to keep my attention on my arriving at the end, my destination. I held in my mind the sacred symbol of the pentagram. After what seemed an eternity I was gushed out into a dazzling light. Exhausted I allowed the current to wash me up on a shore of sand, and I knew not where I was. I could not open my eyes. I only knew I had made it through the labyrinth.

How long I lay there with the water gently washing over and around my body, I remember not. Time had ceased and I was in a blue realm where I felt a peace that I never wanted to leave. Within my mind I heard a voice telling me, "My beloved daughter, you have done well. Go now and heal the sick. You are to minister unto the poor."

Vaguely I remember being lifted gently onto a litter, and being carried back to the Temple of Isis. I languished for many days between life and the netherworld. At times I heard voices murmuring over me and I remember being gently bathed. There came a day when I knew I had to return to this world to fulfill my destiny. With that realization, recovery came quickly.

Why do I tell you this? This was my initiation into my ministry of healing and teaching.

Chapter 8

CONNECTING KNOWLEDGE

All truths are easy to understand once they are discovered;
the point is to discover them.
- Galileo Galilei (1564-1642)

We had just heard the latest translation of the scrolls.

"A magnificent woman," Sebastian said. "The more I translate, the more in awe of her I am."

There was so much to digest. "No wonder she was called a Sophia; she was born to greatness," I said.

"Knowing what I do about reincarnation," Jill said, "she planned this life before she was born, and she chose the family she was born into. I wonder who she was in previous lives?"

"Perhaps she was the Queen of Sheba," Peter offered. "It has been written that some choose to be reborn into a certain genetic lineage so they can complete lessons not yet learned."

Sebastian sat there listening. Finally he said, "You amaze me with your knowledge. There could be much truth in what you say. It will be most interesting to see what the next scroll divulges."

"Somewhere I had heard about mystery schools. However I didn't realize how hard they were," Jill said in a wondering voice.

We sat for a few moments letting what we had just listened to soak in. Peter asked us, "Have you read the book *Three Sevens*?"[1]

None of us had.

"It is supposedly the true story of an initiation of a young Spanish man who was from a wealthy family. As part of his initiation he was sent to the New World, and when he arrived there, he traveled to a mountain, which could have been

---

[1] *Three Sevens: A Story of Ancient Initiation* by William Phelon

in the Southwest. Inside the mountain he was taught the mysteries and he underwent some arduous tests. The Magdalene's initiation reminded me of that book."

"Perhaps when I return to the States I'll read it," I said, "and it will be all the more interesting after reading The Magdalene's story of her initiation.

"Have any of you read *The Kybalion?*" The others shook their heads no.

I continued, "*The Kybalion* is a story of the Hermetic Philosophy of ancient Egypt and Greece. The authors are only given as Three Initiates. In this book, it tells of the Laws The Magdalene gave in this scroll. In the book there are seven Principles. As I remember, they are Gender, Mental Gender, Rhythm, Polarity, Causation, Vibration and Planes of Correspondence. Within each Principle there are seven levels.

"If I remember correctly, it goes like this: A Master can change what she or he wants into other desires at higher levels of vibration instead of going by the human desire which is based on some feeling, mood, emotion, or environmental suggestion. In other words, she or he uses the greater Mind."

Peter was the first to reply. "They would seem similar to the few laws she gave. What I hear you telling us is that there were more, and even though she said there were some things she could not tell, it is too bad she didn't give us more of what happened during her time at the mystery school."

Jill and Sebastian agreed. "In other words," Jill said, "someone can change his thought by consciously willing to do so. It would have to be a discipline of becoming aware of what one is thinking and choosing what one wants to think."

"Ah, oui, the scrolls are saying the same thing. How simple it is!" was Sebastian exclaimed.

"I agree," said Peter. "'As a man thinketh, so he is,'[2] and 'It is done unto you as you believe.'[3] And there is the old saying, 'There is nothing new under the sun.'"[4]

"So true. So true," murmured Sebastian.

---

[2] Proverbs 23:7
[3] Galatians 6:7
[4] Ecclesiastics 1:9-11

"What the paragraph in the book meant to me," I said, "is that we can manifest whatever we want by changing our mental attitude from wanting to having."

"Ellen my love, you got it. It seems we live in a mental universe." Peter reached over placing his hand on mine.

With a bit of a sigh, Jill gave us another aspect to contemplate. "We can easily talk the philosophy, but it is another thing to apply it. I find myself each day listening to some hypocritical statement I have made or thought, and I wonder how long it will take before I get it and live it."

I appreciated Jill's insight. "You are so perceptive. I have also wondered about that myself. Some days I think I am applying what The Magdalene has written and other days I feel I have taken two steps back."

Then Peter said what I needed to hear. "I don't think we should be too hard on ourselves. We have been asleep as flatlanders for so many years, so how can we expect to get it all at once? I liken us to an athlete who first begins with a desire and trains over and over. Some attain the gold medal and others don't. I also have days like you have described. And each time I am aware of lapsing into past thinking, I make a conscious choice to move back into the mode of thinking that I want."

"Ah, Peter, what I am understanding everyone to be saying is that we are in training to become that which we desire and are meant to be," Sebastian offered.

Jill gave a chuckle and said, "We are in training to become enlightened beings."

Peter stood up and stretched. "I am going outside to smoke my pipe and contemplate all this. Good night my friends."

I followed Peter and we kissed. There was much to contemplate and I told him I was going to turn in also. Jill and Sebastian went back to the computers.

୧୨ଡ଼   ୧୨ଡ଼   ୧୨ଡ଼

ALEXANDRIA
Scroll 8

After regaining my strength I was told that I would be sent to Jerusalem in the land of Judea. There was need of a priestess in one of the smaller Temples of Isis established there. In Jerusalem there were several temples. One was the Temple of the Hebrew god; and the other, the Temple of Isis dedicated to Wisdom. The priests of the Hebrew religion were attempting more and more to suppress women. At one time women had equal rights with men and now these rights were being taken away.

I began to ready for my departure. First I was sent to Alexandria for further training, and upon completion I would be sent to Jerusalem. I traveled by barge down the Great River with one of the priestesses of the Temple from Alexandria, who had been sent to accompany me.

With anticipation and excitement I arrived in Alexandria where my destination was the Temple of Serapis. Here was housed the Great Library. It was not the original Library as Caesar had burned the original when he was staving off an attack from the sea some years before. This was a tragedy. The Library had been immense with the overflow being stored in Serapis. What remained in the Temple of Serapis was extensive.

I caught my breath when I viewed the Pharos Lighthouse. It was a beacon of truth and wisdom, and had been built to be a guide for travelers to know it was a safe harbor for learning wisdom and truth for the common man and woman.

At the Temple I was assigned my place to sleep and given duties. It was emphasized we were called Gnostics because we were seekers of truth, and a Gnostic knew.

I was given a teacher by the name of Ioannes, who came from time to time from the lands of Judea, Samaria and Galilee to teach promising students at the mystery school. I was indeed blessed.

My schooling with Ioannes was not accomplished within the Temple. He accompanied me to small villages outside the city where he taught me the refinements of healing. At first I observed him and soon he stepped aside, observing as I applied what I knew of healing.

I became adept at reading the minds of the people I healed, and some I knew were not open to healing while others were. I learned nothing could enter a closed mind.

Ioannes taught me the rite of immersion in water that was an ancient rite of cleansing. As with all rites, the cleansing is symbolic of letting go of old hatreds, fears, and beliefs that keep one ill or unhappy.

Ioannes loved the common people. He dressed simply and his greeting was sincere and warm, and I immediately liked him. I knew I was in the presence of greatness.

After my apprenticeship, Ioannes and his wife Anya accompanied me to Jerusalem. I looked forward to this next adventure, knowing I had received excellent training.

Chapter 9

A HEALING GIFT

With ordinary consciousness you can't even begin to know what's happening.
- Saul Bellow

It was early one morning when Jill heard a vehicle drive up. For a moment her tendency was towards panic, thinking that we had been discovered. Looking out the window, she saw an old truck with garden tools in it. At that moment Sebastian came into the room and she told him of the visitor.

He looked out the window and then smiled. "There is no need to worry. It is only Vieux Fouchet, the gardener Paul hired to come once a month to take care of the plants and trees. I think it not wise for him to see me here. It would perhaps raise questions because I have already informed him that Paul's house was rented while he is away."

I had walked into the living room just as they were talking. "Sebastian, is 'old man Fouchet' his actual name?"

Smiling, he replied, "Non Ellen. He is of an undetermined age, and who knows how old he is. Someone gave him the name of Vieux Fouchet and he doesn't seem to mind."

Peter joined us and Jill told him of the latest turn of events. We discussed how to change our plans for the day, agreeing it would be unwise for him to see all of us. It was determined Jill would be the visible one and she would pretend she was Paul's renter. Sebastian would continue to translate the scroll, and that left Peter and me at loose ends. We dared not go out for our daily walk.

Jill went out to introduce herself to Vieux Fouchet, and Peter and I decided to strip the beds, wash the bedding and clean the house. We had just put the first load of wash in the dryer when Jill came back inside.

"What a delightful old man!" she exclaimed. "He managed to understand my French and we had a long discussion about the flowers and nature. He has such love for plants and trees and he talks to them. I swear, when he began talking to the individual plants they seemed to perk up. He told me they were living creatures."

I asked her if he had talked about the devas and the fairies. "No," she answered, "but I have no doubt that he sees and talks to them."

"I've sensed them in the woods when Peter and I walk through, and also near the stream. When I was a little girl, I spent a summer with my maternal grandmother who lived in the country. She told me that if I would become very quiet, I could see them and talk to them," I said.

"Did you?" asked Peter.

"I thought I did, and then as I grew older the experience seemed more of a dream."

"Perhaps it wasn't a dream," he replied.

"Ummm, I'm beginning to think that also, and I suppose with practice I will see them once again."

"I know you will," commented Jill. "I am going to get to my translations. I think the gardener will be here a few more hours. He told me Paul had paid him ahead of time."

Those hours passed quickly. The laundry was done and the house shone from the cleaning Peter and I gave it. We worked well together and he commented on that.

Before we knew it, it was time to make preparations for dinner. Vieux Fouchet had finished his gardening and left. Peter was now outside smoking his pipe.

I walked out to join him, and saw him looking down at something on the ground. As I grew nearer, I saw it was a small bird and it appeared to be dead. "Oh. Peter what kind is it?"

"It looks like a goldfinch to me, but here in France it could have another name. Poor little thing and so soon after Vieux Fouchet left."

I stooped down and gently picked up the little creature. "Peter, I think there may be some life left in it."

"No, I don't think so. Let's dispose of it."

Shaking my head no, I walked to the glider and sat down with the small bird between my hands. Closing my eyes, I silently asked if it wanted to live, and I received an indication it did. As I held the bird cupped in my hands, I sank into a deep meditative state. I began seeing images of the small bird flying. Time seemed to stand still and I was unaware that Peter went inside to finish getting things ready for dinner.

There came a moment when I felt the little bird move in my hands. As I continued with my meditation, the movement became stronger. Slowly I opened my eyes, and after they adjusted to the daylight, I opened my hands. A small pair of eyes looked up at me. There was a brief moment when the bird and I became one, and I knew it would live.

Glancing up, I saw Peter watching. He had a look of awe on his face. I was the first one to speak.

"Peter, this little bird wants to live." As if to confirm my words, the bird gave a chirp and flexed its wings. I opened my hands wider and as we watched, the bird flew up to a nearby branch, gave a few chirps and winged its way off into the woods.

Jill and Sebastian had come into the kitchen while Peter was there, and he told them about what I was doing. When Peter came out to check on me, they had followed him as far as the kitchen door and watched the final stages of the healing. We were all in awe.

After washing my hands, I joined them for dinner. They wanted to know what had prompted me to hold the bird and concentrate on it. I had to say I didn't honestly know. I only felt a compulsion to do it and I followed my instinct.

Sebastian looked at me. "Ellen, it would appear you have the gift of healing. I am honored to have been present when you brought that little bird back to life."

I thought about that for a moment. "I will say it seemed to be a natural thing to do, but doesn't everyone have this ability?"

Jill said she thought we all did but pointed out that it is something rarely taught and most people grow up thinking it is impossible for them to do. She made the statement that she was surprised that the supposedly dead bird appeared so soon after Vieux Fouchet left.

"Ellen and I talked about that, too," Peter chimed in, "Perhaps it was no accident. What if the bird was a gift from the Holy Spirit to bring out Ellen's healing abilities?"

"Oui," said Sebastian. "I think you will find the latest scroll most interesting."

Peter got up and began clearing the table while I poured coffee for each of us. It was a rather short scroll and it didn't take long for Jill to read it. As usual, we were quiet for some moments afterwards.

Peter was the first to comment. "I was taken with her statement that she learned to read the minds of others to know if they were open to healing. Ellen, is that what you did with the little bird?"

"Yes, however I wasn't aware I did it on purpose. It seemed to be a natural part of the entire process."

Jill asked me, "Can you accept this is a gift and that perhaps the bird was in agreement to play its part?"

Thinking about what she had just said, I sat silent for a moment. "Yes, I can. And by accepting this, it indicates to me that we are all connected whether it be to birds, animals or people."

Sebastian said, "By being with all of you, I am getting a new perspective about life. I forgive myself for thinking I had nothing to live for when the doctors said I only had a short time. I am realizing life is something to be valued, and I thank each of you with all my being." The dear man had tears in his eyes.

Jill sensed it was the moment to ask Sebastian if he had come across a person by the name of Ioannes in his work as a translator for the Vatican.

"Oui. Ioannes is the Greek name for John. Ioannes the Immerser can be translated into John the Baptist."

"John the Baptist?" Jill queried. "But this means she knew him before she went to Jerusalem. This gives an entirely different perspective on him than what is given in the Bible."

"Oui, it does." Said Sebastian.

At that moment, I had an insight. "I don't know how much you have read, but I have read many books on the Knights Templar as well as on Leonardo da Vinci. What has puzzled me is the emphasis they place on John the Baptist. I always felt there was more to the him than was is in the Bible."

"I agree," said Jill.

"Perhaps she will say more in another document," Peter replied.

≈∾ ≈∾ ≈∾

JERUSALEM
Scroll 9

Arriving in Jerusalem, I felt as if I had been cast into an unreal world. Although I had been told of the plight of women, I was not prepared for what I observed. The women coming to the Temple of Isis came for the most part covertly. They were in fear of being seen entering the Temple.

There was no joy I could see here in Jerusalem. The women were being forced into a life alien to them, and this was the opposite of the world I had been born into. My background was of women wielding power that was used for the good of all. The atmosphere felt heavy here.

The men were domineering, looking upon the priestesses of the Temple with scorn. The Romans were occupying Judea, as well as Galilee and Samaria, and they gave off an air of superiority. Those I saw upon the streets were swaggering with their arrogance of dominance over an occupied land.

The Emperor Tiberius had placed Pontius Pilate as governor of Judea by the time I arrived. Archelaus, son of Herod the Great, was the King of Judea. Other sons of Herod the Great ruled the nearby countries of Samaria, Galilee and Golan Heights.

The Romans, as a whole, were tolerant of people's religion, rarely interfering; however the governor was not all that tolerant. The Romans were not tolerant of any hint of rebellion or insurrection, and any man found guilty of rebellion against their authority was sentenced to die by being nailed to a cross. It was the rite of crucifixion,[1] which seemed a barbaric custom to me. I had heard of it before I arrived in Jerusalem. This was totally different from what I had experienced in my own country, as well as in Egypt.

Among the men there were different sects and there were two dominant political factions. The Pharisees were primarily from the middle-class although there were some from the aristocracy. They were closer to the common people and

---

[1] From my research, there was no Greek word for crucifixion. I am using crucifixion as it is of general acceptance.

were considered the educators. This did not make their treatment of women different from that of the other sects.

The second faction was the Sadducees who controlled the priest caste. The high priest of their temple was a Sadducee, and there were a few Pharisees that were priests. The Sadducees were of the wealthy families of the aristocracy. They held beliefs that there was no bodily resurrection of any person. They rejected the oral law and held only to the law of the Torah. This was totally the opposite of what I knew to be true. The Sadducees also controlled the Sanhedrin.

The Sanhedrin was considered the supreme council and the court of justice. From my observation they meted out little justice. The Pharisees kept a tenuous balance because they had the ear of the common people. The Sanhedrin was feared by most of the populace.

There was also a third sect known as the Essenes. They did not occupy the temples, keeping to themselves in their communes. Within this group was another group called the Nazoreans. The Temple of Isis was aligned with the Nazoreans. These were learned people who lived the Presence of God, and they taught the lesser mysteries. In addition there were smaller sects.

Jerusalem and the surrounding territories spawned many different points of view in the midst of the Roman occupation. It was indeed a society of seething controversy, much like a boiling pot.

This was the society I was plunged into, and there was much to learn. Fortunately the High Priestess Salome welcomed me with warmth and acceptance. My duties were to minister to the women, healing where it was necessary. There would be times when I would be sent outside of Jerusalem to heal and this I gladly welcomed.

One of the women who came openly to the Temple was Mariamme the wife of Joseph of Arimathea. She was of royal heritage and so was Joseph. Their lineage came from Levi and the line of David. I was invited into their home where I met their children, James, Salome, Josepheus, and Simeon. I was told there were twins named Yeshua and Thomas who were not home at this time. My heart leapt when I heard the name Yeshua. Ah yes, Yeshua ben Joseph.

I learned Yeshua was the legal heir to the throne of the Jews. He was a descendant of the House of David. The Romans had placed the first Herod on the throne which was not in keeping with the law, and this created grumbling and unrest among the populance. The Jews were expecting a Messiah to come who would take on the mantle of King because they believed in an old prophecy.

When Joseph departed on one of his many trips to the land of the Keltoi[2] and to Breton,[3] where he had tin mining interests and traded in other goods, Mariamme came more often to the Temple. She shared much of herself with me.

Mariamme had been in training in the Temple, and at the age of twelve she participated in the Rite of Sacred Marriage that is the celebration of the season of rebirth, which is an ancient rite. At this event she, as a virgin, was mated with one of the priests whose title was Gabriel. From this mating she became pregnant and Joseph of Arimathea had already agreed to wed her. He did so before the birth of the twins, and from their marriage came other children.

I was well past the age of twelve and I had never known a man to enter me. It did not trouble me because I knew one day it would be. Until that day arrived I had my work to do.

It came to my awareness of people who were ill with a disease called leprosy. They were much feared, having been banished to caves near Qumrum. These people were called unclean and they were shunned. Women were predominant in this group, along with their small children. They survived on very little, which was the small amount the kindhearted people of the Essenes left on the outskirts of their cave settlement.

With the blessings of the High Priestess Salome, I went forth outside the temple to heal. I journeyed to Qumrum with Martha, a novice priestess. Martha asked if I was fearful to be going to this condemned place. I answered her thus, "No, Martha I have no fear as I have no belief in this disease. We are all gods from the Divine Source. Whatever one has can be healed."

---

[2] Keltoi, an ancient name for Celts
[3] Ancient name for Britain

In reply, Martha asked me another question. "Mariam, you say we are all gods. How do you know this?"

"I know. How else can you explain our presence? In the scriptures of the Tenakh[4] it says 'Know you are gods.'[5] The ancients knew this before it was suppressed in human knowledge. We are here on a discovery of an unknown aspect of the Divine Source that is within each woman and man. How else can it know itself unless it created and experienced all these facets of itself?" Martha cautioned me in saying this to other people. The Sanhedrin would consider it a heresy.

Arriving at the foot of the caves, the people covered their faces, shouting for us to go back. They were so fearful. Resolutely I climbed the path, coming to a cowering woman, and I could see the flesh on her arms was eaten away, oozing with blood.

Closing my eyes, I silently asked her if she wanted to be healed and I received a resounding yes. Opening my eyes, I looked into her eyes, touching her while our eyes locked. I was seeing her as a healed and whole woman. As the others watched in fearful silence, her skin became radiant and whole.

Gently I bade her to go and never believe as she had before. I told her the old way of thinking had brought on the disease. Now she has been reborn into a new life, and she must think anew. I bade her each morning to give thought to what she desired for the day and each evening to remember everything that had happened during the day with as much detail as possible. She was to go over all the thoughts and actions she had while watching her responses. I bade her to ask these questions: What have I done this day? What could I have done differently but failed to do? Which of my actions do I regret? Which of my actions made me happy? By doing this she could change her old way of thinking.

I further told her all is forgiven and she must forgive herself. I told her the purpose of this healing was to change the old way of thinking. By doing what I had told her to do, the disease would not come back. With tears rolling down her face, she hugged me before she departed.

---

[4] Tenakh: ancient name for Old Testament of the Bible
[5] Psalms 82:6

One by one they came. All day long I healed the poor lepers and I gave them the same instructions as given to the first woman. I restored their dignity, and they became my followers with many becoming my apostles. Wherever I journeyed, they followed while I healed and spoke what I knew to be true.

As I had spoken to Martha, I spoke to them. I told them they were god's outer garments. I told them what I could do, they could also do. My fame grew with much grumbling among the Sadducees and the Pharisees. They denounced me in their congregations and called me the "black whore."

One day, while in a small village outside of Jerusalem I stood at a well speaking to women. A large group of men came shouting for me to stop and calling me "black whore." Soon a multitude of voices began shouting, "Stone her! Stone her!" They began collecting stones.

Contemplating my choices, I remained where I was. I heard a resounding voice coming from the back of the crowd, "Stop! I command you to stop!" A path cleared as a tall beautiful man with copper hair, piercing blue eyes and skin the color of dark sand strode through them to the well.

Turning to the enraged crowd of men, he purposefully spoke in a strong commanding voice. "You call her the 'black whore' yet she has never known a man. You, who have never bedded with a whore, you cast the first stone. You, who have never defiled the maidenhood of an innocent girl, you cast the first stone."

The men were shocked into silence, and one by one they departed leaving a group of smiling women with me at the well. I looked into the eyes of one I had seen only once in my childhood and I knew him to be Yeshua ben Joseph.

"Hail Mariam of Magdala."

"Ah, you know my name Yeshua ben Joseph. I say hail unto you also." With a big smile on his face, Yeshua replied, "We meet again and I notice you have become a most lovely maiden." We were both remembering our passing each other on the Nile when I was not quite six years of age.

"I suppose I could say thank you for saving my life."

"No Mariam. You and I both know you could have handled this yourself." We began laughing and Yeshua invited me to walk along with him, and the small band of men he had with him. I agreed, calling to my followers, "Follow me."

Walking together we began talking in Egyptian and we were quite oblivious to the others following along. It was like a breath of fresh air to be able to speak with someone who had also gone through the great Initiation at the Mother Temple of Isis in Egypt.

Yeshua asked me where I intended to go now. When I told him my plans were to travel to the home of Martha at Bethany, he told me he was also on his way to Bethany to see Martha's brother Lazarus.

Upon our arrival, Lazarus greeted us and we talked well into the night. We drank wine, ate and shared stories. Lazarus begged Yeshua to teach him the deeper mysteries. Yeshua smiled replying, "Soon enough you will be sent to a great mystery school. Now is not the moment."

The following morning, I departed with my followers returning to Jerusalem while Martha remained at her home attending to the household. Yeshua and his band were on their way to Arimathea where his father and mother had a spacious home.

As I continued to go out and heal, my band of followers grew larger. This did not sit well with the Sanhedrin. When it was known I was of royal blood, they dared not harm me for the time being.

It was a challenge to refrain from telling the people the god they worshiped was not in the temple or outside of them. I wanted to tell the people to read their scriptures, which said, "Know you are gods." I dared not at this point in time.

The Emperor Tiberius, it was rumored, was failing and had retired to an island named Caprae.[6] Unrest grew as the people were being taxed more because the kings of Judea, Samaria and Galilee also had to pay tribute to Tiberius. There was increasing political unrest and there were revolutionists called zealots. It was rumored Yeshua was one of them. These zealots wanted to throw off the yoke of Rome but the Romans were not tolerant of the zealots and some were taken and crucified.

---

[6] Caprae is an ancient name for the Island of Capri.

My great teacher Ioannes was also traveling the lands of Judea, Samaria and Galilee. Yes, it was Ioannes the Immerser, and his message to the people was also that they must change their old ways of thinking. He was teaching also that god resided within them. They were not to pray to a god outside of themselves. He was particularly teaching against Herod Antipas and urging people to overthrow this King and this angered Herod.

In the midst of all this turmoil, I heard tales of Yeshua accomplishing great things. There was another called Simon the Magus, also known as Simon the Magi, who was also creating miracles. I knew Simon had been an initiate at the mystery school in Egypt and an apprentice to Ioannes. The challenges were great for all of us because we were all proclaiming there had to be a new way of thinking. We were heralding a change from the old ways. Most of the people wanted the messiah, who had been predicted, and they were looking for a savior. We knew there was no one who could be a savior, because becoming one had to come from within each person.

Chapter 10

IN THE TROUGH

Prediction is very difficult, especially about the future.
- Niels Bohr -1885 -1962

Peter and I continued walking in the woods as part of our daily regime. Summer was upon us and the trees, flowers and fauna were in their full radiance, their scents everywhere. We enjoyed spending time in nature and being aware of her many faces. Sometimes we would just sit and listen to the sounds of the woods.

Jill was seemingly happy with her translating. And when Peter and I offered to relieve her, she always turned us down. I realized she was a woman with a mission. Sebastian as always was engrossed in his work. So Peter and I were free to explore the many facets of our personalities.

Our days were peaceful and we enjoyed the camaraderie of our meals with Jill and Sebastian. It was so easy to slip into the mode of complacency.

One morning I awoke with a sense that all this was about to come to an end, yet I didn't feel fearful at that moment. I was more interested in trying to figure out the future. I asked myself, *What is it I want to happen?* Of course, what I wanted was a long peaceful life with Peter. I smiled inwardly because nothing about marriage had been mentioned, and I knew I wasn't going to bring the subject up.

Continuing to contemplate, I saw myself as a piece of floating debris riding the waves of a vast ocean. The moment in the trough between waves was the period of calm. *Perhaps I am in one of those troughs,* I thought.

I tried to imagine how the translations of the scrolls would end and could come up with nothing valid. I heard Jill stirring and looked over to her bed. "Good morning. Isn't it a glorious day?"

After stretching, Jill sat up and looked at me. "Now it is a good morning. Tell me, what's on your agenda for the day?"

I shared with her my contemplation of the future. One thing I love about Jill is that she does not interrupt me.

Jill thought a moment and then said, "Perhaps we are in a trough – a peaceful calm. I had never looked at it that way. It certainly is making the translating easier. I have to admit that I will probably be sorry when this ends. It has brought a purpose to my life, which I never had before. Therefore I am making a conscious choice right now to let the future take care of itself."

"In other words, what I am hearing you say is to live in the moment?"

Jill chuckled. "You got it. Somehow I know it will all unfold. Right now it's time for breakfast and a hot cup of coffee, and as you know, I'm one of those people who like that pick-me-up-and-get-me-going coffee." Laughing, I agreed.

When we got to the kitchen Peter already had breakfast prepared and the table set. "You are a man after my own heart," I told him.

After kissing me, he handed me a cup of coffee and then poured one for Jill. Sebastian came in and joined us. I was noticing that with each passing day he looked happier and happier, and his coloring looked healthier.

During breakfast Jill announced the latest scroll was finished. While she went to get the translation, Sebastian and I cleared the table. The dishes could wait until later. Peter had gone out for his pipe smoking. Jill returned and we called Peter in. I poured another cup of coffee from the fresh brewed pot and we settled down to hear what The Magdalene had written.

We became so mesmerized that time flew by. The gnawing pangs of hunger later reminded us that we had missed lunch.

⚝ ⚝ ⚝

MARRIAGE
Scroll 10

I did not see Yeshua again until the Rite of the Sacred Marriage which is celebrated at the end of harvest. The High Priestess Salome told me that this time I was to partake in this particular rite. She began preparing me for the great marriage. I knew not who the great one would be, but I knew possibly I would receive the seed from the male chosen as my bridegroom. I knew this was part of my destiny. I had not been told of this until the eve before the Sacred Marriage, as it was the custom so the virgin bride could not dwell on it for too long.

Most of the brides were usually the age of twelve to thirteen and I was two and twenty, which is considered already old by some. That night after contemplating and performing the disciplines of mind I had been taught, it came to me. It would be Yeshua who would be the bridegroom. I smiled in anticipation and slept.

The morning of the Sacred Marriage came and I was awakened by the High Priestess herself. She brought me a most beautiful robe of white linen trimmed in gold. Handmaidens came with her and I was bathed, perfumed, and dressed. The handmaidens, being priestesses in their own right, seemed to me to chatter incessantly. My eyes were painted with kohl and my lips and cheeks rouged. At last a wreath of laurel was placed upon my head.

Usually brides were masked as well as the groom. However the High Priestess told me that with my two eyes, my identity could not be hidden. The hieros gamos sacred marriage was taking place outside of Jerusalem, it being the rite of fertility with the purpose being to celebrate life and a bountiful harvest from the fields. It was also an age-old rite in remembrance of Isis and Osiris as well as of Inanna and Tammuz. I was given a goblet of red wine to drink, and now the great moment was near.

Tents had been erected for my temple priestesses and me. I could hear the pipes, and the drums were pulsating through my body. Towards dusk it was determined I was prepared and I was led out to the middle of a circle of friends, followers, priests and priestesses coming from afar. There were great fires burning and intense excitement coming from all the people.

Slowly maidens began to dance and soon men began to join them. The drums grew louder along with the music from pipes, flutes and lutes. I stood in the center, and with his people escorting him, Yeshua came to join me. He was naked in keeping with the custom. It was magic when our eyes locked.

Yeshua was placed on a stool before me. The sacred fertility ceremony began as I unbound my hair. With the sacred oil of spikenard, I began to anoint his hair. I moved my hands down his body, and with my hair I wiped the oil from his feet. I felt the energy growing in my loins. Rising I began to dance with Yeshua joining me.

A high energy flowed from all. The people knew something magical and sacred was happening. After the first dance we stopped, and each of us was given a goblet of wine. Locking our arms together, I drank from his goblet while he drank from mine. We began dancing again. The intense drums and music pulsated through me. The moments were timeless. There was only Yeshua and me.

At last, picking me up in his arms, he carried me to the bridal tent where a bed had been prepared. The tent was softly lit from oil lamps. Slowly he put be down. We stood gazing into each other's eyes. Then gently he removed my wreath of laurel and I removed his. Yeshua untied my sash, beginning to take my robe off while kissing my neck and shoulders.

The energy pulsating through me went beyond my experience. Slowly, removing my undergarments, he stood looking at me and lifting me up, he carried me to our marriage bed, laying me there.

At first we kissed tenderly, then moved into passion. I did not need anyone to tell me what to do. It was as though a power greater than us took over. I know he kissed every part of my body and I his. His manhood was stiff and erect, and my nipples were hard where he had kissed them.

Slowly, without hurry, he entered me. Knowing I was a virgin, he gently broke through my maidenhood, and as he thrust into me over and over, he touched my place of arousal. I felt the energy rushing up my spine. It exploded out of the top of my head in a burst of ecstasy at the same moment as his did. It was a true marriage of two gods.

We were spent while not replete. Our lovemaking continued through most of the night and our union became one from the two. Yeshua whispered, "My beloved, I have a confession to make. I know you are my other self and I love you in a way words cannot express."

I replied, "My beloved. I also know you are my other self and I love you. I always have." We both wept tears of joy while continuing to consummate our union again and again.

As the night drew close to the morning, we slept. I awakened to the sound of the drums. At the same moment we both sat up and started laughing. "I think it is the call for us to emerge to hold up the marriage cloth for all to see that indeed you did consummate the sacred marriage with a virgin," said I.

"Mariam, my beloved, I will wed you. I will have you to be my true wife and partner."

"Yes, Yeshua ben Joseph. It is meant to be."

We washed each other and dressed to meet the gathered throng. Yeshua swept the marriage cloth from the bed, and as we emerged, he held it up for all to see. There was a great roar of laughter and clapping.

The High Priest and the High Priestess intoned the blessing for the great harvest to be received from the planting season. The drums and pipes began again along with the musicians. Yeshua waved the marriage cloth over his head and we began to dance the dance of fertility and new life. When we stopped, we joined the others to break the morning fast with bread and wine and we toasted to an abundant harvest to come.

Holding my hand, Yeshua led me to the High Priest and the High Priestess telling them we wanted to truly be wed. Already it was surmised there could be no other husband for me, or a wife for Yeshua. Having the wedding take place this day was not in keeping with the Law of the Jews and I would soon learn Yeshua was known for not keeping many of their customs or laws.

Quickly Yeshua searched out his mother and Joseph, telling them of this intent to wed me. As the word spread, there was a great uproar of laughter and more clapping. I was swept up in the arms of Thomas his twin, given a resounding kiss and was told he was delighted. James followed, then Simon and Josephus. His sister Salome embraced me.

Others clasped me in their arms, including Lazarus and Martha. Then I noticed a tall powerful looking man. Yeshua introduced him as Simon who is called the Magus or Magi of Samaria. I told him I had heard of the marvelous miracles he did. He replied, "And what I do, you also do, as I have also heard of you."

I then saw Ioannes. Here in this area he was called the Immerser. He came up to me and taking my hands, he kissed each one and then spoke to me. "I honor you, a Sophia." As I gazed into his eyes, I saw his destiny was not to have a long life. He smiled and said, "Yes, you know and I know. I am only a messenger of change. I have said there is one greater than I that comes."

"Ah, but I foresee a greater destiny for you, dear Ioannes."

"You are a Sophia and you know."

At that moment, Yeshua's mother, Mariamme came to him and spoke, saying there was no more wine left. I looked at Yeshua, and said "Beloved, will you join me in changing this water into wine?" Smiling he replied, "Yes." The empty wine jugs were soon filled with water and placed before us. We placed our hands over the jugs and closing our eyes silently prayed while within us we saw wine. When the first jug was poured, the wine was deemed to be of an exquisite vintage of red wine. The mind is powerful and with intent, it can do anything.

The marriage took place that afternoon with the celebration continuing for several days. The music played and dancing, singing and feasting were done with a great joy that had not been experienced for a long period of time by the multitude gathered. With this marriage, Yeshua now could be called Rabbi.

Yeshua and I spoke in our private moments and it was determined I would return to my temple where he would stay with me. When he felt the call to go out to teach, I could go with him to heal, or stay attending to my duties. We vowed not to make our marriage an enslavement of one to the other because we each recognized the divinity in the other and that each had a destiny to be fulfilled.

Joseph and Mariamme offered us a small group of rooms for our needs, when we chose. We knew we could also stay with Martha and Lazarus in Bethany when necessary.

Traveling separately or together, lodging and meals were made available to us. Our following was growing larger in numbers with each of us having our own group. There were twelve apostles who were closest to Yeshua in his large following. Two brothers named Simon and Andrew were his guards to keep him from being crushed by some of the crowds coming to hear him. Yeshua gave Simon the name of Petros, which means rock. Yeshua laughingly said Petros was thick in the head. Yeshua told him, "Upon you, the rock, I begin building my ekklesia."[1] Yeshua's meaning of Petros was that he was at the first door in understanding. Yeshua's purpose was to build an understanding in his ekklesia for this group to enter other doors in the nous, and Petros did not have the ears to hear or the understanding. In his limited thinking Petros understood this to mean that he would succeed Yeshua.

It became obvious Petros disliked me intensely and he was jealous of the attention I received from Yeshua. Even though Yeshua and I were married, Petros resented that Yeshua would kiss me on the lips in front of them. It was easy to note Petros was a lover of men only.

---

[1] Ekklesia: Ancient Greek word meaning gathering. During the estimated lifetime of Mary Magdalene and Jesus there was no word "church." See *Theology Today*, Oct. 1962.

Chapter 11

HOLY BLOOD

*The beginning of knowledge is the discovery of
something we do not understand.*
- Frank Herbert (1920-1986)

We sat transfixed while Sebastian read the translated portion. When he finished, there was stunned silence.

I was the first to speak. "Oh my gawd! How beautiful! Is the hieros gamos rite of fertility something like the pagans used to do?"

"It was an ancient practice until Christianity stamped out most of the earlier practices," Peter responded. "As I recall, these were very sacred rites. The people in ancient times didn't have the hang-ups regarding sex like people do now. Today corporate America promotes sex to sell its products. Sex has lost its sacredness."

Jill had remained silent. "Hmmm, you're right in that. However something that struck me was that when she wrote of changing water into wine, she was teaching about the power of thoughts. The thoughts you send out return to the sender. In other words, what we observe manifests and returns. We are the ultimate observer."

"What do you mean about the observer?" asked Sebastian.

"Well, in quantum physics, it has been proven that the observer of anything, by thoughts or words, determines his or her reality. In the laboratories of quantum physics the observer determines the outcome of the experiment. Therefore, we are constantly creating our reality by what we think, by our attitudes and by our beliefs," Jill explained.

"How do you know so much" Peter asked.

"My father was a physici s knowledge rubbed off on me. In som um

117

physics is the closest thing to God, in fact, that it explains the true Creator."

"Tell me, Jill," Peter went on, "in what way do quantum physicists arrive at this concept?"

Smiling, Jill answered, "As I understand it, everything has its origins in the quantum world. Physicists are going from a cell, down to a molecule, down to an atom and down to the components of the atom. Then each component of the atom can further be broken down into the sub-atomic and the very, very tiny where it is still beyond the scope of the physicists.

"I read William Lyne's book *Occult Ether Physics.* In it he writes about the omni particle. From my perception this is the God particle. In fact, there's another book titled *The God Particle* written by a physicist named Leon Lederman."

"What you say is most interesting," Sebastian said. "Most think God is some being outside of themselves. And the Church encourages this as well as most religions. So, what you are saying, if I understand you correctly, is that God is really a principle."

"Well, perhaps the word principle is better than thinking of God as somewhere up in the sky keeping count of whose naughty and whose nice," Jill said with a chuckle.

Sebastian then asked us, "What does the word occult mean to you?"

Peter responded, "From my perspective, occult only means something hidden. It has been polluted by saying it means something dark and evil."

At this point, I joined in and agreed with Peter. "The sacred truth has been carried down through the ages by secret societies because the knowledge had to be hidden from those who would destroy it. As I understand, keeping God outside of oneself keeps mankind enslaved. This means a person always has to have an intermediary to intercede between the person and God. So, if one thinks God is punishing him or her, then by that belief they bring it about. I agree with Peter that the word occult has been used to keep people from looking beyond what is told them by religionists."

We all laughed and Peter picked up the ball. "No wonder the world is in such a mess. Almost everyone is giving their power away and placing their divinity outside of themselves. It is something like a hamster running on a wheel. Mankind is born, dies, is reborn, lives and dies."

"It is sad," I added. "No wonder the Church repressed the truth about Mary Magdalene and also about John the Baptist. If people had lived what she taught them, the world would be entirely different."

"Oui," said Sebastian. "This also applies to Jesus. Instead he was placed on a cross and kept there. I always wondered how one man could die for everyone's sins. What a heavy burden to place on one man!"

Then it dawned on me. "Oh gawd! We have missed one of the most important aspects of these scrolls."

"What?" Peter asked.

"It is so obvious now. The piece of linen with no scroll inside – you know, the one with a rust stain on it? Well, the realization just came. Oh, gawd! It must be a piece of the marriage cloth with her virgin blood on it!"

Sebastian was quick to understand. "Oui! Oui! It is most apparent now."

"Then this cloth would have her DNA on it, and perhaps that of Jesus from his sperm. There must be some residue of his sperm," Jill said.

Peter's voice was full of realization. "This cloth is priceless and it must never get in the hands of the wrong factions."

"Yes," I said. The implications were becoming evident. "The Knights Templar and the Priory of Sion, as secret organizations, have a history of protecting the bloodline of Jesus and Mary Magdalene, and I want to know what evidence they found or acquired to become committed to protecting the bloodline."

Peter said, "From what I've read, the bloodline comes through the Merovingian lineage and some have traced it to the Stuarts of Scotland, but I don't know what their basis is for this allegation."

Jill interrupted, "But Peter, the bloodline coming from only one birth could spawn one million people who are part of that bloodline. How can it be traced through a specific lineage? It doesn't make sense."

"Why isn't there a way?" Peter asked. "I believe there were some scientists who found a common ancestor to us all, one who had lived in Africa somewhere in the neighborhood of 200,000 years ago. As I remember, they named her Eve. I read a book on the subject a few years ago."

I interrupted by asking, "Isn't this through the mitochondrial DNA?"

"Yes, but without going into the sketchy details that I remember, I do remember that according to the scientists' findings, lineage is passed on through the maternal line only." With that, Peter sat back and looked at all of us.

Sebastian cleared his throat and we all looked at him. "Ahem, perhaps as I recall reading, the Merovingians were known for their . . . for lack of a better word, supernatural powers. They were known to be healers and to have other powers. Could it be that someone knew that lineage would be passed down through the female? I do not know of any substantial evidence for their connection to The Magdalene and Jesus."

"You're right. What Peter said and what you said is a very interesting hypothesis," I replied. "Unless, when the Templars looted, for lack of a better word, the Temple of Solomon, they found something that must have given them some reason to revere Mary Magdalene. It must have been something as powerful as these scrolls are indicating."

"Or that 'something' may not have been an object or objects. What if they found other documents giving the truth about her? I mean, the truth that she was a great initiate and every bit the equal of Yeshua, if not more so?" Peter said.

"Perhaps," Jill interjected, "they learned that the bloodline is passed down through the woman and somehow the Church knew this and that is why the roles of women have been reduced to make them seem unintelligent and worthless."

Peter spoke up, "This is all very interesting and this cloth was placed with the scrolls for a reason, which we do not have the answer for now." Turning to Sebastian, he asked him to bring out the cloth for us to see.

Returning soon, Sebastian reverently and carefully unrolled it. The stain was on the edge of the cloth, as if it had been torn into two pieces.

We were silent for a moment and then we all began speaking at once. "Hold it!" came from Peter.

"This cloth is a potential. However let's not jump to conclusions. We do know this is an extremely valuable item and if word leaked out that we have found it, it could be a volatile situation."

Then Sebastian spoke his mind. "You are correct. This is indeed a dangerous situation. I must say at this point that if any of you want to expose this cloth for personal glory or monetary rewards, I refuse to do further translations."

We all looked at him. I was, as always, the first to speak. "Sebastian, I can only speak for myself. I have no intention of sharing this information with anyone. In her first scroll, The Magdalene charged the finders not to allow these scrolls to be hidden away, and since I am one of the finders, I have no intention of sharing this yet, and only will if we are all in agreement."

"I feel the same way Ellen does," Jill said. "I have no desire to exploit this precious and sacred artifact."

"That goes for me also," said Peter. "I agree with Ellen, that if the news of this marriage cloth artifact is released, it must be the four of us jointly. Do you agree Sebastian?"

"Oui. I agree. I have seen too much hypocrisy, lies and exploitation in the Church. I can no longer partake of any such endeavors. Then, it is agreed. We keep this sacred object secret until the appropriate moment?"

We all told him yes and I went on to add, "This must be kept in a very secret place apart from the scrolls. But where?"

Peter got up and began pacing in the kitchen. "Sebastian, didn't you tell us that there is an ancient sacred Celtic well on this property?"

"Oui, and it is a short walk behind the barn where the cars are parked. You have an idea?

"Yes I do," replied Peter. "However, if you notice we have sat here most of the day and we all are a bit bleary-eyed. Let's check it out in the morning. We have been here a long time reading and discussing, and I am ready for dinner. In the meantime, Sebastian can you look around for an airtight and watertight container?"

"It's done!" answered Sebastian. "But what do you mean by bleary-eyed?"

Laughing, Peter replied, "It's a slang expression meaning that our eyes are over-tired."

We all had much to contemplate, and we talked long into the night and were eagerly awaiting for the translation of the next scroll.

I spent a restless night and at times lay awake thinking about what Mary Magdalene had written. There was a part of me that wanted to lash out in anger at the men who had suppressed her story and almost obliterated her from history. I realized that my having discovered these scrolls was no accident. A Divine hand had led me to them. How and why, I did not know.

The following morning after breakfast, Peter and Sebastian left to find the ancient Celtic well. It wasn't too long before they returned smiling. They had found a place to put the marriage cloth. Sebastian had found a container in the barn and carefully packed the cloth inside. Since the four of us were in this together, Jill and I accompanied them to its hiding place.

I voiced my concern about the condition of the well.

Sebastian replied, "There is still water in it, however, the container will not be placed in the well. It will be near it."

I felt a presence as Peter and Sebastian lowered the precious container into its place of rest.

It will serve no purpose to describe the hiding place at this point. The container will be moved by the time this story is known. Within me, I know the spirit of Mary Magdalene is watching over it and when the appropriate moment comes, it will be given to the ones who will use it, but not for exploitation or greed.

≈≈≈ ≈≈≈ ≈≈≈

YEARS WITH YESHUA
Scroll 11

I continue my story as I have lived it. Yeshua was an important part of my life. My writings must include him. I will say this about Yeshua, and also myself: we were not meek, passive people. We loved life and we loved people. We loved the poor and the rich, the lame, the sick and the well people. We loved to laugh, dance and sing, along with drinking wine.

We never drank to excess, because we knew the value of the red wine. When we ate, we ate with a love for all food. We blessed all food, as nothing is good or bad in the eyes of the Divine One. All is from the Divine. It is only good and evil in the eyes of man.

One day I was teaching in the Temple of Isis. One of the women asked why I ate meat. She had heard that Ioannes the Immerser did not eat meat. I asked her if she knew for herself this to be true. "No," she replied. "I have only heard rumors of it."

In answer to her statement, I asked, "Know you, all is divine in the mind of the One? It is only in the eyes of the beholder that one way is better than the other. It is only the minds of men that make one thing good and the other evil."

Another woman replied, "But Mariam, it is known the Essenes eat no meat."

"True, some but not the Nazoreans," I said. "Whatever a person chooses to eat has nothing to do with his or her divineness. Whatever a man eats makes him sick or well according to his belief. Know you the Tenakh says 'For as he thinketh within himself, so is he.'"[1]

From time to time we encountered Ioannes with his apostles. There was animosity between the two groups of apostles of Yeshua and Ioannes, as they behaved as if one was of higher learning than the other. I did not have this challenge, because most of my apostles were women. Ioannes, Yeshua and I would move beyond their hearing and have our honest conversations. I felt a kinship with Ioannes, as he was the first one I met in Alexandria after I departed the mystery school. He spoke of universal knowledge with Yeshua and me.

These were indeed troublesome times. Yeshua was being urged by his family to curtail his teachings against the yoke of Rome and also his open dislike for the old ways and laws of the Sanhedrin. The community of the Essenes was equally unhappy. There were two parts to the Essenes. One forbade marriage and required celibacy and the second had a requirement of marriage. Each sect disapproved of the other's views regarding marriage and celibacy.

---

[1] Proverbs 23:7

Yeshua was teaching the lesser mysteries to the common man and woman. His younger brother James was involved with administering the initiations within the Essenes and was not pleased with the acts of Yeshua. Yeshua and his brothers had all been initiated to follow a greater accord. Being the rightful heir to the throne of the Jews, Yeshua had been trained in the mysteries in Egypt. There was also disagreement regarding my status. I had not been trained in the ways of the Essenes and my beliefs agreed with Yeshua's.

The times Yeshua and I were apart, we would commune with each other with our minds and at times we would leave our bodies and meet in a realm of a higher vibration. All this we had learned at the Mystery School using the natural laws available to all. What we did, anyone can do if the natural laws are understood. I never felt separation when we were apart.

Martha was my most trusted one. Along with her being my sister in the priesthood, she was my first apostle. She always went with me when I went out to heal. One day I had gone to a small village outside of Bethany to talk to the women. I had a host of followers with me. In the midst of my teaching, a man came bringing his young son who could have been the age of twelve or older. The son had fallen from a roof he was repairing and broken his arm. A bone was sticking out from the skin.

"Oh Mariam of Magdala, it has been said you are a great healer. I beg you to heal my son." I walked over to the young boy and held his shoulder and his wrist gently. I gazed into the boy's eyes and asked if he wanted to be healed. As the pain was extreme, he could only nod his agreement. I continued to look into his eyes and slowly before everyone, his bone went into place and the skin repaired itself.

There were great murmurs of disbelief. The boy's father asked, "How did you do it? What magic did you wrought?" I replied, "You saw a broken arm. I saw a whole, well arm. This is for those who have the eyes to see and the ears to hear. Go now and guard your thoughts that the mouse does not enter and eat the good."

As I was about to depart and return to the Temple in Jerusalem, I noticed a young woman and I knew her. "Meesha!

It is indeed you!" I cried, going to her and taking her in my arms. As we embraced, she gave a loud wailing sob.

"Meesha, Meesha, how be you here? What has happened in your life?" I allowed her to continue her sobbing and when she was at last spent, she told me the tale. Meesha was given into marriage soon after I left for the Mystery School. He was an older man, but kind. She did not conceive and his family thought it was her fault because he had other children by another wife. The husband died and his family threw her out. She returned to her family and they attempted to find another husband for her, but rumors of her barrenness were spread and a husband could not be found. Meesha had learned I was in Jerusalem and made her way to find me.

When she had finished her tale, I told her to worry no more because she was now a member of my family. Meesha became one of my apostles and when my child was born, she aided me and cared for the little one.

Yeshua and I had a child born nine months after our marriage. It was an easy birth and Yeshua was near me when this male babe made his appearance. His eyes were blue and as the babe grew older, his hair became copper and his skin was much like that of Yeshua's. We named him James. We called him James the Younger.

After six weeks I left my seclusion and resumed my duties as priestess at the Temple. I continued to suckle James because the role of motherhood was one of which I found great pleasure. Yeshua encouraged me to continue my work in the Temple, and when he came to us, he played with James and sang songs for him. These were always happy occasions, with us delighting in the growth of our male child.

Not all the family of Yeshua was in acceptance of our ways. His mother would have preferred us to become more settled in our living arrangements. She admonished Yeshua that now that he was called Rabbi, he had a duty to be a family man as well as a teacher.

Joseph was a great friend, and he loved all his children. Joseph had much power within the Sanhedrin, and his royalty aided him in his vast empire of trading. He had a longing to go and live in the isles called Breton, but Mariamme had been to the isles once with him and had no desire to live among the Keltoi.

Word came to us that Herod Antipas had imprisoned Ioannes. The reason given was that Ioannes was charged as a revolutionary against Herod. Yeshua came to me agitated and we discussed the situation. Together we began our mind exercises and communicated with Ioannes. The message he gave back to us was to leave him alone as he was losing his head.

There is an ancient saying that when one has his head cut off it means the mind has mastered the flesh of his humanity. He has become Kristos.[2] We knew what Ioannes was referring to, and within a week, he mentally sent us a message that he was departing. To us, we knew he had mastered his vibrations and he had returned to the One. He was Kristos.

It is reported when Herod learned of Ioannes' disappearance he almost went mad with rage. He ordered another prisoner to be executed, having the head removed, claiming that was the head of Ioannes. We knew this was not so.

Sometimes Yeshua went out to teach with his group and I went out with my group. At other times we traveled together and we both spoke. One day we were in a small village in Galilee and a family came to us with their young daughter for a healing. They said she was inhabited by demons. Her eyes were wild with fear, and she was shrieking as one who appears mad. Yeshua and I could both see that around her there were departed entities that had attached themselves to her. There were seven of them. One by one we dispersed these beings and sent them to a place where they could also be healed of their desire to remain attached to the earth plane.

We told the young woman to guard her thoughts and feelings always. She must never become angry. The parents were told to allow her to sleep and when she awakened she would be possessed no more.

Chapter 12

SEBASTIAN'S DISAPPEARANCE DISCOVERED

Down, down, down.
Would the fall NEVER come to an end!
- Alice in Wonderland. Lewis Carroll

One beautiful morning after breakfast, Jill suggested that we drive into a small village for shopping. Our supplies were low, and since it was summer, there were many open-air markets. We wanted fresh vegetables, fruits, meat and eggs.

I was driving Paul's car. Usually I drove out and Jill drove in. We hadn't gone too far when she asked, "Your relationship with Peter appears to be a great one. Will you and Peter marry?"

Caught off guard I laughed and replied that our relationship hadn't progressed that far.

Jill countered with, "Do you think this relationship is right for you?"

For a moment I contemplated her questions. "It's different with Peter. In retrospect I know it wasn't love with Walter. But with Peter . . . it isn't because we have terrific sex. No. There is other magic. I ripple all over when I'm with him and I feel like a giddy schoolgirl. We can talk about intelligent things, and when we are silent, it's a comfortable silence. It's like a dance where we are partners perfectly in tune with one another. When I am with him there is no time. It's a magic I wish for everyone. Does that answer you?"

"Ummm, yes."

I looked over at Jill and noticed she was looking out the window. A sudden thought hit me. "Are you getting ideas about Sebastian?"

"No! Whatever gave you that idea?"

I looked at her again and noticed she was flushed. "Well, you two are working closely together. It wouldn't be out of the ordinary for something to click between you."

"Oh god, Ellen! You do get some of the damnedest ideas. Let's get off the subject."

Realizing I had touched a tender spot, I sighed inwardly, changed the subject and began commenting on the beauty of the countryside. But inside I was smiling.

We spent a delightful few hours shopping for fresh vegetables, breads, fruit, meat and of course wine, along with other supplies.

The following days were tranquil with Sebastian and Jill translating while Peter and I explored the woods and paths.

It was some days after our realization regarding the marriage cloth, that we were able to hear the latest translation. With each one we had become more and more in wonderment. So many preconceived ideas had to be abandoned.

Then one evening we sat discussing the latest revelations of The Magdalene's years with Yeshua. "Now I understand why the Templars revered John the Baptist. The Baphomet they were accused of worshiping was representative of John's ascension," I said.

"Mais oui. When properly translated, Baphomet means wisdom. It is also another name for Sophia."

"My god!" Peter said. "This means the Templars knew the Baptist was a Christ and had not in actuality been beheaded!"

Jill was excited. "Oh my! Now I think I understand why Leonardo da Vinci revered John. He not only painted John in the painting *The Last Supper*, but he also painted skulls near Mary Magdalene in his painting of her. I am beginning to see a connection to either John's beheading, or it could refer to the importance of the mind. Interesting."

"Yes," I replied. "And da Vinci always painted one of John the Baptist's fingers pointing up as if it were a message. It could possibly mean, 'Remember me.' And the skulls could also possibly refer to Mary Magdalene's being as great as Jesus."

By now we were getting many revelations. Peter said that Picknett and Prince in *Turin Shroud* wrote of the possibility of da Vinci creating the shroud.

"Non, c'est impossible!" Sebastian said in a disbelieving way.

Peter continued, "Well, they make a pretty good case for it. They point out the figure on the shroud has a severed head. Also, Picknett and Prince did their own experiment indicating da Vinci had knowledge of photography and could have created the shroud."

"Mon dieu! Will surprises never cease?"

We were excited and on a roll when Sebastian gave us another eye-opening possibility. "Supposedly Jesus was crucified at Golgotha, which translates into the Place of the Skull. The actual place of Golgotha has never been found. Perhaps the message is that Jesus reached the same accomplishment as John and he attained Kristos. There was not one Christ, there were two!"

"If it were known there were two Christs, the foundation of the Church would crumble." Peter offered.

"Why not three?" I asked.

The response from Peter was, "But of course. It makes sense."

It was Jill who said, "Hmmm, three Christs. Apollonius lived during that period and became a Christ and so did Simon Magus. That would make five Christs. It must have been a wonderful period. And yet, the people didn't get their message that it was possible for anyone to accomplish becoming a Christ. After all, Jesus is quoted in the Bible as saying 'Greater things than I do, you can do.'"

Picking up on what Jill had just said, I asked, "Who was the fifth Christ? You named John, Jesus, Simon the Magus and Apollonius."

Smiling, Jill replied, "Isn't it the obvious unobvious? I suspect Mary Magdalene also became a Christ."

"Oh gawd, yes, it makes sense!" I exclaimed.

Peter spoke up saying he thought it plausible while Sebastian murmured, "Tragic. Tragic, that this has not been known."

The following morning after we had discussed the latest scroll, I turned on the television in the kitchen to hear the news. We were about to sit down to have breakfast when Sebastian's face flashed on the screen. We sat there in shock. I think Sebastian was the most shocked because he let go an expletive "merde!"

All I could say was "Oh gawd! Oh gawd!" I felt as if I were frozen in time. Sebastian translated the news report for us, which said that when his housekeeper, Madame Françoise Sagan, had not heard from Father Sebastian Gontard for some time and she made inquiries at the place where he was staying while taking the cure at Lourdes.

A police investigation at Lourdes had revealed that an American, who had given his name as Peter Douglass, had visited Father Sebastian. It was after the visit that Father Sebastian checked out of the hotel where he had been staying.

The newscast went on to describe Peter Douglass as being approximately 6 feet 2 or 3 inches tall, slender with light brown hair worn in a ponytail. He was wearing blue jeans and a white shirt.

The commentator continued saying Father Sebastian was a noted translator of ancient Greek texts and had been a professor at the Université of Toulouse. He was also on medical retirement from the Vatican.

Then followed a piece saying that the authorities were investigating a newly found cave near Mirepoix where they claimed several parchment scrolls wrapped in linen had been discovered along with three pottery jars. The commentator said it was thought there were more scrolls. A young boy had led authorities to the cave, where he reported having seen two people emerge from it.

The young boy was not suspected of hiding any other scrolls and an inquiry as to the identity of the two persons was under investigation. An initial examination of the scrolls indicated they were written in ancient Greek.

The commentator added, "Could there be a link between the discovery of the scrolls and the disappearance of Father Sebastian?"

Peter exploded. "How the hell did the police get my description? And, Sebastian, did you leave a note for your housekeeper?"

"Non. I did not think it necessary since she was leaving to go on her vacation to visit a niece in Italy, and she knew I intended to go to the Mediterranean for an extended stay because that is what I told her when I called her from Lourdes the same day Peter came to see me. Something is amiss. She would not have returned on her own. I was explicit in telling her I would call her when I was ready to return. This is not good."

"You better believe it," I said. "Somebody has made a connection between the scrolls and Sebastian."

Sebastian looked devastated. "Mes amies, this in indeed a serious complication. It could be the Church, but then again, it could be members of the Priory of Sion, the Templars, or of one of the archaeology communities. It could even be a hidden branch of the Knights of Malta. Or there is the possibility it could be a wealthy collector of ancient texts and artifacts. The potentials are one or several. We need to make contingency plans."

I told them I thought we should all think about this. I knew I wanted to go off and think, and I realized also that in the beginning I had not fully realized the ramifications when I fell into the cave and found the scrolls. I excused myself and walked out into the garden.

The sun was shining and the aroma coming from the roses was so sweet. Mixed with the wafting perfume of honeysuckle, it was a delicious smell. I sat down in the glider, became quiet and watched the birds. I knew I couldn't panic, because it wouldn't solve anything.

Peter came and joined me, pulling out his pipe and lighting it. We sat in silence for a while until Jill came out, pulling up a chair to join us. Sebastian soon followed and pulled up a chair to sit next to Jill.

"What do we do, mes amies?"

Jill replied, "I don't sense we are in any danger of being discovered. However, it is disconcerting that Peter has been identified. It's most unfortunate we dropped those two scrolls."

I spoke up. "I'm suspicious, because the newscaster made a connection between the two scrolls and the disappearance of Sebastian. I feel as if we are up against a sinister unknown."

"Mes amies, I agree that for the moment we are safe. There is one thing I did not share. When the couple canceled the rental of Paul's house, I failed to notify him. I was so distraught with my own situation of illness. Ah, it is Divine Providence that I did not inform him. Since Paul has rented his home in the past along with his car, the neighbors will not be suspicious of our presence."

131

We all signed with relief. Then Peter said, "I have thought this out and I've made a decision. I'm going to leave, because I'm the one sought after by the police. If I leave and they find me, it could give you additional days or weeks to translate."

Immediately I gasped, "No, Peter!"

"Ellen, I want to keep you, Jill and Sebastian safe. The most important objective is to keep these scrolls from falling into the wrong hands."

"Okay. However, I am going with you."

"Ellen, do realize the danger involved? I want you safe."

"Peter my love, without you, being safe is not important. I'm going with you, and I've made my decision."

There was a silence. "Ahem," Sebastian began, "I cannot make a decision for you. If you feel this is what you want to do, I cannot stop you. However I want you to think this over carefully."

"I don't want to leave here," Jill said. "I want to stay, and not for safety. I have a drive to assist Sebastian in transcribing these scrolls. But, Peter, I don't fully understand why you think it's necessary for you to leave?"

"I want to because I think it would be better for me to continue traveling as a tourist. If I'm discovered, they will find a tourist. If I remain in hiding, it will perhaps cause them to really think I was responsible for the disappearance of Sebastian."

"And since Peter and I have discovered our love for one another, we can be a pair of tourists in love."

"I can go along with that," said Jill. "I can be the one renting the house from Paul. I do think it would be wise if one of you got an e-mail account on one of those websites on the Internet that allow you to check your e-mail from any computer, anywhere. I'll also get one, and that way we can stay in touch."

"That's a great idea, and let's make out a code," Peter responded. Sebastian sat and looked at us in amazement.

"Voilà. I am in awe of how well you respond to such a thing as this. And oui, Jill's assistance is most appreciated. We will continue at a fast pace."

I asked, "How do we leave here without being seen?"

Sebastian answered with a suggestion. "There is the Canal du Midi. It begins here at Toulouse and goes all the way to the Mediterranean. There is a towpath along the canal and if you desire, perhaps you can even get a ride on one of the many boats that travel the canal."

Peter and I liked the idea; we would not appear to be hiding. We would be tourists on our way to Carcassonne. I'd been there before. We would be hikers interested in the Cathars and Templars; and after all, that is the part of France where they are revered.

Sebastian went to his car and retrieved a map. Peter and I studied it, seeing the grand possibilities. It was agreed Jill would take us in Paul's car to where the River Garonne joins the Canal du Midi.

I asked, "Why is it called a towpath?"

"When the canal was built 300 years ago, the barges and boats had to be pulled by horses walking along the path on the bank," Sebastian said. "That is why it is called a towpath. Now there are almost 100 locks on the canal and therefore the travel is slow for boats. I think you will find some charming small villages, restaurants and sites along the way."

Jill and I went inside, and Jill said she would pack us a lunch while I went to pack my backpack. From our walks in the woods, I had an idea of what this hike would be like. Actually, I realized I was looking forward to being alone with Peter.

At times I had felt like a third thumb while Jill and Sebastian did the translating. Sighing, I knew I would miss hearing what the new translations revealed.

Peter and Sebastian had set up e-mail accounts on the Internet. We all agreed our messages would be lighthearted, such as "no trouble" would be "it's a glorious day." "Trouble" could be "the weather is a bit cloudy." Peter and I carried the code only in our heads.

We set out with farewell hugs and kisses for Sebastian, and Jill drove us to the designated point. There was no one in sight and it would be easy to walk onto the towpath.

Hugging Jill, I told her I felt I was leaving her with the burden of translating. Smiling, she replied that she would be doing something she enjoyed. Turning to Peter, she hugged him. With tears in her eyes, Jill returned to the car and drove away.

Sebastian's parting words to us had been, "Find a walking stick because sometimes dogs have escaped their fences and they could be a nuisance." We waved and began our walk on the towpath along the canal, and it wasn't too long before we found a couple of sticks apparently discarded by other walkers.

For the first hour we said little. I was thinking of Jill. Something within me knew she cared more for Sebastian than she chose to disclose. I wondered if Sebastian had any feelings towards her.

Peter broke the silence. "A penny for your thoughts."

"Oh, I was thinking of Jill and Sebastian, and I was wondering if a possible romance is in the offing."

Chuckling, Peter said, "It's possible. I've only noticed that they work well together. Miracles do occur, though. Do you know that according to quantum physics, miracles are natural occurrences?"

"Thank god! We humans always want to give our power away to something outside of ourselves. Of course I welcome divine intervention."

"Yep. Do you mind if we stop a minute while I light my pipe?"

"I can do with a pause. Go ahead," I said.

"Peter, how does quantum physics explain why bad things happen to good people?"

Having lit his pipe, he took a few puffs. "Hmmm, from my knowledge and understanding, everything starts in the mind. The thought reaches into the quantum where it connects with particles, which brings forth the results. This explanation is very simplistic. Also, I would say no one ever knows what is going on in someone else's mind, except an adept mind reader. Therefore, we don't know what is in the mind of the 'good' person. Most of us put on a facade with other people. Each of us has different experiences with other people, while one might see one person as a saint and the other might see the same person as a sinner."

"I know so little about quantum physics, but this makes sense. I covered up my misery when I was with Walter, and I wallowed in my false pride of not wanting anyone to know what a poor choice I had made."

"I did the same thing and it has taken me time to let go of my guilt."

We were now walking again.

"Could it be that some people come into this life to experience certain things, and then when the supposedly bad thing happens, it is what some would call karma?"

"Well Ellen, I had never thought of that possibility. It's something to ponder. If we think of it long enough, the universe will bring us the answer."

Sometimes Peter would get ahead of me. He'd realize I was behind and then he would stop, grinning at me while I caught up. "I'm sorry sweetheart. I keep forgetting my legs are so long."

Sebastian had been right. The walk was lovely along the canal. Great sycamore trees lined each side of it, and there were barges and boats going either way. We waved as they passed. I felt relaxed and I could tell Peter was also, but this didn't mean we weren't alert.

At one point we came upon a tourist boat that had pulled up to the bank and moored. We were greeted as long lost friends and invited on board. We accepted and managed to communicate, with our knowledge of French and theirs of English. It was mid-afternoon and to our delight we were treated to cheese, bread and wonderful red wine. Telling our hosts that we were tourists, we were offered a ride to Castelnaudary, which we accepted.

We sang songs and the time passed most enjoyably. When our hosts learned we were actually on our way to Carcassonne, they invited us to continue on with them and sleep on the deck for the night. We accepted.

They asked us to dine with them, and it turned out to be a two-hour dinner that was a gourmet's repast. We had stuffed artichokes, foie gras, cassoulet, salad, escargots and Brie. Peter and I offered to pay our share of the fare, but it wasn't accepted.

The evening had grown late when we arrived at Carcassonne. The cry went out, "Vous avoir arrivé!"

And we had.

The view of the castle and the walled city lit by floodlights was breathtaking. From the boat the scene was a stunningly beautiful panorama. We sat on the deck for a while and just gazed at the spectacular site. Finally Peter and I laid our bedrolls out on the deck and snuggled before falling to sleep.

The following morning we bade our hosts farewell and set out to tour Carcassonne. The first item of business was to send an e-mail to Jill and Sebastian to let them know we had arrived safely. We found an Internet café and went in for coffee. Peter found a computer that was free and sent the message, however there were no messages yet for us.

Leaving the café, we wandered around a bit and found a sidewalk café. This time we ordered croissants and café au lait. Peter brought out a map of Carcassonne and we discussed what to do for the day.

He had just lit his pipe when I looked up and saw a policeman in a blue uniform approaching. I had a sinking sensation he was headed for us. I was right.

Speaking in French, he asked to see our passports. Reluctantly, we brought ours out and handed them to him. Carefully he thumbed through each one.

In broken English, he asked us to accompany him to the gendarmes. Peter asked if we had done something illegal.

"Non," he replied and again in broken English said that Peter needed to see someone at the gendarmes, which I took to be the local police station.

I stood up with Peter. The officer began to say something and then shrugged his shoulders. We were led to a vehicle with Police painted on the side and we got in. A wave of fear swept through me. I held on to Peter's hand tightly.

"Peter, what have we done? Why do they want us?" While we were on our walk along the canal we had already agreed to play the innocents if we should be questioned.

"Sweetheart, I haven't the faintest clue. Don't worry; I'm sure it will be cleared up. I can't imagine why they want to see us."

The policeman turned the siren on, and it had the mournful wail European sirens do. The word klaxon entered my mind while we were speeding through the streets to the gendarmes.

Nothing had prepared me for the experience to come.

We arrived at a rather nondescript looking stone building and were ushered out of the car and inside. There the policeman, or perhaps he should be called the gendarme, spoke to the woman at the desk. I was told to wait while Peter went with him.

Peter told him, "If you want to talk to me, she comes too. I will not leave her alone."

The policeman looked at Peter, then at me. The officer nodded to the woman. She came over and frisked me while the policeman frisked Peter. Then he waved for me to come along too.

We had to leave our backpacks at the desk where I was sure they were going to be searched, and we were whisked up the elevator to an office on another floor and into a room without windows. It contained only a battered looking table and a few chairs.

The officer left and the door clicked shut. Peter took me in his arms and stroked my hair. "I don't know what this is all about. I only know we haven't done anything wrong. It has to be a case of mistaken identity."

We jumped apart when the door opened. A middle-aged man wearing a dress suit entered. He was medium height with graying black hair cut very short and had a drooping mustache. He indicated we were to sit. His eyes reminded me of a basset hound. Coming in behind him was another man, who had a laptop computer, which I presumed would be used to record the interview.

The man in the suit spoke quite good English. "Let me introduce myself. I am Inspector Bernière. Your passport says that your name is Peter Douglass, an American, and that you entered France from Andorra. I must inquire as to where you have been while in France?"

Peter sat back and told him of our walk from Santiago de Compostela along the Spanish side of the Pyrenees. He said we had entered France from Andorra and walked to Mirepoix where we discussed visiting the famous caves in the area.

Inspector Bernière asked if we had actually visited any of the caves. Peter replied we had visited la grotte du Mas d'Azil as well as la grotte de Niaux. In addition, we had seen la grotte de Bedeilbac.

Peter asked the Inspector if he wished to see his ticket stubs and was told yes.

Pulling out his money belt, Peter produced the stubs. I also said I would be glad to show my ticket stubs if he wished. He nodded yes. I said they were in my backpack and he only nodded.

Peter was queried as to his relationship with Father Sebastian. He told of their chance meeting the previous year at the Louvre in Paris and of their dinner together. Peter said he had been extended an invitation to visit Father Sebastian when he returned to France. He knew Toulouse wasn't that far from Mirepoix. Wanting to renew his acquaintance with the priest, he made a phone call to the number Father Sebastian had given to him. Yes, he knew Father Sebastian was quite ill. The Father had shared this information with Peter the previous year. When the housekeeper told him where the Father was, Peter made the decision to go to Lourdes to see his friend and said I had accompanied him.

The Inspector asked Peter to repeat his conversation with Father Sebastian during their visit in Lourdes.

Peter never deviated in his statement. He said the father appeared quite ill and despondent and said he felt his faith was not strong enough for a cure. He was contemplating a trip to the Mediterranean where he wanted to go into seclusion for a few weeks. The two had parted and Peter had sensed he would not see Father Sebastian again.

There were what seemed to be the same questions over and over but Peter was consistent with his story. I could tell he really wanted to smoke his pipe. Even though the Inspector was smoking cigarettes, he refrained from asking permission.

I was also asked if I had seen Father Sebastian. I said that I had not gone with Peter when he went to see him; instead I had done some sightseeing. The Inspector got up, thanked us and left, accompanied by the man with the laptop computer.

Peter and I didn't speak because we were so shaken. We held hands and Peter reached over, kissing me lightly. "Don't worry Ellen. This will be cleared up soon."

The "soon" lengthened into half an hour before the Inspector returned, carrying sheets of paper. He told us they were our statements and he wished us to sign them.

Peter looked at his and I looked at mine. They were in French. After scanning his statement, Peter said, "Inspector, in all honesty I cannot sign this because my French is not proficient enough for me to know what I am signing. Do you agree Ellen?" I nodded yes.

Peter continued, "We cannot sign these statements unless they are in English. We have to know if they conform with what we have said to know what we are signing."

The Inspector's expression remained cold and aloof. Without speaking he got up and left the room. Again, we were left alone. Peter stood up and stretched, then he bent down and kissed the top of my head. "Sweetheart, I don't fully understand what this is all about and I'm sorry you are involved."

I stood up and went into his arms. "Peter, dearest, I've been with you ever since Compostela and I know you didn't do anything wrong."

Sighing, Peter said, "Ellen, I'm concerned for Father Sebastian. If he has disappeared as the Inspector has implied, I hope he didn't decide to take his life. This concerns me."

The door opened again, and the Inspector returned with the English translations. I was handed mine and Peter was given his. We both sat down and began reading. Mine was shorter and when I finished, I asked for a pen. The Inspector handed me one and I signed my statement.

Peter reread his several times before asking for a pen. He signed the statement and handed it to the Inspector, who then addressed us.

"You are not to leave France until certain matters have been cleared up. I am sure you have nothing to worry about. Until higher authorities review your statements, I request you not to depart France. I will not secure your passports at this time."

Peter and I agreed and we were told we could go and to collect our backpacks at the desk downstairs. By then it was early afternoon. We were escorted out of the room. A policewoman in a blue uniform took us down the elevator to the area where we were given our backpacks. Leaving the building, we walked out to find another shock.

Somehow while we were being interrogated, the news media had been alerted and had gathered outside. "Mr.

Douglass, Mr. Douglass, how well do you know Father Sebastian?"

Stunned, Peter and I stood there with cameras trained on us. We found ourselves being mobbed, but Peter's height was an advantage. He said "No comment," and holding me close, pushed our way through the throng of news media and across the street to a taxi stand. Peter escorted me inside the first available one, climbed in beside me, and told the driver to go, which he did with a screech of his wheels. I thought for sure the police would chase us as we careened away from the shouting news media. Some might call them the paparazzi but to me they were vultures.

Fortunately the driver spoke passably good English. Peter told him to go to the best hotel in Carcassonne. Within minutes we drove up to the Hotel de La Cité in the old walled city. Peter must have tipped the driver excessively. He was all smiles when he pulled away.

The doorman had already opened the door for us and we walked into an exquisite lobby. Perhaps lobby is not a fitting term. There were beautiful stained glass windows, paneling and stone walls. The décor breathed expensive. Peter led me to the desk where he asked for the most expensive suite in the hotel.

With our backpacks and our hiking clothes, I could see the distain in the clerk's eyes. Peter threw down his credit card saying, "Check it out." The clerk was speechless, and then gaining his composure, he said, "Un moment, monsieur." He disappeared and within minutes returned smiling.

"Monsieur Douglass, we have available a suite. If you would sign here, s'il vous plait." Peter signed, leaving instructions there were to be no calls put through to us nor our suite number given out to anyone.

We weren't even asked for our passports. A member of the concierge took our backpacks and led us to the elevator. Arriving at our floor, he led us to our suite and unlocked the door, going through the motions of making sure everything was in order. Peter gave him a tip and the man left smiling. At last we were alone.

For a moment we just stood there still reeling from the shock, and then we began laughing. Peter picked me up and swung me around and gently laid me on the massive bed.

140

Bending over me he said, "Now is the moment. I want to make love to you and to hell with the rest of the world."

And make love we did. Finally, lying in his arms, I said, "Peter, do you realize this is the first time we have truly been alone?"

Holding me closer, he replied, "Yes and you don't know how I have longed to be like this with you." With that he picked me up and carried me to the massive bathroom, where he began running water in the tub and put in some bubble bath. When he thought the temperature was just right, he picked me up again and stepped into the tub. Slowly he lowered us into the delicious steaming water. With my back to his front, we lay back. I was in bliss.

Turning me over so I was on top of him and astraddle his body, he entered me again. There came that wild, wonderful moment of climax and I fell limp on him. Peter whispered, "Ellen, I have a confession to make. I've never done it this way before."

I began giggling. "Neither have I. Let's shower now."

We stood up and turned the shower on, rinsing off the bubble bath. I wanted my hair washed so Peter did it for me and then I did his. All the feelings of fear and anxiety had faded into one of joy and delight.

After toweling each other off, we fell into bed and into a deep sleep. I don't know how long we slept but when I awoke I was ravenous. I snuggled against Peter and soon he was awake too. Wrapping himself in one of the huge hotel towels, he walked out to the sitting room to look for a menu. Returning, he asked me if there was anything in particular I wanted and I said no.

Peter called room service and ordered two meals and two terrycloth robes for us to be sent up right away. When he hung the phone up, we began to laugh at how the day had turned out. Peter whispered to me that he wanted to check our backpacks to make sure no bugs had been put in them. I looked at him quizzically and he indicated he would explain later.

I watched as he took everything out of each pack and checked every item carefully. This included the tents. He then ran his hands over the entire packs. I was shocked when he found two bugs. There was one in his pack and one in mine.

Each one was at the very bottom of a side pocket and quite small. Carefully he managed to get them out and with a smile, poured a glass of water and dropped the bugs in it.

I was about to say something when there was a discreet knock on the door. Peter looked out through the peephole and saw it was a maid carrying the robes he had ordered. He opened the door, taking them and giving her a tip. Fortunately he had put his jeans on. When she had gone, he put the chain on the door.

Donning our new terry cloth robes, we went out on the balcony. It was magic looking over the gardens and seeing the walled city lit up for her nightly splendor. Peter lit his pipe and puffed on it while we enjoyed the view. I asked him how he had known there were bugs in our packs. He smiled and said, "Pure logic. I should have thought of it as soon as we came into this room. When the paparazzi were there before we were released, I knew that someone from the police had tipped them off. It was too pat. Also, having been a voracious reader of spy thrillers, it all came together."

"I see. You never cease to amaze me and that is what I love about you."

Kissing me, Peter said there was a lot we didn't know about each other, however it would all unfold. I agreed and suggested we turn on the television inside to see if there was any news, and there we were, the camera showing us emerging from the police building.

Then I heard the reporter talking about Peter Douglass, the inventor of a certain type of quanta software chip. I looked at Peter with amazement. "You didn't tell me you were an inventor. Then, you are *the* Peter Douglass of the quanta software fame and you sold Future Quanta? When we were sharing our pasts, you didn't tell me about this!"

"Correct on all accounts except one. I did tell you I had sold my company but I didn't tell you what the company was about. It wasn't important to me and frankly I didn't want to tout my horn about being the founder of that company. I was and am having a new experience. Now let's talk about us."

At that moment there was another knock on the door. It was room service. A waitress and a waiter wheeled in our dinner. We chose to sit out on the balcony and they set up a table complete with a white damask cloth and beautiful china and silver. The wine bucket was iced, and the waiter uncorked the bottle, having Peter sniff the bouquet. Inwardly I smiled at the elegant attention we were receiving. It was a far cry from the meals we had had on the trails and here we were, in an elegant suite, dining in our robes. Finally, Peter dismissed them and we were left to enjoy our meal.

Our conversation was light and gay. Neither of us wanted to dwell on what had transpired that day. Neither did we want to discuss Sebastian or Jill. We came around to talking about Peter's invention and his dedication to his business, while we sat drinking wine and looking at the night sky illuminated by the lights of the walled city.

I told Peter that it was ironic that the two most exciting events of my life were happening at the same time. "Before now, my life was on the dull side and here I am in love with you and involved with the scrolls of Mary Magdalene." Peter agreed he felt the same way. There was an ease between us that I had never experienced previously with a man.

We talked of the Cathars and the loss of their lives. All they wanted to do was worship God in their own way. However, they had become too wealthy from their own endeavors and King Phillip wanted that wealth, while the Church wanted to punish them for being different. Their mode of belief was a threat to the Church because they also were supporters of the Knights Templar. The plan of the Church and the King had been to kill them while confiscating their accumulated fortune.

We fell silent and it was comfortable. Eventually we came out of our reveries and went to bed where we made love.

The following morning I was awakened by a kiss from Peter, and we made love again.

It was long and sweet and I knew I was in a heightened state of bliss because I was experiencing the sexual act as so satisfying. I was being brought to peaks of ecstasy I never knew existed within me and Peter said it was the same for him. At last, we were complete and arose to shower together. I dressed in a flowered full skirt with a white short-sleeved knitted top and put on the sandals I had worn only a few times on my trip.

Peter had unrolled his slacks the night before and he had combined them with a knitted top and sandals too. We stopped and looked at each other and began laughing because we were out of our hiking clothes and moving into an unknown. What a turn our lives were taking!

We went down to the dining room for breakfast and the buffet was exquisite. What else can I say? We ate with gusto and planned our day.

Peter said he was going to ask for a hotel secretary and dictate a statement to the press. "I sure as hell don't want them to follow us around."

I agreed and when we finished eating, we went in search of the concierge. The hotel secretarial services were available at that time and I listened as Peter dictated his statement. It was short and to the point. He briefly gave the account he had given to the police about his becoming acquainted with Father Sebastian the previous year in Paris when they met at the Louvre and struck up a friendship. They had exchanged cards, and while hiking in the Pyrenees this year Peter said he had thought of Father Sebastian. When the occasion arose, he called the number on the card the Father had given him. The housekeeper had told him he could find Father Sebastian in Lourdes and gave him the address. Knowing that the Father had been quite ill, Peter made a decision to go to Lourdes to see him. Father Sebastian had looked quite ill. He felt he had failed to get the miracle cure he desired and was despondent. He indicated he was about to leave and go to the Mediterranean for what Peter assumed would be a retreat. End of statement.

Peter asked that the hotel distribute it to the local papers and fax it to the major French news media. With a sigh of relief, we set out to stroll through the walled city and its narrow streets.

Some of the shops were beginning to open and tourists were already walking about. I asked Peter if we could visit the Basilica and he agreed. As we were about to go in I called his attention to a sign posted outside the entrance. In French and English it stated:

Cult? Peter grinned. "I'm so glad they know the truth."

The Basilica was Romanesque-Gothic architecture and supposedly built on a pagan site. Inside I was drawn to a large statue of Joan of Arc in one corner.

"Peter, isn't it odd that the Inquisition burned her at the stake, and then made her a saint?"

"Yes, and this statue shows her in her battle dress. And I mean dress. It is a beautiful statue showing she was definitely feminine."

We moved on, coming to another interesting statue. This was of a young man with painted dark brown hair. His dark short-sleeved shirt was decorated with white seashells such as those worn by pilgrims on the way to Compostela. His short shirt was over what looked like a green tunic, which came to just above his knees. The right side of the tunic was hidden by another short garment, which left the right leg exposed. Blood was running from a wound just above the kneecap, and he was wearing a white and red toga-type cape draped over the left upper arm and the arm was raised. There was a brown club his fist. The right bare arm was holding the red part of the cloak while his head was bent looking down to the right.

At first we thought it was a most unusual statue for a church. There was a small brown spaniel-type dog on his left, looking up at him with something that looked like a scroll in its mouth. I remarked that the wound above the kneecap reminded me that a wounded thigh had meaning in esoteric mystery schools.

It was Peter who remembered that the statue represented St. Roche, revered as administering to the poor and sick.

While Peter was telling me about St. Roche, a bell rang in my head about the wounded knee. In esoteric terms it meant becoming so spiritual that one had evolved beyond having to have sex, and because of the seashells on the shirt, we agreed that the statue represented St. Roche as a pilgrim on his way to Compostela or returning from there. Compostela was the church dedicated to Jesus' brother James.

Then the thought came. *Was this Jesus' brother – or perhaps the son of Jesus and Mary Magdalene, James the Younger?* I shared this with Peter and he agreed it was possible.

Leaving the Basilica we wandered for a short while before making a decision to rent a car and drive south to Limoux and other villages. I thought, *If anyone wants to follow us, they are welcome to tag long.* Little did I realize until sometime later that I would want to pull the welcome mat back.

After renting the car, we checked out of the hotel but not before retrieving our backpacks and the new robes. The hotel staff had been tipped quite well; therefore we were given the royal treatment when we left. We drove down to the lower town, and found a café with Internet service. Fortunately a computer was available. There was an e-mail from Jill. After we decoded it, the gist of her message was that the translations were progressing very well, however they were very concerned regarding the news of Peter and me being found in Carcassonne. We sent a message back that all was well; we were having a delightful time and had rented a car.

We drove through hilly countryside and past vineyards as we headed south. It was only a short distance to Limoux. Parking in the Place de la République, we found a delightful restaurant for lunch and Peter ordered the Blanquette de Limoux, a delicious sparkling white wine. The monks from the nearby Abbey of St. Hilaire developed sparking wine in the sixteenth century, and some say that was 200 years before champagne.

After lunch we walked to the church Notre Dame de Marceille where we found a Black Madonna statue said to have been discovered in a cow pasture. The Madonna was displayed behind a light blue and gold heavy metal grill. At first glance I thought that at the top of the grill there were Roman numerals within in a circle of gold. Upon closer examination, I realized they were the initials MM, and something within me knew the initials stood for Mary Magdalene and that she was the Black Madonna. I pointed to the initials and we both felt a thrill of excitement run through us.

Also in the church, sitting on a shelf, was a small replica of the statue of Joan of Arc that we had found in la Basilique St. Nazaire at Carcassonne.

As we drove to Alet-les-Bains, we discussed what we had seen so far. It was getting late in the afternoon and we wanted to stop to see what was there. I had consulted my worn guidebook, reading that Alet-les-Bains had flourished during Roman times because of its thermal baths.

The ruins of a reputed Benedictine ancient abbey were there also. Now it was known as the l'Abbaye Notre-Dame d'Alet. I commented to Peter that Notre Dame translated into Our Lady. "I wonder if that refers to Mary Magdalene, or Mother Mary?" mused Peter.

We found the abbey next to a church in the center of the small village. It was near the River Aude, which is nestled amidst crags and hills. The main entrance was locked. Looking around we noticed a small visitor's office. By paying a small fee, we were able to enter the ruins through it.

A few steps inside, I stopped. I had seen a transparent stained-glassed window through one of the portals of the ruin and realized it belonged the church next door. I pointed it out to Peter.

Here in the middle of the region attributed to the Knights Templar mystique was a window with what some would call the Star of David in it. I'd read enough history to recognize it was Solomon's Seal. I gasped with a realization. "Oh, Peter! There is another meaning to this star. I have a friend who is deep into symbolic meanings and she told me it is also called the Initiates Star."

Whoever had commissioned the stained glass star must have been aware of its deep significance. The Abbey itself was first built in the 800's. Later it had been almost destroyed and rebuilt and it had evidences of Gothic architecture.

Having made our tour, we were eager to explore the church next door. To our disappointment, it was closed.

However, walking around the outside we found a second Solomon's Seal stained glass window side by side to the one we had seen through the portal. Both were set in circles of stone. We resolved to return sometime to learn more about those windows. It was becoming late and we wanted to drive to Beziers for the night.

Once we were on the road leaving the small the small village, I consulted my guidebook.

"Peter! There is a statue of a pregnant Virgin Mary in the church at Cucugnan. How strange. It is housed in the Church of St. Julien and St. Basilisse."

Laughing, Peter made a comment regarding a pregnant Virgin Mary. We added this to our list of sights for a return trip one day.

My attention turned to the road, which was narrow and winding. I noticed Peter kept looking in the rear view mirror. Finally he said, "Don't turn around, but I think we are being followed."

"Followed? What makes you think that?"

"When we left Carcassonne, I noticed a car behind us. When we parked in Limoux it went on, or so I thought. Now it is behind us again and it seems to be no hurry to pass. I don't like the feel of this."

Chapter 13

KIDNAPPED

*Adversity has the effect of eliciting talents,
which in prosperous circumstances would have lain dormant.*
- Horace

The late afternoon sun was moving lower in the west as we continued to drive. We came to a small clearing where we could pull off and let the car pass; only it didn't. Peter opened the door to get out but the driver of the other car was faster and Peter looked into the muzzle of a gun.

"Monsieur Douglass, please step out. Also, the lady is to accompany you. If you attempt to do anything I will shoot the lady." Peter got out, putting his hands up as he had been directed to do. "Now, Madame Montgomery you are to get out and come around." I did while shaking with terror.

The driver of the black Mercedes was swarthy and powerfully built. He reminded me of a wrestler. He was dressed in a tan knit shirt and black trousers. His lank black hair appeared to have been oiled. Topping the sneer of his lips was a drooping black mustache and his cold brown eyes looked out from under beetle eyebrows.

Motioning me to come in front of him, he put me between him and Peter. "Monsieur Douglass, if you try anything I will not hesitate to shoot your woman."

The man told me to hold my hands out together, and he pulled out a pair of handcuffs and with quick agility snapped them on me. I was told to get in on the passenger's side of the Mercedes.

In a hoarse voice Peter asked, "What in the hell is the meaning of this? Why do you want my woman?"

The man sneered and replied. "It's not her I want. She is my insurance. You will follow us in your car. My patron wants to see you, and it would be most unfortunate if you do not follow." With his gun pointed at Peter, he stepped back and got into the driver's seat. We took off with Peter following.

I asked questions, however the man gave no answers and I was resigned to silence. I could see that from time to time he looked in his rear view mirror, seeming satisfied Peter was behind us. The drive felt like it was taking forever and I sat in a frozen silence.

The sun was dipping behind the horizon and I sensed we were traveling northeast. Passing through small villages, it became apparent they were not our destination.

It was now dark and it seemed we had been driving for hours when we turned onto a small road. The headlights of the car illuminated the terraced vineyards on both sides. Continuing on for awhile, we came to the top of a rise, and there looming before us was a large chateau sitting behind grilled ironed gates. Stopping, the driver rolled down his window and punched a code of some sorts into a keypad on the gate entry stand. The gates swung open.

The circular driveway rose up to the front portico of the chateau. There were four massive dogs sniffing at the car when we stopped. Peter had driven in behind us. The driver gave a command in French to the dogs and they backed off. He then ordered me out of the car. The dogs stood as if waiting for another command. With his gun pointed at Peter he ordered him out of the car and motioned for us to walk to the front door. He followed behind holding the gun on us.

Peter looked at me with painful eyes. I attempted a small smile but could only blink back tears. A very well groomed man opened the door. He had silver hair cut in what one could call the style of the very wealthy elite of Europe. His skin was tan, which made his ice blue eyes stand out. And they did look like ice because there appeared to be no warmth or life in them. He was about my height, which is five feet seven.

"Bonsoir Monsieur Douglass and Madame Montgomery. It is so good of you to come. I've been waiting for you." Before we could say anything he turned and led us through a double door to the left and into a large study lined with shelves filled with leather-bound books.

His large mahogany desk was positioned so he could look out the double French doors and also at the doors coming from the main hall. There were Moroccan leather chairs and he motioned us to sit down.

"Well done, Bruno. Please keep your pistol on Madame Montgomery while we talk. Now Monsieur Douglass I want to know what was in the scrolls you removed from the newly-found cave."

"And I want to know how you know our names. I didn't remove any scrolls from any cave, and I don't understand what you're talking about," Peter replied in a terse voice.

"Oh, I think you do, Monsieur Douglass."

"Who the hell are you to kidnap me and Mrs. Montgomery? I think we are due an explanation."

"Who I am does not matter. Let us say I am a collector of antiquities. I am also short on patience. When you and Madame Montgomery discovered the scrolls you sought out a Father Sebastian Gontard, a Greek scholar noted for translating ancient Greek."

"You seem to be making more assumptions than the police did."

"Come now Monsieur Douglass, I am more thorough than the police. I have methods at my disposal to ferret out what the police did not. I specifically want to know where Father Sebastian is and where the scrolls are."

"I don't know."

"I think you do, and if you prolong your denial I will have Bruno shoot off one of Madame Montgomery's ears."

I couldn't help but gasp. Peter started to rise and then sat down. I knew this man would give such an order.

Peter looked at me in agony as he replied, "Okay, I can't tell you exactly where he is or where the scrolls are. It's near Toulouse and I can take you to the last place where I knew he was."

"Surely, Monsieur Douglass, you do not take me for a fool. Why cannot you give directions?"

"Being a hiker, I can only give you general directions. However if I take you to him, it will make it faster for all of us. I will do this in exchange for the release of Mrs. Montgomery and her safety."

"Ah, you do think I am a fool. I could very easily have both of her ears shot off. But, non. I will send Bruno with you while Madame remains with me. If I receive any indication Bruno is having difficulty, I will not hesitate to kill her. Do you understand me?"

"All right. I'll do it, since you're holding all the cards." Turning to me, Peter said in a choked-up voice, "Sweetheart, forgive me. Always know I love you and we will be together again. I promise."

With tears flowing down my face I could only nod.

"Very touching. Bruno, handcuff Monsieur Douglass and drive him to where he claims Father Sebastian is. If he tries anything, do not hesitate to kill him."

After snapping handcuffs on Peter, the two departed. "Now, Madame, make yourself comfortable, because we may have a long wait." He went over to a bar, poured himself a drink and took it with him to his desk, where he sat down and began reading through some papers.

I was left alone with my thoughts and my fear. I felt drained and numb. Closing my eyes, I began to look at my life. I began to bless everyone and everything that had been in my life. I forgave those that came to mind and I forgave myself. My prayer became a prayer of thanksgiving, and I blessed this man and I blessed Bruno. As I did, a calm swept through me and I felt a sense of serenity. I thought of Peter and the joy he had brought into my life. I thought of the peace that passeth all understanding and I surrendered totally to the God within me.

Abruptly my awareness came back to the present. Standing in the open French doors was Peter with a gun in his hand. Before the silver-haired man could move, Peter shot his left ear off. With a gasp of pain and shock the man reached up to his ear. The gun had a silencer on it, and there was no sound. Next, Peter shot him in his left hand then his right hand.

"You bastard! What you threatened to do to Ellen, I'm doing to you. Get up and move away from that desk." Trembling and with pain and shock in his eyes, the man did as ordered. Peter then shot him in one knee. "Now, I want to know who the hell you are. And make it quick."

Before he could answer, the man passed out. Peter went over to me and taking a key out of his pocket unlocked the handcuffs. Pulling me to him, he kissed me quickly and said, "We have to get out of here, but first, I want to know who this bastard is."

I noticed Peter had on latex gloves and he began going through the papers on the desk, then the man's pockets. He removed some keys from the man along with a money clip.

There was also a leather case carrying credit cards and I.D. Taking these and some papers, he took my hand and led me outside into the night. There were no dogs.

Bruno's car was there and Peter told me to drive our car and follow him. I didn't have time to ask what had happened. I only knew we were free.

Peter drove a few miles and stopped. Getting out, he walked back to me saying, "Sweetheart, I can't explain now but wait here while I fetch Bruno. Then continue to follow me."

The headlights revealed Bruno lying under a row of grapevines by the side of the road. He was gagged and handcuffed with his arms behind his back and his feet tied together with a piece of rope. Peter roughly put him in the car and drove off. I followed.

When we came to the main road, Peter turned in the opposite direction from where we had first driven in. After a few miles we passed through a small village, which appeared to be asleep. Once past the village he stopped and came back to me. "Wait here and I'll be back shortly. Keep the motor running."

Getting out, I watched as Peter turned Bruno's car around so it was headed back towards the village. Stopping it, he left the engine running and pulled Bruno out of the Mercedes. With a blunt bar, which appeared to be part of a jack, Peter hit him several hard blows until Bruno sagged unconscious. I had to put my hand over my mouth to stifle a sound.

As I watched, Peter removed the gag, handcuffs and rope and opened the trunk, placing them inside. He then pulled out a bottle of whiskey; and after he put the unconscious figure behind the wheel, he poured whiskey down the man's throat until he threw up. Making sure the gun with the silencer had Bruno's fingerprints on it, he positioned it on the seat beside him. Putting the Mercedes in drive, Peter slammed the door shut and the car picked up momentum as it was going downhill. There was a curve just before the bridge over a river.

Quickly we got into our car. Peter, as an old saying goes, put the pedal to the metal. We heard the faint sound of a crash behind us and we knew Bruno would be found. What his fate would be I did not know.

We drove in tense silence until we came to the highway that went towards Narbonne. Peter pulled off the road, turned off the engine and took me in his arms. We both began to cry.

"Oh, Ellen. Ellen. I thought I had lost you," he said when our crying had subsided. I looked up into his beautiful wet eyes and thanked God for this miracle and then we kissed passionately. Drawing back, Peter said, "Perhaps we should be on our way. It won't be Beziers tonight. Tonight it is Narbonne." He started the car up again.

I asked him how he had managed to overpower Bruno so soon after leaving the chateau. Peter began telling me that with him handcuffed, Bruno felt it was safe to have him in the front seat. Peter carefully watched as Bruno punched in the code at the gate as they were leaving the chateau. He waited until they were about midway between the main road and the chateau when he made a sudden lunge at Bruno. This caused the Mercedes to swerve into one of the rows of grapevines. By this time Peter was beating him over the head with his fists and the handcuff chain. When Bruno passed out, Peter managed to find the key to unlock the cuffs.

Getting out of the car and taking the car keys, he unlocked the trunk thinking he would put Bruno in it. There he found a regular burglar's kit, including a box of latex gloves. In the kit he found a tranquilizer gun with darts, plus a box of bullets for the gun with the silencer he had taken from Bruno. Helping himself, Peter took both guns along with the ammunition. Returning to Bruno with the rope he had found, he gagged him and then tied his ankles together. Then he pulled him off the road and left him under the grapevines.

Driving back to the chateau he was praying the code he had seen Bruno use was the one that would get him back in and it did. When he had driven a short distance up the driveway, the dogs came out and that was when he used the tranquilizer gun. He remembered the French doors being open to the summer air and the rest was history.

"Tell me, where did you learn to shoot like that?"

Smiling, he replied, "When I was a small boy my grandfather would take me out to hunt. He trained me very well to use a shotgun and a pistol."

Taking my hand, he asked me what had transpired while he was gone. I told him the man had poured himself a drink before going to his desk to read through some papers. I said I closed my eyes and began blessing everyone, everything and had reached a place of calm when he came in.

We drove a bit in silence, which I broke. "I had never realized how important it is to bless and give thanks for everything in life. I understand now what is meant by 'bless those that persecute you.'"

"Sweetheart, it was your connecting with the Divine that brought us through this." He squeezed my hand, and I brought his up to my lips and kissed it.

"Now I understand what Sebastian meant when he said there are people who would stop at nothing." I shuddered when I thought of what had happened. "We didn't find out who that man is."

Grinning, Peter asked me to take the latex gloves off, which I did one at a time. Then Peter put his hand in his pocket and pulled out several cards and handed them to me. "I took his I.D. case. What names do these give?"

"The driver's license says Gilbert Montand." It wasn't a name familiar to either of us. Peter said he intended to have a full check made into the background of Montand. I asked what he thought Montand would do in retaliation.

"I'm not sure. I think I will hold onto these cards. I also pulled an interesting card from Bruno's money belt. Here, look at this."

Taking the card, I saw it was embossed with an eight-pointed cross set in a circle and there was a phone number written on it. "I wonder what organization this is? From my understanding, the eight-pointed cross is a symbol of the Knights of Malta.

"Peter, let's leave Montand alone. What we know from The Magdalene's scrolls goes along with the old saying, 'what we think, we attract.' Let's not accept any thoughts of retaliation from him into our consciousnesses. I know a miracle happened to us tonight and I accept that."

"And so do I. That old saying has been proven by quantum physics, too. 'Whatever we observe, including our thoughts, we create.' If we observe with fear, then we create or attract fearful experiences into our lives. Most people don't understand that they are the observer. I take responsibility and I admit I had some fear and that is why I wanted to leave Sebastian and Jill."

"I admit I also had fear. Tell me, since you invented the quanta software chip, are you a physicist?"

"Ummm, sort of."

"What do you mean by sort of?"

"Yes, I graduated with a PhD in quantum physics; however I soon learned that when one goes into research, there's a hook to it. To get grants or to work for a company, there is control, meaning it usually has to be done their way. I chose to create on my own and quit the establishment."

"I think I understand and that is why I love your way of thinking. After the episode today, I never intend to fear again."

We were approaching Narbonne from the Perpignon highway. "And my beautiful Ellen, I think I see a sign for a hotel."

Glancing out my window, I saw a sign for the Novotel Narbonne Sud. We took the turn-off and were at the hotel within minutes. There was no problem when Peter asked for the best suite they had.

Once we were settled in, we stood for a minute looking at each other. Then we began laughing. Oh gawd, how we laughed and laughed. In retrospect I can see it was our release mechanism from the horror we had just experienced. I remembered that somewhere I had read, "Laughter is the voice of God."

Taking me in his arms, Peter kissed my ears and every inch of my face. "No man is going to have my beloved's ears shot off."

"Much as I want to make love with you my darling," I said, "a shower is first. I want to wash away the energy of this experience."

"All right, my sweet. I will order dinner. Also we will have our clothes washed and returned by morning. Okay?"

"Sure. And speaking of having things done for us, there is something I've been meaning to discuss with you. I have allowed you to pay for everything so far. Don't you think it's about time I began paying my part? I do have money."

"I will make a bargain with you. When my money runs out, you can pay." With that he grabbed me and began kissing me. "You had better say yes."

156

"Yes," I squeaked and we began laughing again.

Reaching for the phone, Peter asked for someone to come and collect our clothes. Looking at the menu, he asked me to make the selection, which I did, and then he called it into room service.

While he was doing this I walked into the bathroom for a long pee. I never knew I could hold that much for such a long period. *It's amazing, what the body can do under stress*, I thought. The bathroom had a large tub. I began the water running and stripped off my clothes, looking at myself in the full-length mirror. *Not too bad for a 34-year-old woman.*

Peter came in and scooped up my clothes. He had just taken his off when there was a knock at the door. It was someone from the laundry service. I watched as he opened the door only wide enough to hand her the clothes.

"Okay, that's done, now for our bath." Peter stepped in and I sat in front of him laying my head on his chest. He began massaging my neck and shoulders and then my breasts. Nibbling one of my ears, he said "I want you now."

We stood up and got out. And when he had laid a large towel on the floor, we lay down and he entered me. Then with his stiff penis, he massaged my clitoris until I was in a frenzy. When our climax came, I shuddered with ecstasy.

A moment later there was a knock on the door and it was room service. Peter got up. Wrapping a towel around his waist, he answered the door telling the waiter to leave it, as we would serve ourselves.

Returning to the bathroom, he saw I had already let out the water and had the shower going. It was such a pleasure soaping each other down, touching the body all over. "Careful," he said. "We might not eat for quite awhile."

He was right.

Chapter 14

JILL'S NARRATION

When patterns are broken, new worlds can emerge.
- Tuli Kupferbery

The morning news gave a report that Peter Douglass had been taken in for questioning by the police in Carcassonne. Sebastian and I were just finishing our breakfast and he translated the gist of it for me.

Peter and a woman named Ellen Montgomery had been questioned and released by the Carcassonne police who were satisfied Peter had nothing to do with the disappearance of Father Sebastian Gontard. The television commentary showed a segment of Peter and Ellen walking out of the police station into a barrage of cameras and reporters. Peter was the Peter Douglass who had founded the software chip company Future Quanta. The story went on to say that Peter, despondent over the death of his wife, had sold his company several years before.

"Oh my gawd!" I gasped. "Somehow I never made the connection he was *that* Peter Douglass. He must have thought me a ninny for spouting off about quantum physics."

"Pardon? What is a ninny?"

"It's a slang expression for fool."

"Ah, Jill, you are not a ninny. In fact I am constantly amazed regarding your knowledge. Do not put yourself, as you would say, down."

I laughed. "Thank you. At least we know they are safe. Maybe the danger is over."

"Oui. It is now my responsibility to complete the translations."

"I'll clean up the breakfast dishes and perhaps take a walk. When you have enough translated from Greek to French, then I will continue. Okay?"

"Très bien."

After my walk in the woods, I returned to the computer and together we continued our work. Knowing Peter and Ellen had been released had given us more zeal.

One evening after dinner I went out into the garden to sit and enjoy the warm summer evening. Soon Sebastian came and joined me. Our talk was mostly about the translations. There came a point where I asked him why he had chosen to enter the priesthood.

There was a long pause and finally Sebastian said, "I may as well confess to you since I have already confessed to Peter." He then proceeded to tell me the same story of a burning desire to get an education however his family was too poor. Sebastian said he had been encouraged to enter the seminary and he had progressed very well. He was posted to the Vatican to become an apprentice in the archives where he stayed for nearly 35 years. While there he translated many old Greek documents and became very learned in ancient history. When the age of the computer arrived at the Vatican he was sent for training and fell in love with the computer.

"Do you regret coming to the Université and meeting Paul?" asked Jill.

"Ah, non. As I have already told you and the others, I had become very disillusioned with the priesthood when I learned of the intrigues and suppression of information done in the name of the Church."

"Sebastian, what exactly was it that you learned?"

"Ah, Jill, one day I came across a statement made by Pope Leo X. It was devastating to me," Sebastian said choking up and stopping.

I prompted him, "Go on. Take all the time you need."

"The statement was 'How well we know what a profitable superstition this fable of Christ has been for us.' Here was a Pope who lived in the 1500's! At a time of the Inquisition! And he had said Christ was a fable! I was stunned. I pondered this for a long time. Eventually I got over the shock and began investigating the so-called learned churchmen we held in such reverence."

By now, Sebastian was letting his pent up anger roll off his tongue.

"I researched back to the very beginning of when the Church began. Non, it did not really start until Constantine convened the Council of Nicea in 325 A.D. Constantine relied upon one of the presbyters who is on record as saying, 'It is an act of virtue to deceive and lie, when by such means the interests of the church might be promoted.' This presbyter is one who has been revered. His name was Eusebius. Mon dieu! I had learned men of ill repute had founded the Church. Men who were charlatans, liars and even thieves! I could not tell my confessor. I knew if I did, I would be labeled a heretic."

We sat in silence until Sebastian felt compelled to continue. "I began to take notice of the ones in power in the Vatican and I observed the intrigues and games they played for power. My eyes and my ears were opened and I felt sick in my heart. I am so ashamed! I am so full of guilt! Oh, there is so much more that I could tell."

The more Sebastian talked, the stronger his voice became. "I met Paul one day at a computer show in Rome. We became fast friends and he suggested perhaps I could be posted to Toulouse. Soon after our meeting, I became ill and was diagnosed with a heart disease. I was given medical retirement. Of course I contacted Paul and he arranged for me to come to Toulouse. When I came here Paul arranged for me to teach part-time at the Université."

"Sebastian, did you hear what you just said?"

"Pardon, what say I?"

"I just heard you say you became sick in your heart over all the things you had learned, and then you said you developed a disease of the heart."

In a surprised voice, he said, "Ah, oui. It would seem there would be a connection. Thank you for pointing this out."

"And why do you feel ashamed and filled with guilt?"

"Ah, ashamed for my Church and the lies it has perpetuated. Guilt? I feel guilt because I did not have the courage to unmask them."

"My dear Sebastian, one should never feel shame or guilt over what others do or did. From my knowledge, guilt is a poison that one hides from others and that creates sickness and death."

"Perhaps it is as you say. It is a relief you have allowed me to unburden my hidden guilt and shame. Yes, how can I judge them when I went into the priesthood with false motives? Ah, I have been such a . . . a . . . as you would say, hypocrite!"

Sebastian put his head in his hands and I could see him shake with sobs. "You have confessed; and if you accept that you are forgiven, you will be free of the past. What is your intention now?"

"Pardon? I do not quite understand your question."

"When the translations are completed, what are your plans?"

"Ah, I have none. When Peter came to visit me in Lourdes, I was ready to leave and go off to die. Now I do not know."

"Do you want to die?"

"Non, not now. Being with you and Peter and Ellen has made such a big difference in my life. And I will confess, especially you."

"Me? How?"

"Never have I been around women in my adult life. I cloistered myself. Non, I did not turn to homosexuality. I became over involved in my work and now, when I am with you I feel a stirring within me that is new and at times it frightens me."

"Sebastian, I have also felt an interest in you. Have you ever known intimacy with a woman?"

"Non. That is why I am frightened. There is a yearning in me that wants to have an intimate relationship with you, but I am embarrassed to talk about it. Please forgive me."

"I am honored you feel that way."

"Are you? I was fearful you would laugh at me."

"Laugh at you! Never. In fact, I would like to have an intimate relationship with you."

"Mon dieu! I never dreamed you would want to be intimate with me. I am wordless. I do not know the first way to approach such a relationship."

"I never married. However I have had sexual affairs with a few men I thought I loved, but I found out I didn't love them enough to marry. Does that make a difference?"

"Non. Non. I am embarrassed that I do not know how to begin."

"Then let me show you. Will you give me this gift?"

"You consider this a gift? My desire?"

"Yes. I will go in and shower, and when I am finished, you shower and come to my room."

I stood up, and so did Sebastian. Shaking, he gave me a brief embrace. I showered and went into my bedroom where I turned back the covers. I was naked. Placing a bottle of oil on the nightstand, I lay down and soon I heard his knock. "Come in."

He entered wearing a bathrobe and gasped when he saw me. At first I thought he might turn and leave. So I got up and went to him, undid his robe and let it fall to the floor. He stood there, his emaciated body trembling. His clothes had hidden how thin he was. Then it was as though another energy came over me. I had no plans as to what I would do. I just did it.

First I removed his glasses, and then I brought his face down to mine. I kissed him full on the mouth. At first he was stiff, then I felt his arousal and I knew his passion was rising.

I led him to the bed and we lay down. I poured some of the oil into my hands and gently began anointing his genitals. I moved my hands over his torso as he quivered and moaned. I told him "Don't talk, but make any noise you desire." I began stroking his penis and I could feel it becoming erect. "Do not ejaculate until I tell you," I whispered.

I kissed him again and he responded with great passion. Then I placed his hand on my breasts and moved his hand to indicate that he was to touch my nipples and I could feel his body quivering under my hands. I was beginning to get aroused. I whispered for him to get on top of me. He complied, shaking all the while.

I told him to think only of the hieros gamos in the scrolls, because he had been anointed, that we were doing our own hieros gamos and it was a new season. I placed his penis into my vagina telling him to go with his feelings. Moaning, he moved back and forth only once before he ejaculated.

Falling on me, he sobbed. "Forgive me Jill. I am a failure."

I cradled him in my arms. "No Sebastian. You are not a failure. This was your first attempt. We will do it again. And now sleep my dearest."

Like a baby he fell asleep in my arms. I contemplated the wonder of it all, and I realized that this time I did not have to please a man or to fake an orgasm. With Sebastian I could show him what I wanted and teach him at the same time. Soon I was asleep also. Some hours later I awakened and got up to go to the bathroom. When I came back, he was awake. "Thank you, dear lady. I must not disturb you any more."

Determination came over me. "Sebastian, lay back down. We have only begun. Now kiss me." He did and with each kiss I could feel him relax and his passion grow. I showed him how to fondle my breasts and kiss my nipples. I guided his hand to my clitoris, and gently he brought me to a climax and because his penis was erect, he entered me again. We continued throughout the night to explore our intimacy. It was before dawn when we fell asleep in each other's arms.

Awakening some hours later, I pondered what had transpired. I knew I loved Sebastian and made a decision to allow this relationship to unfold. I did not want to overwhelm him. I had to allow him to make the next move.

Unable to sleep more, I arose and took another shower. Wearing only my nightshirt, I went into the kitchen to brew coffee. I heard him come in and turned. I noted there was a radiance about him that had certainly not been there before. He smiled a bit awkwardly.

"I . . . I do not know what to say. I am so appreciative of the experience. I never dreamed it could be so marvelous."

I held out my hand and he came to me and without my asking, he kissed me gently and then with passion. I had unleashed a sleeping giant. "The bedroom," he whispered.

We had intercourse over and over throughout the day and by the time late afternoon came, Sebastian was an experienced lover. I was a satisfied woman as well as a bit sore, but it was worth it. Like two kids, we got up after sleeping and showered together. By this time we were both ravenous.

I brewed fresh coffee and made an omelet while Sebastian poured the wine. We ate with great appetites.

"Jill, I am in confusion. One part of me says I love you and another part tells me it would not be fair to you. I am a dying man. I am most grateful you gave me of yourself so I could experience the sexual act and especially in such a loving way."

To myself I said, *Yes, I know I love you also, Sebastian.* "Do you want to die?"

"Non, truthfully not, not now that I have experienced you. I have not told anyone that I also have an inoperable tumor in my head as well as the heart condition." He put his head in both hands and began to cry.

I allowed him his tears. "Sebastian, you went to Lourdes looking for a miracle. It happened, but not in the way you hoped. The miracle was seeing Peter and becoming involved with the scrolls. I think The Magdalene has plans for all of us including you. However, you must make the decision to live."

He looked up at me in amazement. "Oui. It was a miracle. And oui, I do want to live. I must live. But how do I do it? The doctors have given me only six months or less to live."

I reached out for his hand and said, "Why not pray to The Magdalene and ask for her help in healing you. Go and be alone. Pour your heart into her. Somehow I know she will hear you."

"You are correct Jill. I will go now and be alone in nature."

Getting up, he bent over, kissed my hand and went out.

I thought, *It's time for me to be alone too.* I went into the bedroom, changed into my shorts and a knit top and went outside to sit in the glider.

The evening shadows were upon me and I listened to the frogs and the crickets. The sounds were like a song of praise. Closing my eyes, I went within and allowed my mind to be still. A picture of a butterfly entered my mind. To me the butterfly represents freedom and change. In my mind I saw the butterfly become a brilliant electric blue and then it began to fly. It flew to Sebastian and lit on his head and stayed there with its wings gently moving to and fro.

I had never had this sort of visual in my moments of contemplation. Then the butterfly began to spiral upward and out of sight. I remained still, and when I became aware, I saw Sebastian returning from behind the barn.

Smiling, he came and sat in the chair across from me. "Jill, I went to the old Celtic sacred well and sat there. I did as you told me to do. I began praying to The Magdalene. I confessed all and I asked her assistance in my healing. When I completed my prayer, I opened my eyes and there was this very beautiful blue butterfly. It came and sat on my head. I think it must have been a sign from her."

Smiling, I reached out and touched his hands. "Sebastian, it was from her." Then I told him about the butterfly in my contemplation.

"Mon dieu! Mon dieu! I . . . I am overcome. Tell me, is this what 'being born again' is about?"

"I think so. Can you accept reincarnation?"

"I never thought about it. I do know in ancient manuscripts the truth of reincarnation was accepted. Oui. I can accept it. Ah, I am getting a glimmer of understanding."

Speaking excitedly, he continued, "Eh, what I am experiencing is what Jesus taught, 'unless a man be born again.' Oh merci, merci! One must change his mind."

"Oh Sebastian! You have been born again. You have broken down barriers in your mind of shame, guilt, anger and resentment."

"Oui, oui. I have indeed. Therefore I can no longer be the same person I was. Oui, I know I am healed."

Tears were flowing down my face and his. He came over and sat beside me in the swing and drew me to him. Very gently he kissed me. "I have you to thank for this miracle. I love you, mon amour." With my head resting on his shoulder we gently rocked the glider back and forth savoring this wonderful breakthrough.

"Sebastian, I love you, too." Taking me in his arms he kissed me passionately. I had not thought I could be aroused again after our day of lovemaking, however the passion rushed through my loins. There on the glider he and I, after discarding our clothes, copulated again. We were spent and lay there in each other's arms not speaking.

Breaking the silence, he said, "Jill, I must complete these translations. These must be given to the world. This is my gift to her. You will not think ill of me if I leave you now to work on them?"

"Not at all, I understand. Please, go with my joy and my blessings. I will join you shortly."

Getting up, he bent down again and kissed me. "You are my love."

Sitting there, I was in a heightened state of elation. I pondered the turn of events and gave thanks for my life and the part I was playing in getting these scrolls translated. After

165

awhile I dressed and went to the computer to begin the latest translation from the French to English.

Sebastian had a glow about him and he was humming as he worked. *How wonderful*, I thought, *that he could use his talents for this. But of course*, I mused, *we should all use our talents.*

It grew late and I decided to go to bed and sleep. Sebastian glanced up and I reached down, kissing the top of his head. "I'm going to bed. Work as late as you want." Smiling, he returned to his computer.

I slept in a dreamless state and awoke in the morning to the sun streaming in through the window. Stretching, I lay there contemplating the events of yesterday. For the first time in years, I felt truly happy.

Putting on my shorts and top, I padded out to the kitchen. All was silent. *Sebastian must still be asleep.* I set the coffee on to brew and walked out into the garden. I felt like dancing and I did. When I stopped, Sebastian was standing at the kitchen door and he clapped. "Beautiful! Beautiful!"

Walking over to him, I gave him a hug and we kissed. It all seemed so natural. "Let's have coffee," I said. We walked arm in arm into the kitchen. As we sat at the table, I asked him what he thought The Magdalene's primary message was.

"Hmmm. What I can surmise from what has been translated so far, I would say her message is to be careful of what we think because our thoughts could manifest as illnesses and a life full of problems. And you?"

"Could it be our emotions send messages to our bodies, and emotions are triggered by what we think? According to what I understand, our cells can be broken down into the atomic structure and to the very tiny which is quantum physics. If our thoughts work on frequencies, then our thoughts can keep the body healthy; or, if we harbor unloving thoughts towards ourselves and others, the cells break down into illnesses."

"Ah, oui! That makes good logic to me. The frequencies of guilt, shame, fear, anger and resentment are an unloving form. N'est-ce pas?"

"That is correct, from my understanding. Now, I am not a professional physicist, however what I am beginning to think

166

from her story The Magdalene fully understood the quantum field."

"This means Jesus also understood it. It all begins to pull together, so you Americans would say."

Laughing, I agreed. "I am remembering the one segment where she healed the young boy's broken arm. She *saw* the arm whole while the others only saw it as broken. Meaning, it is what we choose to hold in our mind. She was the observer, therefore what she saw effected the arm."

"Ah oui. The boy was in such pain that he would trust her. It was his faith in her that helped to heal his arm."

"Well put. There is a biblical verse, 'It is done unto you as you believe.'"

"Oui. Oui. Oh, Jill, I am so filled with excitement. I am what you would say, turned on to life."

We both began laughing. "You are indeed turned on, Sebastian"

"Jill, I am still in such awe of what I experienced yesterday. I realize I must discipline myself if I am to translate these scrolls."

I reached over and touched his hand. "You don't have to say anything more. When the moment is right, we will both know and we will have our intimacy perhaps on a grander scale. I must discipline myself, too. Please, all I ask is that we each be very open and honest in telling the other what we want."

Placing his other hand over mine, he said, "I agree, with all my passion and all my heart. Voilà, now I will go before I lose my resolve." Picking up my hand, he kissed it and left.

For the next several days we both worked on the translations. There was no more lovemaking. We shared a comfortable relationship. An e-mail came from Ellen and Peter that there had been some stormy weather, however all had cleared up. They asked what were we doing and I replied our vacation plans were in their final stages.

One night after dinner, I asked Sebastian if he had ever danced. He said no and that he would stumble all over me. I took his hand and led him into the living room. "Sebastian, since you have been born again, it's time you learned how to dance."

I found some music CDs of Paul's and put one in the player.

"Sebastian, close your eyes and feel the rhythm. Once you get the feel, begin to move. Move any way you want. There is no judgment. There is no criticism. The primary idea is to feel the rhythm."

He was so trusting and entered into this part of our relationship with zeal. It wasn't too long before he was twirling and dancing around the room. I joined him and we came together and then parted. We bumped hips and we parted. When the piece was over, we fell into each other's arms and laughed.

It wasn't too bad for a start.

"May I be invited to your bedroom now?" he whispered.

"Of course."

We went to my room and I asked him to undress me. I then undressed him and removed his glasses. Gently he pulled me down on the bed where we began a loving and gentle dance of sexual intimacy. He had learned very well and made sure I reached my orgasm. When we were complete, we fell asleep in each other's arms.

After this night there were no more separate bedrooms. We kept to our resolve to translate and we did our work during the day.

In the evenings after dinner we danced. I taught him the foxtrot, waltz and even the tango. I had always loved ballroom dancing. We danced separately and together, and he was such a willing participant. Some nights we made love and other nights we went to sleep in each other's arms.

I felt he was the love I had always searched for.

Chapter 15

A TWIST IN EVENTS

*Many are those who trade in tricks and simulated miracles,
duping the foolish multitude; and if nobody unmasked
their subterfuges, they would impose them on everyone.*
- Leonardo da Vinci

Waking up with a start, I lay still. My heart was pounding and I realized I was in the paralysis of fear. Then the memory of the dream came back. As I lay there, scenes began to play through my mind of men bursting into the house and holding me hostage while they began beating Sebastian. It was horrible. I heard myself gasping for breath. Placing one arm over my eyes, I reached my other hand out to touch Sebastian. He wasn't there.

Lurching out of bed in a panic, I hoarsely called out to him. Sebastian was getting up from his chair at the computer when I staggered into the living room. Falling into his arms, I began crying, "Oh Sebastian! Sebastian! It was dreadful!"

"Ma chère, what has happened? Come, come, and tell me." He sank back to the chair holding me in his lap. Stroking my hair, he held me until my sobs abated. "Now ma chère, tell me what has upset you so?"

Slowly and haltingly I told him about my dream. "Only, I don't think it was just a dream."

"You do not think it was a night you call mare?"

This brought a giggle from me. I sat up. "No darling. But it is possible that this was a lucid dream of the future. A warning perhaps."

I finished telling him of my dream while he listened without interrupting. He then said, "I also have had a feeling of foreboding the past several days." Sighing Sebastian asked, "But what are we to do?"

"Do you think Paul has been contacted?"

"C'est possible. But of course, he knows nothing."

169

"True," I answered. "However, there could be people who leaked information to the news media and whoever 'they' might be, they could come here to investigate."

"C'est possible. Perhaps it is the moment to give up our haven. But where do we go?"

"Didn't you and Peter work out a code or a plan for us in case we were discovered?"

"Mais, oui. We are to send an e-mail to rendezvous with Lisa. Meaning we will meet in Paris at the Mona Lisa in the Louvre."

"Perhaps we should be packing now," I said. "I will send them an e-mail and say that we can be in Paris in three days if that is possible."

"Oui, it can be done. I regret we have not done all the translations, however a fool I do not think I want to be."

"If you remove the programs from the computers, I will begin packing our clothes and cleaning up the house. Sebastian, how do we get to Paris? I don't think driving your car or Paul's is wise."

"Ma chère, you are correct regarding Paul's car. Perhaps we can drive mine to the airport. There is a car park at the terminal. I will pay for a month in advance."

"That sounds good. And why don't I rent a car in my name for our trip to Paris?"

"Good. Good. I like the way you think."

Taking my face in his hands, he kissed me long and lingering. "Ma chère, I cannot entertain any thought of something happening to you. You are my life now."

"I also feel the same way my darling." It would have been so easy to have an interlude of sex, however I felt within me our first priority was to preserve the scrolls and the translations.

Regretfully we pulled apart. I went into the kitchen to make coffee and to assess our larder for breakfast and lunch. I stood at the kitchen door looking out at the garden and the surrounding trees and felt a wrenching in me to be leaving the serenity of the place.

Turning away from the doorway, I poured our coffee and carried it in to where Sebastian was busy at the computer doing what was necessary to remove his translation program from Paul's computer. He still had to remove all the data relating to the scrolls from both the computers, as well as make a copy of Paul's French to English program to take with us. As I set the cups on the desk, he reached for my hand, kissing it. I bent down and kissed the top of his head.

The morning passed quickly once I prepared breakfast. After we had eaten I cleaned the kitchen thoroughly. Methodically I went through the house retrieving what was ours. Since we didn't have many belongings, the packing was easy. I stripped the bed and washed the sheets. Thank god Paul had a washer and dryer!

Sitting outside while having a light lunch, Sebastian and I discussed our next course of action. His car was packed and ready to go. A message had been sent to Ellen and Peter and the scrolls were packed in my large hiker's backpack, which I would either wear or carry with me at all times.

The plan was for Sebastian to drop me off at a car rental place before proceeding to the airport parking area. I would pick him up just outside the baggage claims entrance and then we would be on our way. We knew there was a chance of being discovered however our trip seemed the most viable thing to do.

As I was making a mental inventory of the things to take with us, I thought of the trash. I asked Sebastian to put it in the car while I did the final house inspection. I was finishing and about to go into the kitchen and out the door when I heard a car drive up and park in front of the house. I froze, feeling paralyzed.

Then I heard the door pull jangle. I took a deep breath, looked through the peephole and saw a large man standing there. I did not see anyone else. I called out, "Who's there?" He replied in French, which I found hard to interpret. With my heart pounding, I answered that I didn't understand French very well.

Suddenly I heard a loud thud followed by a groan and something hit against the door. Shaking, I opened the door. Sebastian had come from behind the house with a shovel and hit the man hard on the head, knocking him out.

"Merde! Merde!" Sebastian began talking excitedly in French. He looked at me, switching to English. "Have I killed him?" Making the sign of the cross he began praying.

Bending down, I could tell the man was breathing shallowly. *My god!* I thought, *what if this is a policeman!* I grabbed Sebastian's arm telling him the man was breathing. Sebastian calmed down a bit although he was shaking like a leaf. I told him to look for the man's identification.

"Is he from the police?" I asked.

"Non. He has a driver's license along with the national identity card. It does not give the nature of his business. The name given is Raoul Fournier. Ma chère, in my suitcase is a revolver. I think we have use for it if he awakens."

Before Sebastian could move I ran around to the back going to the barn where the car was parked. Quickly I found the revolver and a box of ammunition. I ran back to front of the house and gave them to Sebastian. He was still shaking as he began loading the gun. While he was doing that, my mind was racing. I knew we couldn't leave the man there. We also couldn't allow him to become conscious while we were there.

I ran back to the barn again to look for rope to tie up the man and an idea came to look in the kit where Sebastian kept his medicine. *Ah, yes! His sleeping powders.* In retrospect I can see I was almost on an automatic pilot. Earlier I had put a partial bottle of wine in the garage thinking I would dispose of it later. I picked it up and grabbed a piece of rope that was there.

Running back to where Sebastian was, I saw the man was still out and Sebastian was standing over him. He had his legs spread apart and was holding the revolver with both hands pointed down at the man. He was still shaking like a leaf.

Getting on my knees I pulled the man's arms behind him and began tying his wrists together. Next I pulled what remained of the rope down, wrapping it around his ankles while Sebastian stood and watched.

Taking the scarf from around my neck, I blindfolded the man because I didn't want him to see us if he woke up. Then I remembered the sleeping powders and rushed inside to the bathroom for a paper cup. When I got back I could hear him beginning to moan so I quickly poured three packets of the sleeping potion into the cup and mixed it with wine.

All the while Sebastian continued holding the gun on the man. Except for his shaking, he never moved. I lifted the man's head up telling him he had had an accident and he must

172

drink the liquid. He was so befuddled he managed to drink it and within seconds he was fast asleep.

When I told Sebastian to put the gun away, he seemed to come alive.

"Mon dieu! Mon dieu!" he exclaimed over and over.

I next told him to bring the car around and while he was doing that, I searched the man more thoroughly than Sebastian had. I found a money belt and in it a card with an odd symbol imprinted on it and a phone number. I purloined the card, leaving the belt on him. He also had a small gun with a silencer. I chose not to take it. Next I looked in his vehicle, finding nothing of interest. I was careful not to leave any fingerprints. When I cleaned the house I had remembered to wipe where our fingerprints would have been.

Sebastian had just driven up when I noticed the shovel. Picking it up, I stuck it in the soil of a flowerbed as if it had been forgotten. As an afterthought, using a tissue, I scooped up some dirt and rubbed it where Sebastian had handled it. There was something nagging in the back of my mind and as I was about to get in the car, it came to me.

"Sebastian, if we set the burglar alarm, how long will it take the police to get here?"

"Perhaps fifteen or twenty minutes, but how will it help when the burglar is already present and trussed like a goose?"

"My darling, we can leave him right here. We will take off the rope and the blindfold."

"Voilà! C'est bien!" With an alacrity he didn't have previously, Sebastian set to work untying the man and managed to move him into the doorway.

The engine of the car was running. Sebastian quickly triggered the alarm and got in the car on the driver's side. I asked him if he felt like driving and he nodded yes. So I got in on the passenger side and we drove off.

Neither of us said anything for a long time.

"Mon dieu! What a woman you are! I lost my head but you kept yours. Mon dieu! What must you think of me now?"

I reached over to touch his leg, "My darling, none of us knows how we will handle a situation until we are thrust into it. Don't be hard on yourself. Remember, you have in many respects led a sheltered life."

He reached down and squeezed by hand. "Ma chère, I am humbled to be in your presence. You have taught me so much. From this moment on I will attempt to be more present. I ask your forgiveness."

"There's no need to ask for my forgiveness. I am in no position to judge you. You are my precious darling and I love you."

"Ma chère, you are generous. I accept your love."

We drove to the airport without incident and Sebastian dropped me off in front of a car rental agency. He drove on to the parking garage while I rented a small Renault and put it on my credit card.

I drove to the baggage pick up and didn't see Sebastian. My heart gave a lurch, so I drove off. I made a circle around the parking area and when I returned, he was waiting for me with our things. Stowing my backpack and his luggage in the trunk, he got into the car and started laughing. I looked at him questioningly.

"Ma chère, I never thought I would laugh again. When I opened the trunk and saw our trash that we had forgotten to dispose of, it just struck me as funny."

For some reason I also thought it was funny. Laughing I asked him what he had done with it. "I put it in the trash bins in the car park garage." I felt like a tightly coiled spring had been released by our laughter.

Directing me to the route going towards Limoges, Sebastian asked if anyone was following us. I looked in the rear view and side view mirrors while making sure I stayed within the speed limit. I didn't see any particular vehicle that would arouse my suspicion.

"Where did you learn to be such a warrior woman?"

Warrior woman? I thought for a moment. "Perhaps it is ingrained in me, however I do have two older brothers, and growing up, I had to defend myself in numerous battles. Or, perhaps I have read too many spy thrillers. I really don't know."

"Did you learn to tie a rope from your brothers?"

"Yes, come to think of it. They were in the Boy Scouts and I watched them practice tying knots. Sometimes I practiced with them; but never did I think I would have a use for that knowledge!

174

"Tell me Sebastian, why do you have a revolver? Do priests or former priests make it a practice to carry one?"

"Non. I purchased the revolver before going to Lourdes. If I did not receive a cure there, my intent was to kill myself."

"Thank you my darling for telling me. Now we know there is no need for that thinking."

"Oui. You have given me a reason for living."

❧❧ ❧❧ ❧❧

It was getting late in the afternoon. We had agreed to share the driving. I don't remember where we stopped for dinner. We both felt drained of energy. I do remember our dinner was pleasant and hearty. We agreed we were feeling energized and Sebastian offered to drive.

It was late evening when we reached Limoges. We were most fortunate to find lodging since it was in the middle of the tourist season.

Grateful we had a place to lay our weary bodies for the night, we carried his luggage and my pack to our room.

A shower was our first order of business and then bed.

Sebastian continued to carry remorse over his behavior with the intruder. I told him I did not think less of him and that only he could forgive himself.

"Darling, please don't let this come between us. I think we each experienced aspects of ourselves we didn't know we had." With that I began shaking. It was a delayed reaction and I began to cry.

It was Sebastian who now began being the one in charge. Cradling me in his arms, he began kissing me. "Ma chère, ma chère, love of my life. We have so much to discover of each other," and he began kissing away my tears.

"My darling, I've always been a strong woman. Perhaps that is why I never married."

"Oui." Our kissing evolved into passionate lovemaking. Then we fell into a deep sleep, happy and complete. When morning came, I lay in bed contemplating our relationship and concluded it was something like a dance. When the need arose,

I could be strong and lead. I knew there would come moments when we would change roles and I could allow him to lead.

Arising, we again showered, dressed and stowed our belongings in the car. I eyed the people we saw but didn't feel like anyone was following us. We breakfasted at the hotel and while waiting for our order to come, Sebastian related that near Amboise, which was close to where we were, was a home of Leonardo da Vinci. The home is now a small museum that has demonstrations of his work and his inventions.

"Really? I had forgotten he lived in France."

"Mais oui. I believe he died here."

"I remember reading about a woman who worked at Bell Labs in the States. She did a computer-digitized analysis of da Vinci's features and those of the painting *Mona Lisa*. She digitized both his self-portrait and the painting. When she merged both digitized pictures together, they matched. This is a strong indication da Vinci was a woman."[1]

"Non! C'est impossible!"

"Why is it impossible? If a woman is a genius and she knows she would not be allowed to express that during the period in which she lived, then it seems reasonable to me that she would masquerade as a man so she could pursue her work. Besides, haven't you ever wondered why the Mona Lisa is smiling?"

"This I must contemplate. It is an interesting concept. I do know there have been a number of women who disguised themselves as men. But da Vinci? Da Vinci had a beard. I will contemplate."

"Well, back in the States I have a married friend a few years older than me, and she has to shave twice a day. She wears heavy makeup to cover her beard. It may be unusual, but it does happen."

Sebastian chuckled. "Perhaps it is a homosexual marriage."

"I doubt that. They are both devout Catholics."

---

[1] Lillian Schwartz, a consultant for AT&T's Bell Laboratories. Working independently, Dr. Digby Quested of the London Maudsley Hospital arrived at the same conclusion.

Our breakfast had arrived, so we turned our attention to our food.

Sebastian offered to drive the first leg of our trip. And we spoke of wanting to know how the man we left at Paul's had fared.

On any other trip I would have suggested stopping to explore the sights along the way and especially the da Vinci museum, but that was not the trip.

Perhaps it's good I didn't spot any suspicious people. Little did I know what would occur in Paris.

Chapter 16

RECOVERY

Every exit is an entry somewhere.
- Todd Stoppard

Peter and I woke up in Narbonne the morning after our escape from Gilbert Montand and his henchman. I realized I was having a reaction to the stress we had been under, and I ached all over. I told Peter how I felt and he said he also was feeling lousy. He ordered coffee with croissants and bottles of Vichy water from room service. The one thing we didn't want was to become dehydrated from the stress. We slept off and on all day. In the evening we felt better although we were both lethargic.

I looked at the room service menu and ordered soup, bread, cheese and wine; neither of us wanted anything heavy. Peter turned on the television news and there was a report that Gilbert Montand had been attacked and robbed at his chateau. He had been transported by helicopter to a hospital in Paris and his condition was serious. "Due to the way Montand was shot," the reporter said, "it could have been a vendetta."

The culprit, one Bruno Alvarez, had been apprehended. He had crashed his vehicle into a bridge near Montand's chateau and was hospitalized in serious condition. He was under police custody. Montand's money clip and identification papers were inside Alvarez's car. He would likely be charged with robbery and attempted murder.

Both of us sighed. "Oh Peter." I began to cry. Peter held me. When I stopped, I told him we had to talk about our thoughts and feelings of what had transpired.

"You're right. I guess I'm shocked at what I did. I didn't realize I had it within me. It was a side of myself I never knew I had, and I have never considered myself a violent man. I don't regret what I did. All I knew was I had to get you before any harm could come to you. No. I have no regrets and under

178

the same circumstances, I would do it again. Does that shock you?"

"No, my dear one. I don't condemn what you did and I'm grateful to be alive and safe with you. But, I never want to go through anything like that again! Never. And, my love, I trust you with my life. I trust you for the decisions you make."

"Thank you. There has to be complete honesty and trust between us. I like that I can share my feelings and my thoughts with you. I like that I can cry with you. And I love that I can make love with you."

There was no desire for lovemaking that night. We both knew it was okay, and after dinner, we went back to bed where I fell asleep in his arms. Just before dozing off, I silently told myself I only wanted sweet dreams that night. No nightmares.

I woke up first and Peter still had me in his arms. I reflected on how my life had changed. Something within me said that life would always be an adventure with him. My body urges became a priority so I slipped out of his arms and made my way to the bathroom. When I climbed back into bed, he stretched and then grabbed me. Our lovemaking was so tender and sweet.

While showering together, we talked of our plans. Peter said he did not want to stay in Narbonne, so I suggested we drive south to Perpignon and he agreed.

After breakfast we checked out of the hotel and headed out. Perpignon was not too far from the Spanish border; however we had given our word we would stay in France.

In Perpignon we located an Internet café and there was an e-mail from Jill. In it she indicated they were progressing and that it would be probably several weeks before they were finished.

Realizing we were very close to Collioure, a small village on the Mediterranean, we decided to go there and spend the night. We easily found a hotel, the Casa Pairal. Once we were registered, we set out on foot to explore the village.

That day there was the weekly market in the square, and we leisurely wandered through the various stalls and tables as we worked our way toward the sea.

The beach was most unusual. It was littered with stones with gold flecks in them. Peter and I picked up a few to examine closer. Then I spied stones of pale blue, sand and orange, which to me were the colors of the Mediterranean. I felt like we were walking on treasure.

It was evident the Templars were remembered there because restaurants and hotels were named for them. Jutting out into one of the two coves was a large stone fortress named the Royal Chateau. We were able to walk through it and learned it had been built as a summer home for the kings of Majorca. One wing had been given for the use of the Knights Templar.

When we emerged from the Chateau, we realized we were hungry. We had read in some of the literature that Collioure had an anchovy factory, which was open to tours, and we thought we would check it out after we had eaten. I was about to suggest one of the restaurants when Peter bent down and said in a low voice, "Don't look behind you, but I think we are being followed."

My first reaction was a sinking feeling in my stomach. Pretending to pause and look in a shop window, I asked him why he thought that. "Let's just say I noticed a man this morning when we were checking out of the hotel and again at the gas station when I filled up the car. And now, here he is again. It's too much of a coincidence."

We strolled on, coming to the San Vicens Vieux Remparts restaurant, which faced the water. We were seated at a table with a view of the sea. Peter sat where he could see who entered the dining area. Smiling, he said, "Let's forget our shadow for now and enjoy the food and the view."

We ordered the paella along with a bottle of the Rosé Collioure. Our talk turned to the history of the area. The small village had been visited by the Phoenicians, Romans and Greeks and was later occupied by Wamba, King of the Visigoths. It had a long history of being an active trading port. The Chateau had been built around 981 A.D. We both knew we were keeping away from discussing the shadow and the scrolls.

Afterwards we walked leisurely toward our hotel. Peter stopped and kissed me, whispering that our shadow was still following us.

"I have a plan. We will pay for an additional night and leave by a back way. Then we will get our car and drive to Perpignon." I squeezed his hand.

At the hotel Peter paid for a second night and made small talk about the village and how much we liked it. We went to up our room, and since we had not brought our backpacks up, simply left the key there and found a back way down to the ground floor.

We heard voices at the desk, and looking outside we could see no sign of our shadow. We got in the car and as silently as he could, Peter slowly let it roll backwards. At the very moment he was ready to turn on the engine, a couple got on a motorcycle and revved it up. Peter took the opportunity to start our car. He drove as fast as he dared, and we arrived in Perpignon in a short time.

Looking at our rental agreement, I found that we could return the car there. The rental place was not too difficult to find, and I remained outside while Peter completed the necessary paperwork. We had already fueled the car when we arrived in Perpignon.

When Peter emerged, I told him I had seen nothing suspicious while he was inside. We began to walk, stopping at a small café to purchase a soda. Peter asked for directions to the rail station and learned we could walk to it. We kept to side streets because Peter's height made him stand out.

Approaching the station, I looked up at the roof and was amazed to see an art form figure of a man on top of the cupola. He was leaning back with his arms spread out wide, his legs straight out, and he was laughing!

Jill and I had purchased first class Eurail passes before leaving the States and I now learned Peter had done the same. From Narbonne we could find connections to other cities.

There was a half hour wait for the train. I picked up a tourist brochure. Perusing through it I spied a photo of Salvador Dali. "Peter, listen to this. Dali had a fascination for this station. He is said to have exclaimed: 'It all became clear in a flash: there, right in front of me, was the center of the world.' Before Peter could reply, our train was called.

Dusk was falling as we arrived in Narbonne. We had studied the schedule during our ride. A train for Paris was due to arrive from Barcelona in an hour.

Sitting in the waiting room observing people, we spoke very little. I felt drained of emotions and energy. So far we had seen nothing suspicious, however we knew that eventually our trail could be picked up again. We had only bought time.

The train arrived and we boarded. Our compartment was almost empty. We distanced ourselves from the others so we could talk. As the train was pulling out of Narbonne, I felt a sense of relief. Our arrival in Paris would be early in the morning. Leaning against Peter I fell asleep.

In the darkness of the morning we arrived in Paris and even at that time of the day found a crowded station. One of the things we had agreed upon was changing our appearances as soon as possible. We thought perhaps Peter's height might not stand out so much in Paris.

Finding the entrance to the Métro, we chose to head for the Left Bank where, in all probability we could find a small hotel. At this point I was exhausted and was so grateful for Peter's stamina. However, once we got on the Métro train, we unwittingly fell asleep and rode to the end of the line. Choosing to remain on the same car as it made its return trip, we fell asleep again and rode to the other end of the line.

By then, we decided to cover our tracks by riding the Métro and changing lines at various stations. We had purchased day passes so it was no problem. This resulted in our walking up and down stairs many times. I can honestly say the Métro in Paris is a maize of climbing up and down stairs. It turned out to be more of a workout for us than hiking in the mountains.

Finally Peter noticed we were at the Place de République and it seemed a good spot to get off. Emerging into the bright sunshine of the morning, we spied a nearby sidewalk café where we stopped and ordered café au lait with oeufs jambon and croissants. The café also had a computer we could use for a fee, so Peter asked me to check our e-mails, which I did with alacrity. I read Jill's e-mail, but all we could discern was that they were progressing. I sighed and told Peter that it was frustrating not to know what was actually going on with them. I had no idea of what was about to occur and I'm glad I didn't.

I know I had high hopes, yet I also knew the translations, even with the programs used, would take time. Leaving the café we began walking. Peter bent down and kissed the top of my head. "Sweetheart, let's make the most of our time together."

"You're right, my darling." We were passing by a shop with the sign Coiffeurs, and Peter steered me in. He ordered a shampoo and set for me and a shampoo and haircut for himself and a shave. Several hours later we walked out feeling refreshed and like new people.

We took the Métro to Pont Neuf, emerging on the Rue de la Monnaie. Our destination was La Samaritaine. As we made our way to it, Peter told me this elegant store had taken its name from an old water pump near the Pont Neuf. It is said the pump was decorated with a woman replicating the woman of Sameria[1] giving a drink of water to Jesus. It is also said La Samaritaine has everything and I believe that. Our first order of business was new clothes for both of us. We had decided to shed the image of hikers.

We made it fun and were like two kids on a wild shopping spree, which included a stop in the luggage department where we purchased two suitcases on wheels.

Taking them to the restrooms, we changed out of our hiking clothes and stowed our backpacks and extra new clothing in the suitcases. I thought we looked rather elegant. For lunch we chose a well-known café on the rooftop of the second building of the store where we had a light lunch. We had an exquisite 360-degree view of Paris and as we ate, we talked over our plans.

"To hell with trying to shake a shadow!" Peter said. "We're going to be visible and enjoy Paris."

"Really Peter?" I realized I had been holding tension in my body. It would be good to forget the scrolls and to forget Gilbert Montand.

"Oh yes!" I exclaimed. "I'm ready to let it all go."

Laughing, we paid the bill and went to find a bank in the department store, where we cashed some travelers checks. Peter was low on euros and we had just spent my cache.

Feeling uplifted and lighthearted, and pulling our cases behind us, we got on the down escalator to the street where Peter hailed a taxi. Once our luggage was stowed in the trunk,

---

[1] The woman at the well from John 4:5-26

he told the driver to take us to the Hotel Cambon. The driver nodded and within a few minutes we were there.

While Peter was checking us in, I looked around at the charming yet elegant lobby and thought, *My, how times have changed.* Once in our room I told Peter that my mother had stayed at an old hotel on Rue Cambon when she came to Paris in the early fifties.

Peter looked at me saying, "I've never heard you speak of your mother. Is she living?"

"Yes, she's still alive. Oh Peter! I haven't been open and honest with you. Please forgive me. I'm such a hypocrite." And I broke into sobs. This time Peter didn't take me into his arms; instead he allowed me to unleash the emotions I had been holding in.

"Would you care to tell me about you and your mother?"

When I could get my eyes open, I looked at him and saw no anger and no condemnation. I only saw love emanating from his eyes. Taking the tissue he offered, I began.

"I adore my mother and I've done her a great wrong. It was always my father who demanded my attention. I admit I loved it and I put him up on a pedestal and my mother allowed me to do that. I became a lawyer because he wanted me to. I hate being a lawyer! I never admitted that before to anyone." I stopped to blow my nose on another tissue Peter offered me.

"I was his precious princess. Now I can see that my mother was relegated to the background. She was merely his hostess. When he died I was devastated, and I was caught up in my own misery with Walter. I can see now that I was callous and unfeeling towards what my mother was going through.

"My father had only been dead for a year when Mother told me she was going to remarry. I was shocked and angered, and I said many unkind things to her. I called Jill and we arranged to hike the Pyrenees where I met you. Oh Peter! I am so ashamed! What an ass and a bitch I've been! My father smoozed me just like he did his juries and judges! Oh gawd! What a fool I've been!" I began crying again.

Quietly Peter spoke. "Ellen, my love, you can call her and make amends. Can you bring yourself to do that?"

Nodding yes, I took the phone he handed me. The hotel operator placed the call to the last number I knew for Mother.

184

It had been transferred to an answering service and soon an operator came on. I gave her my mother's name and last phone number. To get her to forward my call I had to tell her it was an emergency. At last I could hear the ringing and I was about to hang up when I heard a sleepy male voice answer.

"Hullo. Who's calling?"

"This is Ellen. May I speak to my mother?" In a moment she was on the line.

"Ellen! My darling! Oh Ellen! I've missed you!" We both began crying and laughing. I was able to ask for forgiveness and she gave it to me. We talked for what seemed like hours. And I told her about Peter, and of course he had to speak to her. She didn't mention anything about seeing us on the news, and we didn't mention the scrolls or our adventure. I could at last be happy for her being with her new husband, Jim.

When I finally hung up, Peter took me into his arms and kissed me. He then said, "I promise never to smooze you." And we both broke out laughing. I knew the healing power of forgiveness because I had also forgiven myself.

We realized we were starving, and it wasn't hard to find a good restaurant with Paris being full of them.

Over dinner I told Peter about my mother. When she was twenty-one she had gone to Paris to work for the U.S. Embassy. When I was growing up she would regale me with stories of what Paris was like in the early fifties. When I was twelve, she took me there without my father and she introduced me to her old haunts that were still around. It was a magical trip.

I told him it was ironic we were staying at the Hotel Cambon on Rue Cambon because the first hotel she had stayed in was the Metropolitan on Rue Cambon, but it was no longer there.

Peter was attentive and I was so appreciative he had urged me to talk about her. I realized I was feeling animated and had the sense a burden had been lifted from me.

After I told my stories of Mother, we turned to the subject of what we were going to do in Paris. I suggested we find a capable and reliable lawyer there in France and I placed a call to my father's former law firm. A receptionist answered and I asked to speak to the secretary of the current senior law

185

firm member. After identifying myself, I was put through to Selma Parkins who knew me.

There was the preliminary chitchat before I told her the nature of my call. Selma gave me the names of two lawyers in Paris, reminding me that in France they are called avocats. I thanked her and hung up. Turning to Peter I gave him the two names and a decision was made to make calls the next day.

The following morning I called the first avocat who was unavailable for some weeks. With the second number I hit pay dirt. Monsieur Alain Delacroix had an opening that afternoon at 3:30 P.M. and yes, I was told, he did speak English.

Sighing with relief, I turned to Peter and told him about the appointment. Picking me up and swinging me around, he laughed, saying the first order of business was to love me and then eat.

Over breakfast I told Peter we had to discuss finances, and he said, "You're really serious about this aren't you?"

"Indeed I am."

Looking at me quizzically, he cocked his head and folded his arms. "All right. We share and share alike. However, there is one thing I insist upon."

"What is that?"

"When we marry, I will not sign a property agreement because there has to be absolute trust between us."

For a moment I looked at him. *Marriage?* "This is the first I've heard of marriage."

Peter actually blushed. "Ummm, I've been thinking about it since I almost lost you to Montand. Ellen, will you consider marrying me?"

"I wouldn't be truthful if I said I didn't love you because I do. Yes, I will consider marrying you, based on a few conditions. No, don't say anything yet. I deceived you about my mother and I am asking that neither of us be hypocrites. As painful as it may appear to be, we must be truthful to one another. I know I am speaking more about me. Can you accept those terms?"

"My sweet beautiful Ellen, I accept those terms."

❧ ❧ ❧

The interview with Monsieur Delacroix went quite well from my viewpoint. I had our questions written out which made it smoother.

He began by giving us a brief outline of how the French laws are created and how they work. Without mentioning our involvement with the scrolls, Peter related about his being taken into custody and our being questioned regarding the disappearance of Father Sebastian. I felt we were developing a rapport, and Delacroix agreed to sign an agreement that as his clients, he would by law represent us if necessary. A fee was arrived at and Delacroix agreed to make inquiries regarding the investigation of Father Sebastian.

Peter and I returned to the hotel and talked of our meeting with Delacroix. Both of us agreed we were surprised that he appeared younger than expected. I had thought he would be in his late fifties or sixties.

The man we had met was almost as tall as Peter and had dark brown hair with a touch of gray at his temples. He was very trim and tanned and actually quite good-looking. There was something familiar about him although I couldn't pinpoint exactly what it was.

We began planning our stay in Paris and looking at our options for the future, such as continuing to travel or renting an apartment or house. Returning to the Toulouse area or its environs just didn't seem wise. Both of us expressed a sense that we were being followed and that it was a bit disconcerting.

Our days were spent exploring Paris together. Even though we had been here previously, but separately, we were like kids seeing something new. We spent hours at the Notre Dame Cathedral looking at the esoteric symbols placed there by the builders, and we concluded it was the obvious unobvious. We both marveled that with new knowledge, we were seeing things that we had never noticed before.

Little did we realize Jill and Sebastian had become embroiled in their own adversity. Daily we had checked for e-mails but there was no change in their status that we could surmise. Peter had purchased a laptop computer; so it was not necessary to go to an Internet café. One day I clicked on our e-mail site and there was a message from Jill. "Oh my gawd Peter! Come quick!"

Looking over my shoulder, he read, "We are departing. Will rendezvous with you at Lisa's in three days at the same time. Love." Giving a low whistle, he said, "It means they are in trouble and must leave."

"Oh gawd, no! I know you and Sebastian agreed on a code of some sort. Refresh my memory."

"It means we're to meet them at the Mona Lisa in the Louvre in three days. 'At the same time' means when Sebastian and I first met there last year, around 11:00 A.M."

Sitting in silence, I felt my brain churning. "Peter, why don't we ask Delacroix discreetly to locate and rent a place for us where we can all live perhaps anonymously?"

"My darling, a brilliant suggestion, but let's not call from the hotel."

"Okay, I'll get dressed and since we know the Métro system so well now, we can play 'me and no shadows.'"

Laughing, we dressed, and went out to find a phone. Delacroix was in court that day, and his secretary wanted to set up an appointment for the next week. Peter insisted we had to consult with Monsieur Delacroix as soon as possible because it was an emergency.

Apparently his demand surprised the secretary. Peter told me later she sounded frustrated; however she said she would attempt to contact Monsieur Delacroix. She said for Peter to call back by 4:00 that afternoon and she might have an answer.

"Ellen, why not take in a movie while we're waiting."

"A movie?"

"Yes. We can hold hands and we can eat popcorn."

"Oh Peter! Do you really want to go to a movie?"

"It's better than twiddling our fingers waiting for four o'clock to come."

"You're right."

"Of course, we could spend the time making love."

"Love sounds better. Oh I wish we knew what's going on with Jill and Sebastian," I said as we were returning to the hotel. We had an exquisite session of lovemaking.

ADVENTURE IN THE LOUVRE

Chaos: every event or action is the inevitable
result of preceding events and actions.
- Anon.

The day arrived for us to meet at the Louvre. Jill and Sebastian had spent the previous night at a small hotel on the Left Bank in Paris after Sebastian had driven them to Orly Airport where Jill returned the rental car. They had caught a shuttle into Paris and transferred to the Métro.

The morning of the meeting, they had showered, dressed, and found a small café where they had coffee with a croissant. They said their excitement was high at the prospect of seeing us again. Hoping they would blend in with the tourists, Jill wore jeans and a blue cotton top and Sebastian wore slacks with a knit polo shirt.

In our rental house on the outskirts of Paris, we had arisen tingling with excitement also. I could hardly contain myself. Both of us were wondering what had prompted Sebastian and Jill to come to Paris so suddenly.

Delacroix had found us a quaint little house. A high wall, which gave us privacy, surrounded it and it had a lovely garden. He had also managed to get us a loan car. For a moment I had been tempted to tell him the entire story.

While driving to the car park at the end of the Métro line, I asked Peter, "What if they don't show? What will we do?"

Reaching over and touching my folded hands, Peter replied, "Relax sweetheart. They will be there and let's not add worry to our meeting. What we fear the most has a way of winging itself back to us."

Laughing, I squeezed his hand, thinking how blessed I was. Taking a few deep breaths, I found myself relaxing. The one good thing about the Paris Métro system is that it is on time. We rode in comfortable silence and had only one train change to make.

At ten o'clock in the morning we approached the Louvre from opposite sides. Jill and Sebastian arrived from the

Left Bank. Peter and I arrived from the Rue de Rivoli. The tourist line was already long, however it was moving at a rapid pace toward the entrance.

With Peter's height, I knew Jill and Sebastian would spot us. I looked around and didn't see them. As we were nearing the entrance of the glass Pyramid, I wondered why the architect Pei had chosen the pyramid design. It was impressive and I remembered it had been around 1981 when President Mitterand commissioned him to design the entrance.

After we walked in, we took the escalator down to one of the ticket vendors. Peter and I both were acquainted with the Louvre. I continued to look for Jill and Sebastian while we were walking to the section where the Mona Lisa resided behind her glass case in a roped-off area. Holding my hand, Peter led me up the stairs and we passed through various exhibits.

We had just entered the section where the Mona Lisa was when I spotted Jill. I was about to raise my hand in greeting when all hell broke loose.

Jill began screaming for someone to stop a man who had stolen her pack. I was in the way of the culprit's escape and he could not avoid knocking me down. Peter took a flying leap tackling the man. Another man was about to take the backpack when Sebastian ran over and jumped on his back. Somehow I managed to get up.

It was a melee. It was chaos. Tourists were recording the scene with their flash and video cameras. I then threw myself at the man Sebastian had jumped on, and when the man fell, I sat on him, causing him to drop the backpack. We were all shouting for the police.

A security door immediately shut off the entrance to the Mona Lisa room. Within minutes security guards were there with their weapons drawn. The man who had actually taken Jill's backpack was attempting to tell the guards it was all a mistake and that a crazy American had attacked him.

Tourists were trying to put in their two cents worth and Jill quickly retrieved her backpack from the floor. The four of us came together and huddled together watching the security guards as they took charge of the situation.

The upshot of it all was that a tourist with a digital camera stepped forward showing the security officers a picture he had taken of the man cutting the strap and pulling Jill's backpack off of her. Then all cameras were confiscated.

Security personnel took the two men away to hold them in custody until the police arrived. We were asked to show our identifications, and our information regarding what happened was taken down. Most of the tourists were taking this in a good-natured manner, while a few were grumbling. Of course the gallery leading to the Mona Lisa stayed closed until everyone had been interviewed.

Gradually the people were released. One of the security officials came over to us; and since we were primarily the ones responsible for apprehending the culprits, he said we would be escorted to the Office of Security where the police of the Prefecture would speak with us.

After what seemed like a long hike and an elevator ride down to the level where the security offices were located, we were ushered into a reception room outside the security office. The official told us to sit down and to give him our identifications, please. We complied. The receptionist looked at us with interest.

Jill and Sebastian sat next to each other and I noticed they were holding hands. *My gawd!* I thought. *They've fallen in love.* I wanted to go over and hug them, but I refrained. Just then the inner office door opened, and a tall burly man came out. His body reminded me of a bear. Even though he was shorter than Peter, he was impressive.

"Messieurs et Mesdames, I am Inspector Gauthier of this Prefecture. There are certain matters which must be cleared." Speaking in French, he asked Sebastian to follow him.

With the receptionist sitting there, it was not feasible to talk. We sat in silence, Peter and I holding hands. Jill had closed her eyes and I knew she was in meditation. My mind was churning with a multitude of thoughts and I wanted to know who was behind it all. *No one in his or her right mind would attempt a theft such as this in the Louvre. Had Jill been singled out? Who would know we would meet here?*

The door opened. Sebastian came out looking subdued. An apparent assistant to Inspector Gautier asked Peter to come in next. Squeezing my hand, he arose and went into Gautier's office. Sebastian sat down next to Jill taking her hand. I took notice of the looks of love they gave each other, and I was so happy for them.

I could see the receptionist looking up from her work from time to time, so I closed my eyes, going within, and using my meditation method that had helped me when Peter and I had been kidnapped.

It seemed as if only a moment passed when the door opened and Peter came out. The look on his face was non-committal. Jill was the next to be called. Peter sat beside me, putting an arm around my shoulder, giving it a gentle squeeze. Jill was not kept long. It was my turn.

As I went into the office, Gauthier half rose from behind the desk. His frame seemed to dwarf it. A policewoman was sitting at a laptop computer while the man I had called the assistant stood by the window. It could have been an intimidating experience, however I chose not to accept that.

The questions were similar to those asked of me in Carcassonne. I carefully chose my words, as any good lawyer would do. I could see Gauthier was also was choosing his words carefully. When he wasn't sure of the English, he would turn to the man standing by the window who interpreted. *Of course*, I thought, *there would need to be an interpreter*. When the interview was over, I was told not to leave Paris, as there would be more questions later. When asked for my address in Paris, I gave him Alain Delacroix' name and phone number.

Escorting me out of the office, the Inspector reminded us again that we were not to leave Paris because we could be called in for additional questioning during the investigation.

I felt boxed in. First, I couldn't leave France and then I couldn't leave Paris.

Chapter 17

THE FAME OF IT ALL

We are confronted with insurmountable opportunities.
- Pogo

A security official came to escort us out and Peter asked if there was an unobtrusive exit by which we could leave. The man nodded, escorting us through another maize of corridors. After an elevator ride, we were at the back entrance to the Louvre that opens out on to Rue du Louvre.

Giving a sigh of relief, we started on our way to the Rue de Rivoli, but first we stopped to hug each other. There was so much we all wanted to say. It was Peter who suggested we have lunch and we agreed. He suggested Les Ambassadeurs in the Hôtel de Crillon since he felt we would have more privacy there. Hailing a taxi, we four got in and within moments arrived at the hotel, which was across the street from the American Embassy at the Place de la Concorde.

Laughing, I told them that if we were being followed perhaps whoever it was would think we were going to the Embassy.

When the taxi pulled up in front of the Crillon, a doorman opened the passenger door for us. Before Peter could put his hand in his pocket to pull out money, I handed the driver the fare along with a generous tip. Peter grinned at me as we walked into the hotel.

We were directed to the restaurant and were seated at a table located where we had privacy. The room had some lingering diners, but for the most part we were alone. I could hardly contain myself while we ordered. I was bursting to discuss the situation.

With our orders taken and the wine poured, we began first with Jill, who started with her dream and intuitive feeling of the need to move from Paul's. It took her and Sebastian some time to relate their whole story. They stopped only when the waiter came to take away dishes so another course could be served or to pour more wine.

Jill remembered she had taken a card from the intruder and pulling it out of her jeans pocket, she passed it over to us.

Together we stared at a regular size business card with the emblem of an eight-pointed cross enclosed in a circle and a telephone number written on it. I gasped! It was identical to the one Peter had removed from Bruno. Sebastian was the first to speak.

"It would appear to be the Opus Dei, only their eight-pointed cross usually has no circle around it. There are so many secret societies. Who knows which one this is."

Peter pulled the identical card out and showed it to them. "Isn't the eight-pointed cross also a symbol for the Knights of Malta?" he asked.

"Oui. This is most interesting and unusual. Perhaps it is a separate organization with connections to both the Opus Dei and the Knights of Malta."

It was Peter who brought up the question as to the whereabouts of the scrolls. Sebastian smiled. "This warrior woman has brilliant ideas."

Touching his hand, Jill shared what she and Sebastian had done. On their way to Paris, realizing there could be complications if they were caught with the scrolls in their possession, Jill came up with an idea. "I suggested we mail them to ourselves in Paris."

"You what!" I exclaimed.

"I asked Sebastian where could I exchange some money and he told me I could do it at any French post office. We stopped in Orleans so I could change travelers' checks into euros, and we also purchased boxes and packed the scrolls in them. We packed the translation programs in another box and the translations in another."

"Oui. It is so simple. I mailed them to myself, to Jill, to you and also to Peter. The main post office in Paris is open 24 hours a day, 7 days a week and will hold packages for 5 days for them to be picked up."

"And," added Jill, "The main post office is on the same street as the back entrance to the Louvre."

"By god! You both are brilliant!" exclaimed Peter. "Ah, but there is one item apparently the police did not find."

"And what is that Peter?" asked Sebastian.

"The gun. Where did you put it?"

Jill began laughing. "We thought it might go through an x-ray of some kind if we mailed it, so we brought it with us to Paris. We placed it in a locked case we purchased in Orleans and left it in the safe at our hotel."

We all looked at each other and burst into laughter. Oh gawd! It felt so good to laugh and be with loving people.

It was over coffee when I suggested that I call Alain Delacroix. At our request the waiter brought us a phone. While I was waiting for the call to go through, Peter gave a brief overview of why we had secured the services of an avocat.

Surprisingly, I was put through to Delacroix immediately. The first thing he said was to ask where I was. When I told him, I could hear him breathe a sigh of relief.

He informed me our escapade at the Louvre was splashed all over the news.

"What?" I exclaimed. "Yes, yes I understand. We will be there within the hour."

Hanging up, I turned to Peter and then to Jill and Sebastian. "Well, it seems as though one of those tourists didn't surrender his or her camera. Delacroix said our faces are all over the news and Paris is buzzing with it. He wants us in his office within the hour."

We sat for several moments in stunned silence. Peter suggested that before going we should tell each other about our experiences when we were interviewed by Inspector Gauthier.

Sebastian told of his interview first. Neither he nor the Inspector mentioned the scrolls. Primarily the Inspector wanted to know if Sebastian had disappeared voluntarily or against his will. He told the Inspector of his illness and his despondency. He truthfully told him of going to Paul's house to get away. For the moment it appeared to be a satisfactory explanation. He had been asked if he wanted his Archdiocese informed of his whereabouts and Sebastian had told him no.

Our interviews were all similar in content and we agreed it had been too easy. A thought came to me, "I heard the thief say to one of the security guards something about 'it was a crazy American.' How did he know Jill was an American?" None of us had an explanation for that.

We also discussed whether it would be wise to inform Delacroix about the scrolls. Now we had decisions to make. Peter suggested we not mention them unless it became necessary and we all agreed.

Peter signaled for the bill and thank god for credit cards! After signing the charge slip, Peter asked the waiter to get us a taxi. Gathering up our belongings, we went outside to the waiting taxi. Fortunately no one that we could see had picked up on our being at the Crillon. Having had one episode with the paparazzi, we didn't relish another one.

Delacroix' law office was located on the Avenue Hoche near the Arc de Triomphe. As we entered, the receptionist smiled and buzzed his secretary.

Earlier I had learned her name was Michele and we warmly greeted each other. Then I introduced her to Jill and Sebastian. Leading us to a small conference room, she told us Delacroix would be with us shortly. We found fresh water and glasses already on the table.

Within minutes Alain Delacroix came in. That day he was dressed in the uniform color worn by most lawyers, charcoal grey. His suit was silk and he wore a white silk shirt. He had a presence of success about him.

After introductions to Sebastian and Jill, we sat at the table. In almost flawless English he asked Jill to begin with her story regarding the incident at the Louvre. He nodded from time to time, making few interruptions. When she had finished her story, he asked Sebastian to tell his.

After Sebastian told his story, Delacroix asked Peter and me for our versions. I remembered to tell him about the thief's comment, "a crazy American." He made a notation of that and then wanted to know what questions the Inspector had asked us. By that time we were all on a first name basis.

We asked him what the news reports had said and Alain began laughing. "Whoever it was with the video camera had some excellent shots. I like the one of Peter tackling the culprit as well as the one of Sebastian jumping on the back of the second man. It was almost a . . . what do you Americans call it . . . a keystone cops scenario."

I put my elbows on the table and put my head between my hands. Shaking my head, I said, "So much for anonymity."

I could just hear my mother if this made the news back in California. I think we all groaned.

"So what do we do now?" asked Peter.

"This is a most interesting situation. We have a French priest who disappeared and we also have two lovely American women and one very tall American man. The news said it was an unknown American woman with the priest whom the thief tried to rob."

Turning to Sebastian, Delacroix asked, "Are you so valuable to the Church?"

"Non. I was diagnosed to be dying and I was placed on medical retirement."

Delacroix tapped his pen on the tablet before him. Leaning back in his chair he looked at each of us searchingly. "It would seem there is more here than you have spoken of. Are you sure Father you do not wish to contact your Church authorities?"

In the beginning Sebastian had requested we all speak English so Jill, Peter and I would know what was being said.

"Non. It was at Lourdes that I became honest with myself. I admitted to my friend Peter, that I had lived a lie for many years because I knew the lies and deceits of the Church and I became sick at heart. I am going to renounce my vows. I can no longer support the hypocrisy of the Church."

"This is a very serious step Father. You have thought it out carefully?"

"Mais oui. Yes. It is my decision to officially inform the Church authorities."

"If you would like, I can have my secretary create documents of resignation and renouncement for you to sign. Would that be agreeable?"

"Oui. Merci. I will agree and sign."

"Now to other business." Alain looked at each of us. "I strongly suggest you consider what else needs to be revealed to me. If I am to represent you, if it is necessary, I do not enjoy being unaware of what may be hidden."

For a few moments the four of us sat as if carved in stone, and then I spoke up. "We too want to know why the interest in Father Sebastian. It has been unnerving for us to have been be singled out on two different occasions. Peter and

I have been told we cannot leave France, and I, for one, want to know what the hell is going on."

Backing me up, Peter said, "I agree with Ellen. Is there any way you can find out why the interest in Sebastian?"

"Since it is I that appears to be the center of this excitement, may I confer with my friends?" asked Sebastian.

Delacroix sighed. "Of course. I will leave you alone to discuss this situation. I can only emphasize again that it is necessary for me to know what the entire situation is. Please inform me when you are ready to continue." Getting up, he left the room.

For a moment we were quiet. Then Jill asked, "Do you trust him?"

All I could say was, "I honestly don't know. I'm in a foreign country and not familiar with the ins and outs of their laws. Something in me wants to trust him but in all honesty, I'm not sure."

"I agree with Ellen," Peter said. "She contacted her deceased father's former law office and Delacroix's was one of the names given to her. Apparently he has done work for her father's old firm. Trusting him? I have reservations about that, but I don't have any alternatives either."

"Thank you. Sebastian, being French, do you have any suggestions?" Jill asked.

"Non. This situation is totally foreign to my experience."

"Well," Jill said. "It looks like we may be up the creek without a paddle."

"What? What?" asked Sebastian.

"My dear, what I implied is that we are caught in a situation with no viable solution at this moment. I feel like we are damned if we do and damned if we don't. I suggest we lay our cards on the table and tell Monsieur Delacroix about the scrolls."

"Lay what cards on the table?" interjected Sebastian.

This time I spoke. "It is an American idiom meaning to be honest with Delacroix. What's your feeling Peter?"

"I have listened to all that has been said and this is an unknown. Let's trust The Magdalene to guide us because she directed Ellen and Jill to the cave. I don't think her spirit will allow the scrolls or the translations to be lost."

198

"Are we in agreement to bring Delacroix in on this?" I asked. We were. Peter volunteered to go and find him, and in less than three minutes they were back.

"Peter has informed me you have more to share with me," Delacroix said as he sat down.

I was compelled to speak first. "Since it all began with me, I will begin." Thus I told my tale of falling into the cave and finding the scrolls. I spoke with trepidation as I felt as if I were on slippery ground. This could have been the beginning of an avalanche or we could walk safely. There came a point where I turned it over to Jill, and her story from her perspective dovetailed into mine.

All this time, Delacroix sat immobile for the most part, except when he would from time to time make a notation on his pad. Peter picked up the thread from us, and told of his acquaintance with Sebastian.

When Sebastian was relating his part, I realized I was inwardly praying to The Magdalene to guide each of us and to bless each of us. Later Jill shared with me she was also doing the same thing.

Looking at each of us, Alain asked, "What is your intention regarding the use of these scrolls?"

"In answer to your question, all we want is to have them made available to the world once they are all translated. We do not want them languishing in some basement or archive while the authorities haggle over them. This happened with the scrolls found at Nag Hammadi as well as the Dead Sea Scrolls," I said. "In addition, in the first scroll The Magdalene gives a mandate to the ones finding them, and it is that her words must not be hidden away."

There was a pregnant silence. Alain looked at each of us as he said, "Would you consider informing the Bibliothèque nationale of your find? By doing this, you may avoid further unpleasant experiences."

"Oui, c'est possible," murmured Sebastian. "We have no desire to retain the original scrolls as we have expressed. If my friends agree, I would like to stipulate that I translate the remaining scrolls including the two they hold. However, the translations must be released to the public."

Alain asked, "Is this agreeable with all of you?"

Jill spoke, "It is agreeable with a provision that there will be no prosecution of any of us."

I said I agreed. "The original scrolls must belong to the people of the world."

"And you Peter?" Alain asked.

"I also agree with the provision that the scrolls, along with the materials they are written on as well as the cloth they are wrapped in will be authenticated by a committee of bi-partisan people approved by Sebastian and the Bibliothèque."

"I will go over your points," Alain said. "It is agreeable for me to meet with the head of the Bibliothèque nationale and negotiate the following: 1) There will be no prosecution of any of you. 2) Sebastian will have the first opportunity to translate any scrolls remaining to be translated, including the two scrolls in possession of the Bibliothèque. 3) The scrolls will be made available to the world, and 4) the scrolls, including the material they are written upon, will be authenticated by a committee of bi-partisan people approved by you and the Bibliothèque. Is this what you agree to?"

Alain looked at each of us as one by one we gave our assent. "One other item. Where are the scrolls now? Apparently they were not with you when the attack took place in the Louvre."

Jill smiled and answered saying, "Sebastian and I mailed them to ourselves, and to Peter and Ellen. They may have already arrived at the main post office here in Paris."

With his eyebrows raised, Alain said, "If you will give me your receipts for the poste, I will send one of my employees to gather them and I will have them brought here."

We all looked surprised. Alain smiled, "With the paparazzi looking for you it would not be wise for you to be seen. Gauthier has probably already placed a tail on you, therefore how are you going to retrieve your packages?"

"We hadn't considered that," Jill said. "Very well." She reached into her bra, pulled out the receipts and handed them to Alain. Shaking his head, Alain took them. "Apparently there was no body search. You are a most resourceful woman." He rose up from his chair and left the room.

"This man is so smooth," Jill said. "How do we know we can trust him?"

By now we were all exhausted.

Peter spoke first, "I don't think we have any choice at this time. It's like we're between a rock and a hard place."

"What mean you by a rock and a hard place?" questioned Sebastian.

"Another meaning is we have our backs against a wall."

"Ah, je comprends."

At this point I stood, telling them I was going to find Alain to ask him some questions regarding our possible arrest. Peter wanted to come with me but I told him since I had made the initial contact, it was up to me to find out what I could.

I left the room and in the reception area met Alain coming out of his office. Smiling, he said he had sent his secretary to do the errand.

Looking at him, I asked "Why are you going to all this trouble for us? Do all lawyers in France assist their clients to the degree you're helping us?"

"Perhaps we need to talk. We can talk better in here."

I followed him into his office. It was elegant. My eyes took in chairs and a deep maroon leather couch. The carpet was silver with the overall effect being elegance with simplicity.

Asking me to be seated in one of the chairs, he pulled up another to sit facing me.

Chapter 18

A SHOCKING SURPRISE

Once the toothpaste is out of the tube,
it's hard to get it back in.
- H.R. Halderman

"Ellen, I am going to tell you a story. And I ask you to listen without interrupting. Agreed?"

I nodded, indicating I agreed.

"Many years ago when my father was a young lawyer just beginning his law practice, he married, but not for love. And his wife became pregnant. She lost the child and it was discovered she could never have more children.

"It was here in Paris in 1954 when my father met a young American woman who worked for the American Embassy."

Something within me began going off like bells. There were electrical currents running up and down my body, and I gripped the arms of the chair while he continued.

"They fell in love and had an affair. From that affair, the young woman became pregnant. My father went to his wife, asking for a divorce. Being a practicing Catholic, she refused. In the 1950's divorce was not a common thing. And abortion was out of the question for the two lovers. The young woman agreed to have the child, allowing my father and his wife to adopt it."

"Alain, are you telling me my mother had an affair with your father and...." I broke off in mid-sentence.

"Yes, Ellen. I am your brother."

Stunned! I was at loss for words.

"My mother never told me any of this! She never even hinted she had another child." As if speaking to myself, I mused out loud, "So she had the baby, resigned from the Foreign Service and returned to the States where she became a legal secretary."

"True. My father's wife, whom I called Mother, had a stipulation to the adoption. My birth mother could never see me or reveal to me who she truly was."

I had gotten up and walked to a large window that had a view of the Arch de Triomphe. It was now dusk and the monument's lights were on. I looked out for a moment.

"Alain, how did you learn of this?"

"My father felt he was not bound by the adoption agreement. When I was eighteen, he became quite ill. Being close to death, he asked to speak to me alone. He told me the entire story and he made me promise I would take care of my birth mother and her child if necessary. After those many years, he still loved Margaret."

There! He had said her name.

"My father recovered and we never really spoke of it again. Becoming curious, I sought to find out all I could regarding my birth mother. This included you, my sister. And now I am keeping a promise I made to my father."

"And, your mother? What will she think?"

"She died a few years ago. She never knew I knew. We were never close. My father is retired and he lives in the country growing roses and reading. We do not discuss Margaret. However, after my mother died, he gave me a photo of my birth mother and him together."

I looked at him. *Yes, he does have my mother's blue eyes. Now I understand why there was something familiar about him.*

"Alain, I'm in shock. It may take me some time to get used to the idea of having a brother. And I've already been through so much these past few months that I'm having difficulty adjusting to this bombshell you just dropped on me."

"I have wanted a sister and I have longed to know you and Margaret, so please forgive me for rushing into this. But by revealing this to you, I feel a burden has been lifted from me. Now you know why I have wanted to do all I can to help you."

"Thank you Alain, and I think I understand. This is all so unexpected. And I feel I must share this with Peter and the others. Please come with me."

When we returned to the conference room, Peter could tell something was different. I walked over to him with Alain following behind me.

"Peter, I have something to share with you and everyone. And I'm still in shock."

Peter had risen and I went into his arms. Jill told me later it was if all in the room had become frozen energy in motion.

Looking up at Peter I said, "I have just learned something more about my mother. I . . . I want you to meet my half-brother."

I swear Peter gawked at me and then at Alain. "My god! You're certain?"

It was Alain who suggested we all sit down at the table.

"Will you tell them what you told me?" I stammered.

Again, Alain related the story of my mother and his father. Peter held my hand during the entire recital. Alain ended with, "When Ellen came to me and asked why I was doing so much for her, I knew it was the moment to tell her. I have yearned for many years to identify myself."

As I heard him telling the story for the second time, I had a question. "Alain, why did my father's office have your name and phone number?"

"It is simple. I searched for my birth mother after my father told me. I located her and she had married your father. After I became an avocat I ingratiated myself with your father's law firm. It was one way I could keep track of my true mother and the sister I learned I had, you. I have done legal work for the firm as a consultant on French law. I have also handled legal matters for the firm."

I picked up the thread, "Therefore, when I called my father's former law firm it would only be natural for your name and phone number be given to me. For some reason the other lawyer whose number I was given was unavailable and so I called you. When I phoned, did you know who I was?"

"Yes. Over the years I have managed to keep up with you, your marriage and divorce. I was also aware of the news coming out of Carcassonne when the police interviewed you and Peter. I had also hired a firm to track you. But once you arrived in Paris, you were lost, until you called me."

Jill speaking softly said, "Yes, you do have Margaret's blue eyes. Yes, I do see a resemblance."

Peter questioned Alain, "Did you hire someone to tail us in Perpignon and in Collioure, too?"

"Yes," he answered.

"It is going to be a long night and I have many things to go over with you. First, we must eat. I have a meal waiting for us in my apartment above. Shall we go?"

We all gaped at him. "You have an apartment here?" Jill asked.

"The top floor is my home. Please allow me to escort you there."

I felt as if it was all a dream. We followed Alain and took the elevator to the top floor. Using a key, Alain opened the elevator door. Before us was a foyer and beyond that was a large room subtly lit. *Alain must love the color silver*, I thought as we walked into the room. The carpet there was plush silver like his office and the room's color scheme was sky blue and silver with accents of midnight blue. In the center was a massive round glass coffee table flanked by two blue couches and two midnight blue chairs making it an obvious conversation center. Off to one side was a dining room. All the rooms were geared for comfort. I later realized the room was similar to half of a hub.

The entrance to Alain's rooms was through a door to the right facing the foyer. To the left of the foyer was the entrance to the dining room and behind that, I presumed, was the kitchen and servants' quarters. Facing the dining room and to the left was a door leading to the four guest bedrooms, each with its private bath. I realized he had the entire floor, and surmised that in all probability he owned the entire building.

He indicated the guest room wing and said, "I am having the four of you stay here for the present. You may choose which rooms you will have. I will now see to it that our dinner is served."

Our bedrooms each had a queen size bed and the décors were almost identical. Peter and I chose the first room on the right with Jill and Sebastian taking the first room on the left. Closing the door, I went into Peter's arms. Our kiss was long and lingering.

Sitting down in the one chair in the room, Peter pulled me down on his lap and said, "Now, tell me what you are feeling." Gently he kissed me again.

"Oh my darling, I'm not sure what I'm feeling. What am I feeling? All I can think of is the story of the man falling off a cliff. On the way down he catches a bush branch and as he's dangling there, he spies a wild strawberry. He reaches for the strawberry and eats it and enjoys the taste. I guess I am feeling shock and surprise, along with a little fear. Yet, I also feel a warmth for Alain."

"Do you trust him?"

"I want to hear more of what he has to say before I give him my trust. I also want to speak with Mother. And I want to meet his father. Oh, he told me he has a photo of his father and my mother. I think I need to see it."

Picking my hand up, Peter kissed the palm. "One thing certain my love, life has never been boring since I met you."

At that moment the phone by the bed rang and we both jumped.

Getting off Peter's lap, I walked over to answer it. Alain was calling to inform us dinner would be served in fifteen minutes. Smiling, Peter came over to me and kissed me lightly on the lips and then he said, "Perhaps we will learn more."

Walking into the room to join the others, I noticed the drapes had been pulled back and the large windows overlooked the floodlit Arch de Triomphe. Jill and Sebastian were already there.

The coffee table held generous platters of hors d'oeuvre and a wine caddy with chilled white wine. Alain was present, too, and had changed into a pair of light blue silk lounge pants and a white silk pullover.

I realized Sebastian had spoken very little since Alain and I dropped the bombshell.

Alain said he was having our belongings from the rental house brought to his apartment, and the car parked at the Métro station would be returned to the house. None of us thought of getting Jill and Sebastian's belongings from their hotel.

Perhaps we all felt like we were walking on eggshells because none of us seemed to want to refer to the scrolls. Dinner was pleasant with the conversation confined to general topics. His valet, or maybe it was his butler, served us discreetly.

I have no memories of what we ate but I know we returned to the living room for coffee. Looking at each of us intently, Alain's manner changed. He was all business now.

Picking up a pad and pen from the coffee table he began by saying, "My sister and friends, I am going to question you about certain events and I implore you to answer me honestly. I am here to be of assistance; however there can be no holding back. Do you understand?"

I think we all nodded yes. I know I did. Continuing to speak Alain began, "You must have a guardian angel watching after you. Ellen and Peter, I ask you to tell me of your movements after leaving Carcassonne."

Sebastian and Jill swiveled their eyes to look at us. There had been no time to tell them of our encounter with Gilbert Montand. I began with our traveling to Limoux and Alet-les-Bains and I spoke of our being kidnapped. There were exclamations by Jill and Sebastian. At this point I asked Peter to continue.

He began to relate our adventure with Montand. I could not take my eyes off his face and could hear gasps coming from Jill and Sebastian who was saying "Mon dieu!" a lot.

Alain did not interrupt. Peter finished the story of what had happened. Alain referred to the notes he had made and began asking us to clarify certain points. We were asked to describe Montand and Bruno again as well as Montand's home and grounds. From my standpoint, Alain was most thorough. At times I knew Jill wanted to say something, however Alain held up his hand as if to say no.

Remembering the cards, Peter pulled the one taken from Bruno out of his pocket and handed it to Alain. Taking it, Alain made no comment.

When he had finished with us, he turned to Jill and Sebastian, asking them what had led them to come to Paris. Reaching over to hold Sebastian's hand, Jill said she would begin.

We all listened to what she said had transpired with them. When she had finished, it was Sebastian's turn.

Clearing his throat, he wet his lips. "Mon dieu, how do I begin?"

Painstakingly he began to tell what had happened, from his perspective. It was evident it was extremely difficult for him. Having heard their story at lunch, I was still shocked to hear what they had gone through. I looked at Jill with amazement. Even though I had known her since we were first roommates at the university, I had no idea she could act so fast or do what she did. Later she shared she had felt the same way about me when she listened to our story.

At the end of his account, Sebastian reached into his pocket and pulled out a card identical to the one Peter had handed to Alain. Taking the card, Alain sat back in his chair with one ankle resting on the opposite knee.

"My friends, you are most fortunate in being alive. These scrolls must be of great importance to you."

Sebastian spoke up, "Tell me, are you a Catholic?"

"I was brought up in the Catholic Church by my mother. This does not make me a practicing or a believing Catholic."

Sebastian continued, "Do you believe in God?"

"I have mixed feelings about believing in God. I recognize there must be a supreme force in the universe and that is about all I can tell you. Tell me Sebastian, why are these scrolls so important to you?"

"A good question and you deserve an answer. I went into the priesthood for selfish reasons. It was a way to move out of the poverty I grew up in. It was also to further my education. During my seminary studies it was found I had an affinity for the Greek language. I was schooled in modern and ancient Greek. My abilities brought me to the Vatican where I worked in a section of the archives. It was while there, that I became disillusioned and I began researching when and how the Church was founded. I learned it was all based on fraud, lies and misconduct.

"When Peter approached me, I was sick and dying. I was also curious as to the content of the scrolls. After I translated the first one, I felt I had been given a chance to be of service to the world. Here at last was a woman writing a truth that the world has a right and a need to know. I was given an opportunity to move away from my selfish past, to do something for the world."

"Tell me Sebastian, do you really believe these scrolls are authentic?"

"Oui. I do. In the past, I have had the privilege of translating ancient scrolls, which have been suppressed by the Church. These scrolls of The Magdalene have the ring of authenticity. As I progressed, I saw each scroll was written on a different, ah, a varied type of papyrus. The inks were not the same throughout. But the handwriting was consistent."

Sebastian paused, waiting for Alain to respond. Instead Alain turned to me asking why I felt these scrolls were so important and why I felt it necessary to take the risks I had.

I told him those were good questions. I took a moment to think about my reasons. "I will attempt to answer your questions, but first I will give some of my background and perhaps you will have a better understanding.

"Interestingly it was while I was in law school that I was introduced to what some would call metaphysics. I call it my searching period and I became a seeker of knowledge. I had grown up more or less an agnostic. Although my mother exposed me to various religions, none of them made sense to me.

"I was always a researcher of history. The more I read, the more I became disenchanted with religion. From my perspective it was an evil cancer preying on simple people, especially women, who were excluded from having any voice in religion or society and were relegated to being breeding bitches for men's pleasures.

"This led me to become an advocate for women's rights. I had learned from my studies that it is the women all over the world who are the most oppressed of all. It doesn't matter if they are white, black, red, brown, yellow or blue.

"I researched religion even more and I read the Bible. What I read in the New Testament indicated to me that people were more concerned with the words of other so-called apostles or neo-apostles than living what Jesus taught."

I paused. "Perhaps I am being long-winded, but it became very apparent to me something was amiss regarding the women in the life of Jesus. I felt compelled to seek out what information was available regarding Mary Magdalene.

"Somewhere along the way I read about the Knights Templar and the Black Madonnas. I began to see that there was a noble group who had wanted to preserve her memory. There have been Black Madonnas for nearly two thousand years. Here in France the great cathedrals were designed and crafted by master craftsmen incorporating symbols of her for the entire world to see.

"When I fell into that cave and got over the shock of the fall, I felt a presence, which is hard to describe. It was a sacred presence. I had no idea what was in those jars. I only knew I had to find out."

Looking at Jill, I continued, "Bless Jill, she really didn't resist our bringing the scrolls back."

Reaching for Peter's hand, I went on, "Jill and I had been hiking in the Pyrenees with Peter being part of our group. I thought of him when we discussed finding someone to help us get the scrolls translated. We sought him out and asked if he knew how we could get them deciphered. I told him I was pretty sure they were written in Greek.

"And it was through Peter that we met Sebastian. When Peter told me Sebastian was a priest, I resisted placing the scrolls in his hands. In fact, I didn't want them in the hands of anyone connected with religion. After Sebastian translated the first scroll, I definitely knew I didn't want them to leave our hands before they had all been translated.

I paused again. "There, I think I'm finished except for one last thing. I have felt this sacred presence a number of times since."

Turning to Jill, Alain asked her why she felt the scrolls were so important. Clearing her throat, she began, "As Ellen said, we have the same interests. We were roommates at the University where we discovered we had similar views on religion as well as a common interest in history. I was a history major and already involved with women's issues. After graduation Ellen went on to law school while I took post-graduate studies and became a history teacher.

"Ellen and I have traveled in Europe, especially France, a number of times previously, attempting to trace the trail of Mary Magdalene. After the deaths of Ellen's father and my mother we decided to do something different. We joined a group hiking the Pyrenees, which is when we met Peter.

"When Ellen fell into the cave and discovered the jars, I was more concerned about not reporting it to the authorities than she was. But I didn't protest too much because I also felt a sacred presence. Speaking for myself, I had a growing need to know what they were before relinquishing them. There was also a reluctance within me to allow a Catholic priest to look at them."

Jill groped for Sebastian's hand. "Once I met him I felt a presence around him also. I felt as if I were being carried away on a wave I knew I had to surrender to. Perhaps it doesn't make sense but that is the best way I can describe it at this time. Like Ellen, when Sebastian translated the first scroll, I knew we had been led purposefully to them. One might call it divine intervention."

Alain had not given any indication of what his reaction to our stories might be. He now looked at Peter. "Besides being in love with Ellen, what are your reasons?"

Peter leaned forward with his fingers laced together. "Actually it was love for Ellen that first motivated me. She didn't know it at the time but I had fallen in love with her while we were hiking. When Ellen and Jill contacted me at Mirepoix and told me the story, I asked if they had considered the repercussions of not turning the scrolls over to the authorities. They had, and Ellen gave a convincing argument for having them translated first since it was possible they could be a hoax.

"Sebastian came to mind. I had met him here in Paris last year, and learned then that he was a Greek scholar as well as a translator of ancient manuscripts. I threw the information out to Ellen and Jill. At first there was a great resistance, then they agreed to meet him and now we are here.

"My feelings about the scrolls? I was dubious in the beginning. After reading the first translation, I knew within me it was no accident that Ellen and Jill discovered them. I have a background in quantum physics, and I know that nothing happens by accident."

Alain had been very quiet and still. He shook his head in amazement. "Mon dieu! It is truly a wonder none of you have been killed before now. I am amazed you have gotten this far. Tell me Peter, when you called Sebastian's home to locate him, did you place your call on either a credit card or phone card?"

"I placed it on my phone card. However, there was no need to use it again once we contacted Sebastian. The reason I left Paul's house, besides the fact that I was the one being sought, was that I felt I would be easy to spot with my height. Ellen chose to come with me."

"I am asking these questions because even though these odd cards are links between the two attacks, there must be something more that will lead us to who has been creating havoc in your lives. Did you or Ellen contact anyone once you left your friends in Toulouse?"

"No." Peter said. "Wait. Ellen did call her mother after we arrived in Paris, however she did not mention the scrolls or the events leading up to our arrival in Paris. And, I would like to know how you managed to put a tail on us."

"Inquiries revealed you rented a car in Carcassonne. My agents had begun a discreet investigation of possible cities and hotels where you might register. It was in Narbonne where your trail was picked up."

I chimed in, "Alain, why would you want to track us?"

"Forgive me, my newly-found sister. As I said earlier, I have had a passion to meet you. It was my thought that by finding you I could arrange a meeting. Never did I dream you would seek me out."

Turning back to Sebastian, Alain asked him if he had contacted anyone.

"Non. I was acting as an agent for my friend Paul Leseur. He had been informed his house had been rented for the summer. When I met Peter, Ellen and Jill, there was no need to inform Paul the rental had been canceled and Jill became the pretend renter."

"Jill, did you contact anyone?" She shook her head no.

"Tell me Sebastian, under what name did you register your car at the airport car park?"

Suddenly looking crestfallen, Sebastian replied, "My own. My driver's license and I.D. were requested." Smacking his forehead, he continued, "Mon dieu! I am the guilty one! I also paid with my bank cheque."

Squeezing his hand, Jill muttered, "What is done is done."

Alain held up his hand indicating for us not to become embroiled in this. "It is a possibility that some actions were unwise, however let us not jump to conclusions. Briefly, we have Monsieur Montand acting swiftly when your questioning by the police in Carcassonne made the television news."

Interrupting, Peter said, "I think there is something to be added to our story. The report that the cave and scrolls had been found was not made known in the media until a few weeks after Ellen and Jill were there, and it was another few weeks before the story of the missing Father Sebastian was reported. However in that newscast, an association between the scrolls and Sebastian was made. We thought it suspicious at the time."

"Yes, it appears odd that someone made the connection. Sebastian, please give me the name of your housekeeper as well as your home phone number and address, and I will have discreet inquiries made. This is indeed an interesting situation all of you are in. In the meantime I suggest you be comfortable for the night. Tomorrow may bring new revelations."

After Sebastian gave Alain the requested information, I asked if I could call my mother. For a moment Alain appeared a bit taken aback. "But of course. You are free to do as you wish. You may use my phone, as my guest." Standing up, Alain bid us goodnight and left the room.

We remained silent for a few moments. "Mes amies, are we guests or are we prisoners here?"

Peter spoke up. "I want to think we are guests who do not totally trust their host. Let's not read anything dire into this. After all, he told Ellen she was free to call her mother."

Jill let out a deep breath as if she had been holding it. "I agree with Peter. My head is twirling with the turn of events. What puzzles me is why anyone would be dumb enough to attempt a robbery in the Louvre?"

Then I voiced a thought. "Perhaps someone wanted to flush out the scrolls. Maybe whoever thinks we have them wanted it to be brought out into the open."

"I do not understand," Sebastian interjected. "How would they know we four were going to meet at the Louvre?"

Peter had a plausible scenario. "May I offer a hypothesis? I'm going back to the beginning when the young boy reported to the authorities he had seen two people leave a cave and the authorities investigated finding the two scrolls. Let's assume it was the local police in Mirepoix. They, in turn, recognized the importance and relayed the information on to whatever government archaeology department would need to be notified by law. It and the Bibliothèque nationale probably are one and the same. Regardless, when whoever it was received the information, the information was shared. Someone notified 'friends' with interests in ancient parchments and someone set up a search for the scrolls."

"Well, that makes sense," I said. "But, how did the connection with Sebastian come about?"

Sebastian answered by saying, "It could be that when the two scrolls left behind were examined, it was realized they were written in ancient Greek. In the past various people have contacted the Vatican seeking a translator of ancient languages. Perhaps my name was given to someone who would have been inquiring as to who could translate the scrolls. And I was tracked from Toulouse when I left my trail at the airport."

"This is all excellent reasoning, however I'm exhausted. I need to go to bed. Good night all," and with that Jill got up, giving Peter and me a kiss on the cheek.

"Ma chère, I will depart with you."

That left us alone in the living room. I suggested we go to our bedroom where I could place a call to Mother. Before leaving, Peter asked if we should put out the lights. Taking his hand, I said, "I think we will leave them on. Somehow I think there will be a clean-up fairy coming along soon."

Once in the bedroom, I found Mother's new phone number. Since California was about nine hours behind Paris time, I hoped she was not out. Fortunately she answered.

"Mother, this is Ellen."

"Oh my god! Ellen, where are you? We've been sick with worry. When I saw your and Jill's picture flash up on the television screen, I almost fainted. Are you in jail?"

Chuckling, I replied "No, Mother. I'm fine. It's a long story. I don't want to go into it now."

"Ellen, please don't shut me out. I have to know you really are all right."

"I'm not shutting you out, Mother. We're guests of a lawyer and we're in Paris. Mother, does the name Delacroix mean anything to you?"

There was a gasp from the other end of the phone. "Why do you ask Ellen?"

"I'm in the apartment of Alain Delacroix, the son of Maurice Delacroix."

There was no answering reply although I could hear Mother breathing heavily at the other end of the line.

"Mother, I know this is going to be a shock for you, however I'm in the apartment of your son."

Mother was audibly sobbing and I began to cry too. Stifling her sobs, she spoke, "Oh, Ellen. Oh, Ellen. How did you find out?"

"Mother, let's say it was divine providence that brought us together. I suggest you fly over here because he's been waiting to meet you for many years."

"I signed papers long ago that I wouldn't reveal myself to him. Maurice's wife has to be considered."

"Mother, she died a few years ago and your agreement died with her. We all have much to talk about."

"Yes, we do. And yes, I will catch a flight out as soon as I can."

Giving her Alain's office phone number, I suggested she leave word of her airline and flight number with his secretary. We murmured our love for each other, and I hung up.

Turning to Peter, I said, "My love, she's in shock. Perhaps I was too blunt with her but I didn't know how else to tell her," and I began to cry again.

Taking me in his arms, we lay on the bed while I sobbed my anguish out. I knew I had shocked Mother. I hadn't intended to hurt her and I cried for all the attention I had not given her. Perhaps I was also cleansing myself of all the fear and tension of the past few weeks. I sobbed myself to sleep and vaguely recall Peter undressing me and putting me to bed.

The following morning I awoke wondering where I was. Then the reality of the situation came back. I rolled over to discover that Peter was already up. Emerging from the bathroom, he grinned and lunged for me in bed. "I thought you might be wakening up soon so I have the shower ready. Okay?"

Of course it was. It was becoming a ritual for us to shower together and Peter could sense I wasn't in the mood for lovemaking. While toweling each other off, I told him I wanted to meditate for a few minutes. Saying he understood, he joined me.

The quieting of the busy mind and the stilling of the body works wonders. I began blessing my life as well as those who were in my life. I was finding the discipline of blessing enhanced my life. I had shared this with Peter and he had adopted blessing, too.

When we were done, we dressed and went out to the main room. Jill and Sebastian were already there drinking coffee. She said a buffet had been set up in the dining room but they were having coffee first. Gladly we joined them.

Over breakfast I told them of my conversation with Mother. I also told them she was flying over. Before anyone could comment, Alain walked in.

"I take it you each had a good slumber?" Not waiting for us to reply, he helped himself to the buffet and sat down.

It was difficult to read his countenance. Before I could say anything, he told us the packages had been retrieved from the poste. "I am having them brought up to you. They should arrive momentarily. I also have made an appointment for myself to meet with the Director of Antiquities of the Bibliothèque nationale. Inquiries are being made into the nature of the police investigation, plus some other discreet inquiries are being made on your behalf."

"Thank you, Alain," I said. "And I want to share with you my phone call to Mother last night."

Alain's fork paused in mid-air. Slowly he laid it down and looked at me questioningly.

"I told Mother we were staying in your apartment, and I told her we knew you are her son. She is flying to Paris."

Apparently this was a wee bit of a bombshell. His facial expression ran a gamut of mixed emotions. "I see," he finally said and quietly asked, "When is she arriving?"

"I don't know yet. I gave her your office phone number and she will leave her airline information with your secretary."

"Forgive me if I appear to be emotional at this piece of news. I have dreamed since I was eighteen of meeting her. Please excuse me." Quickly getting up, he left the room.

"Well!" exclaimed Jill. "Life is full of surprises. I didn't expect Mr. Cool-as-a-Cucumber to have a reaction like that."

Nor did I. Turning to Peter I said I was going to seek out Alain because I wanted to see the photo of my mother and his father together. Smiling, he said for me to go ahead and for his own peace of mind he wanted to pick Jill's and Sebastian's brains regarding the translations.

Walking out into the living room, I saw Alain standing with both hands in his pants pockets and looking out the large picture window.

"Alain, may I intrude?"

Turning around, he gave me a wan smile and motioned me to the conversation area where I sat on one of the chairs and he sat on one of the couches. He leaned forward and clasped his hands together.

"Forgive me, Ellen. I have lived the moment of meeting my mother for years. Now I find I am terrified. What if she rejects me? I have never felt this terrified in my entire life."

Reaching out, I touched his hands. "Alain, don't you think Mother is terrified also?"

"Really? I had not considered that possibility. I am also terrified of informing my father about this. Yet I know it is ridiculous."

"Ridiculous, no. You told me yesterday you had a photo of our mother and your father. May I please see it?"

"Of course. Remain here while I get it."

In a moment he returned with a 1950's-style snapshot. Some of his previous tenseness appeared to have lessened. Handing me the picture, he sat down and waited for me to study it.

It was definitely my mother. The picture had been taken along the Seine River in front of one of the bookstalls. Oh gawd, they looked happy. I felt a lump in my throat as I continued to study it. "Yes, they were definitely in love, and Alain you were conceived of that love. You are truly blessed."

Taking a deep breath, he relaxed more. "Thank you for telling me that. I needed this confirmation. My adopted mother was always stiff with me, and distant. I did not understand why until my father told me the story when I was 18. It was not love I received from her."

Handing the photo back to him, I asked if he had found out when Mother was arriving. My question brought him back to the present. "I will check with my office staff."

"Are you going to meet her flight?" I asked.

"No. I would prefer to meet her here. Will you go?"

"Of course. Actually I think it best if I go alone."

Getting up, Alain went into the dining room and asked the others to join us. Again we sat around the glass table. I had moved to the couch to sit next to Peter.

"Before I go to my office, is there anything you wish?"

"There is." Peter said. "What freedom do we have if we leave this apartment? Second, is there a secure house I can rent where we four may have privacy? Sebastian and Jill are eager to continue the translations."

Leaning forward, Alain responded, "It is not wise for any of you to move freely around Paris. The paparazzi will find you and dog your steps. It is a probability the police know you are with me. Regarding a house, perhaps this is the solution to keep you away from the paparazzi. I will have information by the end of the day. Is this satisfactory?"

We all said yes. Then Jill asked Alain if she could go pick up their belongings and check them out of the hotel. She needed to go herself because she also wanted to get a package she had left in the hotel safe. Alain said it would be best if one of his staff at least accompanied her. For safety, he requested Sebastian stay at the apartment.

After he left we continued sitting in the conversation area. It was as though none of us knew what to say. I took the opportunity to ask Sebastian about the Vatican and what it was like to work there.

"Ah, Ellen, it was not at all the spiritual place I had thought it to be. Soon after my arrival, disillusionment came quickly. It was filled with ambitious autocratic men. And I soon learned it was a cauldron seething with politics and vindictive gossip. As I have previously said, it did not take me long to realize that to survive I had to become – how do you say . . . invisible."

"Did you have any interaction with the Pope?" asked Peter.

"Non. He kept to his apartments. The few times we saw him were the moments he appeared on his balcony or on television. From my perspective his secretaries and the cardinals, who for the most part are vicious in their pursuit for control, controlled him. And yet, I do not think any of the popes were weak. They would have to be strong to gain the office."

218

I asked, "Were you there when John Paul I died? It is said he was murdered."

Shrugging his shoulders, Sebastian replied, "Oui, I was there. He could have been murdered. Again, it could have been natural causes. It may never be revealed as to who found the Pope's body. There were many conflicting rumors. If he were murdered, his close associates would have been in fear of their lives.

"It was common knowledge the Vatican Bank was involved with the Mafia, and it had become a scandal within the walls of the Vatican. It was said this new Pope John Paul I, who took office after Paul VI, was intending to make changes in the positions of some of the cardinals, perhaps even removing the cardinal who was head of the bank. It was also said Pope John Paul I had not sought the papacy, however he also had a dream of restoring the Church to follow the teachings of Jesus. He wanted to return the Church to be for the poor, and that would mean major changes. Oui, it could have been murder. There were a number of murders in connection with the Vatican Bank or so it is rumored.

"There were over a thousand priests working in the Vatican. It was rife with rumors appearing to be inspired by self-interests. There were ones who seemed bent on creating gossip for motives I do not know. No one wanted to take responsibility for any mishap. They are very concerned about how they will appear to others. Much, much later the rumors said Pope John Paul I was quite ill and was a very weak pope who had a death wish, but I do not believe this. From what I observed at the beginning of his papacy, this was not so."

Jill began speaking, "'Alas! Constantine, how much misfortune you caused. Not by becoming Christian, but by the dowry which the first rich Father accepted from you.'"

Sebastian smiled, "Ah, Jill, you have studied Dante."

"Yes I have. He wrote that in the *Inferno*. Constantine, when he created the Christian church, gave an extremely large amount of wealth to Pope Silvester I."

"Then, Silvester was the first rich pope," I commented. "What else can you tell us?

"Ah. An example of a pope becoming rich was Pope Pius XII – the Pope during the World War II. He operated on both sides of the fence, as you Americans say. It is said he took money from both sides. Not only that, but he was not a kind pope.

"It is documented he had a deep hatred and contempt for the Jews, and he did nothing to stop the holocaust of Hitler. Not only Jews, but also Gypsies were exterminated. Most people have knowledge of the Inquisition doing horrible acts of the Church and this was a form of an inquisition.

"The popes of history used many tactics to eradicate Jews and Gypsies. The holocaust in Croatia is an example. The Vatican spawned it using the reasoning that the Jews killed Jesus. The Gypsies? They were considered inferior humans. It was the Church in medieval times that first made Jews wear yellow stars for identification. If one were to truly study the hidden history it would be devastating." Sebastian was becoming agitated, however he continued.

"Pius the IX, the pope in office around 1846, became involved in a scandal after he had been in office about twelve years. The papal police kidnapped a small Jewish boy because his parents had not converted to Christianity. The Pope adopted him, playing with the boy often and it is documented he was seen hiding the boy under his soutane[1] while calling out 'Where's the boy?' The public became outraged over this display and the incident made international news. Even the third Napoleon of France and the Emperor of Austria begged the Pope to return the boy to his parents, to no avail. The Pope retained him in a monastery. Later the boy, having grown up, became a priest."

"Sebastian," I asked, "are you indicating this Pope was possibly a pedophile?"

"Oui." Sebastian stopped to compose his agitation.

I could not contain myself. "There apparently has always been a history of pedophilia in the Church and it probably has always been rampant. Thank god it is being revealed more and more."

"Oui Ellen. What can I say? I knew and I observed, while saying nothing."

Peter spoke up saying he had heard that living in the Vatican was very much like living in a goldfish bowl. Smiling,

---

[1] Soutane: refers to a priest's or pope's habit or cassock.

Sebastian answered, "Oui. The goldfish bowl effect does not reflect outwardly to the world and is not well known. Among the priests it has been described as a palace of eunuchs. The description most fitting is 'a decadent palace that floats on a flood of lies and deceit.'"

Softly, Jill entered the conversation. "No wonder you became ill. From what I have read, historically the Church has never been a spiritual organization. It was created on one man's desire for power and control. Constantine created the Church, not Peter. It wasn't founded on the teachings of Jesus either because Jesus' message was one of love and truth."

"Oui. It is true. I will have to say in defense of those few priests who have motives of living what Jesus taught, they are in a minority and often hidden away in obscurity. It is said John Paul I was a pastoral priest who cared for the people. It is my sense he was treading on entrenched toes."

I couldn't help it and I still wanted to know about the promiscuity of the priests and nuns.

Sebastian said he didn't have any firsthand knowledge. Again, there were many rumors and gossip.

"One might say it was common knowledge many were not celibate. In the writings of old documents, this was alluded to. In fact, Pope Julius II had numerous mistresses resulting in three daughters that are known. It is written that from one of his various lovers he contracted the disease known as syphilis. One of the eyewitness accounts written is that syphilis was 'very fond of priests, especially very rich priests.'[2] I cannot verify those rumors of today. What I observed were priests who were heavy drinkers and smokers. Beyond this, I have no firsthand knowledge."

"Thank you Sebastian, for enlightening us with what must be painful for you to talk about," I said.

"I will tell you this, it has been Jill who has helped me redeem my soul. I feel as if I have been born into a new life."

Peter had been listening and with a smile said, "Sebastian, you don't have to answer this, but were you one of

---

[2] From *At* the *Court of the Borgias, Being an Account of the Reign of Pope Alexander VI Written by His Master of Ceremonies, Johann Burchard,* ed. and trans. Geoffrey Parker (London, Folio Society 1963)

those drinking priests? We've been drinking a lot of wine since we came together with you."

We all laughed and Jill, with a twinkle in her eyes, told us she had been thinking the same thing.

Looking a bit sheepish, Sebastian told us he had done his share of drinking, however he also knew he could do without it every day.

Nodding his head in agreement, Peter changed the subject and asked, "You and Jill told us about your miraculous healing. Have you considered having a medical checkup? This would prove to the world you have been healed."

"Oui. Jill and I have discussed this. Do you think now is the time?"

"Indeed I do," Peter said.

"Since it is apparently known you are no longer missing, let's ask Alain for the name and number of a physician here in Paris. It will be to your benefit," I interjected.

"Oui. I agree. This I will do. Merci."

The timing couldn't have been better. The elevator door opened and Alain's secretary Michele came in with the packages retrieved from the poste. Sebastian stood up, barely containing his excitement.

I think we all breathed a sigh of relief when he began taking them from her. "Merci for retrieving these for us. All appear to be in order."

Michele nodded acceptance of his appreciation. Speaking English with a French accent, she had messages for us from Alain: Ellen's mother would be arriving the next morning at nine o'clock and Alain would have a car ready at six-thirty.

She also said, "Monsieur Delacroix requests you consider speaking with the press. If you agree, he will set up the meeting with him attending with you. This can be discussed this evening at dinner. In the meantime, he is speaking with Inspector Gautier regarding developments. He is also making inquiries regarding a Gilbert Montand, and I am to await your reply."

I told Michele we would discuss the press conference amongst ourselves. I thanked her for coming and said we looked forward to dining with Alain that evening.

Peter chuckled. "Alain appears to be a mover and a shaker."

"What is a 'mover and a shaker?'" asked Sebastian.

"It means someone who operates fast and gets things done."

"Ah, oui. He does seem to operate at a fast pace. What are your thoughts of a press meeting?"

I said, "Well, it has its advantages and its disadvantages. On the one hand it might take the media pressure off us, thereby giving us more freedom to move about. On the other hand, well, it could be disastrous. I want to hear what the rest of you think."

Jill spoke up. "I am petrified of a news conference. All I want is to be in a quiet place where Sebastian and I can finish the translations."

"Mes amis, I am in agreement with Jill. I too am petrified at facing the news media."

Leaning forward, Peter spoke. "I suggest before we come to any decision we get Alain's input regarding why he suggested this. Like Ellen said, it could alleviate some of the pressure, and we would be satisfying the media for the time being."

"Since we have most of the day before us, I want to hear about the translations Jill and Sebastian did after we left."

"Ah oui. Perhaps Jill will assist me in opening these packages; and if we are able to secure the use of a computer, it will be done as you requested Ellen. Un moment."

The bell rang announcing the arrival of someone. The butler/valet answered the elevator door, and a member of Alain's staff came in with our belongings from the rental house, including the laptop computer. Sebastian's request for a computer was fulfilled. Providence was with us again.

Introducing himself as Louis St. Pierre, he informed us he was also there to take Jill to the hotel to retrieve their belongings and to check out.

Sebastian and Peter said all was working out perfectly. While Jill was gone, they would install the programs on the computer. I felt like I was getting cabin fever, so I elected to go with Jill.

We accompanied Louis down to the lower level where cars were parked and were escorted into a four-door black sedan with darkened windows, which gave us privacy. Skillfully Louis made his way through the Paris traffic to the hotel address Jill had given him. We didn't say too much during the ride because Louis could hear everything. Our conversation was primarily on Paris and our last visit there.

Pulling up in front of the hotel, Louis got out first. He came around and opened the door for Jill. I could see he was looking around to see if there were any suspicious characters nearby. I felt like we were in a cops and robbers movie.

Casually he followed her into the hotel after first locking me in the car and within 15 minutes they were back. Jill had speedily packed their luggage and checked out after retrieving the box left in the hotel safe.

After Louis unlocked the car, she got in smiling. Quickly he stowed the luggage in the trunk and we were on our way back to Alain's.

By the time we arrived at the penthouse apartment, the French to English and Greek to French programs had been installed on the computer, as well as the files containing the translated scrolls. While we had been away, Peter had spoken with the butler. (I've decided to call him a butler; and his name was Jean-Pierre.) He had brought in a plate of petite sandwiches with wine and glasses, so we had a light lunch waiting for us on the glass table.

Noticing that Peter's computer didn't have a printer, Jill volunteered to read the next scroll in sequence from the computer screen.

But first, we toasted to the completion of the translations.

THE FINAL DAYS OF YESHUA
Scroll 12

We each knew we had a destiny and we knew there would come a time when we would part. We talked of it often, as it was a tumultuous period of unrest. We knew Yeshua was bringing forth a change from the Tenakh of the Hebrews into a new way of belief and we were planting concepts and ideas long suppressed for eons in humans. We knew we were to plant seeds in the minds of the forgotten gods to awaken a suppressed memory. Each one is a god. There is not one God, because all people have been birthed from the Mind of the One. Thus we were committed.

There are levels to initiations. I have already committed to papyrus that there are in our body seven doors. Each door leads to a higher vibration for another plane of awareness. The first three doors are below our mid-body. These doors must be opened and mastered before we can open the remaining four.

The fourth door is the door of love and it resides next to the heart. This love is love of self, for all people and love of all life. There can be no judgments or prejudices. At this door, the initiate is mastering good and evil.

The fifth door is the door to truth and to go through this door, the initiate must master speaking what one knows to be truth. It is a difficult door to go through because men have been taught since birth to hide their thoughts and feelings and so have women.

The sixth door is the door to knowing beyond what the lower man knows. The knowledge that the mind attains is beyond the understanding of lower man. By not understanding, lower man will attempt to destroy that which he does not know. The sixth door is in the head along with the seventh door.

The seventh door is the door to reunion with the One from whence we come. This door can only be entered when the initiate is able to control his or her body by using the mind and understanding the power of will. The initiate must be in tune with every nerve in the body because the body is being tuned to a very high vibration.

Many have attempted the final initiation and only a few have attained it. Usually the final initiation is given in the Temple in Egypt. However, there are initiates such as Yeshua and I who can initiate another as a testing to determine if the one wishing to be initiated is ready to be sent to Egypt.

One day Lazarus came to Yeshua and asked to be initiated. Yeshua denied him. A few days later Lazarus approached Yeshua again requesting initiation. Again Yeshua denied him. When Lazarus came a third time and requested initiation, Yeshua could not deny him because he had asked three times.

The initiation required Lazarus to be placed in a tomb for three days and three nights. During this time in darkness, all of his inner thoughts would come to him. Some say these are demons and some have gone into this initiation and have not come out alive. All parts of the body are challenged as well as the brain.

The tomb selected was near the home of Lazarus and Martha. Lazarus was placed in the tomb with the entrance sealed. No one could go near it for three days and three nights. When the three days and three nights were up, Lazarus was to emerge and Yeshua, as part of the initiation placed his mind on Lazarus, and Yeshua called him forth. Yeshua opened the tomb and Lazarus emerged. He had accomplished going through the fifth door, but not beyond. Lazarus told us that he felt like he had been born again. In one way he had. Lazarus asked that his name be changed to Ioannes as he had great reverence for Ioannes the Immerser as well as Yeshua.

Initiations are not to be taken lightly and only those with the strongest desire should call for an initiation. Some who think they are ready but are not, come out and regress to their old ways or they can go forward with the knowledge they have. Some have even been known to die. I know because I had failed an initiation in a previous lifetime and died.

I found I was again with child, however I continued with my duties as a priestess in the Temple. I curtailed my travels and I did not travel unless I was with Yeshua. He had a large following and I never tired of hearing him teach. During one of our journeys, we were on the north shores of a lake called Galilee. A great multitude of people began to gather. Yeshua along with his apostles, and I with mine, began walking to a nearby slope where Yeshua could talk with them. The people were clamoring to see and to hear him.

It was afternoon when we reached a place where Yeshua could stand and look out over the multitude. He was adored and worshiped by these people and I knew he was having inner turmoil. It is easy to fall into the trap of being worshiped. This was the temptation within him.

Yeshua began to speak and he mesmerized the people. Suddenly he stopped. I could sense he was struggling with this temptation. He had to make a decision. Would he speak as the son of man or as the Son of God? If he spoke as the Son of

God, he knew he would be killed for this heresy. Knowing his thoughts, I was also battling them with him. He stood there for what seemed like hours while the people waited patiently for him to speak. I knew I could only observe his mind but I could not intrude.

The late afternoon sun was beginning to make its descent when he spoke. "This one thing you must do. Love the God that you are with all your heart, mind, soul and life." I gasped, because I knew he was now speaking as the Son of God. Tears flowed down my face and I knew he would surely be put to death. There was a part of me wanting to scream No! Yet I also honored him for his decision, for it was his alone. He was willing to die for what he knew to be truth.

There was a sound of a nighthawk as Yeshua continued with his voice becoming stronger.

> *Blessed are the poor in spirit for they possess the land.*
>
> *Blessed are they that mourn; for they shall be comforted.*
>
> *Blessed are the meek, for theirs is the land.*
>
> *Blessed are they which do hunger and thirst after justice, for they shall be filled.*
>
> *Blessed are the merciful, for they shall obtain mercy.*
>
> *Blessed are the pure in heart, for they shall see God.*
>
> *Blessed are the peacemakers, for they shall be called the children of God.*
>
> *Blessed are they which are persecuted for righteousness' sake, for theirs is the kingdom of heaven.*
>
> *Blessed are you, when men shall revile you, and persecute you, and shall say all manner of evil against you falsely, for my sake.*
>
> *Rejoice and be glad, for great is your reward in heaven; for so persecuted were they, the prophets which were before you.*

As he spoke, my tears continued to silently flow down my face. I had my small son at my feet and another child in my womb. James the Younger plucked at my robe and looking up at me, asked, "Momma, why cry you?" I could only bend down and kiss the top of his head and somehow I managed to whisper, "My tears are of joy for what your father is speaking." I knew for one to speak as God delivers people from the bondage of a vengeful god.

Yeshua continued on. "Let your light so shine before men that they may see your good works and glorify your Father in Heaven." His teaching was lengthy and it is inscribed in my mind. He told us to love one another and to love our self. I knew he was truly inspired to impart the truth of God, which is in everyone. I also knew my greatest ordeal was to come.

Again, the sound of the nighthawk could be heard. The sun was waning. One of the apostles brought him a meager meal of 5 fish and 2 loaves of bread. Yeshua looking at him said, "Feed my people." The apostle replied, "Master, we have no food but this. Send them away to find their own food."

Yeshua looked at him replying, "Give me the loaves and the fish," which the man did. Slowly Yeshua began breaking the fish and the loaves into pieces. He placed the pieces in a basket, telling his apostles to go out and feed the people. The multitude was great and I assessed them to be five thousand in number. When the basket was returned to Yeshua, he filled it up again and asked for more baskets. When all the people were filled, there were baskets left over. He was magnificent in bringing forth more loaves and fishes and he was a Son of God.

Yeshua turned to the multitude, telling them that what he did, they could also do. He told them he came not to bring peace on earth, but a sword of Truth. He was the sword bearer of Truth. The Truth being that they were all forgotten gods of the Great One, the Creator of All. He told them the old must fall away to make way for the new, for one cannot put new wine in old wine skins.

As darkness settled down like a shroud, Yeshua told them, "I must go now." He reached down and he pulled me up from the ground. He bent down, kissing James and also me. The multitude dispersed and we made our way to a lone spot where we laid our cloaks down to sleep upon. I was cradled in

Yeshua's arms and James was in mine. We didn't speak but soon sleep overcame us. When I awakened, I knew Yeshua was also awake.

He spoke. "You already know there is a possibility I may die. As much as I love you and my children, I must live my Truth."

Stifling a sob, I gently moved James and sat up. I looked down at Yeshua. "My beloved, Truth and the love of God must come before all else. What will be will be." We embraced and then arose.

We met with all the apostles. Yeshua was urged not to go into Jerusalem, because he would be put to death. Petros was the most vocal and Yeshua smiled and asked Petros if he loved him. Petros replied, "Oh yes, Master." Yeshua asked again and his answer was the same. Yeshua was quiet for a moment, and then he asked the question again. Petros again replied, "Yes, Master, I love you."

I kept silent, because I knew this was Yeshua's journey. Within me, my heart felt heavy as a leaden stone. Yeshua told us he must go to Jerusalem, because it was the beginning of the Passover. Thomas his twin spoke, saying, "If he is to die, then we should all be willing to die and go with him."

Before the gathering dispersed, Yeshua charged young Ioannes with looking after me, and our children. Ioannes questioned this and Yeshua replied, "If it is to be, it will be. I want to ensure my wife and children are taken care of. Be with her at the birthing." Ioannes agreed saying, "Would that I could go with you."

"That cannot be for I go where you cannot follow yet." All left with mixed emotions. Several were saying among themselves, "The Master sounded as if it was certain he would be taken by the Romans. Does this mean that we will be also?" What Yeshua had spoken on the slope apparently had fallen on deaf ears and they did not hear his message.

We traveled to Jerusalem with heavy hearts. I asked Meesha to take young James and return to the Temple while I continued on with Yeshua. Before entering the city, Yeshua was given an ass to sit upon and ride. This was an ancient rite of a king riding into a city to be crowned. I walked behind him as throngs turned out, waving palm fronds.

Going to the house of a friend, his apostles and I followed him to an upper room where a table had been set. This could perhaps be our last supper together. I had carried with me spikenard and I bent down to anoint his feet when he took the spikenard from my hands and bade me to be seated.

Yeshua began anointing each of our feet. One of the apostles cried out that we were not worthy to have our feet anointed by him. Yeshua said, "Why deny me this privilege? The least of you among us is the greatest and the greatest among you is the least." He returned to the anointing. When he came to me, in a voice full of emotion, he said, "The last shall be first and the first shall be last."

Our meal was meager. We had bread, wine and bitter herbs. Yeshua spoke to us regarding Truth as the message he came to teach, and the greater Truth is that each of us is god. He told us we should honor ourselves. He again said, as he did on the slope by the lake of Galilee, "Love the Lord your God with all your heart, soul, life and all your mind."

Yeshua broke the bread, giving each of us a piece. "Eat of this bread and honor your body as you honor me. Think of me when you eat, as it represents my body. This is also your body."

Yeshua asked that our goblets be filled with wine. He told us the wine represents the Spirit. Always revere the wine as the gods brought the grapes here. "When you drink of the wine, remember me because I am the fruit of the vine." He went on to tell us water is symbolic of the Soul. "Honor your Soul and complete its journey. For those of you who have the ears to hear and the eyes to see, remember, I am with you always."

Yeshua said by morning one of us would deny him. Peter cried out, "Not I!"

Yeshua smiled, again saying, before the cock crows, one would deny him three times. With that he arose to leave, asking that no one follow him, as he desired to be alone. I could see he was filled with anguish and I chose not to intrude on his moments. I was having my own anguish.

Yeshua went to be alone in a garden near the Mount of Olives, while I returned to my quarters at the Temple to be with our son. I was weary and of heavy heart. Upon arrival I went into prayer until morning when I heard a cock crow. With a feeling of alarm I arose at the sound of Meesha knocking on my door.

"Oh Mariam!" she spoke with anguish. "They have taken the Rabbi!" I was asking for details when the High Priestess came in and she asked Meesha to take young James and to give him something to eat and drink. James clung to me. I kissed him and I whispered all was well and for him to go. With tears streaming down his face he left with Meesha.

Salome told me what she had learned. Judas Iscariot went to the Romans and betrayed Yeshua. It seems Judas had gone to the Romans, agreeing to point out Yeshua for a sum of money. He led them in the dark of night to the garden where Yeshua was praying. He entered the garden and gave Yeshua a kiss as a way of marking him. The soldiers seized Yeshua taking him to the Fort of San Antonio to see Pontius Pilate.

My calmness was shattered and I wept in Salome's arms, and as I wept, all the pent up sorrow, anger and anguish poured out of me. At last I slept.

Chapter 19

THE MESSAGE

Know the truth and the truth will set you free.
- Bible John 8:32

When Jill finished reading the scroll, I was in tears. Each of us was touched deeply and we sat for a few moments without speaking. Peter handed me his handkerchief and I noticed I wasn't the only one touched. He had a few tears in his eyes, and Sebastian and Jill had tears rolling down their cheeks.

Haltingly, Sebastian spoke. "She wrote the words of the Beatitudes from the Sermon on the Mount."

"Yes," commented Peter. "If all religions taught and lived what Jesus spoke, there would be no hypocrisy, jealousy or prejudice."

"Why is it humanity ignores his teachings? Have we become so debased that we are immune to the horrid effects of war, power and prejudice?" I asked.

"Ellen, you speak the truth, and I think perhaps the reason for inventing a devil was to turn one's attention away from these teachings. In my research I discovered, or realized, that the idea of the devil or Satan was invented when Christianity was created," Sebastian replied.

"I agree," Peter said. "A devil is a very convenient scapegoat to avoid taking responsibility for ones actions. It also keeps one's focus on fear, which diverts attention away from the real teachings. I think it was the television character Geraldine whose excuse was 'The devil made me do it,'" and we all chuckled at that. It brought a little levity to us.

Jill had remained quiet until now. "We can say that the Buddhists do not promote war, however they do not include women as equal to men. Therefore the teachings of Buddha have also been debased. It is my understanding that Buddha revered women and didn't make his teachings exclusive for men."

I agreed. "All religions are prejudiced against women. I think it most odd since women are the ones who birth the men. Sometimes I wonder if some of these religionists think they were birthed in an incubator."

Before I could continue in this vein, Jean-Pierre came in to say dinner that evening would be at seven o'clock with Alain joining us. He asked us if we would like to have a light lunch and we agreed.

Sitting at the dining table, we were treated to steaming French onion soup and wonderful bread. The cheese on top was stringy and delicious, and Jean-Pierre kept our wine glasses filled. Salad and fruit followed the soup. We declined dessert, opting for coffee in the living room where we continued discussing the scroll. We agreed it was most interesting that Lazarus changed his name and became known as John.

"Could he be John the Beloved?" I asked.

"Oui, it is an obvious conclusion. The Old Testament has name changes. Abraham's wife's name changed from Sarai to Sarah. Another notable name change was Jacob to Israel."

"I wonder?" I mused. "What if the name changes denoted the completion of an initiation?"

The others thought that was an intriguing possibility. And we wanted to hear what the next scroll said.

కించ్ కించ్ కించ్

THE CRUCIFIXION
Scroll 13

Suddenly I was awakened by the anguished cries of Mariamme as she burst into my quarters. "Mariam! Mariam! They have taken him!" She fell upon my bed sobbing. For a moment I could not move. My body was like a stone. I willed myself and I reached out to her saying, "Yes, I know."

When she realized I had been sleeping, she sat up, and began chastising me. "How can you sleep while your husband is being scourged!"

At that moment the High Priestess entered saying, "Mariamme, she was up all night. Why deny her a few moments sleep for she and her child yet to be born?"

Still sobbing, she replied, "Forgive me. I am so distraught. Pilate has condemned Yeshua to be crucified."

Moaning, I said, "How can that be?"

Another priestess had entered the room, giving Mariamme a soothing drink and handing me one also. Trembling, Mariamme drank. "I have learned when the soldiers took Yeshua to Pilate, Pilate asked him if he were the King of the Jews. Yeshua said 'You say it is so,' and not once did he acknowledge he was truly the King."

Upon questioning her more, the High Priestess drew out the story. Pilate had him scourged 72 times. At this point I cringed because I knew that he was whipped with a leather thong with small balls of metal attached to the ends of each thong. I had seen a scourging of a criminal and he had his flesh cut to the bone. I sobbed as I listened.

When the scourging was finished the soldiers dressed him in a purple robe, and then a crown of woven thorns was placed on his head with the thorns being pressed into his skull. Pilate had not wanted to kill Yeshua and the scourging was Pilate's act of punishment. He asked the Sanhedrin to agree to his release but they refused.

Herod Antipas, the Tetrarch of Galilee, was in Jerusalem for the Passover so the Sanhedrin conferred with him as Yeshua was considered a citizen of Galilee. Herod did not give approval of the release.

Upon hearing of this, Pilate went to his balcony where a huge throng had gathered. Most were the same people who greeted Yeshua with the palm fronds when he entered Jerusalem. The mob shouted for his death until Pilate said, "I wash my hands of this affair," meaning he would not take responsibility. The Sanhedrin demanded his death and Pilate gave Yeshua over to the Sanhedrin.

I asked Mariamme what was occurring now. She said he would be taken to the Place of Golgotha for the crucifixion. I arose to put on a clean robe and I made sure Meesha would care for James while Mariamme and I went to the prison where Thomas joined us, and after a short wait, the soldiers brought

Yeshua out, making him carry a heavy wooden beam on his back.

I held back my utterance of horror. With blood running down his face, he slowly began his walk and I could see the blood seeping through the purple robe. It looked to be the color of dark wine. At times he staggered. There came a moment when the centurion in charge halted, calling forth a great Nubian called Simon Cyrene, to carry the beam for Yeshua.

Laborious was the walk, and I, along with Mariamme and Thomas, walked the way with him. At times tears blinded my eyes. Oh how I wanted to reach out to him, but the soldiers kept us all away. This was Yeshua's final walk, and he was willing to die for his Truth because he knew he would be a false teacher and a betrayer if he did not live and die for Truth.

After what seemed to be an endless journey, we came to the Place of Golgotha. There were two thieves to be put to death also. Yeshua's stauros[1] was in place between the two. The people gathered were silent. Simon Cyrene laid the crossbeam on the ground in front of the stauros. Yeshua was commanded to lie down with his shoulders on the crossbeam and with his arms stretched out. Yeshua's wrists were tied to the crossbeam. The wrists were not nailed. Of the two ways, I was relieved the nails were not used. I later learned this way was used because he was already near death. He was bleeding heavily.

When the lashing was secured, he was raised to the stauros that is always kept in place for crucifixions. The crossbeam with Yeshua lashed to it was placed on the stauros. My tears blinded my eyes as he was being raised. The stauros and the beam looked like the sign of the Tau,[2] and above his head was placed a sign in both Greek and Latum reading, "King of the Jews."

At times I felt faint but I would not leave. The crucifixion's purpose was to suffocate the person into death. To keep breathing, the victim had to try and hold himself upright.

---

[1] Stauros: an upright pole or stake
[2] Tau: the indisputable sign of Tammuz or Tammus; the young Sun incarnate, the Sun-divinity incarnate

For three hours or more we knelt there waiting for the death to come. The priests of the Sanhedrin stood and watched also.

A moment came when one of the thieves spoke saying, "If you are the King of the Jews, why don't you save yourself and save us all?"

The other thief said, "Remember me when you reach Paradise."

Yeshua spake to the second thief, "You will be with me in Paradise."

The sky was becoming darker as the day was approaching sundown. Yeshua said, "I thirst," and he was given wine mixed with vinegar on a branch of hyssop.

Under Jewish law there could be no one left on the Tau after the sun went down. This was the beginning of the Sabbath, a holy day for Jews. The soldiers began to break the legs of the thieves because it would hasten the suffocation. Then Yeshua cried out, "Oh God, Oh God. Rescue me." [3]

My heart lurched, because I knew it was the beginning of a psalm in the Torah. It was a cry of anguish along with a song of praise. Silently, I began saying it with him. The sky grew darker and before the soldiers could break his legs, Yeshua spake, "Father, into your hands I commend my Spirit." With that he was gone.

A great wind came up suddenly with the sky becoming almost black. There was thunder and the earth shook and the ones watching were filled with fear. Not I, as I knew he was not truly dead.

Joseph had asked Pilate for the body of Yeshua and it was granted unto him. The body was taken down and carried by Joseph's men. I walked behind, along with Mariamme and Thomas to a nearby garden with a tomb for burial because this had to be done swiftly before the Sabbath began.

Joseph was waiting for us and just outside the tomb I saw a large rock was there. Hastily Yeshua was placed in the tomb without the ritual of anointing and we knew it would have to be done after the Sabbath. Pilate had ordered two soldiers to stand guard to prevent anyone from moving the

---

[3] Bible: Psalms 71:4

body. Joseph had engaged a host of strong men to move the large rock to cover the front of the opening.

As Thomas accompanied me back to the Temple, I remarked that Yeshua had been betrayed by most of his family as well as his apostles. Thomas replied, "Not all his apostles, because I am one also."

Upon entering the Temple, I stopped and prayed before I sought out Meesha and James. I knew by his eyes that James knew his father was gone. There was no need for words. We embraced each other and James asked if he could sleep with me. I could not deny him that.

Meesha brought a light supper and I knew I had to eat something for the child within me. I fell into an exhausted sleep. When I awakened, I lay abed as if I were dead, as I could not move my body. When my awareness became clearer, I realized James had risen and was gone. Blessed be I for Meesha was my thinking. I was bereft of tears.

When I at last had the strength to arise, I cleansed myself and I put on a clean robe. I then sat by an open window gazing out into the garden. I realized the sun was overhead and I knew I had slept long. I felt a stirring in my belly and I rejoiced that I had something of Yeshua within me. I began speaking to the child in a soothing voice. The child had been through much the past few days. I placed my hands on my belly while singing softly a song.

On the morning after the Sabbath I went to the tomb to anoint the body for its final burial. I was entering the garden when I heard a loud noise followed by a flash of light and I stepped aside to allow the guards to run past me in fright. As I continued on, I saw the rock had been moved. With a leap in my chest, I stopped and saw two strange looking men emerging with Yeshua's body. I was transfixed as a beam of light surrounded them and in a moment they were gone. It was as if a beam of light had come down from the sky. I stood transfixed for some moments.

Without thinking, I entered the tomb. There I saw a radiant being whose countenance lit up the tomb. The being spoke to me. "Mariam, why do you mourn? Yeshua has returned to his Father, who sent him. Rejoice. Go and tell the others he is risen. They will see him again." He disappeared before my very eyes. Again, I was transfixed. When I came back to the present, I went to Joseph who waited with James the brother and great was our joy. We called the apostles together sharing the news of Yeshua who had risen from the dead.

The apostles, when they learned of Yeshua's ascension, wailed and bemoaned because they had not been there to witness it. I particularly watched Petros. He had been seen in the Hebrew temple and it was reported he was pointed out as an apostle of Yeshua. Three times did he deny Yeshua just as Yeshua had said he would do. There were accusations hurled at me and also at Judas Iscariot but this was to be expected.

I placed no thought to the accusers because I had the children to think about. I was so blessed to have Meesha with me. There was little support from some of Yeshua's family. James the Younger was old enough to understand so I told him what had happened. "Mother, I won't leave you," he said as he placed his arms around me.

Chapter 20

THE MEETING

We are born for love.
It is the principle of existence and its only end.
- Benjamin Disraeli

After Jill had read the latest translation to us, we sat in silence for a few moments. There was so much to digest mentally. Peter stretched his long legs before standing up. With his hands in his pockets, he walked over to the windows. As he turned toward us, he said, "She's one hell of a woman. It's hard to imagine a wife watching her husband being crucified."

"You are so right, Peter," I said. "In addition, she was pregnant, carrying their second child. Jill, thank you for reading this. The Magdalene's writing about this makes it more real for me."

"I really don't need thanks because I enjoy doing this. When I first translated this scroll, the crucifixion became more real for me, too. I am intrigued that she did not write of him being on a cross. She called it a Tau."

I asked Sebastian what he knew about the Tau and the cross.

He thought for a moment. "From the research I have done, the Greeks had no word for cross. The Tau is also the nineteenth letter of the Greek language. It is also correct, as she wrote, that the Tau cross is a very old symbol used by many ancient civilizations as a symbol for sun deities. Constantine used it too, and the Egyptians used it in the form of an ankh. Based on historical information I can accept the Tau.

"I feel privileged to do these translations. These scrolls must be released to the world!"

Jill reached over and took Sebastian's hand. "Let us hope the world is ready for them. For hundreds of years great ones have attempted to tell the truth. Those who want control over the people conduct wars, inquisitions and holocausts to

239

destroy truth. I am seeing that truth never dies. It is a sleeping dragon waiting to be awakened."

"What you and Jill are saying may be true, and I think we should look at our own situation. The main assassination method today is character assassination. Are we strong enough to withstand persecution and ridicule?" When he finished, Peter looked at each of us.

I was the first to reply. "I couldn't live with myself if I caved-in to caring what others think. I know there are thousands of people who are out there waiting to hear something like this. No. I'm not afraid." Standing up, I walked over to Peter and placed my arms around him.

"I agree with Ellen," Jill said. "After what we each have already gone through, I think we all have the courage to see this through."

Sebastian was smiling. "Bon, mes amies. There can be no turning back. We must complete these translations." Turning to Jill he asked, "Ma chère, will you accompany me to get a medical examination? I wish to know my condition even more so now."

Laughing, Jill hugged him. "Of course, my darling. I know your old condition has disappeared."

Michele called to say Sebastian's statements of resignation from the priesthood and renunciation of his vows to the Church had been drawn up, and that she was having a staff member bring them up for his perusal. She also suggested he read them and wait until Alain arrived before signing them.

Soon a courier arrived with an envelope. Sebastian signed for it and began reading the documents that were written in French. "This appears to be what I want to say, however, I will await Alain's arrival before signing." He thanked the messenger for waiting while he read.

After the courier left, we chose to go to our separate bedrooms to rest before dinner, and Peter and I were not in the mood to check the news on television. We both chose to take a nap. I was dreaming when the jangle of the telephone intruded, bringing me back to awareness. Peter answered it. Jean-Pierre was calling to say cocktails would be served at six o'clock. Peter turned to me saying we had half an hour to rise and shine.

For once we were in the living room before Jill and Sebastian, however they followed us in shortly. For the four of us, wine was preferable to cocktails and Jean-Pierre already knew that. Within minutes Alain came in from his rooms. Greeting Jill and me with a kiss on the cheek, he shook hands with Sebastian and Peter.

He asked if we were comfortable and of course, we were. Turning to Sebastian, he asked if the documents had met with his approval. Sebastian replied they had and that he was prepared to sign them. He pulled the documents towards himself as Alain was handing him a pen, and with a flourish, they were signed.

"My friend, with the stroke of the pen you are no longer a priest," beamed Alain.

Jill proposed a toast to freedom and we gave a grand one. Alain went on to tell Sebastian the documents would be sent to the Vatican with a copy to the Archdiocese.

"Now to other business. I have been in touch with Inspector Gauthier. The two men apprehended at the Louvre appear to be petty thieves hired by an anonymous person or persons. As your avocat, I strongly suggest you relate to the Inspector what you have told me."

Jill was the first to speak up. "I choose not to do that until after there is an agreement with the Bibliothèque nationale. My gut feeling is there is a strong chance the scrolls would be taken away before we can negotiate."

"Oui. I agree with Jill. This is not acceptable," Sebastian added.

"Since the two of you are the ones attacked," Alain replied, "I will abide by your decisions. Will you agree to my giving a statement to the press on your behalf, to the effect that you have nothing to say at this time? I will also state that anything you would say now could impede the police investigation."

Sebastian looked at Jill. She nodded. "I think Sebastian and I can accept that."

Alain looked at us. "My inquiries regarding Gilbert Montand indicate he has been dismissed from the hospital and has returned to his home in the Languedoc region. He has no known record of affiliation with any organization that could be suspected. Of course, this does not rule out other organizations. I am intrigued with the two symbols on the cards you gave me. The Knights of Malta are known for the eight-pointed cross

241

which is better known as the Maltese Cross, although I have not seen present-day evidence that it is used enclosed in a circle. But since there are many secret societies, I will continue to make inquiries."

Turning to Sebastian, Alain asked him if he wanted to pursue a medical checkup.

"Oui. I do." answered Sebastian.

"I will have my secretary make an appointment for you. Now, there is another matter to be discussed. I have found a small chateau available for your use. It is on the outskirts of Paris. This should satisfy Inspector Gauthier since he gave you orders not to leave Paris. You may begin residing there tomorrow."

We were all delighted, and Jill asked if there were connections for computers. Alain smiled, saying they were being installed that day.

"The chateau has five bedrooms with separate baths. There is also a room that used to be a library. It is being converted into an office for your work."

Peter told Alain he was most grateful for such expediency, and that he wanted to purchase two new computers with printers. The two discussed computer technicalities, and Peter decided he would shop for them the next morning while I was meeting my mother at the airport.

Sebastian and Jill were listening to all this with obvious joy in their eyes, and I felt a sense of relief that we were going to be less confined. It was agreed they would move to the chateau the next morning and I would return to Alain's apartment with Mother for their meeting. Then we would all meet at Alain's that evening for dinner.

Peter and I bade them good night.

The night passed slowly for me and my brain was churning with thoughts of Mother meeting Alain. *Would she want to meet Maurice, her old love, now that she was remarried?* All sorts of scenarios played in my mind and at last I slept. It was Peter who woke me up. "My love, your chariot will arrive in one hour. Awaken, my love."

Opening my eyes to see his face bent over mine, I reached for him. Embracing and kissing, we both felt our passion growing, culminating in a most satisfying orgasm for me. Reluctantly I left his arms because it was shower time.

Once we were dressed, we went into the living room where coffee and croissants awaited us. I found it hard to eat.

"Peter, I feel like I have butterflies in my stomach. I wonder where that saying came from?"

Laughing, he replied. "It probably came from a mother wanting to quell the feelings of her child."

"Ummm, I can accept that."

Just then Jean-Pierre came in to inform me the car had arrived. I told Peter to enjoy selecting computers and kissed him good-bye.

Down in the parking garage, a limousine awaited. Denis, the chauffeur, was approximately 40 years old and a bit younger than our previous chauffer Louis.

Making our way easily through the early morning Paris traffic, the ride didn't seem long. We arrived at Orly half an hour before Mother's plane was scheduled to land. The chauffeur had given me a paper with Mother's flight number, airline, arrival time and gate on it. Alain's secretary had written a notation that I was to meet Mother and her husband at customs. I realized I hadn't considered that Jim might be accompanying her.

Standing near the customs billets, I observed the multi-ethnicity of arriving passengers. It wasn't long before I spied them. Jim appeared to be less than six feet tall and reminded me of an older Richard Gere, the actor.

It didn't take them long to pass through customs and soon Mother and I were hugging one another. We were both crying. Pulling apart, I looked at Jim. "Hello, Dad." He engulfed me in a hug, and I swear there were tears in his eyes.

Little was said until we were in the limousine. Jim sat on the jump seat while Mother and I sat side-by-side holding hands. I was hesitant to bring up Alain until Mother spoke of him first, which she did. Before they were married, she had shared that episode in her life with Jim.

He smiled and told me they had made a pact that there would be no secrets and relief flooded through me. Then it was as if the floodgates had opened.

Mother wanted to know about the news regarding the Louvre and I suggested we wait until we arrived at Alain's. I maneuvered them into telling me about their life since their marriage. I also told them what I knew about Alain as well as some of the circumstances leading to his informing me he was my half-brother. I knew Mother and Jim were bursting with curiosity about Peter and Jill, and I briefly mentioned Sebastian, as the newest love interest for Jill.

Fortunately Denis' skillful driving soon had us back into the parking garage. As the elevator rose to Alain's apartment, I again felt the queasiness in my stomach. Jean-Pierre answered my ring and the doors opened. We walked through the foyer and into the living room where Alain stood waiting for us.

Mother and son stood looking at each other. Finally Mother began walking towards him with her hands outstretched. Never taking his eyes off of her, Alain began walking towards her. As they met, Mother touched his face with her hands. I realized I was holding my breath and let out a sigh. Jim took my hand squeezing it gently.

Softly Mother said, "My son, my son." Alain enfolded her in his arms and they both began crying. I was crying, too, and so was Jim. It was a moment to cherish, with its beauty and love. At last, pulling away from each other, they held hands while gazing into one another's eyes.

Alain was the first to speak. "Ma mère. My mother. I have awaited this moment for many years. I . . . I am honored you have greeted me so warmly. I...."

Mother placed a finger on his lips. "No, my darling son. It is I who am honored. I have wanted for so long to know you. Never did I dream it would come to pass." Alain kissed both of her hands and led her to sit on one of the couches. He sat beside her.

Jim and I had walked over to the windows because these moments were theirs and we didn't want to intrude. We stood looking out at the Arc de Triomphe and neither of us felt like talking. Finally Jim whispered, "Do you think we could get a cup of coffee?"

Smiling, I took him by the hand and led him into the dining room where I rang for Jean-Pierre who came immediately. I requested coffee for us and said we'd sit at the table there.

Jim and I sat down and began sharing. I told him of my realization that I had been smoozed by my father. He laughed saying he understood. I felt a warmth as well as acceptance from the man my mother had married. It was a comfortable camaraderie. The coffee came along with a plate of small pastries.

I learned Jim was a widower, his wife having died ten years before. He had two daughters, one son and four grandchildren.

It was evident Jim wanted to get up and move around, and fortuitously Mother and Alain came looking for us. We all returned to the living room and sat in the conversation area. Alain and Mother shared with us her desire to see Maurice. Alain said that first, though, he had to tell his father of the miraculous turn of events and get his permission for a meeting. Alain apologized to his mother that he had not already told his father because he had not thought she would want to see Maurice, however he was very happy she did.

Mother then expressed her desire to meet Alain's son. *Son?* I hadn't thought to ask Alain if he had a wife or children. Looking at him I asked, "You have a son?"

"Yes. His mother and I are separated, and Paul lives with his mother near Fontainebleau. He is eighteen and will soon live with me while he attends the Sorbonne." Turning to Mother he said, "Yes, I will arrange for you to meet Paul. It will be my pleasure."

Mother chuckled, "Here I was, wondering if I would ever experience being a grandmother. Now I find out I have a grandson."

Turning to me she said, "Ellen, I think it's about time you told me about your escapades here in France. Alain said I would have to ask you."

Taking a deep breath I retold my story of falling into the hidden cave and finding the scrolls. I went on to tell of contacting Peter who led us to Sebastian, a disillusioned French priest who had now renounced his vows. Sebastian had the expertise to translate the scrolls. As agreed, I omitted the kidnapping and why Jill and Sebastian felt compelled to leave Paul's. This was followed with questions as to why someone would attempt a robbery in the Louvre and especially try to rob Jill.

Alain remained silent the entire time. My Mother should have been a lawyer. I remembered the cross-examining I received as a child when I did something I shouldn't have.

Inwardly groaning, I silently asked Peter to come and rescue me and, as he would say: "It's quantum law. What you ask for you get, as long as there is no doubt." Shortly, Jean-Pierre answered the bell from the elevator door.

Sighing with relief, I stood up and went to greet my great love. Giving me a hug and a kiss, he grinned. Taking his hand, I led him over to Mother and Jim. With introductions out of the way, we sat down.

My loving mother gently began inquiring about Peter's family. He had already told me that when he was a child, his parents had died in a car accident and his grandparents had raised him. He was an only child, and both grandparents were deceased.

At the first opening in the conversation, Alain inquired about the computers. Two had been purchased and they had been installed at the chateau; and Sebastian was busy installing the programs. He and Jill had opted to remain at the chateau that evening instead of returning to Alain's for dinner.

Dinner was a gala affair and it was interesting to observe Mother interacting with her newly found son and potential son-in-law. Alain encouraged her to share her memories of her early days in Paris.

Her description of Paris in the early fifties was of buses with open platforms on the back where people got on and off. If the bus was crowded, the excess passengers stood on the platform; and the gendarmes directing traffic had impressed her. She said she felt safe riding the Métro at night. She did shift work at the Embassy and sometimes she worked late.

Some of her fondest memories were of finishing work in the Communications Center at midnight and going with fellow co-workers to Les Halles for onion soup and escargot. At that time the marketplace was in the city and not on the outskirts of Paris as became later. Her memories were of a city of gaiety and love. It was in her second year in Paris and during the month of February that she met Maurice. They met not in Paris, but while skiing at Gstaad, Switzerland. Their romance bloomed once they returned to Paris.

There was a question nagging at me and I had to ask, "Mother, why was it necessary for you to give up Alain?"

Tears came to her eyes. "You have to understand the era I was living in when I became pregnant. According to

American morals and prejudices, if a woman became pregnant out of marriage, she was condemned. For some women, their families disowned them. No matter what the circumstances, it was considered the woman's fault. Maurice's wife would never consider divorce nor would Maurice's father have approved of it. A mistress was all right, but never a divorce." Daubing at eyes with a tissue she had found, she continued.

"Maurice's father would not support his education if he pursued his desire to marry me, and becoming a mistress was not an option for me. I was working in a sensitive position in the Foreign Service at the American Embassy and back in the States, Senator Joe McCarthy was going full speed with his witch hunting. His ferreting out communists spilled over into one's sexual life. If Embassy officials knew of my pregnancy, it would mean an automatic firing and an immediate return to the States in disgrace. I was fortunate in having a supervisor who shielded me. Neither Maurice nor I had the courage to proceed with his leaving his wife. By Maurice and his wife agreeing to the adoption, the baby would at least be with one of its natural parents."

The morning following my reunion with Mother, Peter and I moved into the chateau with Sebastian and Jill. Mother and Jim came out in a day or two and stayed for a few days to visit. During that time Alain went to see his father and also his son to tell them of Mother's visit.

It was a relief to be away from the center of Paris. Here I could walk outside in a beautiful garden with a pond and a waterfall. And there were also nearby woods to explore.

I could scarcely believe it was early September. There was evidence the leaves were beginning to turn although the roses and flowers were still in bloom in the garden.

Jill and Sebastian concentrated on the translations. Mother and Jim again came for a few days before departing for the States. She told me of her meeting with Maurice alone. Alain had driven her to see his father. She and Maurice agreed that the passion of love was no longer there, only fondness remained.

While she related her story, I felt tears welling up in my eyes. Both she and Maurice were at last free of that hidden part of their lives and agreed they could be great friends. Maurice told her he knew her presence would benefit not only Alain, but Paul as well. His only regret was that his wife had never shown affection for Alain, and that now perhaps love would bloom for him. The following day after her touching meeting with Maurice, Alain brought Paul to meet his grandmother. I was not present, however Alain told me later that it was love at first sight for grandmother and grandson.

During Mother and Jim's visit, Alain had a dinner for all of us, which included Maurice, Paul, Mother, Jim, Peter and me. Fortunately Paul and Maurice spoke English and our conversation was lively. Jill and Sebastian opted not to come and to let it be a family dinner.

Mother told me I would fall in love with her grandson and so I did. With total acceptance I realized Paul was my nephew. I wondered if The Magdalene had had a hand in the reunion.

Although we had enjoyed their visit, when they left Peter and I gave a sigh of relief. Now we were eager to hear the translation of the latest scroll.

⟪⟫ ⟪⟫ ⟪⟫

THE CRUCIFIXION AFTERMATH
Scroll 14

I did not pursue Yeshua's apostles; because I knew when they were ready they would come to me. For the time being they needed the reassurance of Yeshua, the risen Kristos, to appear to them. I also wanted this reassurance.

In time they came, and they were grieving and mourning greatly. I was asked, "How can we go out among the Greeks[1] and teach of the kingdom of the son of man? How can we be spared if he was not spared?"

I thought a moment. Then I stood, greeting them all. I said to my brethren, "Do not mourn or grieve or be irresolute,

---

[1] During this period the common word for non-Jews was Greeks or Greek. John 7:12:33-35 and John 16:19-23. The word Gentile came into usage at a later period.

for his spirit will be with you all and will defend you. Let us praise his greatness by living what Yeshua taught. He taught you well and only as you live what he taught can you go out and teach."

At this they began to discuss the words of the Master. Petros turned to me, "Sister, we know the Master loved you more. Tell us the words of the Master which you have in mind since you know them and we do not, nor have we heard them."

For a moment I thought of what to say. Petros' first name was Simon. Yeshua began calling him Petros with affection, because his mind was hard as a rock. It was difficult to open his mind to new ideas. Yeshua and I had each spoken of the same things over and over. Yet I knew I must tell them something so as not to discourage them.

I began to speak. "I saw the Master in a vision and I said to him, 'Yeshua, I saw you today in a vision.' He answered and said unto me, 'Blessed are you, since you did not waiver at the sight of me. For where the mind is, there is your countenance.' And I said, 'Yeshua, the mind which held the vision, does it see out through the soul or through the spirit?' Yeshua answered and said, 'It sees neither through the soul nor through the spirit; but the mind that sees all, lies between the two, and holds the vision, and it becomes.'"

Andrew interrupted and shouted, "I do not believe that the Master said this! For certainly these teachings are of other ideas." Petros agreed with Andrew and there was much disagreement among the group.

Levi spoke up and said to Petros and the others, "Petros you are always irate. Now I see that you are contending against the woman like the adversaries. But if the Master married her and made her worthy, who are you to reject her?" Turning to me, Levi continued, "Mariam, pray do continue."

I said to them, "Mind is the tally of all your words, deeds and thoughts. Their carrier is in the head that lies between the soul and the spirit. Whatsoever you sow in words, deeds and thoughts, returns to you."

Phillip asked, "But where does the soul lie? This is all confusing to me." Everyone turned to look at me.

"I say what Yeshua has said. The soul lies in that part of the body next to the heart. The spirit is all around you and

249

within you, however its path comes from the back of your head at its base."

There was a great silence. Andrew said that there was much to think about and we dispersed. I withdrew with Meesha and my son, and I also had much to ponder. I was learning and I realized it was much easier to worship the messenger than it was to apply and live the message.

One night Yeshua appeared to me. He told me not to touch him because he was in his radiant body.

He spoke of where he had gone and this I cannot write about, as it is Yeshua's story. He was now God-man realized, and I rejoiced and wept not. We spake of many things.

Yeshua also appeared to his apostles. He taught them many of the mysteries. He bade them all to go out and be a light unto the world. Each was to be a beacon for Truth. It is not enough to speak of Truth. One must live the Truth.

Thomas the twin had inherited the throne of the Jews, and he was a threat to Rome and the Sanhedrin. Thomas was urged to leave before he could be killed. With my blessing and that of his family, he departed for Egypt.

Chapter 21

MORE INTERROGATIONS

Every problem that comes to you
has a gift in its hands.
- Richard Bach

After Jill read the scroll about the times after the crucifixion, we all agreed we were in awe of the courage Mary Magdalene had. A woman born into royalty who had experienced supposedly great wealth was persecuted not only by the religious authorities, but also by some of Jesus' disciples.

"In addition to that," Peter said, "she was the mother of one child and pregnant with another."

"Oui, she is truly amazing. It would appear she was not allowed a proper period of mourning." Sebastian commented.

"I wonder what modern day woman would have the strength and courage to do as she did?" I pondered.

Jill's commented, "Women must be free of the yoke placed on them eons ago. No longer must they continue to be beasts of burden like asses. It's hard to love my 'neighbor' when I know they defile and debase women and children. I have anger and I admit it."

Looking at Peter, she continued, "Yes, I know, quantum mechanics and the aspect of being the observer . . . but damn it! It's time for women to have the respect of equality!"

None of us responded. We knew we had to allow her to vent her anger.

"Thank you for not chastising me. My anger is something I need to work on."

Peter told her that it was understandable, and when Jill acknowledged his statement, he turned to Sebastian and said, "I am amazed that apostles so caught up in their petty prejudices could change the course of the world."

"Ah, Peter, we must not forget that it was Constantine that set it all into motion. It was not the apostles because they

251

lived and died several hundred years before Constantine. They were only the pawns in this charade named Christianity. There are a few learned scholars who claim it a myth. What a travesty it is that has been perpetuated upon the world," Sebastian observed.

This scroll gave each of us pause to reflect on our own feelings. I also had anger. When we were next alone, Peter and I discussed this and I told him I felt so blessed to have the freedoms I have. We both came to the understanding that we could not change the world. We could only change ourselves. By so doing, we could be like ripples on a pond affecting the consciousness of the whole.

∾∾ ∾∾ ∾∾

Sebastian had an extensive medical check-up, resulting in a clean bill of health. His doctor in Toulouse had sent his records to Paris. The healing had to be a miracle, his Paris doctor said.

When Sebastian related the results to us, we had a wonderful celebration. This confirmed what we already knew.

Alain was negotiating with the authorities regarding the scrolls. We had hoped to keep their existence quiet until the agreement was finalized. Then we received a call from the office of Inspector Gauthier.

Apparently his investigations had brought up a link between the four of us and the scrolls. We surmised there had been a leak from the Bibliothèque office. The following day Alain accompanied us to the Prefecture office at 9:00 A.M.

One by one the Inspector interviewed us again with Alain accompanying each of us. That time Peter was the first to go in. We had agreed we would volunteer no information per Alain's instructions, and the questions we were asked were to be answered truthfully and to the best of our knowledge.

When Peter came out of the office, he looked tired. He had been in there over two hours and I was next. I had no fear when I went into the interview room. (I prefer to call it the interview room instead of interrogation room.) It was similar to the one I had been in at Carcassonne. Inspector Gauthier shook

252

my hand and asked me to sit. A man was there with a laptop computer to take down my information.

The first thing I was asked was if I had been in Mirepoix in late May or early June. I answered yes because that was something I could not deny. He asked me if I had come across a cave, and I told him I had visited a number of caves in that area. Gauthier then specifically asked me if I had found an unmarked cave. I asked him to clarify. He said he meant a cave not previously known by the authorities. Again, I answered yes.

The questions became more explicit. He wanted to know what I had found and who was with me. I told him Jill was with me and I told him I had found pottery jars, and then the questioning led to whether or not I had opened them and removed any of the contents.

I answered I had. His questions led to my admitting I had found the scrolls. However I said that at that time, I did not know exactly what they were or their value. He asked if I was aware that under French law all discovered artifacts had to be reported. My answer was that I was not aware of that at the time.

Inspector Gautier wanted me to account for my time in France after finding the scrolls, so I gave him the places I had been and omitted the kidnapping. My statement, or deposition, lasted almost four hours.

Even though I had gone to law school and was a lawyer, I had never defended or prosecuted a case, and I had never been a defendant. I was a research lawyer. I was exhausted by the time it was over, and I think the Inspector was too. Jill and Sebastian were asked to return the next morning.

Alain had an officer take us out of the building by a back way, and thus we avoided the awaiting news media. Alain suggested we go to his apartment to discuss what had transpired. We were all too exhausted to do otherwise.

We were quiet through the late lunch Jean-Pierre served us. No one was very hungry even though we had not eaten since breakfast.

After lunch all I wanted to do was return to the chateau and contemplate, however Alain wanted to go over the depositions step by step. He felt it was still a great possibility someone from the Bibliothèque department in charge of antiquities had leaked the information to Gauthier.

As Alain was completing his assessments, he found it odd that I had not been asked about the number of scrolls or their condition. We really didn't have an answer to that. On the other hand, he was pleased with the way Peter and I handled our responses.

It was Sebastian who lifted our spirits. "Let us not forget the message of The Magdalene. We stand by our truth and persevere regardless of the opposition."

I could have kissed him. And I did. "Sebastian! Thank you for pulling me out of my doldrums! I bless you."

Blushing, he asked, "What are doldrums?"

"The meaning is gloomy or being low in spirit."

"Ah, merci. I understand now. This we must not do. We have much work ahead of us."

When we returned to the chateau, we found the housekeeper Alain had hired for us was there to greet us. Madame Bouchard was a plump motherly type. Her dark hair streaked with gray was pinned on top of her head in a bun, and her dark brown eyes sparkled with warmth. She asked us to call her Marie.

Her husband Jacques was our groundskeeper and handyman. He was as thin as she was plump, with balding hair and dancing brown eyes.

They were both competent and they were just what we needed. I sensed our stay at the chateau would not be short.

Each of us wanted to contemplate what the potentials and possibilities had become due to Inspector Gautier's questioning. We had a quiet dinner, well prepared by Marie. The next day would be difficult for Sebastian and Jill. Peter and I were not required to return.

We were relieved the following afternoon when Alain brought them home. The interrogation had been more grueling for Sebastian than for Jill. This could have been because he is French.

When the questioning came to their departure from Paul's house and the man left in the doorway, Alain had advised them against answering at that time. At the chateau he asked us if we would like to contact the American Embassy.

Oh gawd! I thought. *Is this going to become a diplomatic affair?* We declined.

Peter asked Alain if charges were going to be brought against any us. He replied that at that moment he could not say. Under French law the intent to commit a crime determined whether the charge would be a misdemeanor or a felony. He now felt it was crucial for the Bibliothèque committee to agree to the terms he had placed before them.

In retrospect, it was a difficult time for Alain also. He was giving up so much of his time to represent us, beyond what I suspected he would do for other clients. There was continuing pressure on him from the news media for interviews with us, and Alain encouraged us to allow him to issue another statement to the effect that still no statement could be made at that time due to the on-going investigations. We agreed.

In the ensuing days, Alain met with officials of the Bibliothèque. With the news media now aware there were scrolls other than the two we had left behind, the pressure was mounting. There must have been a leak from the office of the Bibliothèque or Gauthier's office.

⤝⤞ ⤝⤞ ⤝⤞

UNREST AND A DECISION
Scroll 15

Ah, it is late into the night. I have been compelled to write down my thoughts.

My days were full because there were many requests for healings at the Temple. I also traveled to Samaria, Galilee and into Judea to heal and to teach. Often Meesha and James traveled with me. Martha and the women traveling with me were well aware of my views regarding living the message.

Soon some of Yeshua's followers became members of my ekklesia and this became a joining of Yeshua's followers and my followers. There were moments of friction with Simon Petros beginning to show his dislike of me with more animosity.

There were times we would meet at Mariamme and Joseph's home, and other times when we were near Bethany, we would meet in the home of Martha, Miriam and Ioannes the Beloved. Other homes were open to us as well. I found the women were quicker to grasp what I was teaching and these women coming to me were yearning for a change.

It was difficult for some of the men such as Petros and Andrew to accept women as being equal to them and I discerned they were lovers of men only.

There was increasing unrest throughout the region. James, the brother of Yeshua, came to me, urging me to take my son and leave the country. He said I must also preserve my child yet to be born. He feared for our safety as the Sanhedrin was voicing louder complaints against the ekklesias and me.

Chapter 22

WHAT IS SIN?

*It is an old habit with theologians to beat the living
with the bones of the dead.*
- Robert G. Ingersoll

There was a lull while the committee from the Bibliothèque was making its decision. Sebastian accompanied Alain to the meetings and never once did he waiver from our conditions. The change in him from when I first met him was as if another personality had taken over. Sebastian knew he was healed and he knew he had a purpose to fulfill. His energy was astounding and with his enthusiasm, we were all buoyed up.

One evening after dinner, when we heard the latest scroll, a very short one, Jill commented, "I would think The Magdalene knew she would be leaving soon."

"She mentions her pregnancy in this scroll, therefore she must have been close to the end of it," I added.

Peter commented on her again mentioning Petros was a lover of men. "I would say he was a homosexual, using today's terms."

Nodding in agreement, Sebastian spoke of the travesty done to humankind over hundreds of years. "The Church has spoken of morality, yet very few in the hierarchy live what is requested of the people to live."

Agreeing with Sebastian, Jill went on to say, "The word sin is one of the most misused words around. From my research, Socrates defined 'sin' as ignorance. Another ancient definition was 'missing the mark.'"

"Ah," said Peter, "what is 'God's will' if sin means ignorance or missing the mark? Then the standard phrase 'It's God's will' doesn't make sense."

I laughed. "Every culture has its own definition of what is right and wrong. If we are all aspects of the one God or Creator, then to my way of thinking, Socrates' definition of sin as ignorance rings true to me. Going against God's will means, as has been indicated before, going against that big guy in the sky keeping tabs on the billions of us on this planet."

"However, with so many religions in the world, each vying with the other for the 'true interpretation,' it would seem they are the ones in true ignorance," Jill added. "If each human born is an aspect of God, how can a baby be said to 'be born in sin,' unless it really means we each are born not remembering who we are or what our purpose is. We each are ignorant in that we don't remember."

"Oui, you make sense. Therefore Jesus could not have died for anyone's sins and to say so is truly ignorant. One only has to reason it. Then what has been done to mankind is an enslavement of the mind to keep them in ignorance."

Softly Peter said, "That is correct, Sebastian. In reality, Jesus died for his Truth. Do any of us have courage such as that? I've been asking myself that. I think the situation we have chosen to be in is an opportunity to see if we have the courage to stand by our truth."

"Well put my darling," I said. "Each of us has our truth. And I also have been questioning my courage."

We lifted our wine glasses and toasted, "To Truth, may it free us and as ripples spread to all."

❧❧ ❧❧ ❧❧

DEPARTURE
Scroll 16

Some in the Sanhedrin were calling for my arrest, and word was being spread that the different colors of my eyes were evil. James, the brother, told me that Petros was openly calling for my death. This stunned me. I asked myself, how could any follower of Yeshua's have malice in his heart? This was against what Yeshua and I taught. To follow the way of Truth is to have no malice towards another. For what one does to another returns to the sender. I was troubled and I was also learning not all men want to live what is taught. The words they speak are empty of meaning. They want to worship the messenger and not heed the message.

At first I thought not to leave, but one night Yeshua appeared. "Beloved. Peace be unto you. The moment has come for you to depart Judea. There is a need for you elsewhere. There is danger for you here." Then he was gone. I pondered this and the following morning I sought out Joseph and when I arrived, James was with him.

The three of us talked well into the day. I was a threat to Rome and also to Herod, James pointed out. I carried the seed of Yeshua, and James the Younger's life was also endangered.

Joseph had prepared for this moment and a decision was made to disperse his and Mariamme's family to various places. I would take James the Younger and go first to Egypt to await the birth of my child. Mariamme and my apostles would come with us if they so chose. Joseph would also come for a time and at a later time he would go to Cornwall in the isles of Breton.

James has said he would stay in Jerusalem holding the ekklesia together by becoming the episkopos.[1] James felt Josephus and Salome wanted to go to Ephesus because both were now married and had relatives living there. James, already a High Priest, said he would ask all of Yeshua's apostles to carry the word to areas of their choice. This would indicate James was now head of the apostles, and this would remove some of the pressure of danger from me.

I sought out my apostles, Martha, Miriam, Miriam the Leper, Elizbeth, Mari Salome, Zara, Leah, Janeen, Bekah, Mari Jacobe, Sarah of Bethany and Abigale and I told them of the danger to me, and I asked if any would accompany me to the place where I was going. Each was told to make their choices of coming with me, staying or going away to teach the word.

The women apostles voiced a desire to accompany me to Egypt but we knew Egypt was not our final destination. We had heard of the druids in Gaul[2] and we felt that we, as women,

---

[1] Episkopos: Ancient Greek word denoting 'overseer.' After the Council of Nicea 325 A.D. the meaning became 'bishop.'
[2] Gaul: Ancient name for France

would be more welcomed in Gaul by the Keltoi. Ioannes, the Beloved of Yeshua, sought me out, voicing his desire to come with me as he had promised he would, and I welcomed him.

Gaul was pulling me and within me I knew there was something I was to do there. Being with child, it was pointed out to me that the long voyage to Gaul would not be feasible, nor would going overland, because I would be vulnerable to capture by the Romans or Herod. Joseph advised me to travel the shorter route by sea to Egypt and I foresaw it would be wise to do as Joseph had said.

With what few belongings we chose to take, we set out in caravan to the port of Joppa to board a ship Joseph had prepared for carrying goods to trade in Egypt. It was not unusual for his family to accompany him to the port to see him off. While there, we would visit with some of his and Mariamme's relatives.

We went on board the ship Joseph had waiting. It was considered large for a merchant ship and Joseph had chosen his best. It had sails and oarsmen numbering perhaps 100. The seas became rough after we left Joppa.

Many of the women were ill from the rolling motion of the ship. I gloried in it, and so did young James. We never tired of looking at the water and the birds following the ship. When there was relative calm I taught the language of Latum. Some knew the language and assisted me. Egypt was also a possession of Rome and I contemplated what we would find upon arrival, as Claudius was now the Emperor.

One of the sailsmen told tales of the Keltoi. I had heard they had once been a fierce, noble tribal people with a great leader named Vercingetorix who had brought unification of the many Keltoi tribes. They had fought Julius Caesar with Vercingetorix and his warriors, almost winning. The tale told was that he surrendered to Caesar and he was imprisoned for a number of years before being executed. This act seemed to have broken the will of the Keltoi and for the most part, they were now slaves of Rome. I felt I was to minister to these noble people but I knew my first concern was for the birth of my child and Egypt would be a safer place to be.

RETURN TO EGYPT
Scroll 17

Returning to Egypt, I carried within me mixed thoughts since my life with Yeshua had come to an abrupt halt. Standing at the rail of the ship with James at my side, I told him of the lighthouse we would soon see as we were nearing Alexandria. I caught my breath when the Pharos Lighthouse came into view. I told young James that it was a beacon of truth and wisdom. It's purpose was to be a guide for travelers to know it was a safe harbor for learning truth and wisdom for the common man and woman. I told him, "Always remember this as a symbol for truth and wisdom my son."

Once on land, I felt as if I had come out of a dream. Looking down at my swollen belly and holding the hand of James reminded me it had been a real happening and I allowed myself to think of Yeshua.

The Essene community welcomed us and we were given our own house, because Joseph and Mariamme already had friends and relatives there. It was good to see Thomas again and to share our thoughts of Yeshua. I was welcomed along with my followers. It was Martha who managed the household. A bower and birthing room were made ready for me when my time came upon me.

This was far different from the birth of James. There was no father here for this babe and I knew this one was to be a girl. Yeshua and I had spoken of it and Yeshua wanted this child to be named Sarah. The birth was easy, and there were women in addition to Meesha and Martha to assist me.

When Sarah came out of the womb, the cord was severed. My thought when I began to suckle her was: from out of Egypt has come my daughter. She was so much like Yeshua and later her skin would become almost as dark as mine. During the following six weeks, I continued to suckle her and I talked to her, telling of her father. When I sang to her, she would open her green eyes and I swear she smiled. At the end of the six weeks, I left the bower still suckling her because I was reluctant to release her to a wet nurse.

I had included young James when I talked and sang to Sarah. She was liken unto me with dark skin. His skin was the lightness of Yeshua. I swore to myself and to the god within that these children would be brought up to know Truth and to speak it, so I began to teach them.

One day Mari Salome came to me. "Mariam, how can you be so happy when it hasn't been a year since Yeshua went elsewhere?"

Replied I, "Life is for living and Yeshua chose to complete his destiny. Why should I be sad at that? We are each here to continue the journey towards our destiny. Why would I choose to grieve or be unhappy? I have been given two children therefore I am truly blessed."

In my group there was a woman named Sarah of Bethany. To make a distinction between the two, we began calling my daughter Sarah the Egyptian.

As the months passed, I could see a complacency setting in. Thomas had departed for India. Within me I knew my journey was to continue on to Gaul so I called my women together and I shared my plans. Elizbeth, Zara, Leah, Janeen, Miriam the Leper and Bekah chose to remain in Egypt. I blessed them and kept to my resolve.

Joseph had returned from Breton with goods to trade. Within a few weeks he was ready to depart for Gaul, with Mariamme coming with us reluctantly. In my ekklesia, journeying with me were Meesha, Martha, Miriam, Mari Salome, Mari Jacobe, Abigale and Sarah of Bethany as well as Ioannes the beloved of Yeshua.

Upon our departure, Leah who chose to remain asked me why I was compelled to continue on to Gaul. Answered I thus, "When complacency sets in, one does not grow in spirit. Therefore I am compelled to go. The spirit within is telling me I must go and make known the unknown."

Chapter 23

FIRE

*Courage is the art of being the only one
who knows you're scared to death.*
- Harold Wilson (1916-1995)

Sometimes the days passed swiftly at the chateau and others seemed to drag. There were moments when I felt the progress we were making was inch by inch. We were now nearing the month of November and the Bibliothèque committee, from my perspective, was dragging its feet.

These had been busy weeks. According to Alain, Gauthier was continuing his investigation. Sebastian had been called back to Gauthier's office to refine some points in his deposition. He and Alain had attended meetings with the committee, and with Sebastian busy elsewhere, the translations were going slowly.

Finally an evening came when the four of us heard the two scrolls that had been transcribed.

I sighed, "At last she decided to leave Jerusalem." Again we commented on her courage to travel while pregnant.

"Of course," Jill pointed out. "In those days, women were probably fit for harsher conditions than we are in today's society. She has already written that she traveled around Judea, Samaria and Galilee. She certainly didn't have a coach or a wagon, therefore she probably walked."

"An amazing woman. She returned to Egypt to have her baby, a daughter," I commented. "It really could be Sarah who is referred to as the 'Black Egyptian.'"

"You're probably right," Jill said. "After our last discussion when we were at Alain's, I went on the Internet to do some research about the Church and came across information regarding the WWII pope Sebastian spoke about and that made me interested in the Gypsies. What I learned is that the Gypsies probably originated in India. The first mention of them came in the 800's. It seems they were from basically

263

three tribes, and the captives from the tribes went to Afghanistan as slaves. After a few hundred years, the Gypsies were freed by the breakup of the dynastic rule there. Some went to Turkey, Greece and then to Eastern Europe."

"Did you find a connection between them and why they would have a Saint Sarah as their patron saint?" asked Peter.

"No one really knows." Jill answered him. "However it stands to reason. In India the gypsies worshiped the Goddess Kali. By the time the Gypsies were known in France and Spain, the Black Madonnas were already established here in Europe. I don't think it would have taken much for them to accept the Black Madonna as Kali. I know this is taking us far afield."

"But," I replied, "If some of the Gypsies in France also came from Egypt, perhaps they already knew about The Magdalene. They didn't appear in France until the 1400's."

"True," Jill said. "However, from my research there is no proof they went to Egypt. There are researchers of the Gypsies who say they claimed to have come from Egypt because they thought that would take some of the burden of discrimination off them. The Gypsies have been known for their oral histories instead of written documents, but perhaps they were aware of her. I also have read the Gypsies supposedly brought the Tarot cards from Egypt and yet the cards' actual origin is a mystery, too. I haven't had time to pursue that but I will after the scrolls are all done."

❧❧   ❧❧   ❧❧

Sometime during the night, I awakened with a foreboding feeling. I lay still beside Peter, pondering why. At last I leaned over and gently placing my fingers over his lips, I whispered into his ear, "Wake up my sweet. I think someone is in the house who isn't suppose to be here."

Immediately he was alert. Reaching for the phone, he whispered that there was no dial tone. My first thought was of the scrolls, and I knew the transcribed ones were under lock and key in a bank vault. The remaining scrolls and Peter's laptop were locked in a safe Alain had had installed in Sebastian and Jill's bedroom.

The computers! The programs! But how did the intruder get in? The security alarms were tested yesterday and they were working fine.

Reaching for his robe, Peter got up. Alain had purchased a revolver for us, and Peter took it from the bedside stand. I was up and had a flashlight in my hand. Peter whispered to me to awaken Sebastian and Jill, so I gave the flashlight to him knowing I could feel my way to their room. Part of me wanted to creep downstairs with Peter, but I knew his idea was correct.

As quietly as I could I went across the hall to their room and quietly opened the door. I gave a small cough, and Jill sat up. I managed to find my way to their bed and whispered that someone could be in the house. Immediately they were up. Sebastian got his revolver and their flashlight, and we were creeping down the stairs when I smelled petrol. *Oh gawd no!* I thought.

At that moment all hell seemed to break loose. Peter tackled the intruder and both went down with a crash. This time Peter's height was a bonus. It helped him subdue the invader.

He had managed to get the man down before the petrol was lit. I went to turn on the lights and found the electricity had been turned off. Jill left to wake up Jacques and Marie. They had a cell phone and Marie called the police. Jacques found some rope, and he and Sebastian helped Peter tie up the man.

We left Sebastian holding the gun on the intruder while we gathered up all the flashlights in the chateau because the stench of the spilled petrol told us we dared not use candles for light.

The intruder was a small man with eyes set back in his pudgy face. They were darting all over the computer room. His nose was almost flat and if he had had whiskers and pointed ears, he would definitely have looked feline. He was dressed all in black and wore a black ski mask, which Sebastian had removed to reveal sparse, short brown hair.

Peter and Jacques left to explore the grounds because of the possibly he had an accomplice. While the search was going on, I called Alain on the cell phone. During our conversation, I followed the smell of the petrol to where it had been splashed and stifled a gasp when saw it had been poured on the two computers. Marie and Jill let out a gasp when they saw what I had discovered and I heard Sebastian mutter "Merde." Alain said he was coming out to the chateau immediately.

Spying my camera on a nearby table, I began taking pictures. I had no idea if the local police would bring a photographer to the scene of the crime, so I took a full-face shot of the man. He never moved or said a word. From his mode of dress, I guessed he was a hired professional.

It wasn't too long before Peter and Jacques returned. Somehow the intruder had managed to get through the security system around the property. If there had been an accomplice, he or she was long gone. Within minutes of their return, the local police arrived and Jacques left to open the gate to let them onto the grounds.

Knowing it would be a long night Marie went into the kitchen to make coffee. Sebastian and Jacques were our interpreters for the local police, and it was a grueling night. The intruder refused to answer any questions. Unbeknownst to us, Inspector Gauthier had requested the local gendarmerie to keep an eye on us. In retrospect this turned out to be a blessing because the local police notified his office, and Gauthier arrived in time for the questioning.

In short order, the local police with Jacques' help had the electricity restored. We were requested to sit in the kitchen until we were called individually for questioning. It was a relief to sit down. The kitchen was quite large and inviting with a round table to one side. Marie had made a fire in the ancient wood cook stove, and we were on our second cup of coffee when Alain came in. When he arrived at the chateau and identified himself to the police, he was told they were searching the nearby woods.

Alain asked us what had transpired. I told of my foreboding, and we each related what had happened. Letting out a sigh he said, "It would seem someone does not want these scrolls translated. Or perhaps it was a crime of vengeance to ensure your deaths?"

Gilbert Montand came to mind immediately. Later Peter said he had had the same thought.

Excitedly, Jacques asked, "Who would want to kill these beautiful people?"

Alain shrugged his shoulders, "That is what we want to determine." He asked Peter and me to step outside for a minute.

The nip of a frosty November early dawn hit me. Alain said we wouldn't be outside long. He urged us to tell the police about our encounter with Montand. Peter said he had already come to that realization. He felt none of our lives were worth withholding that information, and I agreed. Holding hands we followed Alain back into the kitchen. He asked Jacques and Marie if they had seen anything unusual within the past few days and they said they hadn't.

The last scroll of The Magdalene came to mind. She had written of her group becoming complacent. I realized I had fallen into complacency. I shared my thoughts with the others. They agreed that our false sense of security was a form of complacency.

The police had taken over the living room and Peter was the first to be called in because he was the one who actually found the intruder. Alain went in with him. We were left in the kitchen with a young police officer.

None of us felt like talking, and Marie made sure the police officials had coffee. Something was nagging at the back of my mind, but I put the thoughts aside when a plain-clothes policeman called me into living room where Inspector Gauthier greeted me and told me that the local police had asked him to conduct the questioning.

Again I spoke of waking up with a foreboding feeling. I said I had awakened Peter who found the phone line dead when he tried to call down to Jacques and Marie. I told of Peter taking his revolver and a flashlight with him when he went downstairs to investigate while I awakened Sebastian and Jill. Apparently Peter had found the intruder in the act of spilling petrol in the computer room.

I was questioned as to who might want our computers destroyed or any of us dead. Taking a deep breath, I gave a number of potentials, including perhaps someone from the Bibliothèque nationale who became aware of the two scrolls dropped in the cave and who didn't want the scrolls translated, or possibly organizations that would not want the contents released. I said that even I, with a slight knowledge, recognized they had been written in an ancient form of Greek.

Gauthier asked if I knew a Gilbert Montand. I answered I had met him briefly, and Gauthier asked me to describe our encounter. Taking a deep breath I described our kidnapping and how we were taken to Montand's chateau. I told him that Montand had demanded to know where Sebastian and the scrolls were. I said he threatened to shoot off my ears if Peter didn't comply and said that I was handcuffed and kept hostage in his office while Peter took the kidnapper to Paul's house outside of Toulouse. I held nothing back. Oh gawd! It was a relief to tell it all.

"Madame Montgomery, why are these scrolls so important when they could cost you your life?"

I looked directly at him and said I had memorized the first scroll, which stated very clearly that the finders were not to allow the scrolls to be hidden away from the world. As I told him the contents of the scrolls, he never once took his eyes off my face nor did he show any emotion.

Before dismissing me and having me escorted back to the kitchen, he showed me a business size card embossed with an eight-pointed cross in a circle. He asked if I had seen this card or one similar to it. I told him Peter had found a similar card on Bruno. I wanted to ask him where he got it, but I didn't dare. Perhaps one day the mystery will be revealed.

Next Gauthier called in Sebastian, then Jill, Jacques and lastly, Marie. With the policeman in the kitchen with us, no one felt free to discuss anything. We were all bleary-eyed and exhausted by the time Marie returned. She had been told the petrol could now be cleaned up. The police had finished taking samples and photographs.

Gauthier, with Alain following behind him, came into the kitchen and said we were not to discuss the episode with anyone outside of that household. In particular, he said we should not speak to the press, and we all nodded our acquiescence. He indicated there would be more questions later and for the time being there would be surveillance around the property 24 hours a day.

After the police departed, we went into the computer room to examine the damage. There was a possibility the programs had not been damaged, however, the keyboards were a total loss. Alain told us he was leaving and would return later in the day. In the meantime, he said he would have two new computers and keyboards sent out. Smiling wanly, he told us we were to sleep and rest. He told Marie and Jacques specifically they were not to give out information to anyone. In addition to the police detail, Alain said he was sending out his own security personnel. Kissing me on the cheek, he told me it wasn't as bad as it seemed, and he went home.

Peter and I stumbled upstairs and into bed. My sleep was deep. When I awakened, Peter was gone, and I lay contemplating the events of the previous night. I felt relieved I had told Gauthier about Montand. Whatever the consequences, I knew we would weather the storm.

As I lay in bed, I began blessing everyone involved and I blessed even Montand, sending him love and joy. I was beginning to return to wakefulness when I heard the door open.

Sitting up, I saw Peter walking in with a cup of coffee in his hand. Setting it on the bedside table, he sat on the edge of the bed. Taking me in his arms, he kissed me deeply. "My darling," he murmured. "I am so blessed to have you in my life."

"My dear, I also am blessed, to have you in my life." I knew our love and our closeness did not need sex as a reinforcer. I asked him what time it was and learned it was almost two in the afternoon. We had gone to bed at eight that morning. Peter handed me the coffee and while I drank, he related his interview with Gauthier.

He had also told him about our kidnapping, including his shooting Montand. I told him about my interview and we both felt as if we had a new lease on life. Nevermore would we allow that specter to haunt us again.

Peter said he had been up since eleven, and that just before he came upstairs with my coffee Sebastian had come down to check further about the damage to the computers. Together they re-examined them. It didn't appear the petrol had gotten inside the casings, however the keyboards were not workable. Sebastian was beside himself, and Jill was sleeping in as I had.

While I was finishing the coffee, we discussed more of the night's events. I commented on what a blessing it had been that the laptop computer had been put in the safe with the scrolls because we hadn't lost it, too.

In trying to figure out how someone knew where we were, we concluded our whereabouts had only been known to Alain and Inspector Gauthier's office. There was the possibility that Alain had been followed, or someone had picked up our trail in some way. Reluctantly, I got up and Peter told me he was going back downstairs.

After showering and dressing, I went down to see by daylight what damages had been wrought by the petrol. The double French doors were wide open to air the room out. Jacques had already been in and cut out the damaged piece of carpet. I heard a noise and turned. Jill entered and came to stand with me. Reaching out for the hand of my dear friend, we were soon in each other's arms, crying. When we finished letting out our pent up emotions, we left in search of Peter and Sebastian.

Outside the computer room, we met Marie whose face was filled with woe. She stopped when she saw us and began crying. "Oh, Madame Ellen and Madame Jill, I have remembered something I did not tell the police last night. I fear I am the cause of all this!"

Taking her hand, I pulled her towards and into the kitchen. Jill was close behind. By now Marie was sobbing. Sitting her down on a chair, I asked Jill to go find Peter and Sebastian. Both men were outside, and the three came in a few moments later with Jacques following along.

Gradually through gentle questioning, Marie's story emerged. It seemed that the week before a strange deliveryman had brought the weekly order of groceries. The truck had the same markings as the usual delivery truck. When Marie questioned the driver as to the whereabouts of the regular driver, she was told he had gotten ill and the driver that day was a substitute. Apologizing for not telling us, she said she had gotten busy and forgot about it until late this morning.

Jacques called the local gendarmerie, and told them of Marie's remembering the substitute delivery driver. Then I called Alain with the news. When I hung up, I realized my stomach was rumbling so I announced my hunger. Marie said she was going to cook something for us, however we overrode her. Jill and I cooked while Marie freshened up for her interview with the local police who were coming to take her statement. We made extra coffee.

When Jacques went out to let the police in through the gate, we assured Marie that she and Jacques would not be fired. While Marie was being interviewed, we four sat down to eat.

After Marie's information had been taken down and the police had gone, we went into the living room to talk. Jacques had a warm fire going in the fireplace.

Peter was the first to speak. "We have choices. We can live in fear or we can gain wisdom from this latest event. I, for one, am not going to lapse into fearfulness. I understand quantum physics too much. I take responsibility for some of this."

Sebastian asked, "What do you mean?"

"I'm the one who shot Montand and in all probability incurred his wrath and his desire for retaliation. When he threatened to shoot the ears off of Ellen, I went into fear and anger such as I have never experienced before. I set into motion something that caused repercussions."

"Peter, I was also in fear," I said.

"I understand that, my darling. However, you handled yours differently. You began blessing and becoming thankful."

"Perhaps by my doing so, it enabled you to overcome Bruno. And I also have a confession to make. Something began nagging at me last night, and this morning I remembered what it was. I had a fear of something dire happening."

Jill confessed she had experienced the same feeling. "After all, Sebastian and I also contributed too some of this when we were leaving Paul's. I think we have all been participants in creating repercussions. I certainly take responsibility for my part."

"Oui. I also. Fear is, how do you say . . . insidious, and I also have had fear. Perhaps we can follow Ellen's lead and begin blessing our enemies. Didn't Jesus give a statement, 'Bless those that persecute you?'"

"That's right, my dear," answered Jill. "This talk of blessing reminds me of research done by a Japanese man. I think his last name is Emoto. What he did was place words such as love and gratitude on bottles of water. The samples were from distilled, polluted and unpolluted water. Photos of the water's crystals were taken before the words were placed on the containers and then the containers were frozen. Photographs of the frozen water crystals showed astounding molecular alterations. The molecules responded to the words of "love" and "gratitude" by showing harmony and beautiful geometric forms. The water not having these words placed on the containers indicated disharmony and chaos. When the words such as hate were placed on the containers, the results were that the crystals became distorted and ugly."[1]

"Vraiment? I have not heard of this particular research. Mon dieu! It is proof that kind, loving words do have an effect," exclaimed Sebastian.

Peter questioned, "I wonder if the water Yeshua and The Magdalene changed into wine at their wedding was changed by using the same principle? Words are powerful, and the mind is powerful."

The thought had come to me, "Apparently from what has been translated so far, The Magdalene was well aware of the power of thoughts and words, and she has written of her knowledge. Can you imagine the difficulty she went through during the crucifixion? She must have had powerful control over her mind and emotions. It's almost beyond imagination."

"Oui," said Sebastian. "Also the travesty is the emphasis placed throughout the years on Jesus' suffering. I think it is time he was removed from the cross."

"I agree," Jill said. "I would like the world to place an emphasis on what he taught. These scrolls of Mary Magdalene reinforce his teachings as well as hers, and go beyond what has been fed to the world."

At that moment Alain arrived, and he looked tired. Greeting us with warmth he shook his head and said how amazed he was that we had come through the latest episode unscathed.

"I have contemplated what I know, and these scrolls must be powerful. I am not a religious man, however I have concluded Mary Magdalene is looking after you."

I told him that I thought he was correct. "Alain, I have to tell you how grateful I am that you are assisting us. In addition to your being our avocat, I feel most fortunate you are my brother, and I will never take you for granted."

---

[1] *Messages From Water* by Masaru Emoto

Smiling, he replied, "My sister, I treasure your words and I have sworn to myself to assist you and your friends in any way I can." Looking around to the others, he continued, "I also treasure your friendship. I may not understand fully why all of you are so compelled to protect these scrolls, however it is my desire to one day know their importance."

"My friend," Sebastian replied, "perhaps it is time we allowed you to read what has been translated so far. Perhaps when you read some of them you will understand. I can only speak for myself. These scrolls have saved my life."

"Alain," Jill addressed. "You may not understand this, but here is how I feel. Within me I know we are all involved in the translating of these scrolls because of a divine plan, and this includes you. Why else would you be connected with Ellen and her mother in the manner you are? There are never accidents or coincidences."

"Jill, the words you speak ring true within me and yet I do not fully understand. And yes, Sebastian, I want to read the translations, if that is agreeable with the rest of you?"

Peter said he heartedly agreed and so did I. When Alain departed, he said he would return the next day, perhaps with some good news. We felt a new sense of renewal in our quest.

∽ᘉᔍ∽ ∽ᘉᔍ∽ ∽ᘉᔍ∽

GAUL
Scroll 18

At last land was seen. We had sailed through many storms since our departure from Alexandria and our destination of the port of Massalia[1] was near. There was an excitement running through all of us. We had experienced stormy seas and were eager to put our feet on land.

Massalia was much larger than I had envisioned and we stayed aboard until Joseph returned with litters for our party. Standing by the rail of the ship, I was amazed at the activity on

---

[1] Massalia is an ancient name for Marseilles, France

the docks. There were other ships anchored, and some were much larger than Joseph's. The sounds were interesting because I was hearing many different languages and dialects. The port was busy with traders coming from many places.

We waited until Joseph returned with our litters. Passing through the streets, we saw the Roman culture and influence everywhere. From time to time we saw what must be the Keltoi because these people were much taller than the Romans. Their hair was varied in shades of copper to yellow. Whereas I was accustomed to people of the color of my skin, these people had very pale skin with a light rose tint. I thought them beautiful while many in my party thought them ugly.

Joseph had hired the litters to carry us out of Massalia to the large home of Joseph's friends, where we were made welcome and led to our quarters. Our countenances were light with laughter, and we appreciated this home with the Roman style baths. At last we were in Gaul.

The change from Judea was intense for those who accompanied me. Only Joseph and Mariamme had traveled outside of Judea and Egypt. It was a glorious time of the year when we arrived with the trees in full leaf and the vineyards held the promise to give a bountiful harvest.

I did not find the oppression as intense as that in Judea, Samaria and Galilee. There were no Pharisees and Sadducee's or Sanhedrin to give forth their opinions of a wrathful and judgmental god. The Romans had their temples for their gods and were tolerant of other beliefs as long as they did not interfere with Rome and each home had its own altar. From my knowledge and discernment, over a long period of time, the Romans adopted and integrated gods from other cultures. Their basic religious ethic when followed was pietas, meaning a sense of duty, honor and respect for their deities and it mattered not the moral character of the priest. What mattered was that he performed the ritual with the proper pietas.

I could now understand the Roman's tolerance of many religions. They had many gods who were integrated into the Roman religion from the religions of the peoples they conquered; and instead of a vengeful and wrathful god, the Roman's approach to their gods was an agreement of sorts, their view being that the gods were responsible for all natural phenomena. We had much to learn.

There was not total freedom because the Keltoi were enslaved beings and there were also slaves from many countries. Whenever Rome conquered, their captives became slaves. This was interesting because it was not that way in Judea. Many slaves were learned and highly prized in Roman homes and I wanted to learn more about them. Before I could pursue this, Joseph found us a suitable home with servants.

Joseph acquired a villa for us on the outskirts of Massalia. There were gardens filled with many herbs such as myrtle and rosemary. There was also a small body of water filled with fish. The garden carried the heavy scent of roses and lilies and it was a place of rest. It was a place of renewal.

One of our servants was a Keltoi woman found by Joseph. He had bought her at the market of the slaves, and when he brought her home, he freed her. Never, said he, would we have slaves for servants. Her name was Briaca and she told us she came from the people called Vasconnes[2] by the Romans. She was tall in stature and almost as tall as me. She was of golden hair worn in braids and of rosy skin.

Briaca merged into the family. She had warmth about her and she was giving and caring. She taught me much about the Keltoi, telling me Keltoi was a name the Greeks placed on them. Within the Keltoi were many tribes and each with their own form of government, which was of loose structure. The Keltoi lived in small settlements and they were fiercely independent. Or, before they were conquered by Caesar, had been.

Under the tutelage of Briaca I soon learned there was no one Keltoi language. What I had learned on the ship was only one dialect. With my speaking more than one language, I picked up the different dialects easily. She also taught me about the great druids who were the priests and law determiners of the various tribes. There were no written parchments, because their history was handed down in stories. An apprentice druid would study twenty years before mastering the oral history.

I am compelled to write of my life journey as I have foreseen its necessity in the future. I bless the beings that

---

[2] A tribe of the Keltoi

discover my writings. My blessings will be fruitful to their lives.

Word spread of my arrival and many were brought to me to heal. I had trained my apostles well and they assisted me. We were gathering people to our ekklesias and with the ekklesias growing, there were others formed. I evolved into being the episkopos for Gaul. Word came from Judea of the success of James who was the episkopos for Jerusalem in addition to being a High Priest. Throngs were coming to hear the teachings of Yeshua as given by the apostles James, Philip, Bartholomew, Peter, Andrew and the other men of his apostles. I was gladdened for them. Here in Gaul, Mari-Salome, Miriam, Mari-Jacobe and Abigale along with Sarah of Bethany went out to various villages that were near our villa and began their own ekklesias. Two years sped by quickly.

One morning I was in the garden alone when Joseph approached me. Joseph stated he had a longing to go to Breton and settle. His fleet of ships was growing and he wanted to expand his businesses in Breton. I already knew this was in his heart.

When this was announced to Mariamme and others, she told Joseph she cared not to go to Breton. In her heart she longed to go to Ephesia because she had two other children living there. Sarah and young James would miss their grandparents and I felt a sense of loss, however I knew each had their own journey. It was not up to me to change their minds.

Ioannes the Beloved made the decision to travel with Mariamme, seeing to her safety, and he was unsure if he would return. In his mind he felt he could spread the teachings by forming ekklesias. He shared with me that in his heart he knew he was not ready for the Mystery School in Egypt. Ioannes had been a brother to me and I had taught him all I could. I knew I could not hold him here.

Within weeks they were gone. Joseph had given me the villa and paid the servants to stay. Remaining with me were Martha and Meesha along with my children. We continued with our healings and our teachings but I was becoming restless. I also was aware that our status in Massalia was delicate.

A Roman woman had heard of our ekklesia and came to me with her young daughter who was gravely ill. The name of the woman was Olivia. What she had heard touched her heart and I was asked to heal the child. When I looked into the daughter's mind, I saw a broken spirit. I silently communed with the child and said to her that she had a choice. She could die and be reborn, to experience again what she was avoiding. Or, she could live and choose to make a difference in this world. It was her choice. The child responded by saying she chose to live. Instantly her color returned to her. Her fever abated and upon opening her eyes, she reached for her mother.

The healing of Olivia's child brought forth a change in her also. Her husband was a member of the Roman Magistrate's staff and he had not been kind to her or their daughter. Olivia resolved to come to our ekklesia and learn all she could. The times under Claudius' rule were more freeing than under the previous rulers. More and more slaves were made freedmen and granted citizenship. He was admitting men of the Gauls into the senatorial order. There was a sense of fair play and improved government.

I had foreseen a change in the near future. From Briaca I learned much of the Keltoi tribes in the Narbonnese province as well as the Vasconnes. My desire to travel to these areas grew and I knew I would soon depart.

Sarah and James had grown and both were tall like my people. At the age of ten, James thought he was a man. Life here had been a respite for me. The ekklesias were established and I was ready to have another person become the episkopos of Gaul.

One day Olivia came to me with the news of Claudius' death. His successor was named Nero and Nero sought the suppression of all Gnostics. In Rome he was having them executed. If he learned I was the wife of Yeshua, the rightful heir to the throne of the Jews, he would seek out my children and me, with orders to execute us. Thus I made a decision to journey to the province of Narbonnese.

Chapter 24

A SURPRISING REVELATION

History is made up of the lies agreed upon.
- Voltaire

It was three days after the break-in before Alain came back to see us. The new computers had arrived and Peter and Sebastian had installed the Greek to French and the French to English translation programs. Jill and Sebastian were delighted to get on with their work.

Peter had ordered a third computer because he wanted to create a web site for the scrolls. I spoke to Jill regarding my concerns about her doing all the French to English translations and told her I felt I had not done my part. Smiling, she told me to get over that guilt because she secretly had been delighted I hadn't been there to share the computer work. She told me she was thriving on it and it brought her and Sebastian into a wonderful relationship. I always enjoyed the fact that she and I had open and honest communications.

Thank god for Peter's laptop! With the other three working on the scrolls projects, I surfed the Internet for information. I learned that it is a virtual encyclopedia. And when I tired, I walked the grounds. The November weather was cold and damp and most of the time skies were overcast.

I was delighted to see Alain when he arrived. Marie insisted we have lunch before talking business. On this visit he looked rested and had a liveliness about him. After lunch we adjourned to the living room where a blazing fire was going in the fireplace. Alain leaned forward in his chair and began telling us his latest information.

"My sister and friends, my investigations are becoming fruitful. First, I have had a breakthrough regarding Montand. It is most difficult to secure information about secret societies. However, my contacts tell me Montand was once a member of

278

the organization Opus Dei. Are you familiar with this organization?"

Opus Dei? We all nodded. He went on, "Apparently Montand had become disenchanted with their leniency about the practice of self-flagellation. Leaving the organization, he and some other disenchanted people formed their own secret society called the True Sons of Christ and they shortened the name to T-1. They use the Maltese Cross as their emblem, but placed it in a circle. My contacts tell me this is an ultra fanatical group."

"Oui," interjected Sebastian. "It could be something like the P-2 organization operating in and out of the Vatican."

"What is P-2?" asked Peter.

"It is supposedly an organization based on freemasonry, however it is a cover for many illegal activities. It really has nothing to do with freemasonry. The founders purloined the Freemason title."

"In other words, they took a legitimate organization and bastardized it, thus giving the true Freemasons a bad name?" Peter inquired.

"Correct," answered Alain.

I asked Alain how they connected Peter and me with the scrolls so fast.

"Well, my dear sister, it took some deep investigating. What I have learned is that one of the members of the antiquities committee of the Bibliothèque nationale is a member of the T-1. When the police in Mirepoix reported the information about the two scrolls to the authorities, this member relayed it to the organization and it would not be difficult to track you as I have done it myself."

"How did you track them . . . us?" Jill wanted to know.

Alain smiled. "Simple. I hired investigators. The registers of hotels, and bed and breakfast places, were checked. It wasn't difficult to locate your names on the register at the Maison de Larche. After you told me of the discovery, I had the area investigated. The owner was questioned and it was learned he gave the three of you a ride to Foix, where he had let you off to catch a bus. I think you are now getting an idea of how easy it was to trace you. However, once you picked up Sebastian, the trail became cold until Ellen and Peter were questioned by the police in Carcassonne."

"I can accept that, Alain, however, how did they track Sebastian and me to Paul's?" Jill asked.

"Again, with the right questions to the Université. It would not be too difficult to inquire about Sebastian and learn he had a good friend named Paul and get Paul's address and telephone number. Recently I called that number and Paul answered. He is most anxious to get in touch with you Sebastian."

"Mon dieu! Has Paul returned?"

"He has. With your permission, he wants to travel here to see you."

"Ah oui! I will call him today."

Peter had been absorbing all this. "Tell us, what are our chances of being prosecuted?"

Giving a chuckle, Alain spoke, "I have been saving the best for the last. I have been in touch with the Committee regarding your terms for giving the scrolls to the Bibliothèque nationale. As you Americans say, I did a bit of arm-twisting by telling them you are having them authenticated yourselves. I also mentioned the name of one of the members who could be charged with Peter and Ellen's kidnapping. They accepted your terms including no prosecution."

For a moment there was silence, and then we burst out laughing, and crying. I was doing both. Jill and Sebastian rushed to embrace Alain. Peter and I kissed and embraced each other. Next it was our turn to embrace Alain. We were all talking at once. Marie opened the door in the midst of this and Peter asked her to bring in champagne and seven glasses. He told her she was also to return with Jacques.

While Marie was gone, Alain informed us there would be a ceremony Friday morning at ten. It was planned that we would give the translated scrolls to the committee and they in turn would loan Sebastian the two in their possession. In the meantime, he was to get our signatures on the agreement. Once he left us, he would take it to the chairman for his signature.

At that moment Marie came in with the champagne. Jacques was right behind her. They were now aware of the scrolls and our negotiations with the Bibliothèque.

Sebastian spoke to them in French, telling them what we were toasting. Marie let out a small squeal. Sebastian gave the toast, thanking the god in each of us, and also Mary Magdalene.

Before Alain departed for his appointment with the chairman, he said he was ready to read the scrolls. With alacrity Sebastian left the room to get copies of the French version of the scrolls that had been copied until then. Returning, he handed them to him, and Peter followed him to the car. When he returned he told us he had asked Alain again about prosecution and was told it was most unlikely unless Montand wanted to file charges and that he doubted Montand would. We all breathed a sigh of relief.

That evening, Alain called to say the agreement was now signed, and in our heightened state of joy, Jill suggested she read to us the last scroll translated which was The Magdalene's story of reaching Gaul. It was rather lengthy.

Peter commented that it appeared she had a new beginning and that we were also on the verge of new beginnings.

"Mais oui," commented Sebastian. "We also have had our travails."

"If Claudius was emperor, this will give us an idea of the approximate year she arrived, wouldn't it?" I asked.

"True." Jill went on to say she had gone on the Internet and found that Claudius ruled between 41 A.D. and 54 A.D.

"So," I said, "this is a span of 13 years. She could have arrived in Gaul within that time frame."

Jill told us, "The information I gleaned from the Internet states Nero became emperor after Claudius was murdered. He was emperor until 68 A.D. Hmmm. The two missing scrolls could indeed give us information. However, Sebastian and I will continue to translate what we have until the Committee releases the other two scrolls to us."

Touching her hand fondly, Sebastian said, "Within a few days we will have the two missing scrolls."

"In some books I have read, the authors contend Jesus was not crucified. One said he went to Britain and married again. This would disprove their allegations, wouldn't it?" I asked.

"Oui. I was thinking that also. I have known Thomas was Jesus' twin. Even though I have been a priest, I was not a truly practicing priest. I was a scholar of ancient texts therefore nothing shocks me. When I first became aware of the misleading and outright lies, I began doing my own research. I realized more and more how the Church has covered up its deceptions over these many centuries thereby creating a great lie. I must keep my anger under control. What is it you say, be the watcher?"

We chuckled. Jill spoke, "Watcher is a good definition for an observer. From what The Magdalene has written, she had with her quite an entourage. Do you think the Sarah who is called the saint of the Gypsies was her daughter?"

"Perhaps," said Sebastian. "We know Sarah was born in Egypt. It is possible it became a myth and this child of The Magdalene later became known as the black maid who accompanied her to Marseilles. Such distortion of truth does happen.

"Sometime after the Gypsies arrived in Europe, in the early 1400's, their veneration of Sarah began. In some quarters she is called Sarah the Egyptian. Now each year in May at Saintes Maries-de-le-Mer there is a festival that celebrates her as well as Marie-Salome and Marie-Jacobe."

Peter commented, "I think I have heard of it. There is quite a large gathering of Gypsies attending from all over the world, isn't there?"

"Oui. One of the misconceptions perpetuated is that Peter was the first pope of the Church. How could this be? There was no Christian church until after the Council of Nicea which formed it in 325 A.D."

"You're right," I said. "There were only ekklesias and it wasn't Peter who founded the ekklesias. It was Mary Magdalene! This means she could be considered the first pope!"

"Mon dieu! You are correct. It only makes sense." We all began laughing. "To credit Mary Magdalene as being the first pope would shake the world, however there would be the skeptics and those in denial. One could give them all the proof needed and still they would deny a female pope. However, there is a little known fact that there was a female pope. Her name was Joan."

"Pope Joan?" I asked.

Jill commented, "I've heard of her."

Sebastian continued, "She was Pope somewhere around 854 or 855 after Christ. It seems she held the position for over two years. This knowledge is usually known as a myth, legend or allegory; however, myths and legends are always based on some event."

I was very curious and asked Sebastian to elaborate on her.

"Oui. As you well know, it is men who write history. This Joan, as I recall, is sometimes called the English Joan. I became interested when I first came across an old manuscript that mentioned her. It is said she was Pope John VIII, but many will say she is a myth. I think that is not so. As the story goes according to my research, she could have been born of English missionaries to Germany. It is said Joan was from Germany and went to Athens. Some say she had a lover traveling with her. After she became educated in Athens, she together with her lover went to Rome where she became active in the affairs of the church and she wore men's clothing so she could pass as a man. This led to her becoming a cardinal and then she was elected Pope."

Jill spoke, "I remember there is a novel titled 'Pope Joan.' A movie was made from the book and I went to see it. Wasn't she a curia secretary before becoming a cardinal? I find it interesting there were English missionaries in Germany in the 7th and 8th centuries."

"Oui, she was. There is a misconception of Christianity being all over Europe by then. That is not so. Actually the Christian movement began in Ireland and spread into Europe around 590 A.D.[1] Ireland and Britain sent missionaries out to Christianize the pagans."

Peter was becoming more interested by the moment. "Here is an interesting thought. Perhaps Joseph of Arimathea and James the son of Jesus and Mary Magdalene were responsible for providing the fertile soil of their teachings in Britain."

---

[1] Saint Columbanus, an Irish monk with a large group of monks set sail for Europe to spread Christianity. The Vikings succumbed to Christianity in the 10th century.

Responding to Peter's observation Jill said, "That is an interesting thought, and perhaps it is so. I have no information to validate it. Do you Sebastian?"

"Non. I have no such information, but it is possible." Sebastian continued with his train of thought. "During the period of Pope Joan, when the people elected the pope, it wasn't too long before her true sex was revealed. This revelation was when the rule was changed to where only a small selected group would elect a pope. As with most great women, history has maligned her."

Indignantly Jill said, "I was incensed when I saw the movie about her. So she had a lover and became pregnant. After all, priests and popes could marry during that time. They even had mistresses who had their children!"

"Ah Jill, I understand your point of view. It was after the revelation of her giving birth that popes were required to prove their masculinity before ordination."

"Sebastian, how did they do that?" I asked.

Chuckling, Sebastian gave a shake of his head. "From my research, the Church hierarchy did not want to be fooled by another woman so a chair was constructed which was perforated."

"Wasn't the perforation actually in the shape of a keyhole?" I asked.

"Oui. It is named the porphyry chair. Before the pope was crowned, a cardinal bent down and felt the testicles, making sure he was a man. Mon dieu! Such madness."

"You are so right and I believe this continued for a few hundred years and then gradually the purpose of the chair was changed and another chair was apparently used without the perforation," I added.

"Oui. A new ceremony evolved around the chair. There is one with the keyhole in a corner of the Vatican museum gathering dust."

Jill added, "Yes, I know. I've seen one in the Louvre. Supposedly Napoleon brought it back from Rome."

"Ah Jill, if only the losers or the fallen could write history. What a grand thing that would be."

Jill agreed and added, "I find it difficult to understand how she came to be appointed as Pope."

"During the period of time that the people elected the pope, she dressed as a man and was well received and loved for the works she did, according to documents I have read. It was after Joan supposedly was unmasked when she gave birth on a street that the rules were changed."

"Sebastian, this is rather ironic. Paranoia came along because a woman became a pope. Now we have what The Magdalene has written regarding Peter and Andrew. It could be they were homosexuals because she wrote they were 'lovers of men only.' This could be where celibacy as required by the Church came from. Yet celibacy perpetuates homosexuality. Could this be why so many priests abuse young boys?"

"It could be. However there are many good people in the priesthood who are not homosexual. And thanks to you, ma chère, I am a well man."

Peter and I had sat back allowing the two experts to share their knowledge, and we were learning. Peter commented it was interesting that Mary Magdalene had made a tremendous change moving from Jerusalem to Gaul, and now Mariamme and Joseph were leaving as well as some of her apostles.

"You're right," I said. "Have you ever noticed that when you make a major change in your life, old friends and acquaintances seem to drop away?"

Peter nodded yes. "When I sold my business, it was as though I had never existed to some people."

"I can understand that," Jill said. "It's almost as if we outgrow people, and sometimes it could be that some outgrow us."

Sebastian appeared to be puzzled. "I cannot say I have had the experiences you talk about. I will confess you are among my first friends. Paul was my first. I had not realized how lonely I was until you three came into my life." Jill reached over and gave his hand a squeeze.

Smiling at Sebastian, I said, "I'm glad you are our friend, and it is true about people almost disappearing from one's life when major changes are made. It has happened to me a number of times. I think this is something I want to contemplate on later."

Turning to a new subject, we discussed the arrival of Paul Leseur the following day. I think we were as excited as Sebastian. This was a man who had made a difference in

285

Sebastian's life and their chance meeting in Rome led to Sebastian's love for computers, resulting in the two men developing the translation programs.

It was Jill who said, "Life is like a tapestry. A chance meeting can lead to a beautiful new thread. We are weaving our individual tapestry with each choice we make."

"Well stated," Peter said. "I am going to weave a beautiful thread tonight as I say good night and wish you all beautiful dreams."

Laughing, I agreed with Peter. "I will join you." Turning to Sebastian and Jill, we said good night.

❧❧ ❧❧ ❧❧

I love all kinds of weather, and the morning came with a delightful change. The sun was shining through the windows. Peter and I had enjoyed a long, leisurely sharing the night before after going to bed, followed by passionate lovemaking.

I turned to him and he was awake, looking at me.

"My love, I love watching you wake up," he said. "It gives me an opportunity to give thanks for the blessing you are to my life. I am a most fortunate man."

Snuggling with him, I replied, "Before I open my eyes, I count my blessings and give thanks for finding you. I am a most fortunate woman."

After showering and dressing, we joined Sebastian and Jill for breakfast. That morning Marie served coffee with a continental breakfast. She was busy making the house shine and Jacques was helping her because we could hear the vacuum cleaners going.

We had breakfast in the petite dining room where a round table was placed near a bay window, looking out towards the woods. After breakfast Peter and I chose to take a walk while Jill and Sebastian chose to get more translating done before Paul arrived.

Putting on sweaters, we walked out into the brisk fall day. I asked Peter what he was feeling now that the scrolls were almost completed. "Hmmm, I think I am ready to move on to the next phase of this. I have ideas swirling around in my brain I want to explore. And of course, they all include you."

Smiling, I tucked my hand into his. "I'm happy you said that. There is one point I feel incomplete with, though."

"Montand?"

"Yes. What is your sense about him?"

"It bothers me. I don't think we have heard the last of him. What happened brought out an aspect of me I was unaware of."

"What did you learn from that experience?"

"I learned I would do just about anything to protect my beloved. And, if we have children, it would extend to them. I'm not an aggressive man, however when cornered, I will act. And I have contemplated the messages in The Magdalene's scrolls and I see no point in holding onto guilt, remorse or fear. And you?"

"I sense I would have felt the same way if the roles had been reversed. I learned that in the midst of danger and in a position of helplessness, I can go within and find a calm mind.

"Paul should be here by now. Shall we walk back to the house?"

The rest of the day was spent getting to know Paul, a delightful man and very energetic. Sebastian and Jill had given him most of the background of our adventures with the scrolls. After Peter and I gave our account of what we had experienced, he shook his head in disbelief.

Speaking in excellent English, he said, "From what I have heard, you are divinely led. The change in Sebastian is most beautiful and I am very appreciative of what each of you has contributed to his healing and change."

The day passed all too quickly. Paul told us of his sojourn in South Africa and his ideas for new computer programs. After dinner the three men became engrossed with the mechanics of computers and software so Jill and I left them. I chose to go to bed and read while Jill wanted to go over the scrolls, which had been brought from the bank vault, to make sure they were packed well.

Chapter 25

THE EXCHANGE OF SCROLLS

Adversity is the first path to truth.
- Lord Byron

The day of the scroll exchange arrived and the entire household was filled with excitement. Peter and I were up early and as we came out of our bedroom, we met Jill and Sebastian in the hallway. Both the men wore suits purchased especially for that day.

Jill had gone shopping with Sebastian, helping him select his clothes for the ceremony. They had chosen well and he looked distinguished. Peter was dashing.

Jill and I had purchased winter coats. We wore dresses and heels and oh how we giggled as we practiced walking. It had been such a long time since we had worn them.

Paul soon joined us for breakfast and he looked quite professional. Our spirits were soaring and we all commented in one way or another that it seemed as though we were seeing the light at the end of the tunnel.

The limousine arrived on time and an invitation had been given to Marie and Jacques to attend the ceremony as part of the audience. Jacques had opted to drive them to the meeting. Marie's sister had come in to help clean up the breakfast dishes. Knowing the security patrol was on duty, we departed with a light heart.

The November day had begun with the sun appearing through scudding dark clouds on their way to the northeast. Alain was meeting us at the Bibliothèque. We knew the news media would be there and were prepared for the flashing cameras and shouting reporters. Of course we wouldn't stop to answer.

Alain had asked Sebastian to prepare a statement. At first he said he wouldn't do it. The rest of us did some persuading and he finally capitulated. Following the ceremony there was going to be a press conference. Actually we were all nervous.

It would have been preferable to hand over the translated scrolls quietly in exchange for the two the Bibliothèque had. However, the Committee wanted the publicity and insisted on the ceremony. It was held in the Francois-Mitterand site of the Bibliothèque on the Left Bank because it was newer and housed a large auditorium. The Richelieu-Louvois Bibliothèque site actually held manuscripts and scrolls, however there was no large auditorium or meeting room there.

Driving into the VIP parking section, we entered through a private entranceway. Paul was seated in the auditorium with Marie and Jacques. The stage was quite impressive with banks of flowers and plants. A podium had been placed in the center with chairs behind it. Once the audience was seated, the Committee entered the stage first, followed by Sebastian, Jill, Peter, me and Alain. The Committee was large and there were two rows of chairs for them. The big moment had arrived.

The chairman stepped to the podium and gave a lengthy speech of appreciation for the finding of the scrolls. Of course he spoke in French. I attempted to follow him.

The lights on the stage were bright, and the house lights were dimmed, therefore I was unable to see how full the auditorium was.

Turning towards us, the chairman introduced Sebastian who had the translated scrolls with him. Stepping forward, he handed them to the chairman. Before Sebastian could make his speech, all hell broke loose. I felt something hit against the back of my chair and looked back to see one of the Committee members slumped over with blood running down his face.

There was screaming from the audience. A Committee member had been shot. In reconstructing the event, we realized I had dropped a tissue and Peter must have bent down to retrieve it. I have no memory of it, but if I had not dropped it and he had not bent down, the bullet would have hit him. Again, there was Divine intervention. The one who fired the shot must have been behind the audience because we doubted that he would be sitting in the midst of it.

Later after we had given statements to the police, the press demanded a statement. Alain was reluctant to have any of us speak and Sebastian was too shaken, so Peter said he would speak for us. Oh gawd! I was so proud of him. He walked out on that stage – all 6'4" of him and demanded the house lights stay on.

This is what Peter said, without notes:

"My name is Peter Douglass. I have been involved almost from the beginning in getting the scrolls translated and out to the world. To the press and to the world I say: there is one power in this universe. It is a great power and can be used for good or it can be used for evil. For too long evil has dominated. There have been many blocks placed in our way to stop these scrolls from reaching the public.

"I am serving notice, to those who want to prevent Mary Magdalene's story from reaching the world: you will be defeated. And I am not making idle threats.

"Once they are made available to the public, will these scrolls be free? No. There is always a cost to everything. Your cost will be your time. In the beginning the translations will be placed on the Internet for all to access. Our intent is not to allow these scrolls to languish in archives accessed only by scholars who would take them, dissect them and give you what they think is the right interpretation. No, these are a gift from Mary Magdalene to the world.

"There have always been the naysayers and the skeptics. There is nothing I can say to open a closed mind. This message and these scrolls are for those who hunger for something better in life and want to know Truth.

"What am I getting out of this . . . only the satisfaction of having complied with the directive from The Magdalene in the first scroll and a way to evolve my life so that I can sleep well at night. I am learning what love is. I am learning what forgiveness is. This is my payoff.

"Regarding who did this dastardly deed of shooting Monsieur Ducote, I decline to speculate. This is a police matter. You will have to get your information from them. Thank you."

Quickly Alain and the police escorted us out and into our waiting limousine. As the car sped away, Peter wrapped his arms around me. Somehow Alain had managed to find Paul and he was in the car with us. We were all too shaken to talk. The driver told us we had a trail of paparazzi behind us and Peter told him to let them follow. He was not going to hide from them anymore.

Paul was the first to speak to the group of us.

"Mon dieu! That bullet was meant for Peter! What sort of people would want to see you killed?"

"As far as we can ascertain, it is a fanatical group from the extreme right of a Christian organization," Peter answered. "At this time we have no proof as to which organization they might be affiliated with. Right now I choose not to guess."

Alain had given instructions for us to meet him in his office so the paparazzi could not follow us back to the chateau. Within a short time, we were in the parking garage. Taking the elevator up to Alain's office, I felt weak in the knees. Reaching down, I pulled off my shoes. Jill followed suit and took hers off. When we arrived, we found Alain was already there.

Michele greeted us and told us he was waiting in his office. After kissing Jill and me and embracing the men, he asked us to be seated. Michele had placed chairs in a semi-circle in front of his desk, and he asked her to bring a chair for him to sit on with us because he did not want to sit behind a desk.

After we were settled, he asked if we could remember anything unusual. Paul had been in the audience facing the stage and saw only us and with the house lights dimmed, the stage lights blinded us. Directing his attention to Peter, Alain said, "It would appear Montand has a vendetta against you."

Laughing Peter commented, "That's an understatement. What concerns me is the danger for all of us."

Alain nodded agreement. "I have spoken with the hospital and Monsieur Ducote is in the operating room. Let us hope he does not die because that would be a tragedy."

"You are right, Alain," said Jill. "This has to come to an end. The translated scrolls are in the hands of the committee and I hope you have the other two scrolls."

"I do." On his desk was a package containing two cylinders with the scrolls inside. Handing the package to Jill, he continued. "I have read the translations you gave me and they are powerful. By these being released to the world, history will be changed."

"Oui," Sebastian said. "The lies and deceits of two thousand years are exposed for those who can accept them."

My comment was to the effect that the truth had been persecuted for eons and everyone nodded in agreement. Alain said he was sending us home and that he was sending the limousine we arrived in to a different location to confuse the paparazzi. He had another to take us home. He said he would be in touch later when he had news.

Gratefully we left, descending in the elevator with Jill carrying the precious scrolls and me carrying our high heels. When we arrived home, Marie and Jacques were waiting for us with a lovely fire was in the fireplace. They informed us that word had been sent from Alain's office that we were with him. We asked if they had seen anything unusual. They replied they hadn't because their attention at the ceremony had been on us.

Marie's sister, Yvonne had prepared a lunch for us and gratefully we sat down at the dining room table. It was a challenge to keep the conversation on a light note. Paul intervened by telling some humorous accounts of his trip to South Africa. By the time lunch was over, we were all laughing.

Peter and I went upstairs to take a nap, leaving Jill and Sebastian with Paul. He remained with us for the next week because the police had told him not to leave Paris. As I drifted off to sleep, I wondered if I would ever have the freedom of leaving France. Nestled in Peter's arms, I slept.

❧❧ ❧❧ ❧❧

NARBONNESE
Scroll 19
(The First Missing Scroll)

Within a week of my decision, Joseph of Arimathea arrived from Breton. By agreement with Joseph, I granted the villa back to him. His intention was to allow it to be used as a school for truth seekers. I knew I had taught the apostles all I could and it was an opportunity for them to use their knowledge for the good of others.

Young James came to me asking to go to Breton with his grandfather. Sadness was felt in my heart, and yet I knew this would be the safest place for James to be. Joseph agreed to take him.

Joseph had asked if he could take me by ship to a small trading port on the coast of the Narbonnese Province and I accepted. Once his business was completed, we were to set sail. Traveling with me were Sarah, Meesha and Briaca. The moment to leave came one fine morning. I bade a farewell to Martha, and the others. Each knew we could be in touch by using our nous. I had already sent out messages that Martha now was the new episkopos.

Our departure was far different from when we left Judea. The budding trees were bursting with leaves. It was almost the same time of the year as when we first arrived. We had no sense of being pursued and the voyage by water was a short one. Upon landing in the cove of the small trading port, I was taken with the colors. The stones on the beach twinkled with gold and there were stones with a mixture of pale blue and pale yellow. Ah, colors and warmth.

We had brought meager belongings with us, as we would travel light. I was accustomed to that way of travel, because I had traveled with few things from village to village outside of Massalia.

With sadness, I bade farewell to James and Joseph. Sarah shed tears. She loved her brother deeply and there was a deep bond between them. James looked with intensity into my eyes and said, "My mother, I will remember all you have taught and I promise you I will apply it to my life."

With tears in my eyes, I spake. "My son, thank you for your words. Nothing can harm you when you live from your Truth."

Turning to Joseph, I looked into his eyes and I saw the depth of the man, a noble man who had given a noble upbringing to his children. He had been equal father to those of his loins and also to those who were not. I could see the regret in his eyes of our parting. I told him this was not a final parting, however we each had our journey in life. I thanked him for his contribution to mine.

We would not wait for their ship to pull up anchor because we had our own travels before us.

જ‍ે   જ‍ે   જ‍ે

THE PARTING
Scroll 20
(The Second Missing Scroll)

Gathering our small pack of belongings, Sarah, Meesha and I followed Briaca who was our guide through the trading village. Here were people of many colors from when the port had once been in great use by the Greeks and the Phoenicians. The smells and sounds were different from Massalia. We were dressed in the manner of the Keltoi at Briaca's request. Joseph had secured a Keltoi group of men to guide us and protect us. We were walking into the unknown.

With Briaca's help the Keltoi made us welcome. Moving from village to settlement, we adapted to their customs. We had such freedom! We were away from the Romans and their watchfulness.

Even though the Romans had forbidden human sacrifice, there were some Keltoi practicing the rite and I exhorted them never to sacrifice any man, animal or fowl to any god. I said, "The God you seek is within you. It is a sacrilege to sacrifice a living being because it is an empty gesture. It is blasphemy against the Creator within you."

There was mumbling in the beginning, however the more I traveled among them, the more the idea took hold and became integrated in their lives.

I had been told of the High Druid of Tolosa.[1] His reputation was of a man strict with the law of the Keltoi and I sensed he wanted to see me and was on his way. At this moment I was living in a small village of the Rhaetii[2] near the large settlement called Rhedae[3] and the Chief of this village was called Luernios. We had gradually made our way into the lowlands of the Pyrenees Mountains. Sarah, Meesha and Briaca were with me and it was a new experience for each of us.

My nohmata[4] was correct. Word began being passed around of the High Druid's coming and Keltoi from different

---

[1] Tolosa, an ancient word for Toulouse, France
[2] Rhaetii, a Keltoi tribe
[3] Rhedae, an ancient name for Rennes-le-Chateau, France
[4] Nohmata, an ancient Greek word for intuition

tribes began to enter the village because they knew he was coming to see me.

The Keltoi needed little or no reason for feasting, games, and celebration. Horns were blowing to announce the arrival of the Arch Druid Arc'hantael. Drums began their pulsating rhythm, bringing an excitement among the people because a High Druid had never visited the small village before. I came out of my round abode wearing my plain Keltoi garment. I was told later that I stood regal as a queen.

A tall man with a white beard almost to his mid-section came into the clearing, walking with a purposeful stride. His long white hair was tied back with a leather strap that had a shell of the sea attached to it, and his wearing apparel was that of his countrymen.

Accompanying him was a younger man dressed much in the same manner. Both carried small packs and the younger man also carried an instrument named a harp. Luernios went to greet them. And after the greetings, the Druid continued walking forward toward me. As he neared I could see his eyes were the deepest blue of the sky. In his hand he carried a magnificent decorated staff, which marked him the High Druid. The peoples of the village stood silent waiting for one of us to speak a greeting. Since I was in the host village I spoke first. "Hail unto you High Druid Arc'hantael. I bid you welcome."

His eyes never moved from my eyes as he stopped in front of me. There seemed to be a long pause while he was assessing me. He knew he had met a most unusual woman. At last he spoke. "Hail unto you who be called The Magdalene. I accept your welcome." We both bowed our heads in acknowledgment of one another.

Turning to Sarah, Meesha and Briaca, I introduced them to the Druid. He, in turn introduced his apprentice Brevalaer. Luernios breathed a sigh of relief, signaling the women to bring forth beer and wine. It was the custom to drink, eat and have music before any serious talk was done. The villagers surpassed themselves in welcoming the two men and it was well nigh to the end of the afternoon when Arc'hantael asked to take me aside for speaking.

Brevalaer had picked up his harp and was singing the tale of the news the villagers wanted to hear. Luernios had made his abode available to us and we entered his home. Jugs of beer and wine had been placed on the table.

Arc'hantael bade me to sit down across from him. We each poured our drink into a cup. I am writing of this, as it was a turning point of my time in Gaul. The High Druid could make life miserable for me or he could give me his blessings. Looking at me from under his bushy eyebrows, he began asking me questions. Never once did I stumble. One of the questions was about alchemy and I told him it was the application of the natural laws of the universe. His eyes lit up and with a loud burst of laughter, he slapped his knee while telling me, "You are indeed a true druid yourself. From whence did you learn of these matters? No, allow me to discern. Ah, yes. Your dual eyes tell me you are of wisdom. You have been to the school of mysteries in Egypt."

Smiling, I told him he was very perceptive. From that moment, we conversed well into the night about matters some would call magic. For us they were only natural laws.

When at last we parted, he gave me a ring. By wearing this ring, anyone who saw it would know I had the blessing of Arc'hantael. I was given an invitation to visit him in Tolosa and I accepted. His parting words were, "Beware. The news of you has reached the ears of Herod Antipas now living in Lugdunum[5] and he has asked the Roman Magistrate to arrest you." I nodded and departed for my abode. I had much to ponder.

When early morn came and I arose from my bed, Arc'hantael and Brevalaer had departed quietly. Awakening Meesha, Briaca and Sarah, I told them what I had learned from Arc'hantael regarding Herod Antipas. Having contemplated long into the time before the sun rose, I knew Sarah and I must part. It was a difficult decision to make and this I shared with them.

Sarah voiced a protest in the beginning. "My Mother, how can I part from you? Where will I go? Where will you go?"

Briaca and Meesha were silent. "My beloved daughter, this is a most difficult decision. My knowing has told me you

---

can blend in better if I send you towards Massalia. There are many dark skinned people there. I will send you to Martha."

With tears running down her face, Sarah nodded agreement. Briaca spoke up, "I will take her with your permission. I will speak with Luernios. I will need men to guard us." Arising, she left our abode.

Meesha was also crying. She had been a second mother to Sarah. This parting would be painful for her as well as me. I spoke. "Sarah, your father did not become risen in vain. You and James are the fruit of our union. Guard well your body because it is within you to carry on the lineage of the House of David."

Walking out into the morning sun, I greeted Luernios. He and the people of the village now looked upon me with awe and full acceptance. They knew I had the mark of the Druid.

In two days Luernios had gathered a band of six men to take Briaca and Sarah to Martha. Unbeknownst to them, I had the night before their departure used the ability of being in two places at once. By using my ability of discernment, I knew where Martha could be found. I visited her while I was lying abed and I told her I was entrusting Sarah into her care. I sent thoughts of the danger of Herod.

The following morning I gave Briaca and the Keltoi tribesman, by name of Kaour, who was leading the party, instructions for finding Martha. I felt a sense of peace with their leaving. I knew I could visit Sarah at any given moment and I blessed the training I had received.

Chapter 26

A COMPLETION

Change is the constant, the signal for rebirth,
the egg of the phoenix.
- Christine Baldwin

The days have passed since the attempt on Peter's life, and it is becoming a distant memory. I asked myself if I was in denial. In discussing this with Peter, I had been assured I wasn't. I also shared my experience with Jill and Sebastian, who said they had also felt the same way. Perhaps it was an aspect of trauma shock. I began to feel much more alive. Paul returned to Toulouse and was missed. He had been the spark of laughter in the house, and we were sorry to see him depart.

The good news was Monsieur Ducote had lived through the operation and was expected to recover. The Committee members had sent us an official letter of appreciation for the translations. Independent experts were authenticating the scrolls as agreed and we were to be notified of their findings. Also Peter had hired an independent group to conduct an unbiased authentication. We hoped the results would be in by the first of the year.

Thanksgiving had passed and now it was time to think of Christmas. Sebastian and Jill had finished translating the remaining scrolls we had, plus the two on loan from the committee, and all had been sent to the Bibliothèque as agreed.

One morning after breakfast, Jill read us the translations of the two missing scrolls. I think we all had tears in our eyes.

Speaking first I said, "Not only did she lose her husband, she gave up her children. I don't know if I would have been able to do that."

Peter responded, "Yes she did. However, it was young James who wanted to further his spiritual path and leave. I can see where she would not want to stop him. And regarding Sarah, she sent her away to save her life."

"True. I had not thought that far. Instead I reacted from a maternal instinct which I didn't even realize I had."

Chuckling at me Jill said her first reaction was the same as mine, and she added that she thought there was a maternal instinct in most women. "I said most, but not necessarily all."

"I see this as more greatness in The Magdalene," Sebastian said. "She has shown a great love for her family. From what I have read, she knows each person has a purpose for life. I see her as willing to give up her attachment to them so that they may live and perhaps experience their purpose."

"Brilliant, Sebastian!" I said. "It would be the greater love to sacrifice one's own emotional attachment."

Peter commented that he enjoyed reading of her meeting with the Keltoi Druid. "The Arch Druid recognized her greatness. In fact they all did."

"Oui. Now I can understand why the Black Madonnas have survived these several thousand years."

The conversation turned to the Christmas season. I asked Sebastian how Christmas was celebrated in France.

"I have never given much attention to Christmas. Of course there was always the Midnight Mass. As a small child we had a tradition of lighting a special log called the Yule Log. The meaning of it escapes my mind."

I shared a memory of something my mother told me. "When Mother arrived in Paris, she said she became fascinated by the tradition of the Yule Log. At that time, it was the custom to attend Midnight Mass, and after the mass, many would go to restaurants where there would be music, dancing and for dessert a Yule Log cake. Of course, not all families went to restaurants. Some would go home after mass to celebrate with a feast which included a Yule Log cake."

Turning to Jill, I asked, "Since you have been a history teacher, can you give an explanation of the Yule Log?"

"Actually I can. The Yule Log tradition dates back to pagan or Celtic times. It was a celebration of the winter solstice, the shortest day of the year. This was an important time because it denoted that the sun is at its lowest and weakest point. It heralds the start of winter. The Yule Log was lit to welcome the sun back into longer days and to mark the beginning of a new solar year. In fact, almost all Christmas traditions can be traced back to the pagans, also known as the Celts."

"Oui. Ancient documents indicate Jesus was born in May and not on December 25 as celebrated. Others say it was in March in 7 B.C."

Dryly, Peter made this statement. "It would seem the Christians were very smart. In order to Christianize the pagans or Celts, they adopted their traditions and changed the names. By doing that, they made Christmas appear to be theirs."

"You're right," Jill said. "The Romans also had a celebration of the winter solstice called saturnalia. The Celts used the evergreen in their celebration of the winter solstice. To them it represented everlasting life."

"Alright," I said. "How are we going to celebrate Christmas? Can we incorporate many traditions?"

Everyone said, "Yes!" Jill offered to research the Internet for various traditions of the world so we could choose those we wanted to include in our celebration. Sebastian became the most enthusiastic of the four of us. He and Peter offered to go into the forest and locate a tree. It was agreed permission had to first be obtained from the chosen tree. Then we would bless it, cut it, take it to the chateau and decorate it gloriously.

A few days passed and with laughter, love and high spirits, we had the tree up. Alain, his father Maurice and Alain's son Paul had been invited for the holidays. Mother and Jim were flying over, and Paul Leseur was also joining us.

The four of us had just begun decorating the tree when Marie came in to announce Inspector Gauthier was there to see us. My heart gave a lurch. Having taken his hat and coat, Marie brought him in. I had the impression we were all holding our breaths.

Speaking in English with a heavy French accent, he said, "Excuse this intrusion. I wanted to personally inform you of the latest development in the investigation of the crimes committed against you."

Crimes committed against us? Gauthier continued, "I have spoken to Monsieur Delacroix and it was agreed I was to tell you in person. The body of Gilbert Montand has been found. It has the appearance of suicide. However in these types of cases, it is difficult to determine. Supposedly he shot himself."

The four of us spoke all at once saying it was over and giving out "thank god," "hallelujahs" and so on. The Inspector was smiling broadly and he continued, "The local authorities found evidence which links him to the men who caused you grief. We are closing this case and you are each free to leave France or pursue whatever you choose."

Peter asked, "What about Bruno?"

With a slight shrug of his shoulders, Gauthier replied that it had been discovered that there were a number of outstanding crimes and other charges pending against the man and that it was up to the courts to make a decision as to his fate.

I went forward, shaking his hand, thanking him profusely for coming. Peter, Jill, and Sebastian followed me. I think he was embarrassed.

When the Inspector started to leave he stopped. Turning back towards us he said in a wondering tone, "A most curious room was found in Montand's chateau. It was filled with whips, a bed with nails and videos showing him using self-flagellation. One more item of interest perhaps. The man who attempted to enter your friend Paul Leseur's home near Toulouse recovered and it has been discovered he was connected to many other crimes. I think his prison sentence will be a long one.

Shrugging, he placed a finger to the side of his nose, and gave a nod saying, "Joyeux Noel and Merry Christmas."

I felt we truly had just had a visit from St. Nick.

And it was a Joyeux Noel and Merry Christmas.

We now give you the final translations because we cannot think of a better way to end this book.

❧❧ ❧❧ ❧❧

MY TRAVELS
Scroll 21

We wintered in our village. Briaca returned before the first snow with news that Sarah was safe and secure. I blessed the tribesmen and Briaca who had taken her to safety.

As the white silence fell, it was a time for quiet. For the people it was also a time for storytelling. The wine, the mead and the beer was drawn and helped to keep the cold at bay. The artisans were busy making jewelry, which would be traded in the spring. Their work was of great beauty and skill.

Before my eyes I watched Meesha blossom into a comely woman. What brought this about after all these years was a man of the Ruteni[1] tribe. He was wintering here because of an injury. Meesha had nursed him and love began. His wife having died, Tangi was lonely and ready for another wife.

Meesha spoke with me of their love for one another, and with my blessings, she became his wife. Tangi knew there would likely be no sons or daughters because Meesha had told him of her barrenness. At the beginning of spring the pair departed south to live with his people. How could I feel sadness when Meesha had found happiness? I knew it was also time for me to move on.

Having accepted the invitation of Arc'hantael, Briaca and I set out for Tolosa. Briaca was eager to return to the area of her people, the Volcae.[2] The gift from the people when we were leaving the village was a druid walking staff. It was beautifully carved and I accepted this with deep appreciation.

We walked not the Roman roads, but we traveled through woods, fields newly planted and over low hills. Wherever we stopped, my staff and the ring I wore brought forth hospitality. My eyes of two colors were looked upon with curiosity and reverence.

I had learned the settlement of Tolosa was large and had many Romans living there. Arc'hantael's village was to the south of the settlement. Arriving at the end of the planting season, we were made welcome by his people, the Tolosa as well as the Volcae. Here I would stay for some years. I wanted to study and work with Arc'hantael and his school of druids.

I knew the Roman agents would hear of me and attempts were made to find me. Word traveled fast through the many tribes and I was protected. I realized the arm of the Emperor was long. However, I no longer feared pursuit.

----

[1] Ruteni, a Keltoi tribe
[2] Volcae, another Keltoi tribe

I learned the uses of the different herbs and I learned the uses of the weapons to bring down meat and to snare. The forests were lush with many ever green trees. I spoke with the trees and the plants in the manner I had as a child. I spoke with the birds and other animals. Never did we take an animal for meat without its permission.

I admired the artwork of the various Keltoi tribes with the intricate designs of their ornaments and jewelry. Their metalwork was beautiful. I loved their bawdiness and their great laughter. I also observed when the druids meted out justice. At times I joined them.

I have experienced freedom of movement. I have enjoyed having no responsibility except for myself. I have been free to explore other realms and other worlds and always I return to this one.

I celebrated with them the birth of babes. I healed the sick and the wounded. I celebrated their deaths. I knew it was only the body that died. That which was within them lives forever and will return again and again until the soul is satisfied. I celebrated the coming of the seasons. I celebrated life.

࿄ ࿄ ࿄

MY LAST YEARS
Scroll 22

While I place my thoughts on papyrus, I am hearing the pipes and the drums. My people, and they have become my people, are beginning the celebration of the Rite of Fertility. Do I have a remembrance of Yeshua and I? Yes. I have no regrets. I know I can leave this life with no regrets and nothing to accomplish that is unfinished.

Sarah thinks she can surprise me by arriving unannounced. Silently I laugh. My inner vision is keener than ever. She brings with her my granddaughter Makeda, who was beget during a hieros gamos, the same as I brought forth James. She is a comely maiden and her skin is much lighter than ours. She has the copper hair. I can see the resemblance of Yeshua.

The challenges of other years need not be addressed here because I have written of them. There are many ekklesias

303

throughout Gaul and some have penetrated the heart of Rome despite the persecutions.

I have foreseen the future for some. Petros died in Rome by the order of the Emperor Nero. He was never part of the ekklesias established by my apostles or me. Men are such fools. They come from the womb of woman but honor her not. It speaks of a hatred of self. There is another man named Saul who claims to be an apostle of Yeshua, yet he has already persecuted many of the Gnostics. He is full of his own self-importance. He is no true spokesman for Yeshua. He spied for the Romans and I foresaw his death in Rome.

Beautiful James, brother of Yeshua, had been overly successful in spreading Yeshua's words; for this he was killed in Jerusalem. James, our son, has become a Druid and he travels the roads of Breton. He also has come to the land of the Vasconnes. We have great love and respect for each other. He, with his grandfather Joseph, has many ekklesias in Breton.

All life is to be honored. I have foreseen long into the future. There will be wars, plagues, famines and oppression. I look upon Yeshua's life and my life as threads of Truth. We are part of the tapestry of life. Long have I pondered these things I have foreseen. We have been seeds of Truth. Some will lay dormant for years. Truth is always waiting to be watered by the seeker of knowledge. Only when one tires of the games men play will the seeker emerge.

As my teachings and presence have been suppressed, so has the true status of women been hidden away. I see a new dawn. When my writings are found, it will be a sign of change for women and they will be revered as the wombs of creation. Woman and man will walk side by side, each gifted with minds equal but reflecting the varied aspect of the One. I have seen the foolishness of certain traditions. These will be no more.

Chapter 27

MY LEGACY
Scroll 23

I have foreseen the future and the attempted suppression and knowledge of my existence, however this is not to be. I have placed in the future a finding of these scrolls and the emergence of my truth.

What is my message? Foremost I say that Yeshua's message was love and Truth. The old ways must be done away with. Over and over he spoke the message: Love the lord your god with all your heart, soul, all your mind and your life. Next is to love other beings as you would love yourself.

My message, together with Yeshua's and Ioannes' the Immerser, is Mind. And what is Mind? Mind is the total of all thoughts, feelings and emotions. Yeshua and I were like two hands. One hand was love and the other mind. When clasped together they became the One.

The Truth is available to all. It is for those who have the eyes to see and the ears to hear. If, after reading my words, you desire to know, I urge you to seek a Master Teacher or a mystery school. It is a fool who attempts the mysteries without the guidance of a Master Teacher. To those with an open mind, much is given. I have given you only the lesser mysteries.

My life has been for the purpose to awaken the divine that sleeps deep within each person from one lifetime to another. My teachings have been consistent. By healing the thoughts, the body will be healed. Change is necessary and created by what one thinks and believes.

All learned people can espouse great knowledge. Unless they turn it into experience, it is empty of meaning. I cannot tell you the deeper mysteries. I can only allude to them. If anyone passes this plane by death to the body, they did not master the mysteries. I have taught Truth as I know it and as I have lived it. This is what I taught wherever I traveled.

The Nobleness of Life

I have always honored all members of my family.
I have always honored the place of right and
truth.
I always expect to know greatness in others.
I always expect the unexpected.
I have never sought my name to be praised.
I have always treated servants with honor and
respect.
I have always respected another person's truth.
I have not caused pain to another.
I have caused no man or woman to hunger.
I have never created a cause for anyone to weep.
I have never killed another for I value life.
I have not taken from any man or woman what is
not rightfully mine.
I am pure in spirit and mind.

These are but words. If lived righteously, you will experience the Kingdom of Heaven on Earth. I leave you with three keys to unlock the Kingdom within you.

Forgive everyone. Everything. And lastly forgive
yourself.
Never blame another. Blame withholds the
Kingdom.
Give. Give with no thoughts of return.
Give up hatred, anger, and prejudices.
Give generously of whatever you can. God is a
cheerful giver.

I have lived what I taught. I am ever expanding awareness. I know my Truth. Therefore, I know I am an absolute being. I am complete in all ways. I know I am God I Am.

I have been the wind swaying through a mighty
tree.
I have been the wind blowing across the land.
I have been the soaring falcon.
I have been its prey.
I have been the snowflake as it falls.
I have been the tear on a woman's face.
I have been the sharp edge of a sword.
I have been the breath of a sleeping babe.
I have soared to the highest mountaintop.
I have been the dew upon the rose.
I have been the bleat of a newborn lamb.
I have explored galaxies.
I have danced in the center of the sun.
I have done it all.

Where go I now? I return to the One. I return to the home from whence I came before I incarnated into all my many lives. I say that what I have done, you can do also. It is within each woman and within each man.

All that I leave behind is my legacy. When these papyri are completed and placed in a hiding place, I walk out into the field and raise my vibrations. There will be no one to witness this except for the creatures of nature. In a flash of light I am gone. Until we meet again,

I am Mariam, the Magdalene. I have never died.

EPILOGUE

What we call the beginning is often the end.
And to make an end is to make a beginning.
The end is where we start from
- T.S. Eliot

Ellen opened this story and she asked me to close it, so I get to have the last word. I knew she would be much better at telling the story, except for the adventures Sebastian and I had while we were apart from her and Peter. Mary Magdalene is a hard act to follow so I will keep this brief.

Ellen and I have no regrets over the roles we played. It is the truth that I preferred to translate the scrolls. If I hadn't remained with Sebastian, my life would be a different story.

After the age of the scrolls was authenticated by the papyri as well as the inks used, we launched the web site. The scrolls are a gift to the world. The originals are housed in the Bibliothèque where scholars from around the world can come and study them.

In the spring we had a double wedding in the garden at the chateau. There was no minister because in France religious ceremonies are not considered legal. That suited us, as we are nonreligious. We are spiritual. We are not anti-god; we are pro-god.

The four of us had civil ceremonies the day before, done in accordance with French law which only recognizes a civil marriage performed by a French Civil Authority called an officier de l'etate civil. All marriages are required to be performed in the local city hall, or mairie, by a mayor, or maire.

Now that the explanation is out of the way, I can say we chose to have our own private ceremony at the chateau. Sebastian and I made our commitment before our friends and families. Peter and Ellen did likewise. We each wrote our own commitment vows.

Those attending were Alain with his son and Maurice; Margaret and Jim flew in from the States along with my brothers and their families. Of course Paul, Marie and Jacques were also there for the celebration.

For a wedding gift, Alain presented the chateau to the four of us. With its five bedrooms and adjoining private baths, I don't think we will tread on each other's toes. And we may not all be occupying the chateau at the same time. We are fortunate in having Marie and Jacque remain as our caretakers, knowing there is always a loving reception when we do return.

Our plans are to live in the Pacific Northwest. We are purchasing a home with acreage in the country. Ellen and Peter are purchasing property near by. The four of us have found a community where the people are learning and living the teachings of Mary Magdalene and Jesus. These people are from all walks of life and nationalities.

Sebastian and I are already booked for a number of lectures. We think we have conquered our fears of public speaking. We finally developed the photographs taken inside of and around the cave, of all the scrolls and also the attempt to destroy the computers. Thank god the intruder is in prison for a number of years! We have put together a slide show.

Sebastian and Peter are working on a business project, creating new software for quantum computers; and I really can't say more than that. Ellen chooses not to do public speaking. She has chosen to study quantum physics and is helping Peter and Sebastian where she can.

Yes, our lives have changed. I am conscious each day of my attitudes, thoughts and prejudices. I am learning I can choose to change them to love and allowing. It isn't easy at times. Because of our cultural differences, Sebastian and I probably have had more adjustments in our marriage than Ellen and Peter have. Fortunately we are able to express our feelings and we are able to share what is troubling us. I have observed a deepening love and respect in Peter and Ellen's relationship. Each of us is realizing miracles in our lives as we strive to live what The Magdalene taught.

Since I am putting my thoughts down regarding the four of us, I have to say we have a greater love and appreciation for nature and all life. We have realized this is the plane of demonstration, or as one might say, the plane of opposites. There has always been good and there has always been evil. Despite evil, we were given the keys to live life joyfully by the gift of what The Magdalene wrote.

We have a deeper appreciation for life. It is a gift not to be wasted. Sebastian once asked me if I ever became depressed. I told him that before I met him and got involved in the scrolls, I had many days of depression, anxiety and sadness. I shared with him the words of a song that helped me over some rough times. I now share them with you.

Gifts From Me

Feeling lost and scared,
my mind reached out to God,
asking for a way
to find some peace inside.

A voice came drifting back,
as soft as gentle rain
and calmed my restless heart
with its saving grace.

The voice said,
Everything you see, everything you feel,
everything you sense,
is a gift from Me.

Everything you make,
every breath you take,
all that you can be,
is a gift from Me.

Your soul, created free,
is never from My care.
All is done in Love
as a gift from Me.

All My Children One.
Through them My Kingdom comes,
When they open up their hearts
and share the gifts from Me.

Share the gifts from Me.
Share the gifts from Me.
Share the Gifts from Me.[1]

Before writing this epilogue, I spoke with Ellen, Peter and Sebastian, asking them what they would want to be imparted to you. It is this: the teachings of Mary Magdalene and Jesus are only words and they can only be experienced if consciously applied. If not applied and lived, the words are merely empty words. It isn't a process for the short term. These teaching must be incorporated as a way of life for meaningful changes.

The four of us have repeatedly been asked about the marriage cloth. For now it is in a very safe place. We take our sacred charge very seriously and when the right moment arises, it will be revealed and shown to the world.

Life is so sweet. We bless our lives and we send our blessings to you who read this.

We invite you to seek out our community of like-minded people in the Pacific Northwest, that is, if you are open minded and willing to change.

Jill Ashland Gontard

---

[1] Words by Bill Dallavo

BIBLIOGRAPHY

Abbot, Edwin A. *Flatland, A Romance of Many Dimensions.* Boston: Shambhala Pocket Classics, 1999.

American Revision Committee, Ed. *Holy Bible* (American Standard Version). Nashville, TN: Thomas Nelson, Inc., 1901.

Baigent, Michael; Leigh, Richard, Lincoln, Henry. *Holy Blood, Holy Grail.* New York: Bantam Doubleday Dell, 1983.

_____. *The Messianic Legacy.* New York: Bantam Doubleday Dell, 1986.

Begg, Ean. *The Cult of the Black Virgin.* London: Penguin Books, 1985.

Boureau, Alain; Cochrane, Lydia G., Trans. *The Myth of Pope Joan.* Chicago: University of Chicago Press, 2001.

Budge, E. A. Wallis, Trans. *The Egyptian Book of the Dead: The Papyrus of Ani in the British Museum.* Mineola, NY: Dover Publications. 1967.

_____. *The Queen of Sheba and Her Only Son Menyelek aka The Kebra Nagast.* London: Humphrey Milford, Oxford University Press, 1932.

Bushby, Tony. *The Bible Fraud.* Hong Kong: PacificBlue Group, Inc. 2001.

_____. *The Secret in the Bible: The Lost History of the Giza Plateau and How Temple Priests of the Great Pyramid Preserved the Evidence of Life Beyond Death.* Melbourne, AU: Joshua Books and Stanford Publishing, 2003.

Collins, Paul. *The Modern Inquisition: Seven Prominent Catholics and Their Struggle with the Vatican.* New York: Overlook Press, 2001.

Cornwell, John. *A Thief in the Night: The Mysterious Death of Pope John Paul I.* New York: Simon and Schuster, 1989.

_____. *Hitler's Pope: The Secret History of Pius XII.* Toronto: The Penguin Group, 2000.

Doresse, Jean. *The Secret Books of the Egyptian Gnostics.* Rochester, VT: Inner Traditions, 1986.

Gardner, Laurence. *Lost Secrets of the Sacred Ark: Amazing Revelations of the Incredible Power of Gold.* London: Element Books, Limited, 2004.

_____. *Bloodline of the Holy Grail: The Hidden Lineage of Jesus Revealed.* London: Element Books, Limited., 1996.

_____. *Genesis of the Grail Kings: The Explosive Story of Genetic Cloning and the Ancient Bloodline of Jesus.* London: Element Books, Limited, 2000.

_____. *Realm of the Ring Lords: Beyond the Portal of the Twilight World.* Ottery St. Mary, Britain: Multi MediaQuest International, Ltd., 2000.

Haggard, Sir Henry Rider. *King Solomon's Mines.* Waterville, ME: Thorndike Press, 2003.

_____. *She.* Mattituck, NY: Amereon House, 1982.

Hall, Manly P. *The Secret Teachings of All Ages.* Los Angeles: The Philosophical Research Society, Inc., 1988.

Hancock, Graham. *The Sign and the Seal: The Quest for the Lost Ark of the Covenant.* New York: Simon & Schuster, Touchstone Press, 1992.

Haskins, Susan. *Mary Magdalene, Myth and Metaphor.* New York: HarperCollins, 1993.

Hopkins, Marilyn; Simmans, Graham; Wallace-Murphy, Tim. *Rex Deus: The True Mystery of Rennes-Le-Chateau.* Shaftsbury Dorset, UK: Element Books, Limited, 2000.

Knight, Christopher; Loman, Robert. *The Hiram Key: Pharaohs, Freemasonry, and the Discovery of the Secret Scrolls of Jesus.* New York: Barnes & Noble, 1998.

Lederman, Leon. *The God Particle: If the Universe Is the Answer, What Is the Question?* Boston: Houghton Mifflin Co., 1993.

Leloup, Jean-Yves. *The Gospel of Mary Magdalene.* Rochester, VT: Inner Traditions, 2002.

Lincoln, Henry. *Key to the Sacred Pattern: The Untold Story of Rennes-Le-Chateau.* Oxfordshire, UK: Windrush Press Ltd., 1997.

Lyne, William. *Occult Ether Physics: Tesla's Hidden Space Propulsion System and the Conspiracy to Conceal It.* Lamy, New Mexico: Cretopia Productions, 1997.

Mack, Burton L, *Who Wrote the New Testament? The Making of the Christian Myth.* Harper Collins Publishers, Inc. New York 1995.

Michell, John. *Who Wrote Shakespeare.* London: Thames and Hudson, 1990.

Moreau, Robert. *The Rom: Walking in the Paths of the Gypsies.* Toronto, Ontario, Canada: Key Porter Books, 2003.

Olson, Steve, *Mapping Human History: Genes, Race, and Our Common Origin.* Boston: Mariner Books, Division of Houghton Mifflin Publishers, 2003.

Pagels, Elaine. *Beyond Belief: The Secret Life of Thomas.* New York: Random House, 2003.

Pardoe, Rosemary; Pardoe, Darroll. *The Female Pope.* London: The Aquarian Press, 1988.

Parker, Geoffrey, Ed. and Trans. *At the Court of the Borgias, Being an Account of the Reign of Pope Alexander VI, Written by His Master of Ceremonies, Johann Burchard.* London: The Folio Society, 1963.

Phelon, William. *Three Sevens: A Story of Ancient Initiation.* Quakertown, PA: Philosophical Publishing Co., 1977.

Phillips, Graham. *12 Tribes, 10 Plagues, and the 2 Men Who Were Moses.* Berkeley, CA: Ulysses Press, 2003.

_____. *The Marian Conspiracy: The Hidden Truth About the Holy Grail, the Real Father of Christ and the Tomb of the Virgin Mary.* London: MacMillan Publishers., Ltd., 2000.

Picknett, Lynn. *Mary Magdalene.* New York: Carroll & Graf Publishers, 2000.

Picknett, Lynn; Prince, Clive. *The Templar Revelation: Secret Guardians of the True Identity of Christ.* New York: Touchstone Publishers, Ltd., 1998.

_____. *Turin Shroud: In Whose Image? The Truth Behind the Centuries.* New York: HarperCollins, 1994.

Ramtha; Weinberg, Steven Lee, PhD., Ed. *RAMTHA, The White Book,* Eastsound, WA: Sovereignty, Inc., 1994.

Ramtha. *A Master's Reflection on the History of Humanity; Part I: Human Civilization, Origins and Evolution.* Yelm, WA: JZK Publishing, 2001.

_____. *A Master's Reflection on the History of Humanity; Park II: Rediscovering the Pearl of Ancient Wisdom.* Yelm, WA: JZK Publishing, 2002.

Sitchin, Zecharia. *The 12th Planet: Book I of The Earth Chronicles*. New York: Avon Books, 1978.

_____. *The Lost Book of Enki: Memoirs and Prophecies of an Extraterrestrial God.* Rochester, VT: Inner Traditions, Bear & Company, 2002.

Sora, Steven. *The Lost Treasure of the Knights Templar: Solving the Oak Island Mystery*. Rochester, VT: Inner Traditions, Destiny Books, 1999.

Stanford, Peter. *The Legend of Pope Joan: In Search of the Truth.* New York: Henry Holt and Company, 1998.

Starbird, Margaret. *The Woman with the Alabaster Jar: Mary Magdalene and the Holy Grail.* Rochester, VT: Inner Traditions, Bear & Company, 1993.

Three Initiates. *The Kybalion: A Study of the Hermetic Philosophy of Ancient Egypt and Greece.* Chicago, IL: Yogi Publication Society, 1912.

Thiering, B. E.; Thiering, Barbara. *Jesus & the Riddle of the Dead Sea Scrolls: Unlocking the Secrets of His Life Story.* New York: HarperCollins,1992.

Tolkien, J. R. R. *Lord of the Rings Trilogy.* Boston: Houghton Mifflin Co., 1954-56.

Van Buren, Elizabeth. *Refuge of the Apocalypse: Doorway into Other Dimensions.* London: C. W. Daniel Company, Ltd, 1986.

Wallace-Murphy, Tim; Hopkins, Marilyn. *Rosslyn: Guardian of the Secrets of the Holy Grail.* Great Britain: Element Books Limited, 1999.

Whitworth, Eugene E. *Nine Faces of Christ: A Narrative of Nine Great Mystic Initiations of Joseph, Bar, Joseph in the Eternal Religion.* San Francisco, CA: Great Western University Press, 1972.

Yallop, David A. *In God's Name: An Investigation into the Murder of Pope John Paul I.* New York: Bantam Books, 1984.

Acknowledgements

I would be remiss if I didn't acknowledge the wonderful people who helped me birth this story into novel form. It is with deep and profound gratitude and love that I thank my friends Bill Dallavo, Robert Hoffman, Karolyn Hoffman and Ginny Harris. It was due to their reading and editing, along with their encouragement that brought this book into fruition. I thank them for pointing out the weaknesses in my writing style. I want to acknowledge Bill Dallavo for his enthusiasm and eagerness to read the next chapter before I had completed it. I again acknowledge him for allowing me to use the words to his song, *Gifts From Me*. I thank my granddaughter Myriah Brown for her looking over my shoulder and correcting my sentence structure. I also thank her for not playing the piano while I was writing.

Without Robert Hoffman's computer expertise I probably would have been up the creek without a paddle. His suggestion for the cover design is exactly what I was wanting and words cannot express my deep gratitude for his labor of love in putting the manuscript into book form with his creative genius. With gratitude I thank my son, Ken Brown for his creating the cover. He picked up on what I wanted and with his expertise and love brought the cover into being. From him I never hear a discouraging word. I am so blessed to have these wonderful people in my life as well as the long list of people who have encouraged me and made a difference in my life.

With gratitude and love I bless you who are reading this book, or have read it. Thank you.

I acknowledge my teacher, Ramtha the Enlightened One. He has taught me to make known the unknown and his teachings have restored my worthiness while teaching me to take responsibility for my life and to apply what I have been taught. From him I realized the importance of Truth and research. I honor JZ Knight because without her, I would have never received the great teachings that unlocked my mind. Thank you.

POSTSCRIPT

For this second revised edition, I am forever grateful to my editor, Jo Stockstill, who tightened the grammar, loose ends and inconsistencies of the first edition. I call her "the Quilter" because she has assisted me in having a greater second edition by rearranging pieces to enrich the pattern. To quote her: "sometimes its as if the author is working for the editor." Yep, but it is worth it all.

My thanks and appreciation extend to Mike Wright for reading the revised edition and giving suggestions; to Chantal LaFont for her editing of the French usage; and to Jan Hazelton and Kathleen Hazelton for not only their handling of my website and Kathy's graphic for the chapter endings but also for their enthusiasm, encouragement and suggestions. I want to give credit to my granddaughter Myriah Brown for the photo she took of me on the back cover of the second edition. Last, but not least, my thanks and appreciation extend to my son, Ken Brown, for the cover art and the new back cover; and again, to Robert Hoffman – my savior when in need. Every author needs one.

Bettye Johnson

May 2005

About the Author

Bettye Johnson's background is a woven tapestry of experience. Her first earnings came from picking cotton in Texas as a young girl. She left Texas to work in the Foreign Service branch of the U.S. State Department, with tours of duty at the Embassies in Paris, France and Tokyo, Japan. After resigning, she has been a wife, mother of three sons, government employee, Federal Women's Program Coordinator, program director for a holistic center, minister of a non-denominational church and a writer of short stories for her grandchildren. She has always had a quest for knowledge, enhanced for the past 17 years by being a student at the Ramtha School of Enlightenment, Yelm, Washington. She makes her home in Washington State.